KV-510-006

The Making of Molly March

The Making of
Molly March

Juliet Dymoke

PIATKUS

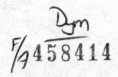

F/458414

First published in Great Britain in 1996 by
Judy Piatkus (Publishers) Ltd of
5 Windmill Street, London W1

The moral right of the author has been asserted

A catalogue record for this book is available from the British Library

ISBN 0–7499–0341–4

Set in 11/12pt Times by
Action Typesetting Ltd, Gloucester
Printed and bound in Great Britain by
Mackays of Chatham Plc

For Jane Conway-Gordon

In gratitude for
friendship, advice, and encouragement

Prologue 1835

The rain was a constant gentle downpour that had gone on all day and showed no sign of abating. The children were restless, inattentive, because there had been no exercise in the yard, even for the short time allowed.

Miss Plumstead glanced at her fob watch. It was ten minutes to four and she would have a wet walk home. At least now that March was nearing its end, there was a little more daylight in which to reach her cottage half a mile away. Reproving Mary Dodds who was pinching the arm of a very scared little girl only brought in last night, she said, 'Put away your books, children, and I'll read you a story for the rest of our time.'

She chose *Jane Sparks*, an improving tale which had little appeal for her class, most of whom stared vacantly without a spark of intelligence, but at least it passed the time and some of the girls listened. They sat in grey rows, their dresses bought from a factory already cut out and then sewn by themselves. Poor little things, Miss Plumstead thought, not for the first time, nothing could be more drab than this dull whitewashed room boasting only three tables around which the girls clustered. They lived a dreary life, but then, Miss Plumstead supposed, you could expect nothing else for these dregs of society, with nowhere to go but the workhouse. Westbourne workhouse was no worse than others, but Miss Plumstead thought the dull grey building a blot on what was otherwise a pretty Sussex village.

Among her class, Mary Dodds was totally destitute, her father killed in a drunken brawl and her mother dead from the

1

scarlet fever. Supported by parish relief she was waiting only to be old enough to go into service. Cecily Jones had a mother in here but they were separated by the regime which was different for men and women, boys and girls; Mrs Jones, as she called herself had no idea who Cecily's father was, had been brought in off the streets by a constable, run away once and was now back, wearing the awful yellow punishment frock. Cecily wept frequently. Joan Wills had settled into a sort of dumb misery, but several were brighter, Dolly Hayes for example really seemed to enjoy Miss Plumstead's lessons. Here at least they were clothed and fed, the grey dresses better than the rags in which most had arrived, and they had decent food, dull and without variety, but on five days a week they were given meat with potatoes and cabbage, bread and cheese on the others, which served for supper as well. Puddings were the greatest treat, reserved for very special days. There was a medical officer who could order milk for the sick and other necessities but for the rest there were no such luxuries. The routine was dreary, the men working in the vegetable plot, grinding corn for their bread, or picking oakum; the girls and women sewed, while the boys made fishing nets, for the sea was only a few miles away. Mr and Mrs Norris were master and matron, acting as judge and jury over offenders, and Miss Plumstead's heart had gone out yesterday to Polly Smith who had been beaten for daring to take a left-over potato.

Sometimes there were as many as eighty souls confined in this grim building with its bulk around two separated exercise yards, and the routine so soul-destroying that many destitute people turned to crime or prostitution to avoid being shut up in here. Miss Plumstead privately thought it was better to be fed and clothed, even in the parish workhouse, than to go on the streets.

She had been accounted a pretty woman when she was young, her hair a soft brown, her eyes grey, complexion delicate, and twenty years ago she had been engaged to a captain in the Queen's Own Regiment, but he had been killed at Waterloo. Unable to bring herself to take his ring off her third finger, for they had been deeply in love, she had not looked at another man. Her father was long dead, and she gave herself to caring for her mother in their small cottage, and to teaching

2

these little outcasts of society. Though frustrating, it was sometimes rewarding, and she felt that at least she was trying to give them a little simple education, a more hopeful picture of the world outside.

The Reverend Henry Newland, Vicar of Westbourne, had obtained permission for the boys and girls to walk the short distance down the road to the parish church on Sundays. Little heathens! had been Mr Newland's first judgement of them, wondering if any of them understood a word of what was being said. But to his credit he persevered and Miss Plumstead was glad. Uphill work though it was little Agnes Fox had actually asked some quite intelligent questions after last Sunday's sermon.

Class over, she put away *Jane Sparks*, said 'good afternoon, children,' which drew some sort of response, and went to find her oilskins. So she was in the main hall when a cart drew up outside and two parish officers half carried a woman through the entrance. Heavily pregnant, without cap or bonnet, rain had plastered the hair to her head, and she was moaning, the sound rising now and then to a cry of pain.

'Poor soul,' Miss Plumstead said. 'Where did you find her?' her ready sympathy rising as she noticed that the wet bedraggled dress had once been made of good cloth.

'In the gutter,' one of the men answered. 'No one could say anything of her in Emsworth so this is the only place for the likes of her. In a fever and near her time too. Excuse us, Miss Plumstead.'

She stood aside for them to take the wretched creature to the infirmary and then went home to the good supper which would be awaiting her.

'You must be drenched and cold,' Mrs Plumstead grumbled as her daughter came in. 'I hope you've changed your shoes.'

'Yes, mother, as you see.'

'Well, I'm sure I don't know why you do it. That dreadful place – and walking there in all weathers. You'll catch your death of cold, or something worse from those creatures.'

'Dr Hicks does his best for them, Mother.' She sat down with her toes to the fire. 'There's no bad sickness at the moment.'

'That's as maybe. But you've no need to do it, the eight

3

pounds a year they pay you is really neither here nor there. And what would become of me if you took sick, I'd like to know?'

Her daughter, who had heard this many times before, did not answer directly but said instead, 'At least I feel I'm doing something for those unhappy children. If Harry hadn't died, if I'd children of my own to care for —' Even now she could not speak of him without the threat of tears. He had died in the famous charge of the Fighting Fifty-Second, commanded at Waterloo by Colonel John Colbourne, who had written to her regretting the loss of a gallant officer and comrade. She had the letter still, locked away in a box with those Harry had written throughout the Peninsula campaign, often read and wept over still.

'Well, well,' her mother said, 'put another log on the fire, my love. Cis is cooking us a tasty crown of lamb to our dinner because I've invited that nice new curate.'

Poor Mother, Miss Plumstead thought, still trying to marry me off, for all I'm rising thirty-nine. But she changed into her mauve silk dress with the pretty pattern of violets embroidered on it, and the evening was pleasant; the curate, a lonely man in his early forties, had some conversation and the dinner was excellent, yet she was glad when he went and she could go to bed. Unable to rid her mind of that poor creature brought in that evening she wondered what had driven her here and in such straits. Alone and seemingly destitute, it must be terrible to give birth without a mother or family to take her in at such a time.

In the morning the rain had cleared away and spring sunshine shone on the first daffodils. Miss Plumstead picked her way across last night's puddles and, as she had a little time in hand, enquired at the Matron's room for the latest admission.

'Oh, her,' Mrs Norris said, 'her bastard was born in the middle of the night of all tiresome things. A girl and well enough, but the mother's likely to die of her fever and not in her right senses at all. We can't even get her name out of her.'

Used to Mrs Norris's heavy-handed ways, Miss Plumstead, who rarely acted on impulse, was moved to ask, 'I wonder if I might see her? Perhaps if I sit quietly beside her —'

4

The matron shrugged. 'If you wish, but it'll be a thankless task. Dr Hicks came in an hour ago and agrees with the midwife – she'll be in her coffin before the day's out. But go if you wish —'

In the woman's ward of the infirmary several beds were occupied, one by a woman with a rash covering her face, another coughing incessantly, but Miss Plumstead saw at once that last night's admission lay in the far corner. Washed and changed into a workhouse nightgown, the lashes were down on a drawn white face except for where two fever spots burned. Yet it was a face that told Miss Plumstead a great deal. Now dry, dark curling chestnut hair framed it, and the hot dry hand Miss Plumstead took into her own was beautifully shaped, the nails delicate. Obviously a woman of some breeding, but how in heaven's name did she come to be in this dire situation? Furthermore there was a wedding ring on the hand she held, so the child could not be a bastard.

'That one's for a hole in the ground,' the woman with the cough wheezed. 'I'm surprised she ain't gone b' now. Kept us all awake last night, she did, hollerin' n' that ...'

Miss Plumstead did not answer but sat quietly, and perhaps it was the soft stroking of the hot hand that seemed to focus the sick woman's wandering mind, for suddenly her eyes, filled with pain and distress, opened to gaze up questioningly. 'What has happened ... oh tell me ... no one came ...'

Miss Plumstead leaned over her. 'You are in Westbourne workhouse, near Chichester. You were brought in last night, do you remember? And now you have a little daughter.'

'A ... a daughter?' The woman stirred but was too weak to do more than pluck at the cover with her free hand. 'Yes ... yes I remember now, the pain ... Oh let me see her. Where is she?'

Miss Plumstead could not help but notice the woman's educated voice which indicated a gentle origin. Quietly she answered the distraught question. 'In the nursery, I expect, and I'm told doing very well.'

Two tears trickled down the pallid face. 'Poor ... poor little thing. No one to care ...'

Miss Plumstead stroked her hand. 'Don't upset yourself, my dear. Tell me where your husband is and I'll —'

5

A shudder shook the form in the bed. 'Gone ... I don't know where ... wicked, oh wicked, to leave me so!'

'Your parents then, your family? Can we not write to someone to come and fetch you? This is clearly no place for you, or your baby.'

But the lucid moment had gone, the dying woman's hold on reality fast disappearing. She began to mutter unintelligibly of a man, of walking, always walking, a blue dress, and once she called out, 'Mama! Mama!'

Desperately sorry for her Miss Plumstead said loudly, 'Can you not tell us your name? For the sake of your child?'

Somehow the word 'name' penetrated, for the woman murmured, 'Marianne ... I am Marianne ...'

'Yes, and your surname?'

But this was too much and there was only low rambling until suddenly and quite clearly the words came out, 'She ... my child ... she must be christened. Call her ... Marianne ...'

'I'll see to it.' Miss Plumstead felt so much sympathy for this poor creature that she said impulsively, 'Would you like me to stand godmother to her? I teach the little girls here.'

Marianne looked up and her face was lit by a lovely smile that showed through all the wreckage of whatever had brought her here that she had been a woman of tremendous charm. Gripping Miss Plumstead's hand she nodded. 'Oh, please.'

'Of course it shall be done at once,' Miss Plumstead went on. 'You must let me summon someone, a member of your family, to take care of the baby. I promise you I will see to it.'

A great sob, half feverish spasm, shook the dying woman. 'No ... no ... they would not. Except ... but she can't. No one ... no one ...' The words faded into a jumble, there was a rattle in her throat and the next minute the cessation of it told Miss Plumstead she was dead.

For a few moments, time enough to send up a prayer for the departed lost soul, Miss Plumstead sat still. Slowly she released the hand she was holding and then on an impulse she slipped the wedding ring off the slack third finger. If she could, she would give it to the orphaned child in due course. Then she went to look for Mrs Norris, ignoring the woman in the next bed who said, 'Well, she's for the churchyard, eh?'

'Dead, is she?' queried the matron. 'No more than I

expected, poor body. And maybe better for her than being a pauper here.'

'However she came to this state, she must have been a lady,' Miss Plumstead maintained. 'Anyone can see that just by looking at her and hearing her voice.'

'If she was then it's mighty odd that she'd no one to care for her,' the matron pointed out, echoing the dying woman's last pathetic 'No one ... no one.' 'Did she say anything to you that might tell us?'

'No,' Miss Plumstead said regretfully, 'Only that her child is to be baptized Marianne.'

'That's a high-fallutin' name for a child on parish relief, because that's what she'll have to be.'

'The name is what her mother chose,' the schoolmistress insisted, 'and I said I would stand godmother.'

The matron cast her an odd glance. 'That's mighty good of you, Miss Plumstead. You don't need to, I'm sure.'

'Oh, but I do. I promised.'

'Very well.' Mrs Norris shrugged at what she thought a nonsensical thing. 'To be sure, you can't adopt all the beggars that are brought in here, you know.'

'Of course not, just this little one, and I only mean to – to —' she was not quite sure what she did mean to do. 'Perhaps the Reverend Newland will come and we can get it done today. She must be called Marianne.'

'Very well, if he has time. But we can't call her a name like that in here. It's to be Mary or Molly. We have several Marys already, so it had better be Molly. Seeing as you got some sense out of the mother, have you any notion of her other name, where she came from?'

'None.'

'She must have had a family. They ought to take care of the child, not us.'

'Not the child's fault,' Miss Plumstead said sadly. 'The poor woman was too far gone.'

'Well, if she was a lady born as you say, what did she do to be cast off, and in that state, eh? Mrs Norris considered that if a woman of standing arrived in the condition of the dead woman last night, there must have been some cause, some unpleasantness or worse. Miss Plumstead had no answers to any of this, only pity for the innocent result.

'We can surely give the child a surname,' she murmured.

Mrs Norris, who had a dozen things to do this morning, considered she had spent enough time over the matter. She was not a hard woman but her intelligence was of the lowest sort and she ruled the workhouse according to the strict injunctions laid down by the authorities in Chichester. She and her husband had to deal with indigent men, rough, ignorant, and all in need; elderly paupers, prostitutes, girls 'in trouble', waifs and strays, and it was not a post many would envy, but they earned fifty-two pounds a year with an extra eight pounds to augment their food, and they ran the place efficiently, having no mind to move on. If the regime was austere, if the punishments for misbehaving were severe, there was no deliberate cruelty, only a lack of warmth, of comfort of any kind, and Miss Plumstead's gentle nature wondered with pity what the future could be for a little waif lying in a cot in the infirmary. What could there be? Nothing but this dreary place until she was maybe ten or eleven, when it would be into service or work on a farm.

'Then as it's March,' Mrs Norris said with a rare concession to humour, 'we'll call her Molly March. Good thing she didn't come last month!' She hurried off, remarking pointedly that it was gone half-past eight, but before going to class Miss Plumstead slipped in to look at the child. Wisps of dark hair escaped from under the plain white cap, eyes shut under dark lashes. She looked healthy, one little fist clenched, the other resting against her cheek. Something about this child appealed to the schoolmistress, though she could hardly have said why.

If only she could take her home, bring her up, but that was quite impossible. As a spinster of nearly forty, with an elderly mother to care for, she knew nothing of raising children, having neither brothers nor sisters and consequently no nieces or nephews. With the sentimentality of the inexperienced she visualized an angelic little girl growing up at Rosemary Cottage, playing in the garden, herself reading bed-time stories. But it could hardly become a reality and putting out a hand she touched the soft skin of the baby's cheek. Well, she could at least keep some sort of watch over the little thing, be a godmother to her which was of course her Christian duty, whatever Mrs Norris might say.

'Poor little Molly March,' she murmured. 'You shall have one friend at least.'

As for the future, who could say? For a workhouse child it was never rosy.

Chapter One

A large figure filling the side entrance of the great barn momentarily blocked out the sunlight, which surprised Molly into looking down from the loft.

She had slipped out to visit a maverick hen which, escaping from the yards and henhouse, was now happily sitting on two eggs in a corner of the hay store. If the master knew she was there he'd shoo her out, taking the eggs, and Molly wanted to protect her. She would have to remove the hatched chicks to the henhouse eventually but for the moment it was her secret. Moving away from the broody hen she glanced at the small doorway, the large doors only opened for the groaning hay wagons, and a warmth crept into her cheeks. It *was* him. No one else was so tall, and so broad and strong with it.

'I saw you come in,' he said with a friendly grin. He had a shock of fair hair and the bluest of eyes. 'What are you up to, Lass?'

Sure she could trust him, she said, 'There's a hen up here, sitting. I call her Betty. I never had no pet before except one of the cowhouse kittens and she were killed by a fox, nasty vicious thing. I bring Betty a handful of meal or corn if I can get it. There's always some gleanings. It's my secret so don't you tell anyone.'

Leaning against one of the sturdy posts, his smile widened. 'I won't. Anyway we'll be cuttin' the last field on Monday. By rights it ought to be tomorrow.'

'Master'd never allow work on the Sabbath, he's that strict. D'you think the weather will hold?'

'Should do. Harvest supper on Monday night, eh?'

And that would mean he would be going. It would be as if a brief brightness had gone out of her life. Why did it produce such an ache in her heart? But all she said was, 'I'll be starting on the baking today.'

The farmer, Mr Wicks, took on casual labour now and then, for haymaking and at harvest time, and this was the second year that Hal had come. Last summer they had spoken only once or twice, the first time when she took the men's food to the fields at noon. When he thanked her for his share she had shyly asked his name.

'Godfrey Hallam,' he had told her, 'but I'm always called Hal. You know how folks shorten names and I could hardly be called God, could I now?'

'That's disrespectful,' had been her answer. 'You didn't ought to take the Lord's name in vain – it's one o' the commandments in the Holy Book.'

'I never meant no harm,' he said quickly, 'and I don't know much about the Bible neither, 'cept what the preachers tell about us all bein' sinners and that, but what with all the travellin' I do, I don't get to church much.'

'You could read the Bible yourself,' she pointed out and he had given a great guffaw.

'Nay, lass, I can't read, nor write come to that, never had the learning. My Ma had ten of us and I were out at work by eight year old, sweepin' yards and such like. 'Tis me 'ands that earn a living.'

She had felt sorry for him, to be so deprived of something she loved – not that she had much time for reading or pleasing herself in any way. But when she left the workhouse to go to work on the farm Miss Plumstead had given her a Bible, the first present she had ever had and it was her most prized possession. At that harvest supper a year ago, Mrs Wicks had kept her busy as usual with the food and the dishes and refilling the jugs. In that lady's opinion the men got drunk and would become too free with young servants and dairy maids and she had eventually sent Molly to her bed. 'Better out o' harm's way,' had been her opinion.

So Molly had whispered goodbye to Hal as she passed him and he had said he would come back. Not believing him, because itinerant workers who hired themselves out all

11

summer came and went all over the country, nevertheless she had dreamed of seeing him walk across the yard, as she dreamed of moving one day out of the narrow confines of the farm into the larger world beyond where she would surely find something better. Her fantasies were fed by a vivid imagination, more real than the long day's work. The stories in the Bible, her only book, filled her head and she laughed and rejoiced with Sarah, sorrowed with Job, fought with David, yearned with Bathsheba, wept with Rachel.

And then, a few days ago she saw him cross the yard and shoulder a scythe for cutting the barley. There was a good crop this year which had put Mr Wicks in a rare good mood. She didn't understand Master. He went to Bosham church every Sunday with the missus beside him, herself and Susan, the dairy maid, perched behind, to sit at the back of the church on the servants' benches while Mr and Mrs Wicks sat nearly at the front. It was the only outing and the greatest pleasure of the week. The Vicar was young and fair, very good-looking and unwed, doubtless able to have his pick of the young girls in the parish. But when a shaft of sunlight turned his hair to gold Molly thought he looked like the Lord Jesus must have done, smiling on them all, for he was a friendly sort of man.

But the farmer mostly seemed as grumpy after the service as before and he had criticized the Vicar for being too soft with Mary Scriven who'd been got with child, some said by the blacksmith's lad, though Mary wouldn't say and spent her days between crying and defiance. Silly wench, Molly thought. But Hal was beginning to fill her head, looking up at her now with an unmistakable expression in his eyes.

'Come down,' he said softly and she turned, setting her foot on the ladder, only to miss the rung and tumble headlong.

A moment's fright and then strong arms caught her and set her on her feet. 'Oh!' she exclaimed, suddenly shy, 'I don't know how many times I've been up and down that ladder and never fallen.'

'It's as well I were here then,' he said. Pausing for a moment to smile down at her flushed face, he kept his hands about her waist and added, 'You've turned into a fine-lookin' woman, Molly March.'

Her colour deepened. Mr Wicks, being very Puritan, did not

allow mirrors in the house which would encourage, he said, the vanity of the women there; her reflection in the glass of the kitchen window being her only guide it did not seem to Molly that she had any cause for vanity. She was either flushed from the heat of the great range, or dusty from the hen-house, but the first thing anyone noticed about her was the irrepressible smile, as if she laughed at life, even when there had been precious little to laugh about. An old woman at the workhouse had once said, 'Born in a ray o' sunshine, that one,' despite Molly's arrival in the middle of a bleak March night. Her curling chestnut hair refused to be subdued under a cap, despite all the efforts of the matron, and then there was her walk. In her miserable childhood she had not grown very much and was pale, insufficiently nourished by the poor food and lacking fresh air and exercise. Just occasionally she went on a Sunday afternoon to tea with Miss Plumstead. A great joy this, to eat pink iced cake which she had never seen before the first visit. But Mr Norris, the workhouse master, said it was favouritism and grudgingly gave permission now and then, because he did not want to offend or lose Miss Plumstead. The workhouse had been a hard school; even gentle Miss Plumstead unable to prevent the girls from hearing the prostitutes' talk, or the tales of women who had cheated and stole. Driven by poverty they were without morals or scruples of any kind, but at least before she was old enough to become part of that hinterland of crime, Molly had been sent to work here. So, from Miss Plumstead's influence, and that of her Bible, she had miraculously escaped corruption.

And six years on the farm with good and plentiful meals and fresh air had worked a miracle. She was now a little above average height and moved easily, swaying a little to a gentle rhythm of which she was totally unaware but of which Hal, for one, was very much aware. His look now showed him more than conscious of her unselfconscious appeal.

'A fine-lookin' woman,' he repeated, and reached out to touch one escaping curl. 'When can you come out and take a walk wi' me?'

Swiftly she said, regretting the words almost at once, 'I don't get a moment, what with the cleaning and cooking and helping Susan in the dairy. And the master's that strict.' There was disappointment on his face and then, despite Mr Wicks's severity, she added in a rush, 'Leastways on Sunday afternoon, if they both go to sleep after the good dinner I cook for them, I can sometimes slip out, so maybe —'

'Then let me walk wi' you,' he said. 'I'll wait for you.'

'Maybe,' she repeated. 'I might still be busy with the baking, though Master wouldn't approve o' that of a Sunday.'

'Just an hour,' he pleaded, 'when they're sleeping. They won't know if you're walkin' or bakin', will they?'

'I'll try,' she said and at that moment a raucous voice bellowed out, 'Molly, where are you? Drat the girl – *Molly*!'

To her surprise Hal bent and gave her a swift kiss on the cheek. 'I guess you'd better go.'

'I better had,' she murmured, her face warm and unaware that her eyes were shining. Giving him a quick smile she sped away across the yard to the kitchen where a tirade of orders greeted her. It wasn't that Mrs Wicks was deliberately unkind. Her tongue was part of her stock-in-trade and, with the passing of time, she had begun to lay more and more on Molly's shoulders. Growing fat, her face reddened and coarsened, she was jealous of her lost youth in this girl's looks. Not that she had even approached these, but the girl's appeal teased her into being rough and demanding. What annoyed her most was Molly's cheerfulness and her ability to do the dreariest of tasks as if it was the one thing she wanted to do. Being unable to understand the private world Molly lived in this only fuelled Mrs Wicks's pettishness.

'Where've you been?' she demanded in a querulous voice. 'Always somewhere else when I want you. Did you get the basket ready?'

'Yes, missus,' Molly said. 'I've not been above ten minutes.'

'What does it matter how long you've been when I want you? Well, get along then, to the south meadow today.' Mrs Wicks hunched a shoulder. 'And hurry back. There's the chickens to pluck and the stuffing for the goose to make, and then the pies, you'd best use the biggest dishes.'

'I won't be long,' Molly promised and with the heavy jug of cider in one hand and the equally heavy basket in the other, she left the kitchen to the last injunction, 'No hanging about talking to the men neither, I want you back quick.'

14

'Yes, missus,' she called over her shoulder and crossed the yards, shooing an unhurried duck out of the way, avoiding Bush, a mongrel and as surly as his master, who stared at her with malevolent yellow eyes. He was on the long chain by his kennel and she kept well out of reach, taking the footpath to the open fields. But she had not gone far when there was a step behind her and with his scythe on one shoulder Hal reached out and took the heavy jug from her hand.

'You might slop it,' he said, and she pointed out that she'd carried a good many such jugs without spilling a drop.

'Happen,' was all he said, but he smiled at her and she wondered why she got this odd sensation when those very blue eyes looked down at her. For all she was a good height for a woman he towered over her.

'I suppose you'll be going after the supper?' she asked.

'Aye. I've to be on a farm up by Winchester on Wednesday, bin there many a time, but it's a fair old walk so I must be off at dawn and walk the drink out o' my head. But maybe I'll get a ride in a farm cart.'

Her heart sank. It was only to be expected. The extra workers at haymaking and harvest never stayed long, moving on to the next job. Several of them eyed her with a grin and a wink – silly lads, she thought them and took no notice, aware of the farmer's disapproval if she stopped too long. Seeing her now, walking up with Hal, he gave them a suspicious glance.

'That scythe mended then?'

'Aye.' Never one to waste words, Hal set the jug down by a great oak tree where there was shade for them all to eat their dinner. From the basket Molly produced a cloth and piled the bread on it with the cheese she had cut into large squares, cheese made in their own dairy and very good. Into tin mugs she poured the cider and handed them round. Hal took a thirsty swig and over the rim his eyes met with hers with unmistakable intimacy. Fortunately at that moment the farmer had his back to them, but as soon as the cider was poured, he said, 'Off with you, girl.'

She turned back to the lane. Sometimes she stayed and handed out the bread and cheese but, seeing her arrive with Hal, he allowed no such liberty today, and she set off back to the house. It was a mixed farm, plenty of arable land down to

15

wheat and barley, but there was a good herd of Shorthorn cattle, pigs in accommodating styes, and the life was constantly busy all through the round of the natural year.

This morning however, despite the mountain of work awaiting her in the big kitchen, she did not hurry. The sun was hot, the air sweet, and she relished these few moments alone. Always longing for a little time just to be by herself, virtually never having it except at night when she was too tired to think of anything but sleep, she relished the short walk. Berries were red on the hawthorn hedge, blackberries ripening, soon to be picked for jelly, while old man's beard wreathed in the tangle of thorns; a thrush was singing and she sang too, a song she had learned years ago from Miss Plumstead – 'Over the hills and far away —' Miss Plumstead, the only person in her eighteen years whom she had loved, until Hal came. Did she love him? Was love like this, looking for a particular face when the men came in, exchanging a quick secret smile, her stomach behaving in an odd way? She didn't know. She had heard tales from Susan of walks in the twilight with a lad from the smithy, Susan's home being so near that she was able to go home every Sunday afternoon. What would it be like to have a home and parents? That was another thing she didn't know.

On Sunday she sat through the morning service with rare impatience. Mr Wicks expected his workers to attend church and she was only too aware of Hal in the side aisle, his hair smoothed down and wearing his Sabbath coat which emerged somewhat creased from the bag that carried all his worldly goods. And this morning the young curate at whom she usually gazed seemed pale and slender beside Hal's large presence.

Afterwards she had to hurry back to the farm to finish off the Sunday dinner and lay it out on the scrubbed table, a piece of gammon, several chickens and some of the goose stuffing made of eggs and suet and currants and apples which she had kept by for today. She had baked raisin tarts, apple pies, and made a custard. The Wicks always ate well and any friend who called shared their good table. The men sat in the back kitchen, Mr and Mrs Wicks in the main kitchen and Molly not at all until everyone was served. Sometimes when she thought of the meagre fare in the workhouse – bread, potatoes and cabbage, with a small helping of pork or bacon now and again

– she was very much aware of her good fortune. If the work was hard, at least she had enough food to sustain her, far more than many poor families in the village, and she wished sometimes she could take a basket of left-overs to one or other, especially to Mrs Brooks who had no man and three young stomachs to fill, but though Mrs Wicks gave the woman sewing work occasionally she never suggested anything else, paying her, Molly thought, very meanly for what she did. But on the Wicks farm there were few left-overs and these went into the pig bucket. Now and then Molly sneaked a piece of bacon and a sausage or two out to the dairy for Susan to take to her voracious young brothers and sisters.

With all its drawbacks, her workload too heavy, she had learned to endure Mrs Wicks's tongue and the farmer's dour moods and grim adhesion to a loveless code. Right was right and wrong was wrong as far as he was concerned, so Molly did what she was told, thankful to be well fed and paid five whole pounds a year for her labours. She had heard horrid things about cities, having only once been to Portsmouth when Mrs Wicks needed her to carry a new set of china for parlour tea on Sunday, but it told her that she would not like to live in such a great sprawling place.

Yet she had an odd and quite unjustified certainty that there was something better ahead of her. Sure she was not destined to spend her life in such unremitting drudgery, marry a farm worker perhaps and live in a cottage with the same round of work, remembering always that she was the daughter of a lady, she was quite determined to better herself. Thanks to Miss Plumstead who had coached her into speaking properly, when she'd a mind to, even the lapses into choice workhouse language were something that could be set aside when her chance came. How she was to achieve this betterment remained a mystery, but it would come, she was sure of that.

The dishes were done at last, the china put back on the big dresser, the kitchen table scrubbed – Sunday or not that had to be done for Mrs Wicks insisted on cleanliness, particularly when she didn't have to do it – and taking the apron off her Sunday dress Molly set off for the bridge over the stream. The dress was blue, a figured cotton with a pattern of tiny white flowers. Miss Plumstead had sent her the material last year for her birthday, of which Mrs Wicks took no account and instead commented that she thought the dress too fancy for a servant girl. In her turn Molly ignored this and finished the sewing of the pretty material. Knowing that she looked nice in it she almost danced her way down to the bridge.

He was there, sitting on the low stone wall. 'Well, girl?' he asked. 'Are they sound asleep?'

She nodded. giving him a shy glance. 'I hope you had enough dinner. You've a big frame to fill.'

'Oh aye, enough – though I'll not say I couldn't have eaten a third slice of that tart. Did you make it? I thought so. You'll be a tidy wife one o' these days.'

She blushed, moving on over the bridge, leading the way towards the village of Bosham.

'How far's that?' Hal asked.

'No more than three mile. Not as far as I walk to see Miss Plumstead at Easter-time!'

'Who's Miss Plumstead?'

'A lovely lady, that kind to us all.'

'Who was she kind to?'

'Us children at the workhouse, in Westbourne.'

'The workhouse?' he exclaimed. 'Whyever was you there? Don't you have no folks?'

'No. The brightness faded from her face. 'No. I was brought up there.'

'Horrid places from all I've heard. I'd rather be dead than –' he broke off, catching her hand. 'You poor little thing. How did you come to be shut up like that?'

'I was born there,' she said, looking away to the shorn fields of Mr Wick's neighbour. Wearing a neat little bonnet, instead of her usual work-a-day cap, it half hid her face. 'I don't know nothing about my Ma or my Pa.'

'Then how —'

She had not talked of this for years, didn't want to think about it. But Hal seemed to care – he did care, for he was looking at her with a warmth in his eyes that somehow made her want to let him into the cold and lonely world of her child-hood. 'Miss Plumstead told me that my Ma was brought in on a March evening – that's why they called me Molly March, though my name is really Marianne. Isn't that grand?'

18

Giving her hand a squeeze he said, 'I like Molly better. Go on, Lass.'

'There's not much to tell. My Ma was so sick that she died in the morning. But Miss Plumstead were with her and she says me Ma was a lady and spoke beautiful, that's why I try to.'

'Well,' he said thoughtfully, 'that's as maybe, but it don't seem as if it's done you any good. Her folks must've had a reason for turning her off – maybe she weren't no better than she ought to be.'

Suddenly indignant, Molly turned on him. 'You shut your face, Godfrey Hallam. You don't know nothing.'

Laughing, he retorted, 'No lady would talk like that. You ain't gentry, Molly March.'

'Maybe not, but Miss Plumstead taught us to read and write and I found out early on that I could copy people's voices. Listen – "Well, Hallam, ain't you finished your dinner yet? Get off about your work." Now who's that?'

He guffawed. 'Missus, of course. Aren't you the clever one!' They were in a lane and he stopped, turning her to face him. 'I'm glad you're not gentry, Molly, because if you was I couldn't –' a brief pause, '– I couldn't think about you the way I do.'

'Oh, Hal,' her anger was gone, for she had fought that battle more than once in the workhouse, 'perhaps it doesn't matter who my Ma was, and she never mentioned my Pa, but she wore a wedding ring, so I ain't no bastard. I'm just me, myself, and I don't mean to work on a farm all my days.'

'What do you mean to be at then?'

'I don't know, but I do know it will be better than slaving for Mrs Wicks from dawn to sunset. Mrs Norris, who was in charge of the workhouse, always said,' and she mimicked the matron's voice, 'You girls must be grateful that the parish feeds you and puts a roof over your heads. Be respectful and obedient when you go out to work. If you get a good place it will be better than most of you deserve.' Her face was sombre. 'If it hadn't been for Miss Plumstead I'd have run away, p'raps done something awful. But I'll better myself, you'll see.'

'I like you as you are.' Bending, he kissed her, his mouth warm on hers, his hands firmly on her shoulders. To be kissed like this was something she had never known. Miss Plumstead had pecked her cheek when she had given her the Bible, but she had known no affection, no love like this.

A man with a cart was coming up the lane and, releasing her, Hal drew her hand through his arm to walk on together. The tide was in and several craft bobbed along in the sunshine. A fine yacht with white sails was out in the bay and pleasure craft carrying people enjoying the afternoon sunshine.

'Fancy having money to buy a boat like that big one,' Molly said.

'I ain't never been to sea but I would surely like to.' Hal gazed longingly as the graceful craft moved outward, then he smiled down at her. 'Shall we do it together, eh?'

Molly gave a gurgle of laughter. 'What, you and me? There's a daft idea.'

The sunshine, his company, the short hour of freedom and most of all his kiss, only brought home the realization that in two days he would be gone. The light seemed to fade and she asked where he would be going after Winchester, Hal answering that it would be to the charcoal burners in the woods near Twyford Down. She had never heard of this place but it sounded a long way off.

Rather forlornly she asked, 'What do you do, charcoal burning?'

He laughed, his eyes on a water rat which had come out of the little stream that wound by the churchyard. It sniffed round the grass and in a swift movement he caught it by the tail and swung it. 'What'll I do with it? Chuck it in the sea and see if it likes salt water?'

'Let it go,' Molly said. 'Water rats don't do no harm. Tell me about the charcoal burning.'

He tipped the little creature back into the stream. 'Well, we make charcoal, for smelting iron and zinc, and it's used for all sorts of things. Rob Tench, who has his own kilns, though he don't own the woods, wanted me back all summer but I were set on coming here. I said I'd go back come September. Soon after that we start cutting and drying the wood for next year's burning. That's when he can do with a big fellow like me to haul and stack the wood. There's always a market for charcoal.'

'I see,' she murmured. 'I don't know much about that, but I

suppose it's a good living. Do you have to go? Couldn't find something about here?'

'I promised,' he said simply. 'First Farmer Miller and then Rob Tench. I can't not go.'

A deep sorrow seemed to settle on her. She had thought he loved her, but how could that be if he was willing to leave her for so long? Yet she liked him for keeping his given word. Glancing at the church clock, she said, 'It's near half past four, I must go back,' and slipped off the wall. He walked close to her, her hand on his. How could that produce such wild hope?

The men were paid and in high good humour, more than ready for the feast. The harvest supper was always shared with Farmer Barton and his wife and all their workers and it was the one day in the year when Mr Wicks was lavish. It gave him standing among his fellows, even if he was a skinflint the rest of the time. A large crowd of labourers, wives and servants assembled in the barn where a vast repast was laid out, an ox roasting outside. There were numerous pies, packed with ham or bacon, or chopped beef, for Mrs Wicks said these went further than too much plain meat, though the ox was cut in large enough slices to fill hungry bellies. There were cheese and Molly's freshly baked quartern loaves. Mrs Barton brought brawn made from ox-feet, apples and pears from her orchard, and several large fruity cakes. It was no surprise to Molly that the food disappeared with great rapidity. Hal made himself useful, filled mugs with home-brewed ale and cider from great stone pitchers and the company grew mellow, the talk louder, the laughter at familiar jokes uproarious.

The tables were eventually cleared and the fiddler who lived in the village began to play a country dance. Hal came straight to Molly and they jigged to the music until they were both hot and sweating. Thankful that this year Mrs Wicks did not send her off to bed, Molly wiped her face on her apron and laughed, revelling in it all, for tomorrow, she thought, could take care of itself. She danced with Dick Ellis who had long cast his eyes on her, but she deemed him no more than a good-natured oaf, while Henry Smith who kept the village shop was openly looking for a wife, or so Susan said. Some of the dances were in sets and she enjoyed the weaving and circling, meeting up with Hal every now and again so that a secret smile could pass between them. He was heavy on his feet and upset Susan in one dance but she jumped up none the worse, for it was all part of the fun.

The noise, the laughter and the singing increased as the great jugs were refilled and emptied many times; farmers' wives and daughters in their best clothes bounced to the music, even Mrs Wicks was persuaded to join in. Her husband merely smoked his pipe at the far end of the barn and talked with old Jacob Downs, Farmer Barton and others of the crops, the good year they'd had, though there was always a voice or two prophesying less good fortune if there was a cold late spring next year.

Catching their breath after a hornpipe, taught them by the blacksmith who had once gone to sea, Hal said, 'I ain't had such a good supper since last year's. Even his lordship's Christmas feast for all his workers, us burners as well, weren't as fine as this.' Glancing round the large barn, seeing everyone occupied with the dancing or slumped on a bench happily inebriated, he caught hold of her hand and led her to the open door. 'Come out,' he whispered. ''Tis a fair night, a moon for lovers, eh?'

She cast a glance at Farmer Wicks but he had his back to her and Mrs Wicks was deep in talk with other farmers' wives. Her heart thumping, she went with him.

Outside the fire was dying, the ox picked clean of meat, though smoke and sparks still floated upwards. Susan was there with the blacksmith's son, kissing by the wall, and Hal grinned. 'See!'

He took her away from the big yard into the further one where the smaller barn stood, Molly hoping no one had gone looking for a private place and disturbed her Betty. But it was quiet inside, moonlight lifting the darkness and it smelled of warm straw. Hal put his arms round her and the kissing began in earnest. To her it was all new and heady and exciting, his arms were strong and comforting, and when he gently pulled her down on to a pile of straw she seemed to have neither the strength nor the desire to resist him.

One large hand was feeling her breast through the thin cloth of her dress and after a moment he murmured, 'You're the girl for me, Moll. I knowed it last year. I ain't never seen anyone I liked better – you're that comely —'

'Oh Hal, that's the cider talking.'

'No, it ain't. I've thought of you all year. An' I bet you've given me a thought or two, eh?'

'I guess I have,' she murmured. To be loved like this was more intoxicating than any amount of cider. 'I do love you too.' He was holding her closer, his hand pulling up her skirt. 'We'll be wed, then? Soon as we can fix it?'

'Wed? How can we? We've nowhere to go,' She was beginning when he laughed and said, 'I'll build us a hut where the kilns are. Burners lived in huts, you know, good solid ones with a proper wooden floor an' all, warmer than any old stone cottage, I can tell you.'

Despite the growing intimacy she withdrew a little. 'I don't want to live in no hut nor in a wood. I want better 'n that.'

'It'd only be for a while,' he pleaded, 'just a little while, until I can do better for you, much better!'

'How? At the charcoal burning?'

'Maybe not. You'll see – I'll find something.'

She wanted to pursue the subject, make him see that a hut in a wood was not what she wanted, even with him. But he had had enough of words and slid above her, his hands having done their work.

'Oh,' she moaned, desperate between fear and desire. 'Don't – don't – t'ain't right.' Innocent she might be but after many years on the farm she was not ignorant. 'Stop, Hal – don't – we ain't wed.'

'We will be – soon – and that's good enough for the likes o' us.'

His mouth was on hers, stopping all speech, his heavy body holding her down. She tried to cry out, instinct recoiling from this intimacy even while her body seemed to be responding. But it was too late. Incredible sensations were flooding her, her arms winding themselves about his neck, all of her on fire with delight.

And it was at this moment that Mr Wicks strode into the barn. He had a shotgun in his hand, Bush growling at his feet.

Chapter Two

'Huh!' His tone was nasty. 'You two eh? I might a' known it. Thought I heard a fox in here and by God, I were right.'

They had sprung up, Hal scrabbling at his trousers, Molly hastily righting her dress, a sudden and unknown terror striking her. What had she done? Or let Hal do?

Hal, however, thrust her behind him. 'We're goin' to be wed,' he said in a firm voice while eyeing the gun. 'No harm done. Soon as I can —'

'Wed! A likely tale,' Mr Wicks sneered. 'I've had your sort 'ere before, seducing innocent girls, or not so innocent maybe, and then goin' off and never seen again. Get off my land, Godfrey Hallam, and don't never come back.'

'Then I'll take her wi' me,' Hal said. 'We'll do all right.'

Sick with shock, Molly looked at him, uncertain what to do. To go with Hal would be all she desired, but they had nowhere to sleep, nowhere to go except to walk to his next farm. How would they manage? But Mr Wicks was not going to give her a chance to decide.

'You ain't taking her nowhere,' he said. 'Do you think I'm going to let you profit from your wickedness? Like as not she'll end up on the streets and it's my Christian duty to stop that.' And he pulled the trigger, though he did aim wide.

The explosion was deafening. Molly screamed and Hal yelped as two pellets ricocheted and embedded themselves in the flesh of one leg. 'You wicked old man,' he shouted. 'Dang you, I'm hurt.'

'No more 'n you deserve. As for you,' the farmer turned on Molly, 'get out of here. Get to your room and stay there, d'you hear? Hallam, be off with you or you'll get some more pellets in you.' Bush, catching the menace in his master's tone, growled, baring his teeth.

With blood running down his leg, Hal saw no sense in getting himself peppered with shot or quite likely set on by the vicious-looking dog. To Molly he said, 'Don't fret, Lass. I'll come back, I'll fix something for us, a place to live, and we'll be wed. Soon as I can.'

Pitchforked from love in Hal's arms into terror that Mr Wicks would use the gun again, she cried out, 'Oh go – please go – I'll wait for you —'

'Enough of this,' the farmer said roughly. 'Go on, Hallam or I'll set the dog on you.'

'I'm going,' Hal retorted, 'but don't you dare touch her. 'Tweren't her fault and I'll be back for her.'

'Huh,' the farmer said again. 'I'll warrant she were willing enough. Now get off my land and you, girl, into the house and upstairs with you.'

Molly fled, Hal's voice following her. 'Don't be afraid. I won't be long.' Then, eyeing the shotgun and the evil-looking Bush he too went out, conscious of the farmer's determination to see him off the premises and out into the night.

In the house Molly ran up the stairs to her attic room to fling herself on the bed, overcome by shattered sobbing. The music, the singing were still going on in the large barn where Mr Wicks leaned his gun against a wall with the laconic remark that, as he thought, there was a fox in the smaller barn.

The harvest celebration ended about midnight, the guests departed with their wives and workers for their moonlit ride home in gig and cart, and the hired men, some already asleep, some the worse for drink, settled down on the hay, prepared to be on their way in the morning. One fellow remarked that Hallam was gone, but merely thought that he'd set off on the long walk to his next place. In the house Mrs Wicks was putting what little leftover food there was into the larder, down a few steps and with stone slabs to keep it all cold, while Susan and her sister cleared the barn of the dishes.

'Where's that Molly?' Mrs Wicks demanded. 'She should be helping.'

'She won't help no more,' her husband said. 'I caught her and Hallam in the barn, and not in time neither by the look of it.'

'Well!' Mrs Wicks exclaimed. 'I'd never have thought it of her – always keepin' away from the lads, as if butter wouldn't melt in her mouth.'

'Not this time, the strumpet. I'll not turn her out, which is what she deserves, but she'll go, soon as I can take her back to the workhouse.'

His wife stared at him. 'And what am I to do with all the work there is?'

'Get Susan into the house, and that young sister of hers to the dairy, she's helped out often enough,' he told her and began to unfasten his belt.

'Well, I don't know. Molly's used to my ways an' she works well,' Mrs Wicks grumbled.

'So she may, but what's begun – where'll it lead, eh? And I'm not having no slut in the house, with her sinful ways.' Wrapping the belt around his hand he stamped off up the stairs and throwing open Molly's door went in without a knock or a pause. She still lay on the bed, and seizing her wrists in one horny hand he held her, while he brought the leather down across her back – once, twice, three times.

Taken utterly by surprise, Molly cried out, 'Oh don't – don't – we meant no harm.'

His breath labouring, he retorted, 'You Jezebel! If the Good Book hasn't taught you right from wrong, I don't know what will. Now you stay there. You're not coming down 'til I say.'

Unable to keep back a cry of pain, she gasped, 'You don't understand. He's coming back for me – to wed me —'

His answer was a snort. The rain of blows had ceased and he stumped out, shutting the door behind him. There was a bolt on the outside and this he shot into place.

Molly lay still, whimpering a little, hardly daring to move. Never having been beaten, even in the workhouse, above a switch of the cane on her hand once for tearing her dress, this was an indignity that hurt worse than the bruises across her back. She had heard of girls beaten by drunken fathers or unkind husbands for some misdeed or other, but that this should be done to her for the few minutes in Hal's arms seemed a vicious punishment. At least he had not used the buckle end and she sat up, grimacing a little, feeling with her hand to see if there was any blood oozing, but the belt did not seem to have broken the skin.

Slowly anger replaced the pain and terror. She wouldn't stay one moment longer in this house, but then realized the door was locked and her window too high for escape. In any case if she ran away how would Hal find her? It was very dark now, the moon gone behind some cloud and she had not thought to snatch her candle from the kitchen when she fled, so she was unable even to look for comfort in her Bible. She thought of Mr Wicks's cruel words and the tears came afresh. Perhaps she was the wicked thing he had called her? Was it a sin to love as she and Hal had loved? But she wasn't a Jezebel, nor a strumpet, she wasn't! If they were married wouldn't that put all right again? She cried his name into the pillow and there, without attempting to undress, wary of her sore back, she eventually slept.

In the morning she woke at the usual time and rose gingerly, the weals smarting. It would, she thought, be too painful to change into her working dress. Then she went to the door. It was still locked and it stayed so all the morning. Her window was in the gable of the highest wall and looking out she saw no one but the stockmen turning the cows out after milking, though she stood there most of the morning. About mid-day she could smell the dinner being cooked and realized she was hungry. A little later the bolt was pulled back and Susan brought in a plate bearing a slice of bread, and a jug of water. Mr Wicks stood outside, watching.

'I'm sorry it ain't more,' Susan whispered. ''Tis terrible downstairs this morning. Oh Molly, what did you do?' But before she could answer Mr Wicks ordered her downstairs. To Molly he said, 'You're to be ready to go in half an hour.'

'Go?' For a moment Molly looked blankly at him and then, sick with dread, asked the almost unnecessary question. 'Where?'

'Westbourne workhouse,' was the terse answer. 'Where else? Pack your things, but nothing that ain't yours, mind.'

'Wasn't the beating enough?' Molly was trembling. 'We didn't mean —' But the door was shut again and bolted.

27

Hardly aware of eating, she chewed the bread, dry from having been left out last night, but she was too wretched to care. Fetching the canvas bag she had brought with her when she first came to the farm, she packed away her work-a-day stuff dress, put in her two nightdresses, comb and toothbrush, her mind too numbed, too shattered by what had happened, to take in what was happening now. Her Bible, unopened this morning, she wrapped in an apron. What condemnation would she find there? Thinking of Jezebel, she shuddered.

Her saved money was in a little purse she had made from a scrap of material and tied with a cord, four pounds, six shillings and tuppence ha'penny – not a great deal, only she was sure she would be unwise to ask for what was owing. But a spirit of rebellion was growing in her. Never, never again would she let herself be treated like this. Last night's beating had seared more than her back, and when the door opened and Mrs Wicks appeared, puffing from the rare exertion of climbing to the top of the house, she raised her head and gave her a defiant look.

'Come along now,' the farmer's wife ordered. 'You know Mr Wicks can't abide being kept waiting. You stupid girl, you had a good place here, and how I'm to manage —'

'I'm sorry,' Molly said truculently, 'I didn't mean to cause trouble. But me and Hal —'

'You don't need to talk nonsense to me about a handsome fellow promising to wed you. They all know how to get their own way. You won't see him again.'

'I will – I will. If he comes back, when he comes back, tell him —' Tell him what? Where could he find her? Not at the workhouse for she'd be sent out again, though at least they would know where she was, and surely he could find the workhouse?

'He won't come back unless he wants his backside full of buckshot,' was Mrs Wicks's opinion. 'Now get along downstairs.' Suddenly she added, 'You've bin a good girl, Molly. You ought to a' known Mr Wicks can't tolerate lads and girls tumbling each other afore they're wed. An' I can't go agin him.'

With one last glance round her little room under the eaves Molly followed Mrs Wicks down the stairs, knowing only too

28

well that uppermost in Mrs Wicks's mind was concern for her own comfort, rather than any sympathy. Suddenly she didn't want to go, beating or no beating.

After the recent fine weather today was overcast, storm clouds rolling in from the west, all adding to Molly's feeling of oppression. Mr Wicks, sour-faced, was in the yard, in the act of getting into the gig and in silence she climbed up beside him, laying her bag on the boards beneath her feet. Mrs Wicks did not come to see her go, only Susan waved from the window of the dairy. It was hard to believe she was being sent away from the place that had been home for more than six years and she looked round the yards, the barns, wondering how Betty the hen would fare without her. The large kitchen had seen no much of her life, baking and roasting, proud of her bread and pies; washing the floor and scrubbing down the big kitchen table had been a daily chore and even if it was a loveless life, she saw it now as a security lost to her.

During the drive to Westbourne Mr Wicks did not speak. Fields slid by, down to stubble now, the crops harvested, and all the while her dread of the future grew. It was not until he brought the horse to a standstill by the gate that he glanced at her to say, 'You'll be punished, but you just remember that you brought it on yourself. Wantons must be punished and pr'aps you'll learn your lesson. Now bide here while I speak to the matron.'

He climbed down and without a backward glance rang the bell at the gate. Admitted by a man in workhouse clothes, he disappeared.

Molly sat still, staring at the grim grey façade, the faceless windows, revulsion growing in her, nausea threatening. They would make her wear the yellow punishment frock and she knew only too well that the other girls would jeer at her, taunt her, that for a few days she would have to eat 'the bread of repentance' instead of dinner, at least until Mrs Norris relented. 'I can't,' she thought, 'I can't go back. I won't. They can't make me.'

Snatching up her bag she jumped down and began to run – across the square, behind the church, down a lane and into a maze of woodland. Stumbling, gasping, she plunged on, into a field of stubble which scratched her bare legs, with no idea of where to go or what to do. Only that she must get away, somewhere, anywhere. There were no sounds of a pursuit and after about half an hour she slowed down, to lean panting against a hay rick. Surely it would do no harm to rest a little, and she sank down against the warm straw.

Here she managed to get her breath back and wipe the sweat off her face. Thirsty now she began to wonder if there was a stream nearby or maybe even a cottage where she could ask for a drink from the well. But she could see neither and instead slid down to lie curled against the comfort of the rick. There she fell into an exhausted sleep, so still that a couple of dormice ventured into the straw to look for fallen grains. The clouds moved in and it began to spit with rain so that, when she woke an hour later, it was falling steadily, almost automatically making her think how relieved Master would be that the harvest was in. And then, thrusting away any thought of him, she sat up to pull bits of straw out of her shawl.

Now the stark reality of her position faced her. Hungry and thirsty, with no roof over her head or work to earn her bread, what should she do? Miss Plumstead, she was sure, would help her, but she daren't go there, for the cottage was too near the workhouse. It was the first place they would look for her, if they were looking at all. Perhaps Mr and Mrs Norris were merely thinking that they were well rid of her, until she was brought in, perhaps picked out of the gutter as no doubt Mr Wicks expected. No, she couldn't involve dear Miss Plumstead, who was getting on and still caring for her ancient and very trying mother, with the help of an equally ancient maid.

If only Hal were here. He couldn't have gone far. He might, she thought, have hung about the outskirts of the farm, hoping to see her. But he probably didn't want to get her into more trouble and had too much respect of Mr Wicks's shotgun to venture too near. Where was he now? Had he marched straight off to his next employment? Abandoned her? But he could not have known she had been turned out, and if somehow he managed to catch Susan, even Susan might not know that she had run away from the awfulness of the workhouse and its dire punishments.

Looking round the fields, seeing no one in sight, she

wondered what to do next. If only he would come striding across the stubble to rescue her, Gideon's sword in his hand! But there was only the empty countryside as far as she could see, all quiet after the labour of the harvest. Setting such store by his given word he must have gone on to Winchester and then Twyford Down, wherever that was, but he'd never mentioned the name of the farm. If she got there how could she find it – and if she did what then? Doubts and uncertainties assailed her. Perhaps after all Mr Wicks was right and it was just a night's sport to Hal? No, she wouldn't, couldn't believe that, but he wouldn't come back for her for a while, not until he'd found a home for them, and she had repudiated the idea of a charcoal burners' hut. Would she not welcome it now? It was all too great, too frightening a puzzle. For a brief moment she wept helplessly. But resolve rose and courage with it. Picking up her bag she headed west. She would go to Portsmouth; in such a busy place there was bound to be some employment to be had, and at least she could pay for food and lodging while she looked.

Trudging off in the now steady rain, a few ominous rumbles of thunder in the distance, she began to feel better. She was young, strong, and ignoring the rain, hoped her best dress was not looking too bedraggled, nor her bonnet, which had been a present from Miss Plumstead on her last birthday. Dear Miss Plumstead, when would she see her again? Bracing herself she felt that, even if wet, she was tidy and presentable for the search for lodgings. She walked on, came to a lane, a village, then another, neither of which she knew, but at a crossroads a signpost showed her the road to Portsmouth. It seemed a long way, but gradually, after rows of market gardens, forlorn in the rain, the way became more built up, houses and shops clustering together and even in her predicament she looked about her, taking in the strangeness of it all. In the narrow streets women were out shopping, children darting about, beggars and garishly dressed girls, soldiers and sailors in uniform strolling along, for this was a naval town which also housed a good many of the military in several barracks. But sailors were the more in evidence, loitering about the public houses and one called out to her.

'C'mon in, missy, out o' the rain, and I'll buy you a nip to keep you warm.'

Ignoring this she hurried on, finding herself in a maze of streets until, passing under a great gateway set in solid stone walls, she came into the heart of the old city. The first thing to do was to look for somewhere to stay and seeing a notice proclaiming 'superior lodgings' hanging outside a clean looking house, she knocked on the door.

A hefty woman in an apron opened it. Looking Molly up and down she asked, 'Well?' in no very friendly manner.

'If you please, ma'am,' Molly said in her politest voice, 'I need a room. Do you have one free?'

The woman did not immediately answer, eyeing Molly from her bonnet, its ribbons limp, to her muddied shoes, the hem of her skirt torn in one place from that desperate run through the field of stubble. Then she asked, 'Who are you? What are you doing asking for lodgings by yourself?'

'I need somewhere to stay while I look for work,' Molly explained, still on the doorstep. 'I had to leave my last place.'

'And why, may I ask?'

'There was a little – trouble.' Molly felt herself flushing.

'And you in it, eh? Well, I don't take in lone women, like as not no better than they should be. So you get on your way.'

The door slammed while she stood helplessly on the doorstep. It had never occurred to her that a decent place might see her solitariness in so bad a light. She would have to look for a less prepossessing house and wandering on came to the High Street. Dusk was falling now and people turning for home, but she could see that the houses here must belong to respectable people, the many shops selling goods of high quality, but there were also plenty of taverns, lighting up their windows, looking warm and enticing for customers. A smaller street, branching off, would perhaps accommodate her better, but it was very short and came out into another that ran parallel to the High street. Here she asked a young woman carrying a baby wrapped in a shawl, where she might find a bed for the night.

The girl, for she was little more, looked at Molly out of tired eyes. 'Well, if you don't mind sharing a sailor's bed, Mrs Dent at no.26 might take you in —'

'I do mind,' Molly broke in. 'That's not what I want.'

The girl shrugged. 'I thought mebbe you was one o' us. It's

32

a way to get food and a bed, if you ain't got much in your purse.' The baby started to howl and she crouched down in a doorway to put it to her thin breast.

Perplexed, Molly stood where she was, wondering what she had best do, and while she looked about her, realizing to the full the awkwardness of her situation, a man sidled up to her.

He was untidy and his chin had not seen a razor for several days. 'Well, miss, all alone, eh? So am I and my pockets pretty well to let, but I've enough for a bite of bread and cheese and you can share that, and my bed as well, if you've a mind to. Two are warmer than one, eh?'

By his voice Molly sensed he had once seen better days but she edged away. 'No – no – I must go, find a lodging house, perhaps you could tell me of one,' adding rather foolishly 'I've enough to pay for myself.'

He eyed her, took in the little purse hanging on her wrist. 'Have it your own way then,' he said casually.

In sudden and inexplicable panic she turned away and would have taken to her heels, but she'd not gone one step when he put out a foot and neatly tripped her. She fell heavily, her canvas bag scattering her possessions into a large puddle. For a moment she lay there, shocked, but almost immediately got to her knees to gather them out of the wet. He bent over her and passers-by, if they paid any notice at all, thought she was with the fellow. But in an instant he had whipped out a knife and slit the cords of her purse, wrenching it free. Then he disappeared into the murk. It had all taken less than a minute. Gasping for breath, one knee bruised and her wrist hurting from the jerk he had given it, she cried out, 'Stop! Stop him!' Only the sound of her cry was lost in the noise of passing carts and riders. She swept all her wet things into the bag, higgledy-piggledy, and got to her feet, fighting the desire to sob out loud. The realization that her money was gone paralysed her. Panic seized her again and with good reason. What could she do without money? She couldn't pay for accommodation or even for supper. Was this, she wondered wretchedly, how girls came to live on the streets?

She was still standing there, utterly forlorn and in dreadful indecision, when a carriage came past, its wheels sending up a shower of muddy water. If anything was needed to complete her misery, it was further mud and rain to cover her soaking clothes. A brief glimpse showed her a face, kindly and concerned, at the window of the coach, before it bowled on down the street.

More afraid that she had ever been in her life, the workhouse now seemed a haven compared to her present situation, for who would take in a penniless girl or give her work? And she was hungry now, so hungry her stomach seemed to rumble with emptiness. Blindly she walked on. She had always thought God looked after waifs and strays, cared for lost folk, but if she was now indeed a fallen woman, how would He look on her? Slow tears ran down her face.

It was then she saw the bakery, candles lit on the counter, a woman tidying up for the night. Drawn in to the light, the warmth, and savouring the smell of bread, Molly saw that there was one roll still lying by itself in a basket. Her stomach seemed to cry out for it. Perhaps the woman might think it would be too stale to sell the next day and would let her have it? Hardly aware of what she was doing, she put out a hand, touched it and then, hesitantly, drew back.

Unfortunately the baker's wife, returning from the back room, let out a screech and shouted as Molly herself had done only a short while ago, 'Stop, thief! Thief! Constable – Constable!'

By ill-luck there was a law officer passing the door, and he came in at once to lay a hand on Molly's shoulder, even as she turned to flee.

'So we have a thief here, do we? What was she stealing, Mrs Beddows?

'That bun,' the woman said truculently.

'I was hungry,' Molly whispered, white and shaking. 'My purse was stolen. Oh, please —'

'Very likely, I dare say,' the woman snorted and to the constable added, 'I'm not saying I mightn't have given it to her if she were that hungry, but stealin' is stealin'.'

''Course it is,' the constable agreed firmly. 'You, girl, where do you live?'

'Nowhere,' The word was dragged out of her. 'Leastways, not yet. I'm looking —'

The constable didn't care what she was looking for. He

wanted his home and his supper on this miserable evening. 'So you're a vagrant then? Well, we can't have such as you cluttering up our streets. Come along with me.' He nodded to the baker's wife and propelled Molly out of the shop.

Outside a little crowd had gathered when the shouting and accusations started, a few boys in rags, the girl with the baby had come to stare, with two young men on their way to the Dolphin tavern. 'Out of my road,' the constable ordered, and holding her arm firmly walked Molly up the street, turning at the end of it to go through a forbidding gateway. There was no use in struggling for he had her arm in a firm grip; in any case she was too shocked, too shaken to do anything.

Next to the gaol there was another large building, one of the city's barracks and two scarlet-coated soldiers on the way out looked curiously at her. 'Another moll,' one of them said and the other laughed. She went without protest – of what use to say she was neither a prostitute nor a thief? She would either be imprisoned in here or sent back to the workhouse and she was numb with awful foreboding. Knowing enough of what sent folk to prison, she was aware that stealing, even a loaf of bread or as little as a bun could be punished severely, and a second or third offence might mean transportation. Even for a first time it would warrant hard labour. Oh no, no, surely not for the temptation to take a left-over bun? Would they believe her if she protested that she had resisted the temptation? If she was to be punished like this it must surely mean that she and Hal had sinned greatly, that what she had experienced as warmth and love with marriage to come was nothing of the sort. Hal was gone and he would never find her now.

In the large hall with grey stone walls, lit by a solitary gas jet, the only furniture was a bare table and some benches. She was told to wait while the constable knocked at one of the several doors. A man appeared, whom Molly later discovered to be the head turnkey, not best pleased at being disturbed in the middle of his supper. He glanced briefly at her.

'Well, we're overcrowded just now. She'll have to go in with another female and be examined in the morning when the magistrate will be here. What's she done? Or is she on the streets?'

'I'm not,' she burst out, 'and I'm not a thief neither!'

35

'I wasn't asking you,' he retorted. 'You'd best keep a still tongue in your head. What's she done, Mr Peters?'

'Tried to steal some bread.'

'I didn't – I wouldn't.' Despite his admonition, she could not keep back the agonized denial. 'I meant to ask the baker.'

'That's as maybe,' the constable shrugged. 'I'll leave her to you, Mr Astridge. I'm off duty shortly and ready for a hot supper. She's a rare cook, my old woman is.' He nodded and went out.

Mr Astridge was barely into his forties and set on being governor when the present occupant of that post resigned. Determined to stop various abuses in the prison such as smuggled goods, he glanced at Molly's bag. 'Open it.' In silence she obeyed, bringing out her few clothes, which looked pathetic, damp and creased as they were. He picked up the package wrapped in the apron. 'So? You can read eh? Or is this stolen too?!'

'No,' she was near to weeping now. 'It was a gift – it has my name in it.'

'If that *is* your name.' But he put the Bible back in the bag, giving her a curious glance. Then, fetching a bunch of keys he beckoned her to follow him down a corridor. 'Inside,' he said, opening a door. 'You'll be examined in the morning, and think yourself lucky there's a justice coming for the Petty Sessions tomorrow and he may have time to consider your case. Now you'll sleep in here with old Betsy Tucker, so you'll probably catch something.' He pushed her in and by the poor light she saw an old woman sitting on a mattress on an iron bedstead with blankets wrapped round her scraggy form. There was another bed, but no covering on it.

'You put that blanket back,' Mr Astridge said to the bundle of rags. 'You've only right to one.'

Swearing in the foulest language, the old woman unwound one covering and held it out to Molly, who took it gingerly and wished she could throw it into the wash tub at the farm.

'Please,' she said to the turnkey, 'please sir, I'm that hungry.'

He shrugged. 'Kitchen's closed now. There'll be gruel and bread for breakfast at six-thirty,' and going out locked the door.

Molly sat down on the straw mattress and let the blanket fall on the end of it. A small oval barred window showed a faint light from the courtyard lamp. Her cell-mate asked what she was in for, making several unsavoury suggestions.

'There was a bun,' Molly said, 'but I didn't take it. I'm not a thief – only a thief stole my purse.'

The woman cackled. 'It's not such a bad thing to help yourself from them that 'as more'n you. I steals summat reg'lar to get put back in 'ere. There's more food an' better than in the work'us. They all know me, magistrates an' all, and they just say, "Here's old Betsy back again."'

'Is this a very big place?'

'Lord love yer, yes. And too many folks in it, what's more. We're supposed to have a cell each but t'aint likely. You and me's only in 'ere until we're sentenced, and then we're put in the women's cells. You never 'eard such screaming and swearing. An' they'll steal yer things as soon as look at you.'

Molly shivered, horror engulfing her. The workhouse would have been better than this, even the punishment frock.

'But you're lucky,' old Betsy went on. 'Leastways, if you wants to get out. One o' the turnkeys told me when I come in that Sir Charles'll be on the bench tomorrer. Second-chance-Charlie, we calls 'im, 'cos he's always saying he'll give prisoners another chance to live proper. Not that I wants it. I wants to stay in 'ere for the winter. They 'eat the cells and there's good food an' it's better nor livin' on the streets. Where d'you live, eh?'

'Nowhere,' Molly repeated, 'nowhere.' Tired, very hungry and worn out with today's awfulness, she lay down, wrapped in her shawl, over which she was forced by the cold to lay the unsavoury blanket. Trying to ignore the old woman's stream of tales, each more lurid than the last, of punishments meted out to men, women and even children, Molly wanted to shut her ears. But eventually Betsy stopped, to snore instead.

Thinking herself too miserable to sleep, attacked by bed bugs, she tried to say her night prayers but the words wouldn't come, her mind numb. How could she sleep in this miserable place, deep in her own misery? Nevertheless, she was so tired that eventually she did doze off.

In the morning, her natural resilience came to her aid, and

after a cold washing of her face and hands under the yard pump, Molly tidied herself as best she could, combed her hair, retied her bonnet and tried to brush the dried mud from her dress. Then she followed the other women, prostitutes, thieves, and vagrants, into the female dining room, where she ate the hot but tasteless gruel as if it was the food of the gods, thankful that talking was not allowed. The Sessions hall was on the first floor of the prison, and after a long wait during which a number of men and a few women were marched in and a little later out again, some looking relieved, others grumbling, some swearing until told to shut their mouths by the prison guard, Molly herself was called.

The large room was occupied by the clerk of the court sitting by a table covered with papers, two officers standing at the back by the benches provided for the prisoners, while on the raised dais was the presiding officer. As she looked curiously towards him she gave a little start of recognition, for there at the head of the court was the man who had looked out of his carriage window yesterday. Sure it was him, she became certain when he gave her a studying glance as if he recognized her. The clerk read out the charge, asked her name, her age, where she lived and when once again she said 'nowhere' he wrote down 'vagrant'. He also put down her date of birth and where it had taken place, further information as to parents she could not tell him, only answering what she could while his pen scratched. The baker's wife had not put in an appearance, informing the constable that she could not give up a morning's work to waste her time on a stupid girl, but the arresting constable was called to explain what had happened.

Molly lifted her head to answer the questions as best she could. Yes, she had been tempted, but she hadn't actually taken the bun and was going to ask the woman if she could have it. Her purse having been stolen she did not know what to do. Sir Charles asked one or two questions himself. If he was as his nickname proclaimed, inclined to give first offenders the benefit of the doubt wherever possible, she began to feel that if her fate lay in his hands, there was some hope for her. No doubt he could indeed be stern enough with habitual criminals, his hand falling heavily where needed, but he looked at Molly with a much kinder expression on his face.

'Well,' he said. 'It seems you are only homeless through no fault of your own, and if your appearance leaves somewhat to be desired that is in part the fault of my coachman.' He smiled at her swift upward glance. 'Yes, I thought you realized it was my carriage that showered you with mud yesterday. You must remember that if you walk in a busy street you would be wise to stay close to the houses. I think there is no great crime here.' To the clerk he added, 'I will give Miss March a second chance, for I believe she meant no harm. I wish to find out more, so send her to my room when I'm finished. Next case, please.'

She stumbled out to wait once more on the bench in the corridor, overcome with gratitude, wondering at the same time why he wanted to see her. Ten minutes later Betsy came out with a toothless grin on her face. 'What did I tell you, eh? An' I've got six months, so us is settled, eh?'

'Quiet, Betsy,' an officer said. 'Get along with you. I don't have to tell you where to go.'

An hour later Molly was admitted to a room used by court officials to robe and read papers. There was an armchair by the hearth, a large desk and a cupboard along one wall. Sir Charles was seated by the desk and now that he was out of his official gear Molly saw that he was middle-aged with greying hair and somewhat corpulent. He had a round chubby face bearing a kindly expression and indicating that she should stand before him said, 'If I am any judge I believe you are not the sort of girl to get into trouble of this nature, so suppose you tell me your story, right from the beginning, in particular why you are not at home with your family.'

Sure somehow that she could trust him, she told it all, beginning with the workhouse and Miss Plumstead, asserting that her mother had been a lady. She kept nothing back, only hesitating, a flush in her cheeks, when she came to Hal's place in her story. But it had to be explained and she ended by saying, 'I did think, I still do, that he will come back, though he won't never find me now. And as you know, Sir, I've been robbed of what money I had.'

Sir Charles listened in attentive silence. He took in her natural bearing that even misfortune hadn't crushed, the hands reddened by work but nevertheless well-shaped, her face

39

showing him an honesty that he was quick to recognize. If he could spot the liar and the cheat, he could also recognize the innocent.

'My poor child,' he said at last, 'it seems to me that you have been somewhat ill-used by fate, and I can quite believe that your mother must have been in the same case to be driven to the workhouse.'

She flushed, almost overcome by his understanding. 'Thank you, Sir,' she whispered. 'Oh, thank you.'

'Well, as I said in court there is no case against you, so you are free to go. But what are you going to do? I don't want you up before me again.'

'I don't know, Sir. If I could find work – but I can't pay for lodging until I do.'

He seemed to be thinking. 'And when you were on the farm you worked in the house, in the kitchen?'

'I did all of it,' Molly said simply.

He pulled a card out of his pocket and scribbled something on the back of it. 'Now take this to Crossley Lodge, it's a white house in the road by Southsea Common, only a mile or two from here and the constable will direct you. Go to the servants' entrance and give this to whoever lets you in. My housekeeper was telling me this morning that we need another girl in the house, though I can't say for what duties. I leave all that to her, but it's employment for you, if you wish it.'

He gave her an encouraging smile. 'I'm sure you will make the most of a second chance, eh? Why, bless me, the child's fainted!'

Chapter Three

Captain Matthew Hamilton was a deeply disappointed man. In the army since he was sixteen and considered a most promising young officer, by now at thirty, he could certainly have hoped for a lieutenant-colonelcy with the cavalry. Instead he was a mere captain in a line regiment. He owed this situation to the fact that he had fallen foul of no less a person than James Brudenell, seventh Earl of Cardigan. He was not alone in this. Well known for his vile temper, his prejudices, his blistering attacks on juniors whom he disliked, the Earl demanded perfection from his men. There must be no speck of dirt on their cherry-coloured trousers which had given them the nickname of 'cherry-bums', no mark on the dashing jacket and pelisse he had designed himself, no speck on the boots, despite a dusty parade ground. All weapons had to be polished daily, all horseflesh of the top quality, harness in mint condition. His theatrically clad regiment must be the best in the army and he looked very poorly on an officer who had neither private means nor breeding, most of whom he had managed to get rid of. Matt Hamilton had both, but his lordship disliked him for another reason entirely. Matt's father had been a major-general of the highest distinction, and a personal friend of the Duke of Wellington. They had served together in India where Matt had been gazetted in his early days. Lord Cardigan loathed 'Indian' officers. One by one he forced them out of his regiment, accused them of sloppiness, carelessness, disobedience, inefficiency, and any other misdemeanour he could think of. He forced one to a court martial, several into resignation for trivial offences, blocked the advancement of others. Complaints were lodged at the Horse Guards, and Wellington remarked acidly that he was very sorry for the General Officer so unlucky as to have the 11th Hussars in his division. Most of the uproar was over such stupid matters as placing a black bottle on the mess table instead of a decanter, and for a while Lord Cardigan was pilloried in the press, booed at the theatre and jeered at in the streets, but he had the hide of a crocodile and the supreme conviction that he was always right.

Two of Matt's particular friends, Captains Tuckett and Forrest had suffered at his hands and three years ago Lord Cardigan turned his attention on Captain Hamilton. The particular provocation that incurred his wrath was nothing more than a cold in the head. Matt had been suffering from a heavy one and going on parade, perhaps a second or two late, had seized a fresh handkerchief, stuffing it inadequately into his pocket before mounting his new mare, Shalima, to ride out on to the parade ground. Most unluckily the handkerchief came loose just as the ranks lined up before their Colonel. It fluttered to the ground, was caught by the wind and floated away to land almost under the hooves of Cardigan's charger, who, taking exception to it, pranced restlessly.

His lordship's prominent eyes bulged as he jerked at the reins, his face turning purple with rage. He shook with it as he shouted, 'You, sir, Hamilton – how dare you insult my parade with your – your disgusting rag? Come forward at once.'

Matt obeyed, edging Shalima ahead to face his furious superior. A verbal assault followed while the whole regiment, some six hundred men, sat their mounts to listen in embarrassed silence, Matt's own company in justifiable indignation. Captain Hamilton was sloppy, like all officers who had served in India, had no idea of discipline, and when Matt tried to protest, was told that he was insubordinate, and instead of ordering a trooper to retrieve the offending object, demanded that Matt should dismount and chase it as it was blown across the parade ground. It was not only humiliating but utterly against army code for an officer to be thus treated in front of the men. There was a further row later in the day when Matt was summoned in front of the Colonel and ordered to rename his horse. Lieutenant-Colonel the Earl of Cardigan would have no Indian-named mounts in his regiment. Unfortunately as Matt started to explain that the animal was a present from an Indian official, a friend of his late father, this only made matters worse and Matt compounded the whole affair by being unable to keep back the most enormous sneeze.

Lord Cardigan screamed at him that he was a clown, a buffoon, and a disgrace to the regiment. Matt forced himself to apologize, angry though he was, and afterwards recounting the tale to Harvey Tuckett, his friend grinned at him and said, 'Even he couldn't court martial you over a handkerchief!' To which Matt replied that he would put nothing past their choleric commanding officer. Some years before Captain Tuckett had had his own run-in with Lord Cardigan which ended in a duel by the windmill on Wimbledon Common in which Tuckett was wounded. Lord Cardigan was summoned to a court martial out of which he wriggled, and Captain Tuckett had left the regiment.

It was most unfortunate therefore that a week later Matt had a letter from his stepfather, Sir Charles Milner, to say that his mother was very ill and that he should come at once. He applied for leave, which was given with a very bad grace, and went home. Lady Milner's life was in danger for a few days, and Matt wrote for an extension of his leave. This was refused, but he nevertheless stayed on at home. Only when she was on the road to recovery did he return to the regiment. Hardly surprisingly, a storm awaited him, and a commanding officer once again purple with fury and threatening a court martial for being absent without leave. This was applied for, but luckily for Matt the Earl himself went home to Deene Park for a couple of weeks before he could receive a reply; and the major, being a friend of Captain Hamilton, put the correspondence in his 'pending' file and left it there. Matt, without a great deal of sober thought, took advantage of this to go straight to the Horse Guards.

There he asked to see the Commander-in-Chief. A harassed staff officer told him that the Duke of Wellington could not concern himself with junior officers who thought themselves ill-used. At this, though in some guilt at doing it, Matt told him that his father, General Hamilton, had been one of his grace's closest friends. He would be grateful for ten minutes of the Duke's time if he had to present himself here every day for a week. On the second afternoon Wellington saw him.

In his late seventies the Duke looked thin and lined but as alert as ever and with no patience for trivia. He had had more than enough complaints of the Earl of Cardigan and if the Earl had not had as many influential friends, including the Queen and Prince Albert, as enemies he would have got rid of him.

'Well, Hamilton, I've very little time,' his sharp opening remark was not encouraging, 'and none to be attending to regimental quarrels. Good God, where would we be if every jackanapes with a grievance came charging up to my office? But I suppose, as you have presumed on our relationship, which is not the behaviour I like, I will nevertheless have to spare you five minutes.'

At this typical Wellington set-down, the habitual crease between Matt's brows deepened as he said in a low voice, 'I beg your pardon for that, sir, but I thought it the only way to see you. And I do consider myself most abominably ill-treated.'

'You do, do you?' Wellington gave a snort. 'I am sick to death of the arguments in the 11th and if there is much more of it I shall disperse all the officers to other regiments.'

This was harsh indeed, but Matt replied that there was a great deal of discontent. 'Captains Forrest and Tuckett —'

'Thank you, I know all about them. I shall write a directive to be read out to all officers. I'll have no more of this.'

Matt stood silent, aware that an interview with the Commander-in-chief could reduce the strongest character to a pulp.

'Well, sir, well? As you are here you had better tell me your grievance.'

'Yes, sir. But first I would like to acquaint your lordship with the fact that I have three times applied for my majority which is more than due, and each time there has been a vacancy Lord Cardigan has put forward a junior officer above me, simply because they were from the aristocracy, and had never so much as seen the Indian coast.'

The Duke looked at him in amazement. 'You've had the infernal impertinence to come to me about that?'

'No, sir, that is only what has gone before. I merely wanted to point out that my colonel is set against me, but the more serious matter concerns my mother.' He was aware of Wellington's eyes beneath the white brows, seemingly boring into his head. 'I went on leave, sir, to see her, having been summoned by my stepfather, to find her very ill indeed. The doctor thought her dying and I wrote at once asking for an extension of leave. Lord Cardign refused me in the most offensive terms. I thought it my duty to stay with her and, thank God, she began to recover, but when I got back he was most unreasonable —' too gentle a word, Matt thought, for his Commanding Officer's attitude – 'and furthermore he chose to insult my late father, into the bargain. He never has anything good to say about any officer who has served in India.'

Wellington gave him a sharp glance. 'Does he not? Perhaps he forgets that your father and I once campaigned there together.' For a moment he stared at Matt who began to wonder if his rash move in coming here had been a fatal error. Then, in a softened voice, the Duke asked if Lady Milner was really recovered.

'More or less, sir, though I doubt if she will ever have full health again.'

'I'm sorry for that. Such a pretty woman, as I recall at her marriage to your father. I stood up with him as groomsman, you know, but that's more than thirty years ago. Pray give her my good wishes for her restored health.'

'I will, sir, and if –' Matt found it hard to force the words out for he disliked asking favours, 'if your grace would consider granting me a transfer, anywhere else, I would go willingly.'

'Oh you would, would you? Well, I suppose if I don't want further trouble I had better do so.' And in a return of his sharper voice, the Duke added, 'Well, I can't have you in the cavalry so it will have to be a line regiment. What do you think of that, eh? All you cavalry men have a great deal of conceit and think you can bring off any job without the infantry, but you are wrong. At Waterloo, I can tell you, it was the infantry that won that day.'

'Yes, sir,' Matt said meekly.

'You had better go on half-pay while your request for a transfer is considered by the Quarter-master's department. I believe the 50th is short of officers.'

'The Dirty Half-Hundred!' Matt exclaimed and then wished he hadn't.

'Not a good-looking regiment,' Wellington agreed icily, 'but devilish steady. Are you refusing it?'

'No, sir, no indeed.'

'Good, because it's all I'm likely to offer at this precise moment, and why I should concern myself with your affairs at all I'll be damned if I know. Well, yes I suppose I do. Tell your mother she has herself to thank for this.' He paused for a moment and then added, 'You are very like your father,' before picking up a letter and his pen to signify that the interview was over. Matt thanked him and withdrew. Having traded on his father's connection with the Duke, it amused him that it was a memory of his mother's pretty face that had softened the Duke's attitude. Half ashamed of his own impertinence, he was at the same time relieved that at least he was free of Lord Cardigan.

All this was now three years in the past. Matt's new commander was a certain Lieutenant-Colonel Henderson, a very different sort of man from the Earl of Cardigan; a disciplinarian certainly, a soldier with a total dedication to his career, but under a brusque manner he was also humane, treating his officers in a manner to earn their respect. He had seen action at Waterloo, and later in India and Ireland. Experienced, tough, he asked nothing of his men that he wouldn't do himself and his soldiers trusted him. He was also a 'character'. He took his wife everywhere with him. She travelled with her maid, her groom, and her tent. They had no children and were totally devoted to each other. The soldiers called him Old Walking Boots because on a long march he often dismounted and strode along with his troops. Matt liked him, and the feeling seemed to be mutual, the Hendersons often asking him to dine with them. The Royal West Kents, the 50th got their nickname in the Peninsula when dye from their black facings got on to hands and faces, and Matt found a stability and good humour in the regiment as a result of Colonel Henderson's sensible ordering. Never a man to be entirely at ease in mixed society, army life suited him. But he felt his career had been if not blighted, certainly halted, and for this he loathed Cardigan, with a hatred that went deep and was never entirely forgotten.

Home now on a week's leave, he joined his family at the dinner table with reasonable pleasure. He was very fond of his mother, now somewhat frail, few traces left of her delicate prettiness, and living a sofa-life. He had been her only child by George Hamilton and she was grief-stricken when her husband was killed, but Selina Hamilton was not the woman to live alone. She was endearing in many ways but without the least idea how to manage without a husband, and shortly after accepted an offer from Sir Charles Milner, a widower with two daughters. The eldest, Henrietta, was only a year younger than Matt, Georgina two years behind Henrietta. The boy, bereft of the father he had adored and venerated, was lost and unhappy. He found it difficult to communicate his personal feelings. Sir Charles was always kind to him, but Henrietta put him down as a nuisance, being very short with him, while Georgina, a lively tomboy, teased him unmercifully until, fortunately, she outgrew that stage. At eighteen she married and now, softened and happy with her husband and two children, she and Matt were on quite affectionate terms. The last member of the family was Toby, the only issue of the marriage of Sir Charles to General Hamilton's widow and the absorbing light of his mother's eye. She did not attempt to understand her elder son, but with Toby there was really very little to comprehend.

It was he who was dominating the conversation this evening. 'I say, sir,' he burst out, 'do but consider it. There is going to be a war, everyone says so. Though why we have to take sides with the rascally Turks – well, everyone says they are, at least those fellows who've travelled abroad – to fight the Russians, I don't know. But that doesn't matter, I must be in on it.'

Lady Milner shuddered. 'What are you thinking of, my love? I can't, I won't bear it. After all the troubles your brother has had —'

'That's nothing to do with it, Mama. Has it, Matt?' He appealed to his half-brother, who merely shrugged and said, 'I can't imagine you would really want to join the 11th.'

'No, well, I hope I've got too much family feeling to think of buying in there, not but what they have a glorious uniform. Wouldn't I like to swagger down the Mall in it!'

Matt permitted himself a wry smile. 'Do you know that the Earl of Cardigan orders men to be stationed at intervals there to salute him as he goes past? How's that for monumental conceit? But the army is more than a uniform, and the cavalry more than the "cherry-bums", you know.'

'Of course I do, but', Toby turned to his father, 'could you not buy me a cornetcy in the Light Dragoons? Peter Shrimpton has gone in and says they're a splendid lot of fellows. I'm sure you could pull a string or two, you know so many people in London.'

'The penalty of having an uncle on the Privy Council,' Sir Charles said lightly, 'but I've been away from London for a good many years now and I'm sadly out of touch.'

'Do see what you can do, please, Papa. There's Colonel Grafton at Winchester. Georgy said only the other day that she'd met him at a ball and he'd spoken of you.'

Toby was sitting next to his mother and she laid her hand over his on the table cloth. 'My dearest, pray put this idea out of your head. I can't have both my sons in danger, and you are so young.'

'Matt was younger than me when he went in, weren't you?' He threw the question at his half-brother, but without waiting for an answer, rushed on, 'I can't spend all my life sitting at home, Mama. Surely you can see that?'

'Well, I think you are being very selfish.' Henrietta Milner was a spinster. She had had one offer and turned it down, and now with her stepmother a semi-invalid, she had decided to devote her life to the care of her father, the house and the invalid, persuading herself she was doing something noble in sacrificing herself to them. The role of martyr, unfortunately, had only succeeded in turning her somewhat sour, and she added, 'You are upsetting Mama'.

Toby had turned his spectacular blue eyes on his mother. 'I don't mean to. Dear Mama, you do see, don't you? You wouldn't expect me to stay at home for ever, and it would be so splendid. Just because Matt was foolish enough to pick a quarrel with Lord Cardigan, who everyone knows has the smartest regiment in the cavalry —'

'I wish', Matt said coldly, 'you would refrain from making remarks on something about which you have neither experience or judgement'.

Toby opened his mouth to retort, but as they had all finished their roast beef and the servants were clearing the dishes he let the matter rest. Almost at once he was distracted by the maid now removing his half-sister's plate. A new girl, and by Jove she was lovely! Tall, with a beautiful figure clearly visible under the black dress and white apron; lovely hair too half hidden by that cap! He watched as, unconcernedly, she took the plate away and brought another from Frederick who was serving the blackberry and apple tart, to lay it before her mistress.

Lady Milner gave a long-suffering sigh. 'No, no tart for me. How can I be expected to have any appetite, I don't know. To be faced with losing you both —'

Matt gave her a patient smile. 'I have been in the army for fourteen years, my dear mother, and come to no harm. It's a good life for a man who is determined to make it so. Whether Toby is only interested in the glamour I can't say, but if I had him in my company I'd soon make something of him.'

'There!' Lady Milner clutched at the straw, 'If you went into your brother's regiment, Toby —'

'Good God, no. Mama, what can you be thinking of? The Dirty Half-hundred? Infantry! No! It's the cavalry for me. Why, Jasper Strange says the cavalry will win the war, if there is a war, without any help from the foot-sloggers.'

'Jasper Strange', Matt said crushingly, 'is an ignorant cub, even more ignorant than you are, if that's possible'.

'Well, he's going into the Dragoons and that's where I mean to go. Mama, don't look like that. Don't you want the best for me? And the cavalry is the best. It's what Matt chose first, and even if he —' he caught Matt's eye and finished lamely, 'Yes, well, never mind that. You know, Mama, I'm not a child any more to be tied to home. And you've got Henrietta to run round and wait on you.'

'Toby!' his father exclaimed with rare sharpness, 'you will not speak to your mother in such a manner, if you please. And I think we've aired the subject enough for one evening.

49

Frederick, I'll have some more of that tart.'

Matt was silent during the rest of the meal. Never one to talk a great deal, he attended to an excellent slice of Wensleydale cheese, but it was an ongoing aggravation when he came home in that disparaging remarks seemed to surface for one reason or another, concerning his affray with Cardigan. It was felt to be a blot on the family reputation and he found this excessively hard to bear, though at the time his stepfather had agreed that he could not have acted other than he did, certainly in the matter of his mother's illness.

At least, for the moment anyway, Toby's affairs had turned their attention from trying to marry him off. At twenty-one he had become engaged to a certain Maria Kingswood, a young lady of good family, and for one blissful summer they had been very much in love. However when his regiment was due to depart to India, she suddenly discovered she neither wanted to be a junior officers' wife, nor to go to India, nor above all to leave her Mama. There were tears, recriminations and the betrothal was called off. For a while he was sadly disillusioned that his goddess had feet of clay, not loving him enough to share his future whatever that might be. However by the end of the long sea voyage he had discovered that his heart was not broken. The scar remained, but life was new, exciting, and the comradeship of his fellow officers did a great deal to assuage the soreness. Occasionally his mother or Henrietta invited personable young ladies to the house, but he was not going to be caught that way again. When he married it would have to be for different reasons. His stepfather had never interfered in his affairs, though he had done his best for the lonely boy, and now they were on good enough terms that after dinner Matt asked for a word with him in private.

They went into Sir Charles's study where he suggested Matt should pour them both a brandy. Then, taking his glass and settling in his chair by the large desk he said, 'Well, my boy? I do trust you are not in any further difficulty?'

Matt sat astride a stool. 'No, and not likely to be, I trust. I've got used to the 50th and they are a very decent set of officers. No, sir, it's Toby, though I'm aware that it's not for me to interfere.'

'Nonsense, I regard you as his elder brother. What has he been up to?

'Any devilment that's going in Portsea, and he's getting a bad name. No doubt you've heard a few things too. While I appreciate my mother's protective feelings towards him, as the youngest of us, and naturally she doesn't want to part with him, nevertheless he must have something to do now that Cambridge is behind him.'

'Where he did precious little work,' Sir Charles agreed, 'and yes, I have heard a few rumours. Nothing is more likely to lead to mischief than being refused the chance to do what one wants to do with one's life. He is set on the army, I see that, and it's only in deference to his mother that I have hesitated.'

'I know, sir. She is by nature somewhat fearful, but with you and Henrietta —'

Sir Charles weighed his paper knife on one finger. 'I've taken care of her fears and fancies these twenty years.'

'You have indeed,' Matt said quickly, 'and I'm aware that I tried her with my affairs, what with the broken engagement and all. But I didn't mean to imply —'

'Of course you didn't.' His stepfather gave him a quick warm smile. 'My dear boy, you and I have always been able to come to an understanding, haven't we? And as far as Toby is concerned, you are right. How the young rascal has escaped being brought up in front of me I really don't know. If the boy is set on the cavalry I'm prepared to buy him in as a cornet. What do you suggest?'

'Well,' Matt finished his brandy. He liked this cheerful rubicund man who was, he knew, devoted to his mother and quite capable of nursing her through her terrors. 'I would advise avoiding Lord Cardigan's command. Although Toby and I have different surnames, someone is bound to know of the connection and enlighten his lordship, which would do Toby no good. It might be worth seeing what is available in the Dragoon Guards, the 1st or the 4th, I should think. I could make enquiries, if you wish.'

'I would be grateful,' his stepfather said warmly, 'though I don't like to use up your last few days' leave.'

'I can go up by train and take the chance to look up one or

51

two friends, especially now that the 11th is back from Ireland.'

'It's very good of you.' Sir Charles regarded him for a moment. He liked this stepson of his, though at times he still found him difficult to understand. Tall, thin, reserved, Matt could look a little forbidding when he chose. He was always scrupulously neat, which made the business of the handkerchief all the harder to stomach, and always courteous, though giving little away on a personal level. Sir Charles had a shrewd idea that his broken love affair, coupled with the disastrous end to his cavalry days, had left their mark, though Matt would never discuss either matter. Even in his concern for his own son, Sir Charles wished that he could lift Matt out of a way of life that seemed to be lived on too cold a level. He had never underrated Matt's abilities, but he was lacking the warmth to counteract a certain harshness – a wife in short, but no one since Maria Kingswood had caught his fancy. It was a shame, but Sir Charles was a great believer in not interfering. Except of course in the case of his young son, and he expressed his feelings on that score in a heartfelt tone. 'I must say I do wish very much that he could go in under you.'

'So do I. I would soon lick him into shape, but I'm afraid he won't look to a line regiment. Well, I'll go to London tomorrow and see what I can do.'

'I appreciate this, Matt.'

Their private talk ended satisfactorily as always between two sensible men, and Matt, finding the drawing room empty, followed the rest of the family up to bed, first putting his head round his mother's door to wish her goodnight. She was seated by her dressing table while her maid Sylvia brushed her hair and Matt was thankful that she could not at this moment pursue the subject of Toby.

He was on the upper landing where his room was when he heard a stifled sound and then a low laugh and a voice, Toby's, saying, 'Come on, you know you'd like it as much as I would. There's an empty room along here and a most convenient sofa.'

'No, sir, *NO* – if you please.'

'I don't please. I can soon make you —'

'That you can't. Let me go at once.' And then a little piece

52

of the workhouse slipped out, 'You're naught but a silly loon with nothing in your head but the tassle below it! Let me go, I say.'

Smothering a rare desire to laugh, Matt had had enough. In a few strides he was up the intervening short flight to the attics and seizing Toby by the collar wrenched him away with such force that his brother fell against the banister. Then he turned to the girl, expecting to see her frightened, but she was not. Her hazel eyes were glinting with anger.

'I'm sorry,' he said sharply, 'I'll see he doesn't bother you again.'

Toby was scrambling to his feet. 'Damn you, Matt, you'd no cause to do that. I didn't mean any harm —'

'I know exactly what you meant. Save that sort of thing for the street molls in Portsmouth, there are plenty of them, but don't you dare to molest any of our maids – do you hear me?'

'Oh I hear you, curse you. But you must agree – a prime piece, eh.'

'Enough of that. Give me your word, or I'll see that your father hears of this.'

Toby's face was scarlet with mortification. 'My God, you *are* being moral. I'll wager you had your fling once, if not now, for all we know.'

'Stop it.' Matt caught his collar and shook him. 'Go to bed at once, you ill-conditioned pup.' He half pushed him towards the stair and Toby went, mainly because in reality he stood a great deal in awe of Matt, who had all the self-assurance he himself lacked. He tried to think of a parting shot and nearly said, 'I suppose you want a clear field,' but not wanting a boot up his backside, wisely thought better of it, and muttering something about Matt being a kill-joy, went away.

To Matt's surprise the girl, instead of scurrying off, stood where she was by the wall, her hands flat against it on either side of her. 'Thank you,' she murmured. 'I wouldn't have let him, I could have stopped him —'

Matt gave his rare low short laugh. 'I'm sure you could. You're a well-plucked female, I must say. What's your name?'

'Molly, sir, Molly March.'

'And how long have you been here, Molly March?'

'Two days, sir, and I got lost going to my bed. There's so many stairs and corridors.'

'This part of the house is a rabbit warren, I grant you. Are you the girl my stepfather told us of, who was up before him after considerable misfortunes?'

'Yes, sir,' she said simply.

For a moment they looked at each other. At dinner Molly had been told that when she took plates around she did not look directly at the recipient, but now she gave him a swift glance and saw a man a good deal taller than herself with almost black hair and very dark well-shaped brows, a slightly hooked nose, and deep-set grey eyes. It would have been a stern face, she thought, if he had not given that sudden laugh. He had bothered to come to her aid and she felt a swift warmth towards him. 'Thank you,' she said again. 'I think I could have sent him about his business, but he shouldn't have – well, I suppose after me being up before Sir Charles, he thought me a bad sort of girl, but I'm not.'

'I'm sure you're not.' He was quite certain of it. There was an honesty about her that he liked. Retrieving her cap from where it had fallen on the floor, though he had no need to do so – she was after all only a servant girl – nevertheless he felt sorry for her. And she had an attractive face, more than pretty, those lovely brown curls loose now. Stirred, though he had no idea why, he had a sudden and overwhelming urge to kiss her himself. Good God! he thought, what was the matter with him? Had he sunk to Toby's level? But he brushed the thought away and in a harsher voice than he meant to use, merely said, 'Get off to your bed now, along here and up that spiral stair at the end, and try to come up with one of the others in future.'

She made a slight bob towards him, took the cap from his hand and walked away, not hurrying, in the direction he had indicated.

Matt watched her. There was something about her, a dignity that she did not lose even in what could have been a nasty situation. When she was hidden from view, the passage dark with only a small gas flare to light it, he went away to his own room. He understood well enough why Toby had been attracted to her and he would have strong words to say to him

54

in the morning concerning where a man took his pleasures. But for himself – what nonsense! He would go to London tomorrow, find his friend Captain Tuckett who now ran an agency for the East India Company in the Strand. Together no doubt they would pass a pleasurable evening, and he could forget about Molly March and his wish to set a kiss on those inviting lips.

Chapter Four

Sir Charles Milner was generous to his servants at Christmas time, and each girl had a length of patterned cotton material to make a day dress, with a guinea as well. Frederick, having been many years with Sir Charles, combining the duties of butler and valet, received two shirts and four guineas, while the cook-housekeeper, Mrs Davies, also of many years' employment, had similar gifts. The scullery maid, Mabel, another recipient of Second-chance-Charlie's kindness, was overjoyed with her half-guinea which went straight to her impoverished parents, while there was five shillings for the boy Jack who looked after the fires and cleaned the shoes.

The senior housemaid, Sylvia, a plain girl who had never attracted Toby's interest, had been in the house for five years, and as well as overseeing the cleaning was Lady Milner's maid. Not an extravagant household, but one with a master who was much respected and a mistress, whose frailty commanded compassion, and Frederick saw that it ran smoothly enough. Molly's work-load was as full as that at the farm, but less heavy. The highest standards of cleanliness were required and Molly was on the run all day, but she didn't mind. She brought her own brand of cheerfulness to her work, her gratitude shown in the only way she could, by keeping the downstair rooms spick and span, which was no hardship, for she loved sweeping and dusting in the beautiful drawing room, handling the delicate porcelain ornaments with loving care. Every morning she shook the curtains and cushions, made sure Jack had a good fire going for when the family emerged from breakfast. The dining room was Frederick's particular charge, but she dusted the sideboard with its collection of silver, entreé and chafing dishes, bowls and candelabra, as well as assisting Frederick in the dining room when Sylvia was engaged elsewhere.

She and Sylvia also had charge of the bedrooms, to make the beds and sweep and dust as downstairs, refill the jugs on the washstand, make sure Jack laid the fires properly. It was a great deal to get through and still to be changed out of her print morning dress into the afternoon black frock, supplied by Mrs Davis, with white cap, apron and cuffs, by half past one. After the first two days and the upset with Toby there was only one awkward moment. Having struggled as always to contain her bouncy hair under her cap, when she leaned forward to set his plate before Sir Charles, a hair-pin fell out on to a slice of baked ham. With swift presence of mind she whipped the plate away and held another out for Frederick to replenish, encountering a severe look. Toby choked down a laugh, Henrietta make a clucking noise, but Sir Charles at once looked up at her and said, 'No harm done, eh?' A little flushed Molly went on with the serving and there was no further comment, though afterwards Frederick said severely that he did not like such mortifying things happening at his dinner table and that she must learn to pin her hair properly.

Sylvia and Molly shared an attic room which contained only two narrow iron bedsteads, a chest of drawers, one hard chair and a jug and basin. As the winter deepened it became very cold and they pushed the beds together, making them into one double bed for warmth. Sylvia told Molly she was the eldest of four and always sent her wages home to her widowed mother, but mostly she talked of the family, of their master's goodness, of Lady Milner's illness three years ago and how Captain Hamilton was summoned home, of Miss Georgy's wedding, and Toby's high jinks when he was on holiday from Winchester school. It was clear she cared for little else but her place here.

Molly dreamed, nursed ambitions of rising to be house-keeper one day in at least a ducal residence, or perhaps of setting up as a milliner. Sometimes she thought of marriage, but since the disappearance of Hal made up her mind that it would never be to a poor man. She liked the life in the servants' hall, the cameraderie, though each one knew his or her place and there was a hierarchy even there, but the companionship was something she had never known, for she could hardly compare it with either the noisy and often lewd talk in the women's day room at the workhouse, or with the often silent meals at the farm.

Toby had not bothered her again, probably, she thought, because he stood in too much awe of his half-brother, whether Captain Hamilton was at home or not. In November, to everyone's relief except his mother's, his commission was purchased as a cornet in the 4th Dragoon Guards and he went off in the highest spirits to join his regiment. At Christmas time he came home, resplendent in his dark blue uniform with its scarlet and yellow facings and tall black shako, insisting on running down to the servants' hall to show himself off to Mrs Davis and Frederick who had both known him since babyhood.

'What do you think, Molly?' he asked mischievously, as she was laying the able for the servants' dinner, and she gave him a little smile before answering, 'Very beautiful, sir.'

He gave her a grin and went off upstairs again as proud as could be, to dash out and see if his friend Jasper was at home. Mrs Bell, Georgy to the family, arrived with her husband Walter and their twin boys of almost two years; while a nephew and niece of Sir Charles's with a cousin of Lady Milner's completed the party for the festive days. It made a great deal of work, but Molly loved it all, seeing the holly and the ivy brought in, and a Christmas tree decorated, a thing she had never seen before. The little boys added noise and brightness to the house and she was simply glad to be part of it all. Farm Christmases had never been like this and she was sorry when it was over.

After the New Year celebrations Sir Charles told Frederick that he was extremely pleased with the hard work put in by all the staff and that each should therefore have a day to visit their families. When her turn came, on a crisp January morning, Molly set off for Westbourne. Soon after coming to Crossley Lodge she had written to Miss Plumstead explaining very guardedly what had happened, though saying nothing about the fracas in the barn, and she had a reply saying she

58

would always be welcome at Rosemary Cottage, adding that Mrs Plumstead had died, though that, Molly thought, was more likely to be a relief than otherwise, even if the old lady's devoted daughter would never say so. It was a long walk, but setting off after the breakfast had been cleared away Molly didn't care, relishing the freedom, the fresh air, hoar frost glistening on the trees, ice on the puddles and streams. Glad she didn't have to pass the workhouse to reach the cottage, she rang the bell, to find the door opened by a new maid.

Miss Plumstead came hurrying out of the sitting room. 'My dearest Molly what a delightful surprise. Take off your cloak and bonnet and come to the fire. You must be cold. Tell me about your new place.'

Molly enthused, describing it all, speaking warmly of her employers and making Miss Plumstead laugh with her account of Second-chance-Charlie. Her friend had grown older since the days when she had taught at the workhouse, her grey hair thin and wispy, her cheeks a little wrinkled, but her eyes were bright as she looked at Molly.

'You will stay for your dinner? You saw I have a new maid? Dear old Polly didn't survive my mother for long, and this girl is quite a good worker.' She rang the bell and told Winifred to put more potatoes and parsnips in to roast with the capon.

After dinner, sipping Miss Plumstead's cowslip wine, Molly said she would have to go soon, to be back before dark, and at once Miss Plumstead jumped up.

'I've something for you, Molly dear, that I meant to give you as soon as I could now that you are quite grown up.' She opened the top drawer of a little chest and brought out a small box. 'There, my dear, this belonged to your mother. I took it from her finger when she died, to keep it for you until you were old enough to have it.'

Molly took the box and opening it saw a plain gold wedding ring. Unaccountable tears rose, for the mother she had never known. 'I'll keep it always,' she said. 'Thank you, Miss Plumstead, thank you so much. It's like having something to show that I did belong to someone.'

'Dear child, I wish we knew more. There must be a family for you somewhere. But at least I am your godmother and we must always keep in touch.'

'Oh yes, yes.' Molly turned the ring in her hand and then slipped it back into its box. 'I don't think much about a family any more, only that my Ma was a lady – and how good you've been to me.'

'You could wear it on your right hand until you marry.'

'We're not allowed to wear rings or any sort of jewellery. Cook told me that the first day, not that I had any.'

'Of course not. I should have known. But keep it until you can wear it.'

'I will, oh I will.' Molly tucked the little box into her purse.

'And,' Miss Plumstead asked a little archly, 'what about that young man of yours? Did he come looking for you?'

'No,' Molly was trying not to think of Hal, but she added, 'I don't even know whether he did come back. I expect he went off to the farm where he was promised and then to the charcoal burning. Maybe he thought I'd still be at the farm, waiting till he was free to find work where we could be together – though I told him I'd not live in a burner's hut,' she added so firmly that Miss Plumstead laughed.

'Well, perhaps when spring is here he'll come looking for you.'

'I did hope so, but I feel I won't see him no more – again, I mean,' she corrected herself, as always responding to her friend's influence. 'Perhaps he was after all just what Mr Wicks called him.' She gave a little sigh and then braced herself. 'I had best go now, I'm expected back by tea-time.'

Miss Plumstead reached out to give her hand a little squeeze. 'You may be right, and in any case you must put it behind you now. But you shan't go without a Christmas present.' And going to a shelf she pulled out a book. 'I'm quite sure you haven't read this – *David Copperfield*, by Mr Charles Dickens. I read all his books when they come out in a magazine month by month.'

'I've never read nothing – anything – but my Bible that you gave me. It's my only treasure.'

'Oh my love, I'm so glad. You can't go wrong while you read the scriptures, not that I suppose you have much time for reading.'

Molly shook her head. 'Sylvia and I can't keep our candle burning for long, there's no gas in the attics, you see. In the morning I'm up by six, but now and then in the afternoons, if there's not too much sewing, I've time to look at a *Ladies Magazine* that her ladyship gives Sylvia when she's done with it. So I could find a little time to read a book, if I had one.'

'Then this is yours. I believe you will like it.'

'I'm sure I shall,' Mollie said eagerly, taking the book and turning it in her hand, looking at the leather cover, the gold tooling, before opening it at random to see the names – David and Steerforth, Betsy Trotwood, Agnes and Dora – people whom she was going to know as if they were part of her own life.

Raising shining eyes, she said, 'I shall keep it always. Thank you, dear Miss Plumstead. I'll try to come again soon,' and she kissed her friend warmly.

Walking back to Crossley Lodge, the ring in its box safe in her purse, and clutching her precious book, she thought it was the best Christmas she had ever had. Briefly her mind went to Hal, brought back to her by Miss Plumstead's question. Where was he? Had he really forgotten her? Well, she would have to set herself to forget him. But it was not easy, nor to bury entirely the guilt, the memory of those moments of bliss standing against it. But she had a good place now, a good wage and kindly people to work for. Other girls had far less.

The winter passed and by February the talk at the dinner table was all of war. Sir Charles read the latest news from the *Hampshire Telegraph* of the happenings in the Balkans. There had been no European war since Waterloo, forty years ago, and taking in some of the inflammatory articles and letters in the paper gave it as his opinion that England was spoiling for a fight. The Russian bear had become the symbol of evil, threatening with her might the Balkan states, while the Tsar was seen as a wicked despot.

'This attack on Turkey is outright aggression,' was his opinion, expressed to his younger daughter and her husband when they came to dinner. 'And to destroy the Turkish fleet in its own harbour was nothing short of a massacre. War is coming and I certainly think it justified. But it will turn the old country upside-down. The paper remarks on our ships assembling at Spithead.'

'Well, we have only to look out of the window to see that!' Henrietta pointed out.

'The *Wellington* came into harbour last week. I thought she was finished,' the master of the house remarked, 'a broken screw, I believe, but she's been made sea-worthy enough to be Sir Charles Napier's flagship.'

'He's a strange old fellow,' Walter Bell remarked. 'I think he originated the saying "a rolling gait"!' He was an awkwardly made young man, never seeming to fit into his chair, but he was intelligent, with a dry sense of humour. Georgy adored him. He had once wanted to join the Navy, but having crossed to the Isle of Wight in a friend's yacht on a very rough day, discovered he was no sailor, and now kept his interest in the seafaring world to naval law. Fast making himself a name as a first-class lawyer in Southampton, Georgy envisaged him as a judge one day, if not Lord Chancellor.

Sir Charles smiled broadly, knowing the Admiral of old, adding, 'Captain Giffard told me the other day that the *Agamemnon* has had to have a false keel put on. As for the *Termagent* he says she won't sail or steam or steer! What a fleet we are assembling.'

Walter too had been bitten by war fever. 'Southampton is in a bustle, I can tell you. I half wish —'

'Don't you dare,' Georgy broke in. 'The Navy can do very well without you, Walter, and I can't.' She was smiling at him, but on her mind were her two brothers, both in uniform.

The staff, serving the dinner, lapped up all this information, Frederick almost regretting that he was not an army man. Molly felt proud to be part of a household that might be sending two soldiers to the war.

'Well, I hate it,' Sylvia remarked later. 'Her ladyship is in such a taking and if Master Toby should be hurt, I'm sure I don't know how she would bear it.'

'Or Captain Hamilton,' Molly said quietly. Ever since he had rescued her from Toby she had felt a warmth towards him and an interest in his doings. She wondered why he was not married. Meeting Toby today on the landing, that young man had said cheekily, 'You've only to say the word, you know. Send a soldier off with good cheer.' To which she had answered, 'Oh, get along with you.' He quite thought himself a lad for the girls now that he was in uniform, but only succeeded in amusing her.

As for the captain she had not spoken to him since the episode on the landing, except one Sunday morning when passing her on the stairs, he had said, 'Off to church, Molly?'

Sir Charles expected his staff to attend church on Sundays, with the exception of Cook who refused flatly to leave the Sunday dinner, saying she would go in the evening, but everyone knew that when the time came she would be nodding in her basket chair by the kitchen fire. Molly had simply answered, 'Yes, sir,' and made as if to go on down the stair, but he paused.

'Do you have family to visit afterwards?'

'No, sir. I don't have any family.'

'None at all?'

'No, sir.'

He remembered then when she first came, his stepfather telling them all something of her background, and feeling sorry for her he gave her a swift smile, 'Molly-all-alone, eh? But not here at least?'

She responded to that smile. 'No, not here, sir.'

He went on up and she went slowly down to the kitchen where Frederick would be waiting in his sombre Sunday clothes. That morning she found herself less than able to concentrate on the sermon. That smile haunted her, all the more for its rarity – and the name he had called her! Molly-all-alone! How appropriate it was, though here, despite the inevitable annoyances, mishaps, sharp words, the staff had become part of her life and she thought herself fortunate to work in Crossley Lodge. Dusting or cleaning, her head was full of David Copperfield's adventures. Having never read a novel before it was a whole new world of adventure and romance, humour and wit, and she loved it. Though her spare time was short she managed to read at least a page or two every day, writing to Miss Plumstead of her delight in the gift.

By the end of March it was war indeed and a large and impressive fleet had assembled at Spithead. Matt, with his regiment quartered nearby and ready to march for the docks, came home for a flying farewell visit, staying only one night, and bringing good news.

'My majority has come through,' he told his assembled family when he walked in on them late at night. 'Major Foulkes has sold out, which I think a reprehensible thing to do on the eve of war. Anyhow I have scraped up enough to buy myself in.'

Amid the congratulations, Sir Charles said, 'This is splendid news. You must let me reimburse you for —' tactful as always, he would not for anything have hurt Matt's pride, 'shall we say half the cost?'

Acknowledging the generosity, so typical of his stepfather, Matt nevertheless said, 'Very good of you, sir, but indeed I can manage.'

Sir Charles smiled. 'I never knew a young man yet who could not do with a little extra. But seriously, Matthew, don't deny me this pleasure, for that's what it will be.' And at that Matt could only shake his hand and thank him warmly, for if the truth were known the purchase of the promotion had sadly depleted his bank account. 'It will be very odd to have the French on our side,' he remarked the next morning at breakfast, 'especially for the older officers who fought at Waterloo.'

'Are there many of them?' Sir Charles asked.

'Too many. There are plenty of extremely able younger officers without sending out men in their sixties who've not seen action since they fought under Wellington. Lord Raglan is, in my opnion, the worst possible person to appoint as Commander-in-Chief. I met him some years ago, a most kindly and courteous man, but a desk soldier. He's been forty years as Wellington's military secretary!'

'Not the best choice perhaps,' Sir Charles agreed, 'but I presume he will have a younger staff.'

'I sincerely hope so,' Matt agreed. 'Anyway for good or ill the die is cast. The army is already half embarked.'

'The town seems to be full of soldiers, and a great many naval personnel too,' Henrietta said, 'I saw so many of them yesterday when I went out. And they seemed so very young!'

'I know,' Matt answered in some amusement. 'I saw a group of cadets all gold-braided caps, shouting, "Peerages and prize money, or Westminster Abbey!"'

'What it is to be young,' Sir Charles sighed. 'It all makes me wish I had not chosen the Bar.'

'Dear Papa,' Henrietta touched his hand, 'Suppose it had been Westminster Abbey – how awful it would have been for us. I had better go up to Mama now.'

'Tell her I'll be up in a moment to say goodbye,' her brother said. 'When is Toby coming? Or isn't he?'

'Now, I should think.' Sir Charles caught the sound of a wild knocking and ringing on the front door. 'He said he'd try to look in.'

A moment later Toby entered, in full uniform, his sword buckled. 'Hello Papa, Hettie. What you too, Matt? I'm glad to run into you before we sail – though it's a miracle that I am here. I never saw such a crush in the town. My friend Larkins' brother is trying to get a bed and I swear there's not one to be had. It'll be straw in a stables, I shouldn't wonder.'

'I'm not really here,' Matt said, 'I must be off at once, but we'll meet in the Crimea, no doubt.'

'Chasing the Ruskies off, eh?' Toby grinned and planted a kiss on his sister's cheek. 'Isn't it all splendid? We're going to war and we're the best in the world at soldiering. I wish we were sailing together.'

'Oh, the line regiments don't sail in the exalted company of you cavalry men.'

'I'm truly sorry you aren't with us,' Toby said in a proprietary manner as if he had been a dragoon for years, and then added in a less than tactful manner, 'But with Lord Cardigan commanding the Light Division and his splendid hussars and lancers turning all heads as we rode down —'

The smile was wiped off Matt's face. 'You are more than welcome to him.'

'Oh, I know you didn't see eye to eye with him —'

'That's an understatement!'

'Yes, well, he'll still be a splendid commander, and to make one glorious charge with him —!'

'Everything to you is splendid at the moment, isn't it?' Henrietta asked, looking from one to the other of her brothers, Toby in the glory of his regimentals, Matt in scarlet coat with black facings and a scarlet line down the outside of his trousers, and for a moment she seemed near to tears, a most unusual occurrence. 'My two brothers! I'm so proud of you. Come back safely.'

As if to underline the real gravity of what they were going to, the thunder of a cannon shook the house, followed by another and then a third.

'The naval gunners at it again,' Matt said. He held out his hand to his stepfather. 'Goodbye, sir.' There was much more he would have liked to say, something to express his affection for this cheerful kindly man, about his care for his mother. Despite her exaggerated love for her youngest born, Matt felt not only protective towards her, but a long concealed desire for a closer relationship. However, he expressed none of this, merely ending, 'If you will be so kind as to look after Shalima for me? No space for horses for us infantry officers, except of course for the Colonel.'

'I will exercise her regularly. My dear boy, I do wish you well. I hope everything is being done efficiently, but I have a native distrust of Authority emanating from Whitehall! One always wonders if the men at home know what they are about! Do you have everything you need?'

'Thank you, Sir, yes.' Matt nodded. His devoted man, Merton, had packed all his small items – spy-glass, compass, watch, spare socks, notebook, and water bottle, with a knife, fork and spoon, toothbrush and soap – in his knapsack while the rest of his baggage would be taken aboard with the regiment's luggage. Safely packed was a Colt revolver which he had bought, being very impressed by it three years ago at the Great Exhibition in the Crystal Palace. Last of all in any available space he stuffed a few cigars, a box being his farewell present from Sir Charles. Shaking hands with his stepfather he gave Toby's shoulder a friendly punch. 'Goodbye, infant. I'll see you in a few weeks' time. And behave yourself.'

Toby chuckled. 'Not much chance to do otherwise, though we have some good larks in the mess.'

'I don't doubt it.' Matt gave him a fleeting smile and went away upstairs to his mother's room. She always breakfasted in bed and Sylvia was in the act of removing the tray. He bent to kiss her. 'A very quick goodbye, Mama. I must get back to barracks.'

'Oh!' her ready tears came. 'It is too much, to say goodbye to both of you on the same day. And to go to war! You've never done that before.'

He laughed outright. 'Dearest Mama, what did you think I was doing in India? We were skirmishing against tribesmen a great deal of the time and some of them were excellent shots! I grant you this is on a grander scale, but I'll endeavour to come back and bring Toby with me. For all he thinks he's going to win the war single-handed, not everyone is in action all the time.'

She began to tear her handkerchief in her fingers, hardly hearing him. 'Toby is too young to go. Suppose he is killed? I shall die too, I know I shall.'

If he was hurt he gave no sign of it. 'Mama, soldiers are exposed to risks, of course, but I've talked to his company major, an old friend from my days in the 11th, and he will try to keep an eye on the boy.' And then, hearing Toby bounding up the stairs, he gave her another quick kiss and left, passing his brother in the doorway, but not before seeing her arms held out to the young dragoon.

'Well,' Frederick said in the kitchen. 'That's both of them off. I don't know how the mistress will go on, I'm sure.'

'Dr Flack has left her some of his calming medicine,' Sylvia said, adding on a sigh, 'Didn't they both look grand? I think soldiers always look so smart and so handsome, even if they are as plain as a pikestaff.'

Austerely Frederick said, 'They're the same men under all that gold braid.'

A bell rang and he disappeared, only to return a few moments later, before Molly had finished laying out trays for the luncheon dishes. He was looking very pleased as he announced, 'The master says I may take you girls into the town tomorrow to see the Queen and Prince Albert, and the ships and all.'

'Oh!' Molly clasped her hands together and Sylvia gasped with excitement. 'Well?' Frederick turned to Mrs Davies. 'What do you think, Cook? Will you come?'

'Me? Good gracious, no.' Mrs Davies was round and plump and complacement. 'Think of all the crowds, pushing and shoving and trampling a body to death, I shouldn't wonder. You take Sylvia and Molly.'

'And Mabel?'

'Dear me, no. I need her to be at her work as usual.' But then, seeing the scullery maid's castdown countenance, the tears of disappointment welling up, she added, 'Oh well, maybe I can manage. You shall go as long as you do the vegetables tonight.'

'I will, I will.' Mabel's tears miraculously dried. 'Thanks ever so much, Mrs D. What a lot to tell me Mum when I go 'ome.'

'Which won't be yet a while after a morning off to see the Queen. She's a mother too, you know, but don't expect her to look like yours,' and Mabel whose humour was of the simplest, lapsed into giggles at this sally.

On Friday, the eleventh of March, 1854 the day was bright and windy with snatches of sunshine, broken now and then by a sudden shower. Frederick in a sober black coat and black peaked cap, collected the three excited girls and conducted them across Southsea Common, joining the crowds streaming towards the docks. Military and naval uniforms mingled with the bright clothes of the women, the blue and scarlet and green of the soldiers, many wives with children hanging on their arms. Highlanders in kilt and sporran, bearskins and red braided coats caught Molly's eye for she had never seen a Highland soldier. Down the High Street the crowds pressed forward to see the Scots Fusiliers in fine trim, followed by the Irish Guards, crack regiments of the British Army, Frederick said, for he had a brother who was a guardsman.

All the shops were opening, particularly those selling freshly baked bread, pies and baked potatoes. Flags had been hung from many windows and the dense crowd, making for the Hard, were cheerful, singing and laughing, though here and there there was the grave face of one who knew what it was all about, and some of the women were in tears. Frederick bought the girls a fresh roll each with a slab of cheese in it and told them to watch their purses as there were bound to be pickpockets in such a great crowd. A way was kept clear by the police at about nine o'clock as the Highlanders of the 42nd marched past, playing the bagpipes, everyone craning to see them, Sylvia envying Molly's height for she was a small girl.

Next came the green-jacketed Rifle Brigade, all carrying the new Minié rifle, a great improvement on the old Brown Bess, and as they marched their band played 'The girl I left behind me', the mass of people taking up the song. The crowds were thickest at the Dockyard gates where the little party from Crossley Lodge had a quick sight of Major Hamilton marching behind his Colonel, Mrs Henderson having already gone aboard with the horses, her husband's Bacchus and her own Lady May, led by their groom, Reid. The 50th were looking their smartest, this morning and Matt felt a surge of pride to be at their head, his greatcoat and blanket in a roll over one shoulder. The party from Crossley Lodge cheered him loudly, even Frederick moved to bellow; 'Good luck, sir.'

'Oh, he does look fine,' Sylvia sighed and Molly thought so too, finding herself suddenly praying that he would come home safe. It was all heady, exciting. Frederick managed to get his party through to the Hard where two ladies in front of them, complaining that the crush was too great, persuaded their disgruntled male escort to get them away. The girls slipped into their places near the steamer pier, Frederick seeing easily over their heads, while Jack dived between the legs of two large gentlemen to find himself a place.

The heaving waters were a sight, thronged with vessels, from the great black and white warships – the *Duke of Wellington*, the *Caesar*, the *Agamemnon*, *Princess Royal*, and the *Royal George* – to steam transports such as the *Simoon*, ready to take two thousand troops. Yachts, sloops, every sort of vessel, down to wherries and rowing boats were taking people out to view the Fleet and charging outrageously for it.

'I wish we could go,' Molly said and remembered how she and Hal had looked out to sea last summer at Bosham and talked of sailing away.

'Too expensive for the likes of us,' was Frederick's opinion, being always careful with his money, 'but it's a splendid sight from here.'

Sails billowed, pennants flew, flags were raised on every church spire inland, and such excitement was generated that Molly thought she would never forget this day.

At noon the word spread like lightning that the Queen had arrived, answered by a salute from the guns of the *Victory*,

Nelson's old ship now in dock, as well as from the men-of-war, ready to sail. The train carrying the Queen, Prince Albert and their children had arrived at Clarence Yard, where a wealth of uniforms received them, among these General Simpson, the garrison commander of Portsmouth, several admirals and a guard of honour formed by the men of the 42nd Highlanders.

The royal party went aboard the yacht *Fairy* and were borne out to sea on the brisk wind, heading for Cowes where they would spend the night at Osborne House, before reviewing the Fleet tomorrow. As the yacht came into view from the Hard the crowd yelled their loyalty and the Queen waved with one hand, the other struggling to hold her hat on her head.

'The wind is no respecter of royalty,' Frederick remarked and Mabel giggled. A royal salute was fired from the Platform battery, making the girls jump, as the *Fairy* sailed between the ships of the Fleet, the sailors manning the yards and cheering.

'I've never seen nothing like it,' Sylvia said, 'and I've lived here all me life.'

'We're privileged to be allowed to come,' Frederick said majestically. The boot boy, Jack, had got into a scuffle with another youth and Frederick had to turn his attention to extricating the rascal. For a long while they watched, not caring for the pushing, jostling crowd, but finally Frederick said it was time they returned home to serve dinner.

Molly was turning away, regretfully leaving the wonderful sight when she suddenly became aware, quite close to her, of a Rifle Brigade uniform, a big man with broad shoulders filling it. Surely unmistakable! It *had* to be him, and as he too turned away, she cried out, 'Hal! Oh, Hal!'

Chapter Five

He had swung round as amazed as she. 'Moll! *Moll!*' Flinging
an arm round her he hugged her close. 'Oh, Moll, my lovely,
I bin lookin' for you, but no one could tell me nothing.' He
became aware of Frederick's astonished gaze, of two girls and
a lad staring at him, and looking a little sheepish he said, 'We
know each other from a year agone.'

'So I see,' Frederick remarked stolidly. 'Are you off to the
war?'

'Not yet.' Hal held out a hand to him. 'Godfrey Hallam, at
your service, 2nd battalion, Rifle Brigade.'

'Then good luck to you. Come along, girls, it's time we
went back.'

'Oh please,' Molly begged, knowing she was blushing,
'May we walk back behind you so that we can talk. You'll
walk with me, won't you, Hal?'

He looked down at her, a broad smile on his face. 'I don't
never want to let you go again.'

'I'm afraid followers aren't allowed in the kitchen,'
Frederick said, but looking at her radiant face, and not being
an unkind man despite his rather severe manner, he added,
'But that's not to say you can't walk out occasionally.' And
then marshalling the other girls, Sylvia and Mabel exchanging
sly grins, and with a sharp word for Jack, who was still
staring at the large figure in green, he set off towards home.

People were beginning to move away now, the Queen's
yacht more than half way to Cowes, and arm in arm Molly
and Hal, both still in a daze, followed a few yards behind
Frederick's little party, only the feel of the rough green cloth

under her hand assuring her that it was no dream.

Explanations were soon made, Hal exclaiming in anger on hearing that Mr Wicks had turned her off the farm, that he'd like to kill the danged old fool. Of her adventures afterwards he said, 'Well, aren't you the one, running off like that! And gettin' your purse stole, an' up before the beak an' all!'

'But in the end that was my good luck,' and she told him about Second-chance-Charlie which made him laugh. For his part, desperate to search for her, he had come back before the charcoal burning and could find no trace of her. Not having the brightest of intellects, nor having met the lady, he had forgotten about Miss Plumstead, and after a few fruitless days he went back to Twyford Down. 'Then, when we all knew there was goin' to be a war,' he went on, 'I came south to Portsmouth – I'd no relish for the burning no more – and I thought I'd be a soldier. They've bin recruitin' here for a while and I said I'd go. There was a sergeant of the Rifles, what a talker he were, about what a good life the army were an' all that, so I joined. I got me uniform three days gone,' he added proudly.

'And mighty fine you look in it,' was all Molly could say, still shaken by the sudden sight of him, seemingly bigger than she remembered, his eyes bluer, his face ruddier.

'I'm in Anglesey barracks,' he told her. 'Most of the 2nd battalion marched out yesterday. We saw 'em go and gave them a mighty cheer, I can tell you. I wished I were with 'em, though not now I've got you back, Moll.' An appalling thought struck him. 'If I had've gone I'd not 'ave seen you!'

'Then if they've all gone, what will happen to you?' she asked, the same thought in her mind. If he was now in the army his life was no longer his own to order.

'Well, we new fellows'll be here trainin' for a while. We might go where the war is – depends. But some wives is allowed. I'll speak to our sergeant 'bout it. You'll wed me soon as we can, won't you, lass?'

She looked into his face, seeing the love there, the smile on his wide mouth. Her mind was in a turmoil, but carried away by this unexpected reunion, she answered, 'Oh yes, dear Hal, yes.'

When they reached the common Frederick sent the girls and

Jack across the road to the house before saying, 'I suppose we can spare you for another half hour, Molly, but no longer. When the church clock chimes one you must come in.'

'Yes, Mr Frederick,' she said at once. 'It's ever so kind of you. I won't be late.'

'See that you aren't,' and he added to Hal. 'I wish you well, rifleman, if you get sent to the war.'

So for half an hour Molly and Hal wandered the common and under one tree, he turned her to face him and planted a kiss on her lips. A thrill ran through her, a sudden resurgence of the feelings she had known in the barn and for a brief moment they clung together until the clock chimed.

'Dang it!' Hal said. 'Wish I could put you under me arm and carry you off this minute.'

Laughing, she answered, 'You'll have to be patient. We won't lose each other again.'

In the kitchen everyone wanted to know how she and Hal had been separated and she told the story without mentioning the barn, making it sound plausible enough.

'So romantical,' Mabel sighed, her command of the English language not particularly good, while Sylvia asked if she was going to marry the soldier?

Mrs Davies said indignantly, 'You can't go off all of a sudden like that. A decent engagement must come first. Nor can you leave Sir and Madam in the lurch, can she, Mr Frederick?'

'No indeed,' he agreed. 'And I should be sorry to lose you, Molly. You're a good worker, one of the best we've had. And there's no hurry, is there?'

She was touched by the compliment, for Frederick did not often praise the maids, deeming it made them puffed up. Still somewhat carried away by the day's events, she was uncertain what would happen now that Hal was in the army.

'You can, of course, be betrothed, as Cook says,' the butler added, 'but you'll have to wait to wed until the war is over anyway. Is he to go out?'

'He doesn't know, though he says maybe, if more soldiers are wanted.'

'Well, don't you think of going with him,' Cook said, 'I knew a woman who followed her man and she had a hard time of it, living in a tent, sleeping on the ground, either too hot or too cold, and terrible food. Imagine that after my cooking!'

Molly smiled at that but said, 'I suppose if a woman loves a man she'd go anywhere with him.'

'He's such a big handsome fellow,' Sylvia sighed, 'and when he looks at you, Molly —' she became lost for words.

'It's no good being silly about it,' Frederick admonished them. 'Marriage is a serious matter and Molly will do well to consider it that way. Most people in service have to make up their minds to long engagements.'

Everyone had something to say about it, Mrs Davies, who had never been married but used a cook's courtesy title, quoting the baker's boy, now thirty, who had just wed after a seven-year betrothal. That night, after Sylvia had plied her with more questions, which Molly answered with guarded caution, she lay wakeful. She was thrilled by Hal's return, of course she was, but part of her did not want to leave this ordered house, the secure position. To marry a soldier, perhaps to go far away – oh, it would be an adventure and to be loved by him surely the best thing in the world?

Why did she have a single qualm? She heard nothing from him for a week, hardly surprising, she told herself, as he could not write a letter, but then one afternoon he knocked on the back door and asked if he might speak to Molly for a moment. Mrs Davies was asleep in her room after the exertions of luncheon, Frederick was upstairs pressing Sir Charles's evening clothes and Sylvia, who had opened the door, gave Molly a conspiratorial look and beckoned her.

Abandoning her sewing, Molly stepped outside into the area where stone steps leds down to the kitchen quarters. 'Oh Hal,' she caught his outstretched hand, 'I was beginning to think it was all a dream, us meeting like that.'

'It were real enough,' he said. 'Moll, I've talked to the sergeant, seen the captain too. Seems like we won't go to the war just yet, and they say we can get wed in the barracks chapel!'

'Oh! When?'

'Soon as we like. Tomorrow, eh?'

She laughed at him. 'Don't be daft. There's so much to be thought of. Mr Frederick says we ought to wait until after the war.'

'Don't see why,' he answered indignantly. 'Anyway what's it to do with him?'

'Well, you must see, I can't go until someone is found to take my place, though there's plenty of girls looking for work, I'm sure. And then – where would we live?'

'In the barracks. There's places for married soldiers and there's other wives there, so's you'd have company.'

'I never thought to marry a soldier.'

'Nor a charcoal burner,' he grinned at her. 'Only me.' Sure that there was no one in sight, he kissed her cheek and then her mouth. ''Tis a good life, Moll, and I like bein' a soldier. Maybe I'll be a sergeant one day, and the pay'll be good then. We've good vittals and I like fine to shoot wi' my rifle. The sergeant says I'm good at it. You'll be happy too, Moll.'

Hesitantly, she said, 'With you, yes, but you might be sent anywhere in the world. What about me?'

'They draw lots,' he explained. 'Six wives to a company. Maybe we'll be lucky. Take a chance on that, eh?'

'And if I'm not chosen?'

'We'll arrange summat,' he said vaguely. 'C'mon, lass, what d'you say? When'll you wed me?' He touched her cheek, kissed her again, let his hand run down her neck.

'Soon,' she whispered, 'soon.'

But there were inevitable difficulties. Molly relayed Hal's news that there was no need for delay, though Frederick heartily disapproved. 'Marry in haste, repent at leisure,' he quoted. 'There's naught to stop you being engaged, but to wait until the means are there is more proper for servants.'

When Molly explained to Lady Milner, that lady said, 'What a pity. But I suppose you must go. You've kept the bedrooms so well, Molly,' but it was easy to see nothing really impinged on her just now but the fate of her two sons.

Sir Charles took a much wider view. 'As long as you are sure, Molly. You can't know this young fellow very well.'

For an inexplicable moment she hesitated. 'Perhaps not, Sir, but he's a good man. He'll take care of me.'

'I'm sure he will.' Sir Charles smiled at her, thinking how she had changed since the day she stood before him in the court, bedraggled and muddy, without any means of support.

Some of the rough edges had been smoothed away, she conducted herself well, and, as always taking an interest in his second-chancers, he hoped the labourer turned soldier was good enough for her.

Miss Plumstead, however, had considerable doubts, about which she felt an obligation, as Molly's godmother, to speak, even though tentatively.

Molly had taken Hal over on the following Sunday afternoon as they were both free, to introduce him to Miss Plumstead. He was shy of her, knowing from Molly that she was clever, had taught the children in the workhouse, and had read a great many books. He answered her questions mostly with 'Yes, ma'am,' and 'no, ma'am,' and sat on the edge of the chair, which she thought likely to overset the legs. At last she asked him if he would go down the garden to the henhouse to collect the eggs for her.

When she heard the back door close, she turned at once to Molly. 'My dear, are you sure about this?'

Sitting very straight, Molly smiled and answered as she had to Sir Charles, that he was a good kind man and that he loved her very much.

'Yes, I'm sure he does. But do you love him in the same way?'

Another infinitesimal pause was not lost on Miss Plumstead, as Molly answered. 'Oh yes. He will take care of me and I can look after him.' She smiled. 'Men are really great big babies at heart, aren't they?'

Miss Plumstead's knowledge of the opposite sex was small but she had loved her long-lost captain who had been an intelligent man and a first-class officer, according to the letter she had received after his death. 'Perhaps so,' she conceded a little reluctantly, 'but I understand he can neither read nor write, while you – I know how much you've been enjoying *David Copperfield*.'

'It's wonderful,' Molly exclaimed. 'And Hal says that in the barracks they've been having classes for men like him. He can write his own name now – well, almost.'

'And read?'

'Not yet, but he will, and I'll help him.'

Their eyes met and Miss Plumstead said, 'My dear child, I

can't hide that I hoped better for you. He will, forgive me, always be a farm worker, or a soldier, or some such thing, though I suppose he may get promotion of a sort. Is he really the husband for you? You've actually spent so little time together, and though long engagements can be wearisome, they are really better than making a dreadful mistake.' She paused. 'And if he should be sent to the war —'

Molly gazed out of the window which faced towards the village street. She had told Miss Plumstead nothing of what had happened in the barn but now, unable to be less than honest with her, she said in a low voice, 'Don't you see, dear Miss Plumstead, I must marry him. We loved each other last summer and I – I am promised to him.'

A bright flush came into the elderly lady's cheeks. 'My dear! But I don't believe you need to blame yourself, not for being perhaps a little carried away.'

'Don't you?' Molly asked a little wistfully, and then bracing herself added, 'Anyway I do love him, and if we have to live in a lowly way, well I suppose that's how it must be for me. And no harm in it either.'

'There is, there is!' Miss Plumstead spoke with rare vehemence. 'Molly, you are changing, growing in many ways – I can see it. And so like your mother. Although I only saw her the once, when she was so ill, you are as like as you could be. You must never forget —'

'That she was a lady?' Molly's smile was a little sad. 'I don't and never will, but how does it help me? I know nothing more of her.'

'Maybe not, but she has left you the gift of being gently born even though you had such a wretched childhood. It was why I tried to give you a little extra teaching, encouragement. There's a whole world of books and learning open to you and if you marry wisely, someone with the same tastes, would it not be for greater happiness?'

Molly gripped her hands together. 'I won't deny I've thought of that. I wondered if I could ever be a governess or a teacher, or marry a parson and teach in Sunday school. But, you see, I have to marry Hal now that he has come back to me. And he needs me to help him to go on well, maybe stay in the army and get to be a sergeant-major, who knows? Perhaps

I shall like being a soldier's wife.'

Miss Plumstead made a helpless gesture. 'Could you not wait a little while?'

'He'll be sent off somewhere soon, perhaps to the war, and unless we're wed, I've no chance of going with him.'

'Then wait until he gets back.'

Shaking her head, Molly said. 'I can't. It would hurt him so much if I said no. Nor do I want to say no, not really.'

'I see you are quite determined.'

'I am,' and as Hal came back Molly turned to give him a warm smile. 'Did you find many eggs?'

'Ten,' he said proudly. 'I've put them on your kitchen table, ma'am.'

Molly rose to go. Nothing further was said, and she kept her doubts to herself. They had been there for some time. In the barn there had been none, and when he kissed her now, there were indeed none. But everything Miss Plumstead said was true, only she would have to be the strong one in the marriage if he was ever to make something of himself. She could do it, she had to do it, to atone for what happened last summer.

The wedding was arranged for the last day of April in the barracks chapel, where the chaplain would marry them. Afterwards Hal said he would be given a few days' leave and he was wondering where they could go, suggesting perhaps an inn on the Fareham road that his friend Billy Jacobs spoke of. 'Good beer, good food, and a good bed,' he told Molly, adding with a grin, 'Better than straw in a barn, eh?'

Molly laughed and said it would be just the place, so that he was as pleased as a child with her praise, although the idea was not his. She was abstracted though, thinking of his love-making in the barn – perhaps after all it would all be all right.

But they were not destined to marry in April. Molly had been to the post box for Lady Milner, who showered it with letters for Toby and the occasional one for Matt, though knowing no more than that the British Army had landed in Bulgaria to drive the Russians back across their own border. The warm spring evening smelled sweet with the tang of the sea in it, and Molly dawdled. One thing she missed was the outdoor life of the farm, for the servants at Crossley Lodge had little time off and were often days without leaving the house. She could see a ship making for the harbour, the evening sun lighting the sails. Where would the life of a soldier take her? Whether the two new companies drilling so assiduously would go to the war or not, one thing was certain – they would be posted somewhere.

Running down the area steps, she found a distressing scene in progress in the kitchen, Sylvia in floods of tears, Mabel snuffling in sympathy, Mrs Davies clucking over a letter.

'Whatever's the matter?' Molly asked, her mind instantly going to the two sons of the house so far away.

'It's Sylvia's Ma,' Cook explained. 'She's fallen down and broke her leg and it seems there's not a single body to take care of her. This is a letter from a neighbour begging Sylvia to come home. Her Ma is in great pain and the boys running wild.'

'I'm sorry,' Molly began as Sylvia broke into fresh sobs. 'What can be done?'

'She must see what Sir Charles has to say,' Frederick said, adding in some exasperation. 'Do stop crying, girl. We'll get this sorted somehow. And you, Mabel you've no cause to snivel at all, so stop it.'

He went away upstairs and was gone some while. When he came back, he said, 'Sir Charles wants you, Molly, in his study, at once.'

'Me? What for?'

'That's for him to tell you. Hurry along now.'

Molly ran up the servants' staircase that led into the passage at the back of the hall. There she knocked at the study door.

He was sitting at his desk, looking unusually serious, and at once he said, 'Ah, Molly, you've heard about Sylvia's trouble?'

'Yes, sir.'

'It's clearly her duty to go home and see what she can do, so I'm afraid we'll have to let her go – not permanently of course, her place will be kept open – but you see the dilemma it puts me in?'

'Yes, indeed, sir. Her ladyship does so rely on Sylvia for everything.'

'Exactly so, and this could not have come at a worse

moment when she is so worried about our two soldiers. To lose Sylvia would be a great hardship, unless —' he paused, his eyes fixed on Molly's face, 'I realize it is asking a great deal of you but as you know her ladyship's health is never good, and she really couldn't be doing with a stranger just now, so I am wondering if you could postpone leaving us for a little while? I know it means changing the date of your wedding but I would be glad if you would consent to that. My wife knows you and trusts you, and I imagine you know a great deal of what Sylvia does for her.' He paused and then without giving her time to answer went on, 'This is rather a shock for you, I'm afraid, but it won't be for long.' He was putting it as kindly as he could, but it was clear he expected only one answer. Servants were there to be at the disposal of their employers and though he generously released Sylvia, he did not expect to lose them both at the cost of his wife's comfort.

But he had judged Molly correctly for she barely hesitated. 'As if I wouldn't do anything for you, sir, after you've been so good to me. I'll tell my young man on Sunday.'

He smiled up at her. 'I hope he won't mind too much.'

'He'll do what I say,' she said cheerfully. 'After all, we've only just met up again and he don't – doesn't – expect to be sent away yet awhiles. He'll understand I must take care of her ladyship till Sylvia comes back.'

'Thank you,' he said. 'It's a great weight off my mind. We've got used to you, you know, and you are doing so well, as I was sure you would.'

'My second chance,' Molly said impishly and then hoped it didn't sound cheeky, but he laughed.

'Oh, I know very well what they all call me, but in your case I was right, eh? And we'll get a temporary girl in to help you with the housework.'

She thanked him and going back down the stairs was aware of oddly mixed feelings.

Hal was less than pleased. 'Ain't it more fitting for us to wed than for you to run about after the old lady. Someone else could do that, eh?'

'Not really,' Molly said. 'You don't quite understand. I do owe it to Sir Charles. He came to my rescue, didn't he? If he hadn't who knows where I'd be now, in that prison or sent to a workhouse or something, and then we wouldn't have met at all.'

'I suppose so,' he said grudgingly, 'but I want you for me wife, Moll. I have ever since I set eyes on you.'

'I know.' She squeezed his arm. 'But it won't be for long.'

He was not happy about it. 'Soon as we're trained, the sergeant says more 'n likely we'll be shipped out to join the brigade wherever they are.'

Uneasily she asked, 'What about the wives?'

'Six to a company is allowed. But unless we're wed there's no chance of that. You do see, don't you?'

'Of course,' she said and to distract him asked if he thought they could manage on his pay.

'A shillin' a day,' he told her proudly. 'And a penny beer money. Wives get rations, not quite as much as hungry fellows,' he gave her a grin, 'but you won't go short. We'll manage. I've to get you a weddin' ring, o' course.'

'No, you needn't,' Molly took his hand. 'Miss Plumstead gave me my mother's and I'd want to wear that anyway. You won't mind?'

He looked more relieved than otherwise, not having much in his pocket. And here, strolling together by the sea on this sunny afternoon, Molly's doubts receded. With his arm about her, his strong body close to hers she felt a surge of love for him, certain in her own mind that it was what they must do, for in a sense she was already his.

During the weeks that followed she was run off her feet and hardly saw him. At Lady Milner's beck and call from morning to night she found herself becoming increasingly fond of that frail lady with all her foibles, gradually convinced that she could do a great deal more but for enjoying her delicate health and the family cosseting that attended it. The whole household hurried to carry out her wishes, from Sir Charles down, and there was something pathetic about the occasional burst of tears that Toby had gone so gallantly to war when she wanted him at home. Molly soon established a very good relationship with her, gentle but bracing as well, and one afternoon Lady Milner said, 'You have become as good as Sylvia at looking after me, and clever at arranging my hair,' which pleased Molly.

There was to be a dinner party at the end of the week, the Mayor of Portsmouth and his lady among the guests. As always when there was the prospect of some entertainment Lady Milner got herself off her sofa, to go through her wardrobe with Molly to choose the most suitable gown. When she was ready she gave a deep sigh and said, 'Are you sure you must leave us, Molly? Even when Sylvia comes back I would like you to stay.'

'It's very kind of you, m'lady.' Molly fastened a necklace of pearls round Lady Milner's throat, thinking how pretty her ladyship must have been when she was young. 'But you have Esther now in my old place, and though she can be a little clumsy she's a good girl.'

'She broke that pretty Wedgwood vase of mine last week,' Lady Milner said rather petulantly. She was used to getting her own way.

'Yes, I know, ma'am,' Molly clasped a bracelet about her wrist, 'but if you remember Sir Charles said it would be quite easy to replace and he would order one.'

'Oh, well, yes. I daresay it will be well enough. But I don't like changes in the staff.'

Molly smiled. 'I know, ma'am, and I've been so happy here, but my young man is waiting for me and if I'm lucky I'll go with him wherever he goes. I'm sure you understand.'

'I suppose so. Off to this horrid war, I expect. You're a superior sort of girl, Molly, and I'm sure you'll be an excellent wife.'

'I hope so,' Molly said softly. 'Oh, I do hope so.'

During the weeks that followed, Frederick, with Cook's approval and appreciating the sacrifice that Molly had made, allowed her out on most Sundays during the time when Sir Charles always took tea with his wife, and sometimes if it was raining even permitted Hal to sit in the kitchen where Cook plied him with tea and fruit cake. He was slightly over-awed, never having been in such a large kitchen or seen so many crocks and pans, china and silver, but he had a natural way of accepting things politely that made Mrs Davies remark later, 'Quite a proper young man, Molly. Knows his place.'

News trickled through slowly. The army was still at a place called Varna. Major Hamilton wrote graphic accounts of their doings and the letters were often in the process of being read out when she brought in the tea.

'"The weather here is very hot,"' Lady Milner was reading the letter out loud to her husband, '"the countryside not unlike dear old England and there is a lake we can swim in. Everyone is very hospitable – we dine with the French and they dine with us, though unfortunately Lord Raglan keeps referring to them as 'the enemy'! Peninsula ways die hard. We are moving up country."'

'Oh dear,' she said, 'I wonder where that will be? but there's more ... "Lord Cardigan took a party of cavalry out yesterday towards the Danube, brought his 'cherry-bums' back in perfect order but without any information. He does not appear to know what a scouting party is for and is totally without battle experience. I shudder to think what he will do with the Light Brigade. We need experienced old soldiers like Sir Colin Campbell who has the Highland Brigade. Whatever he does will be well done. Yesterday two of our men developed symptoms of cholera, and today they are dead."' Lady Milner paused, her face ashen. '"Our chaplain read the service over them this morning. I am well. I hope if I get a moment to look Toby up later, but at the moment we are very busy practising manoeuvres. As he has a horse and I haven't I hope he will ride over to the Line section of the camp."'

Molly listened to as much as she could and later in her bedroom, Lady Milner read it out all over again, pathetically eager to hear more news of Toby, although Sir Charles had assured her that an army camp could stretch some miles.

It was July before Sylvia returned. Her mother's leg had become ulcerated and healing had been very slow. However Sylvia at last felt able to leave and on her return Molly wrote a hasty note to Hal. Hal had not yet mastered the art of reading, but she was sure his friend Billy Jacobs would read out her letter and write an answer. It came very quickly.

'Miss, Hallam says Saturday next would suit at half past ten in the morning. W. Jacobs.'

and he had added, 'if suiting you'.

Chapter Six

Smiling to herself Molly took the ill-written note to Sir Charles. He raised no objection, and unlocking his desk took out a small purse.

'I have been keeping this for you,' he said, 'a little wedding present, and to thank you for changing your plans to help us out of our difficulty'. Pausing for a moment he added, 'You know, Molly, I shall always be interested in your welfare. If ever you are in any trouble or difficulty you may come to me.'

'Thank you, sir,' she answered warmly, 'but I hope from now on my Hal will take care of me.'

'I hope so,' he agreed, 'but remember what I said. You never know what life will bring!'

For her part she had never met anyone like him and accepting the purse went away up the stairs, to find it contained ten golden guineas. She had never seen such a sum in her life. Oh, was he not the most generous of men! And bearing in mind she was going to live in a barracks, made herself a little canvas bag that would tie round her waist and keep her money safe.

Lady Milner, more practically, asked her what she was going to wear, adding that her own gowns would be too small, 'Miss Henrietta's too, I fear.'

Molly doubted if Miss Henrietta would consider giving her a gown, even an old one, for Sir Charles's elder daughter seemed to consider that a great deal of fuss was being made over a servant's wedding, which could well have waited a few years until the young man was more established – unless of course the girl was pregnant. Used to certain signs in her younger sister when she was 'expanding', Henrietta watched Molly closely and came to the conclusion that she was not.

Molly thanked them all but said she would find herself a dress and hunting in the second-hand shops of Portsmouth found a pretty sprigged muslin, pale yellow with little white flowers and plain white muslin at the neck, discarded no doubt by some young lady for a new season's gown. She found a bonnet and bought some yellow ribbons to decorate it; ten shillings for the dress and three for the hat, so that she felt she could indulge in a new pair of shoes. Showing off the outfit in the kitchen she rather tentatively asked Frederick if he would consider giving her away.

'If Sir Charles can spare me,' he answered with his usual caution, but relented enough to add with a rare twinkle, 'It will be an honour to stand up with so pretty a lady.'

Sylvia sighed with envy, having no follower herself and aware that a life in service was likely to be her lot, but she found an unworn pair of stockings which she pressed on Molly, while Mabel gazed at all the preparations, quite carried away, until told sharply that she had the vegetables to peel.

When the day came, Sir Charles insisted on sending her in Frederick's charge in his own carriage to Anglesey barracks. Everyone wished her well and she left Crossley Lodge with regret but on a rising tide of hope. Not many employers, she thought, would treat a servant girl so well.

Miss Plumstead, in answer to Molly's letter concerning the wedding, had bowed to the inevitable, writing to say that she would of course attend, and if the bridegroom had any leave would they care to spend it at Holly Cottage? She was more than due to visit her sister in Bosham and they could have it to themselves, with Winifred to cook for them. As to starting from the first night in married quarters even Hal said firmly he weren't going to have no silly bastards playing jokes on them, and though he had thought of Billy's suggestion of an inn, he liked Miss Plumstead's much better, secretly relieved that she was not going to be there all the time.

The service over, with no hitches, they arrived at the cottage. Miss Plumstead, all blushes, hoped they would enjoy playing at being householders; she stayed long enough to share a wedding feast together, handing Molly a small package. 'A little present, my love, that you may find useful as a soldier's wife.'

Opening it Molly found a roll of embroidered silk tied with a ribbon, that spread out to reveal in small pockets, needles, thread, cottons, buttons, tape, scissors, bodkins and every other necessary that Miss Plumstead could think of.

'A "tidy",' Molly exclaimed. 'I've always wanted one! And this – it has everything I could need.'

'I made it myself of course,' her old friend added, 'extra large and all the time wondering how far it will travel with you.'

'Everywhere,' Molly assured her. 'Dear Miss Plumstead, you have been my good angel. I shall treasure it with your other presents to me.'

Winifred served a crown of lamb with peas from the garden and freshly dug potatoes, followed by a cherry tart. Hal ate enormously and when a finger bowl was placed beside him he was not sure whether to drink it, until he saw Molly, who was used to them on the table at Crossley Lodge, dip her fingers in hers to wipe them on a napkin, which he privately thought a bit of a fuss. What was wrong with rubbing one's hands on one's trousers? Miss Plumstead left after the meal, Hal carrying her bag to the hired carriage, and shaking her hand with some diffidence. Leaving them standing by her wicket gate, she admitted to herself that after all he was a very nice young man, so polite, good-looking in a rough way, and there was no doubting his love for Molly. Perhaps her misgivings had been unfounded and Molly would make something of him after all.

Then she was gone and the bridal pair walked in the garden, the paths edged with small box hedges. 'We'll have a garden one day,' Hal said. 'I'd like fine to grow flowers, though veg'tables is more use.'

Afterwards Molly took him through the village to see the workhouse. He looked at it and then said, 'My poor lass, I hate to think o' you in such a place. We didn't have much at home, but we had our cottage and even if us boys slept four to a bed and breakfast were often no more'n a mug o'hot water, well, we had each other.' He gave her arm a squeeze. 'I'll make it up to you, I promise.'

'You already have,' she said and thought she would never forget the look on his face.

That night as they climbed into the late Mrs Plumstead's feather bed, Hal said, 'Better than straw in the barn, eh?'

'And no one to come at us with a shotgun!' On a long happy sigh Molly added, 'It's all come right now that we have God's blessing.'

'Aye,' he answered simply and wrapped her into his large body.

The few days at Holly Cottage were in a way strange to Molly. Not being a man who thought too deeply about life, her new husband expressed his love very physically, yet like many big men he could be gentle and she loved him for that. But when she tried to talk, to share with him some of her hopes and dreams, she often found he had fallen asleep and was disappointed that he did not respond as she would have liked. The difference between them was only a fine line now, but might it not widen with time? Thrusting the thought away, for this was after all their honeymoon she gave herself up to enjoyment. Their stay was made all the more delightful by the weather which was warm and sunny, allowing them to roam the woods where Molly had once fled from Mr Wicks and the workhouse, and between the fields of ripening corn which made them think of last year and the harvest supper.

Winifred produced good filling meals for them, Miss Plumstead having told her that Mr Hallam had a big frame to fill, and on the last evening, after a supper of beef and dumplings, they stood for a while by the little window of their room, low under the thatch. Moonlight lit the garden, the scent of flowers in the air.

'I wonder if it will ever be like this again?' Molly murmured and Hal, not given to verbal romanticizing, said, 'I 'spect so. Come to bed, Moll.'

And in his arms in the deep feather bed, she was happy, all doubts forgotten. In the morning they walked back to Portsmouth, Hal carrying her bag, his knapsack on his back, and even he was moved to say, 'I'll never fergit this place, never.'

Their reception at the barracks was, as might be expected, raucous, with a number of pranksters among the fellows and a great many crude jokes were cracked. Molly, however, gave as good as she got. 'You hush up, you silly sods,' she told them cheerfully, 'or I'll find a way to pay you out. See if I don't.'

Hal was told he'd married a right 'un, and several wives came to greet her. In particular, she immediately took to Nell Harker, an older woman whose husband was the corporal of their company, a quiet industrious fellow who had seen a good deal of service and was here to steady the new recruits.

Married quarters were no more than curtained cubicles, the only privacy available, and setting down her things Molly hoped Hal's size would ensure that there would be few practical jokes. One fellow did climb on a stool to look over and serenade them with a bawdy song, but Hal reached below the curtain and up-ended him so that the song ended abruptly. After that the corporal told them to stow their gaff and get down to the wet canteen.

Molly sat and talked with Mrs Harker, asking many questions about life married to a soldier. 'As good as any for folk like us,' Mrs Harker told her, adding with a smile, 'It's what you make of it, Mrs Hallam, and I can see you've got a decent sort of man.'

The 'decent sort of man' came up from the canteen somewhat the worse for drink and with a strong smell of beer on his breath. Lying in the narrow bed in the dark Molly thought longingly of their room at Miss Plumstead's. A cubicle this size, the iron bedstead barely big enough for a man of Hal's girth, let alone the two of them, was now to be all the home she would know for a long time and remembering how fiercely she had rejected the burner's hut, she wanted to laugh – if she hadn't cried. For the big fellow now snoring beside her she had thrown up all her plans, her ambitions, for surely to become the lady her mother had been was now a far-off dream. To be an army wife had never entered her head, though, she thought stoutly, it must surely be an adventure. Only now that their brief honeymoon was over she faced the fact that it might be years before she would have a home, a house of her own. And when they had children, what sort of life would it be for them? There was one wife here with three children under five and to bring them up in barracks seemed to Molly the last thing to be desired.

Listening to the combined snores of the barrack room, she faced the future with a very real dread. Swept away by Hal's reappearance in Portsmouth, she had been carried along by his love and her own, for she did love him, though she had not been prepared for such a testing. Her sleep was disturbed, her dreams frightening.

But the morning was the start of a bright new life and her spirits rose as Nell Harker showed her where the stores were kept, and the dishes for cooking their rations explaining that the women took it in turns to make the inevitable stew, meat and potatoes, cabbage and turnips, with bread from the barracks bakery which was sometimes fresh, sometimes not, and Molly hoped that perhaps she would get the chance to bake one day. She watched the men drilling, was proud of Hal, that he moved so smartly, seeming to handle his rifle with the best of the recruits, never dropping it as some cack-handed youths did, though she was disappointed when he said that the reading classes were tiresome and he was not the man for the letters.

'It's for officers to read orders,' he said. 'What for do us men need 'em, eh? Captain Smeaton and the sergeant tells us what to do.'

'But if you hope to be a sergeant one day,' Molly pointed out, 'I'm sure you'd need to be able to read. It can't do anything but good. You could read books for yourself.' In the town this morning she had bought herself a copy of *Jane Eyre* and was longing to start on it.

'Oh, books,' was his vague answer, 'but I ain't likely to get promoted yet, eh?' It was clear he had no inclination for study, though he had seemed to enjoy it when she read aloud to him from *David Copperfield* at Rosemary Cottage. Once he said, 'That David! What'll he get up to next?' But to Molly it was disappointing.

In the evenings the men disappeared to the canteen where they could get happily drunk for a few pence, though woe betide them if they weren't up to their drill the next day. One fellow who fell flat on his face at roll-call was flogged, though he was only given twenty lashes as a warning. In some horror Molly watched from the window of the dormitory and it brought home to her the rigid discipline of army life. Please God Hal never fell foul of the rules. Happy as she was when he was with her she found as the days passed that they were hardly exciting. She liked Nell Harker very much, but some of the women were of a very low sort, thinking of nothing but getting drunk, indulging in obscene talk and cackling laughter, and Molly tended as far as possible to keep away from them. They called her stuck-up, but soon found she was not in the least put down by their mockery. Neither did she like the rowdiness, the noise in the barracks at night, nothing having quite prepared her for this, though Hal seemed to take it in his stride.

He looked very handsome in his uniform. The Rifle Brigade still wore the long-tailed green coatees of Peninsula days with black waist and cross belts, the shako adding to his height. She was proud of him, pleased because he was clearly enjoying himself, but during the day she hardly saw him. Only at night did they have time for whispered confidences that went swiftly into lovemaking. Sewing, talking to the other women, cooking on the stove outside, occasionally walking into the town was not, to her mind, comparable to her busy days at Crossley Lodge.

When after three weeks the news swept through the place that they were ordered for the seat of war in two days' time, she was glad, though quite where it was she was not sure.

'Seems a lot of the Brigade got sick when the army landed,' Hal told her. 'We're to go to make up the numbers. I've put your name down for the draw, Moll.'

'Oh.' She knew sudden fear. 'Oh, Hal, suppose I'm not one of them?'

He scratched his head. 'Maybe you'll be lucky, lass,' he said hopefully, which was no answer at all.

But she was not among the fortunate ones and, as soon as the list was read out without her name on it, she hurried away to her cubicle where she sat on the bed, her hands clenching and unclenching on the blankets. What was going to happen now? She had given up her work, her independence for a few weeks of joy and now Hal was going away for maybe one year, maybe two, three, without her. She knew, for Nell had told her, that some regiments stayed abroad ten years or more without ever coming home, and after praying and praying for the chance to go with him, it seemed as if Heaven was deaf to her pleas. She felt suddenly cold, afraid.

When Hal came in, she said dully, 'What am I to do?'

He came to sit beside her and put his arms around her. 'I don't know, lass. There's nought for wives left behind, unless they have family, 'cept going on parish relief —'

'No – no.'

'Well, I'm not saying I'd like that for you, course I wouldn't, and I don't want to leave you, Moll, not without knowing what you're at.'

'There must be some other way for me to come. Ask the other men, Hal, try to find out. I'll ask Mrs Harker.'

'I spoke to the corporal just now and he said that after the war against the Frenchies – oh, years ago when lots of women went trailing after the army – regulations was tightened up and no more'n six allowed in the draw.'

'Oh.' She stared blankly at the future. 'I don't know what to do.'

'P'raps you could go back to the gentleman where you were and ask him to find you work, like he did before.'

She stiffened. 'How can I? I'd be ashamed to admit they were right, when they said I should wait until you came back.'

'Well, perhaps the lady at the cottage, your Miss Plumstead – wouldn't she let you stay with her, instead of that maid she has?'

Pride rose in Molly, the same emotion that had gripped her after Mr Wicks's beating. 'I won't ask Sir Charles so soon, he was so good to me before, I'd be mortified. As for Miss Plumstead I won't go and sponge on her, nor would I take poor Winifred's place away from her, even if Miss Plumstead agreed – which she wouldn't and quite right too.'

'Well,' he said practically, 'you've got the money Sir Charles give you to help out till you find work – an' all the pay I've got coming,' he added as an afterthought. 'I'm that sorry, Moll. I never thought – I don't want to go without you,' and he turned to kissing her which was better than trying to deal with this sudden problem.

91

Oh, when she was within the protective circle of his arms, she felt hopeful, resilient, but soon it would be no more than a memory. 'We neither of us thought,' she whispered, and then her resolution began to harden. 'I won't be left behind, I won't. I tell you, Hal, I *won't*.'

'I don't see how —'

'I'll find a way to come,' she retorted fiercely, 'You see if I don't. Somehow I'll be on that ship with you, Godfrey Hallam, if I have to hide away for the whole voyage!'

He looked down at her in doubtful admiration. 'You've spirit enough for anything, my lass, but I can't see it's likely.'

'I'll find a way,' she repeated. 'I'm not going to let you go without me. Oh, I wish you hadn't joined the army – you wouldn't have if we'd met again sooner.'

'Maybe not,' he admitted, 'but if it wasn't for leaving you, I'd like it fine. It seems to suit. But I never thought —' he gave up trying to express what he did think and silently held her close against his chest.

But the luck that had deserted her in the draw presented her with a totally unexpected chance. There was a young lad, no more than sixteen, who, in high excitement when war was declared, had volunteered, but he was quickly frightened by what he had done and wept into his pillow most nights. She noticed that the other lads mocked him and were always playing jokes on him, jokes he didn't know how to take, and the next morning while he was searching for a hidden sock and snuffling at the same time, Molly came across to his bed, which was next to her cubicle. 'What's the matter, Will? You seem so unhappy.'

His cheeks turned a youthful pink, very little beard there. 'I was stupid, I was, but the other lads at home egged me on. I hate the army. I want to go home to my Ma and my little sisters – and they need me. No one likes me here, they're at me all the time, they call me Pug and I hate it.'

Molly suppressed a smile. He had just the look of a timorous pet dog. 'It's only silly fun,' she pointed out.

'It's beastly. I hate them all. They poured whitewash into my boots yesterday.'

She put an arm about his shoulders. 'I'm sure that took some cleaning. But if you stand up to them, don't let them see

92

you mind, I'm sure they'll give up in time. And I'll ask my Hal to watch out for you.'

He hardly seemed to hear this sop. 'They won't never stop, because I'm smaller than the rest of them,' and then he added: 'What's more I'm not setting foot on that ship on Saturday. I'm going home.'

'Will they let you go?' Molly asked cautiously. 'I shouldn't think —'

'No,' he muttered, 'I asked but the sergeant said —' the colour deepened in his face. He was not going to repeat the sergeant's cutting words, telling him not to be a snivelling little coward and other harsh things. 'No,' he repeated, 'they won't, but I'll run away, so I will.' He pulled on the missing sock, fear and obstinacy chasing each other across his face.

She watched him and then said, 'If you do, they'll catch you and you'll get a flogging, and more than a few lashes, I shouldn't wonder. Don't do it, Will, they might even shoot you for a deserter.'

'That's what my friend Dick says.'

'Then you have got one friend. You two can stay together on the ship.'

He shook his head vehemently. 'I ain't goin'. Even if they catch me, I'd rather be shot than stay in the army. I'll go to my uncle, he'll hide me, so I won't be shot.'

'How can you run away? I don't see —'

A secretive look came over his face. 'I might jump off the ship, I'm a good swimmer, but – well, I can't tell you, missus, but I've got a plan.'

'Whatever idea is in your head, think better of it,' she advised him, but she had a certain sympathy for him, he wanting to run away, she wanting to stay with the Brigade. But of course he wouldn't do it, he wouldn't have the courage.

She and Hal were both aware the next day that it was their last together for a long time and when they lay close in the narrow bed, hopes shattered, reality a poor bedfellow, she wept though she had not meant to.

'Cheer up, lass,' he murmured. 'Come down to the dock to wave us off, won't you? So's I can see you as I go?'

'Of course,' she whispered. 'I'll go down early.'

In the morning there seemed to be no miracle, the parting

inevitable. All was bustle, everyone getting their kit ready, checking knapsacks to be sure a few precious personal objects were safe. Hal was detailed to carry out and load the officers' luggage on to a wagon, and he and Molly snatched a last kiss as he went. Then he was gone. For a moment she stood there, bereft – and it was then, emerging from her cubicle that she saw young Will's only friend, a lad of his own age but built on solider lines, hastily pushing something under his blanket.

'What are you doing?' she asked suspiciously.

The rifleman, his face red with blatant guilt, whispered, 'He's gone, missus, like he said he would, got out last night. He told me we could trust you. I'm putting his uniform under here and with luck they won't find it for a while. He still had the clothes he come in, you see.'

'But what about roll-call?'

'That won't be till we go aboard and by then p'raps they won't bother about him.'

Molly's brain was moving fast. 'Go down now or you'll be late. I'll see to this.'

The momentous idea was taking swift shape – it was, it must be the answer to all her prayers. The barrack room was empty now and without hesitation she pulled off her dress and petticoat and in a few moments was dressed in Will's abandoned uniform. It fitted her well enough and pinning up her hair she tugged the shako over it. In the knapsack she found only the regulation water bottle, knife and metal spoon, and mess tin, so stuffing her own clothes and all her possessions into her canvas bag, including her Bible and her two books, as well as her 'tidy' and what toiletries she had, she managed to get this into the knapsack. Then, fearful of being late, she ran across the barrack room and down the stairs.

Outside men were milling about the parade ground, grabbing rifles from the piled arms, and she was just in time to take one before the order to fall in. She saw Hal's tall figure towards the front and hoped he wouldn't look round, slipping into a place at the rear where a soldier who had no marching partner received a shock.

'Where's Will Jones?' he whispered.

'Gone,' she hissed back. 'Don't you say one word. I'm going in his place,' and he gazed at her in stunned amazement.

94

Marching out and shouldering her rifle she had had no idea it would be so heavy, but thankful she had always been strong she strode out with the rest behind their company commander, Captain Smeaton. Hal would look for her at the docks, but perhaps not seeing her would think she was too upset to come. A little smile lifted her mouth, anticipating the moment when he would see his soldier wife. But that wouldn't be, she hoped, until they were well away. As they entered the docks there was a cheer from the few people gathered there, not at all like the great send-off back in March, she thought as she lined up with the rest to go aboard the *Severn*, a sail and steam troopship. Never thinking to set foot on the deck of a ship, she felt almost sick between nerves and excitement, looking up at the rigging, sailors busy high above her, others hurrying about their various duties on deck, making ready to sail. The few women who had won places followed with their bundles, several holding children by the hand, hurried along by the sailors to go below.

The gangway was withdrawn and slowly the sturdy little ship moved away, a tug taking her out of the harbour. The sails were still furled as there was no breeze but her screws were in operation. The quay began to recede as she moved down Southampton water towards the open sea. It was beyond anything Molly could have imagined and in leaping excitement she wanted to share it with Hal. The Riflemen were all together on the deck and cautiously, thinking she might now dare to speak to him, she had taken no more than one step in his direction, when Captain Smeaton blocked her way.

'Well,' he said, 'what have we here?'

Brought up short, for she hadn't seen him watching her, she managed to say, 'Rifleman Will Jones, sir.'

'I think not.' With a deft movement he removed her shako. 'What have you to say, eh? It's Mrs Hallam, isn't it? Does your husband know what you're about?'

His voice was stern, accusing, but she answered sturdily, 'No, sir, I give you my word. It was my own idea. When I realized that Rifleman Jones had run off, I took his clothes.'

'You did, did you? That foolish young man will have to pay for absconding on the eve of action! But you – did you really hope no one would observe that you are a woman?'

'I hoped not, until at least we were safely out to sea.' It was better now to be honest.

'Till it was too late, eh?'

'Yes, sir. Oh please, don't send me back. We've only been wed a few weeks.'

Quite a few of the newly embarked company were now aware that something untoward was going on, several sailors giving sidelong grinning glances, while Nell Harker paused at the top of a companion-way, stifling an exclamation. Corporal Harker gave a gasp and said, 'Sir, I'd no idea – Rifleman Jones was in his bed last night – at least I thought he was.'

'But obviously not this morning,' Captain Smeaton observed. 'Rifleman Hallam! Here, if you please, at once.'

Hal had got into conversation with a sailor but swung round on hearing his name. When he saw his wife, her hair fallen down he too let out a gasp and in two strides was beside her, his face scarlet with mortification.

'What're you about, girl?' he hissed. 'Do you want to get me flogged?' And to Captain Smeaton, 'Beggin' your pardon, sir. I'd no idea – I told her – but she's never one for givin' in to what she don't like.'

'Other wives have to stay behind,' Smeaton pointed out. 'There's the cutter taking off the sailors' wives. I'd better ask the captain to signal to them to put back.'

'Please,' Molly begged in a shaking voice, all her exultation running out. To have come so far and then to be sent back was too much to bear. 'Please, sir.'

Hal put his arm round her. 'Captain Smeaton, sir, she ain't got no folk, none at all, nor nowhere to go. Couldn't she stay? She's a good worker, she'll wash and cook an' do anything —'

The captain's hard gaze did not waiver. Hal added, 'We've only bin wed a few weeks.'

Rather sternly Smeaton retorted, 'And I know a young lieutenant who has had to leave the bride he married yesterday.'

They both stood abashed, aware that every minute he hesitated the boat for shore was drawing further away. Under his cold manner he was not a harsh man and privately rather admiring Molly's courage than condemning so preposterous an action, at last he said, 'Do you have any women's garments with you?'

'Yes, sir. All I need.'

'Then get below with the other women and get changed. That uniform – you'd better give it to the sergeant. And you, Hallam, I suggest you keep your wife in better control. Sergeant! Get the men fell in – we're not on a pleasure trip – and see they know where to stow their gear.'

He strode off without waiting for Molly's hasty thanks and a sailor grinned at her. 'That way, missus,' putting emphasis on the last word as he pointed astern.

Hal had to fall in and Molly, glad to escape all the curious eyes, went off to the companion way, but with a singing spirit. She had done it! She was aboard, going with Hal to the war in a place that until last March she had never heard of.

Below in the dimness and stuffiness of the lower deck the women were shown to a rear portion, partitioned off by a wooden screen. There Nell seized her and gave her a hug while the other five from their company gathered round.

'Well,' Nell exclaimed, 'what a thing to do! And I never thought the captain would let you stay. You're a brave girl, Molly Hallam.'

She sank on to a stool, suddenly weak at the knees. 'I don't feel it now. But oh, Nell, I can be with him and that's all I want.'

Actually she did not see Hal until the evening. The sergeant was overseeing the men settling in, finding cots, stowing their knapsacks, and he told the women to stay in their own section. Molly changed her clothes and folded the green uniform – with some regret, for she had liked the masculine clothes. A little boy of five came to watch her open-mouthed, not sure whether she was boy or girl, while on another woman's knee a baby cried until she began to suckle it. The lower deck was airless and oppressive and there they all were, Molly thought, for the weeks it would take to reach the seat of war, but none of that mattered compared to the heady realization that she was on board and allowed to stay.

Later they were told they could go on deck for a while. There the band of the Rifle Brigade was striking up with 'Lilibulero', the men gathered round talking, smoking their pipes, with the evening ration of rum and water in their mugs. It seemed they had all heard of Molly's escapade for there were grins and winks and raised cups. Feeling now that it was all settled and somewhat proud of his wife, Hal came straight over, for he had been watching for her. But he couldn't help saying, 'Moll! How could you? The captain were that good to let you stay, but he mightn't a' been.'

'I know,' she said, 'I know, but I had to try, and now I'm here. Isn't there anywhere we can be on our own?'

He shook his head at her, smiling now. 'Nowhere, I guess, on a ship. But come over behind them steps.' There he seized her by the shoulders and his kiss was worth all the anxiety and the daring that had gone before.

It was a clear night, the sky full of stars, the ship moving across the dark still water, to the sound of the screws, something she would soon become accustomed to. The sails were still furled, the scene peaceful. Giving a long, contented sigh, she said, 'Do you remember how we walked to Bosham, a year ago now, and wondered what it would be like to go to sea?'

'Aye,' he looked down at her. 'You're one in a hundred you are, my Moll.'

Leaning her head against his chest, everything seemed to have fallen into place, her impassioned prayers answered, a great adventure in front of them, nothing wanting. What lay ahead? Would another ship bring them home? No one could know but if a storm should sink their vessel, at least they had this wonderful moment!

Chapter Seven

'Damned Frenchmen!' Matt said angrily. 'God knows what good will come of having them on our side if this is how they're going to go on.'

'We don't know who moved the buoy,' Colonel Henderson answered with almost equal irritation, 'but I don't see who else it could be. It's left us this wretched sandstone cliff. Get the men marched along to a better area of the beach, Hamilton. I see no point in exhausting ourselves at this juncture.'

Annoyed by the whole situation, the buoy having been set up as a line of demarcation between French and British landing space, it seemed obvious to Matt that someone had moved it in the night greatly to favour the French, which the British rightly resented, and he hurried down the shingle to shout orders to junior officers, and then to the sergeant in whom he had more confidence.

The beach for the entire length of the unfortunately named Calamita Bay, quickly named Calamity, was seething with men, stores, arms, the long bay filled with ships disgorging their human cargo. A sunny morning, with little wind, had aided the landing craft manned by cheerful, sweating sailors, who were setting down the soldiers on the edge of the surf, some of them carrying officers through it on their backs. At one point they admonished the Highland Brigade with a 'Come on, girls, don't be afeared to get your legs wet!' The Highlanders in kilts and full dress returned these remarks in kind while on reaching the beach a few held hands to execute an elegant dance across the sand. Matt had seen it and laughed, but in truth there had been little to laugh about since the army's arrival at Varna in Bulgaria some five months ago.

At first it had seemed a pleasant spot, with waters to bathe in, fruit and vegetables easily available, but as the summer heat descended on the place cholera broke out among the troops, decimating some regiments. There was also dysentery, various fevers, and the once splendid army lost its look of vigorous well-being. The unhealthy atmosphere of the place took its toll and men began to look pale and worn, their strength debilitated in some cases by ridiculous orders over frequent drilling and clothes totally unsuited to the heat, including the choking leather stock about the necks of sweating men.

Now, expecting immediate action, the army had been landed with no change of uniform, their knapsacks left aboard, thought to be too heavy for men in their weakened state to carry. Tents were also left because of the lack of transport. There seemed to be no peasants about, no carts brought back by foraging parties. All the men had was what they could carry rolled in their greatcoats.

Matt was in no better case. His scarlet uniform was now stained dark red by sweat, sea water, and a liberal caking of dust and mud. The sea voyage from Varna to the Crimea had, however, been reviving, the air healthy and refreshing, and he had visions of better things now that they were here. He hoped that the French and the Turks were not going to prove difficult allies, and did not envy Lord Raglan having to act in concert with the ailing Marshal St Arnaud and the Turkish commander, Omar Pasha.

On the shore he found Captain Ben Marshall, his immediate junior with whom he was on very good terms, Marshall carrying out the orders to move left with some thankfulness. 'That should have been our beach,' was his resentful comment as he looked right towards a big sandy curve where the French were already smartly in order, the music of one of their bands wafting across the still air combined with the sound of bugles.

'As soon as our band is landed we'd better strike up "Rule Britannia", eh?' Matt suggested. 'Sergeant, get those men away there,' the order sharply given as half a dozen soldiers sat down possessively on some casks of beer.

'I'll leave you to it,' he added. 'Has Mrs Henderson come ashore?'

'Over there,' Marshall pointed to a small group, 'with her usual following. Her groom is trying to get her horse off, terrified, poor beast and no wonder. I don't envy the cavalry.'

'I don't suppose they'll land until tomorrow. If I can find anything passable to dine on you're welcome to join me.'

'Thanks.' Marshall gave him a cheerful nod. 'God knows whether this barren-looking place will yield anything worth having.'

Matt left him to it and went off to escort Mrs Henderson to where her husband was waiting for the regiment to come up. He had got to know her well during the past four years and admired her spirit. She never grumbled, took ease and hardship in equal part and occasionally made comments that went straight to the heart of a matter. It was clear she was indispensable to her husband and that they were never content away from each other. A quiet woman of about forty-five, thin to gauntness, but extremely wiry, Olivia Henderson had a plain face redeemed by keen intelligent brown eyes and was always soberly dressed in a brown riding habit. She was accompanied by her maid, doggedly prepared to look after her mistress who was the least conscious of women of either looks or clothes. Rosalie Brown made it her business to see that Mrs Henderson was presentable wherever they were, though she was beginning to wish they were at home in the Kensington house that seldom saw them for long. The groom Reid simply acted as watchdog over his mistress and was at this moment engaged in calming her mare, Lady May, and endeavouring to persuade her mule to come ashore, the animal living up to its reputation and refusing to get off the landing craft.

Both Mrs Henderson and her husband had become very fond of Matt and in private she called him Matthew, treating him almost like the son she had never had. Such was the Colonel's entourage, but, with them safely ashore in the capable hands of Jim Reid, Matt strode up to join his chief on higher ground where he sat his horse, his eyes on the assembling of his regiment. They had scarcely arrived when the Colonel exclaimed, 'Good God! Look at our welcoming party!'

A small group of men in rough coats mounted on shaggy ponies had appeared suddenly on the ridge beyond and though they paused to take in the size of the huge army landing below, they very soon rode swiftly away.

'Well, let's hope their rumps are all we see of them for the moment,' Colonel Henderson remarked. 'I wonder if they were Cossacks? Tell the sergeant to hurry up those stragglers.' Matt sent a young lieutenant down to the beach where the 50th was still in some disorder, but the first two companies were already clambering over the low sand dunes to the firmer land above.

Matt joined Ben Marshall as the last column set off, but before they left the beach the younger officer exclaimed, 'There's a boatload of women coming in. I thought they were to stay aboard at least until we've established a bridgehead, and especially as we shall have to bivouac tonight.'

Matt glanced across the sparkling water. He could see the cutter Ben pointed out, packed with wives and a few children, heading for the beach. 'It should be stopped,' he said abruptly. 'A campaign is no place for women.' He felt strongly on the subject of camp followers, thinking that for the most part they simply got in the way – a view he was going to be forced to change later on.

'But they still come,' Marshall said. Like many others he had had to leave his own young wife and son at home. Only very few officers' wives were permitted, but he added, 'I wouldn't like to try telling that to our C.O.'s wife and I saw Lady Errol half an hour ago, Lord Errol's regiment being in our division.'

Matt said nothing, looking at the boat. Perhaps a dozen women were in it, clutching at shawls and caps in the fresh breeze, and then, suddenly, he thought he saw the housemaid – what had he called her? Molly-all-alone! But the woman had turned her head away to look back at the ships and he could no longer see her properly. But of course that was ridiculous. It could not be her, merely someone like her, only why did one thing after another bring her into his mind? In a village in Varna he had walked behind a peasant woman who seemed to have the same swinging walk. It was ridiculous – and annoying.

He did not stop to see the woman land, having too much to do to get some sort of order on the higher ground. The regimental band had arrived and struck up a rousing tune, putting the men in good heart as the order was given to march inland, and Matt hoped the cavalry would get as easy a landing tomorrow. He had not seen Toby since the sailing from Varna for they were in different ships, but in Bulgaria Toby had swayed between high pride in the 4th Dragoons and chagrin at what had to be called Lord Cardigan's inept scouting expedition, which at the time brought back no information, achieving nothing but a few acid comments from more experienced officers.

There was too horror at the onslaught of cholera. Even in India Matt had seen nothing like the sickness that so ravaged this fine army, where a man might be fit and well one moment and dead a few hours later. One victim was Colonel Beckwith of the Rifle Brigade, so that Matt's acquaintance Major Norcott had to assume command. Toby had ridden over to see his brother one afternoon, obviously shaken by his first sight of such a death. He had to learn, Matt thought, that war was not all shining accoutrements and fluttering pennons.

After a few shouts of 'Look to your left! Dress the line. Close in to the right,' they marched about four miles inland, the sunshine of the morning vanishing behind thick cloud. Rain began to fall. By the time darkness came it was a steady downpour. The men were sent off to find what firewood they could and in the way of soldiers brought back sufficient. Matt ate his supper of cold beef and biscuit with the Colonel, washed down with rum and water.

'I hope my wife has got her tent up somewhere,' the Colonel remarked, 'but I can trust Reid to see to that. She'll be up with us by morning.' He glanced across at his second-in-command. 'When we go home, Hamilton, it is time and more that you looked for a wife. You see what a joy Olivia is for me.'

Matt's smile was a little wry. 'I should be lucky to find anyone of her stamp.'

'Well, I won't deny that she is a rare treasure, but once we are back home, I'll set her to look for a likely bride for you.'

'Thank you, sir, but I think —'

103

'Oh, you undoubtedly think me an interfering old fool, and I have known you long enough to understand your feelings about wives with the army, but I'm sure Olivia has shown you another side of that.'

'That she has,' Matt agreed warmly, 'but all in all I think I'll look for myself.'

The Colonel laughed. 'Conceited fellow! Well, we'll see. Did the Royals come up to our left?'

'Yes, sir. No doubt Colonel Bell has found some sort of shelter.'

'Well, if there's any to be found trust an old Peninsula veteran to find it. But we can't see anything in this blackness, better try to get some sleep.'

Rolling himself in his blanket and thankful for his waterproof sheet, which he had long found invaluable when campaigning, even in India where, when it did rain, it was torrential, Matt lay down for the first time on the sod of the Crimea while the rain soaked through blanket and greatcoat. But he did sleep in an odd sort of satisfaction. Nothing mattered but that maybe tomorrow or within the next few days they would be face to face with the enemy and he would be doing what he was trained to do.

Molly's landing had been a matter of great amusement for a large sailor who jumped from the landing craft into the sea, grinned at her and said, 'Come on, missus, take a piggy back and I'll get ye ashore with dry toes.'

Molly laughed and settled herself astride him, her skirts caught up and a good deal of leg exposed, which the sailor said was shapely. She had watched with growing impatience as the Rifles were landed, longing to join Hal and was glad at last to be off the ship. It had served them well, though there had been horribly rough weather round Gibraltar and many of the soldiers had been prostrated by seasickness. Hal was one of them; vomiting over the side of the ship. Molly held his head, thankful that her own stomach had no such disposition. Captain Smeaton ignored so trifling an annoyance and every day had his men on deck, drilling, cleaning weapons, employing a large amount of polish on boots and leather belts. The sea air, the wonder of the vast ocean, filled Molly with awe and delight, and the two days spent refuelling at Malta enabled her with Hal and the Harkers to explore the old town of Valetta. It was the first foreign place she had ever seen, discovering that a whole world lay beyond the confines of Westbourne and Bosham and Portsmouth. From this expedition a good many of their company returned roaring drunk and incurred Captain Smeaton's extreme displeasure.

Molly saw little of Hal for the captain had no time for men lounging about and the confines of the women's quarters, with some sick, especially the children, and dozens of men crammed into the lower deck, made the air foul. She escaped as often as she could to the deck, sometimes taking an unhappy child for an airing.

Hal got over his sickness and they stood together as they approached the Dardanelles and the ancient city of Constantinople. The golden domes and minarets glinted in the sun, the whole place looking like a fairyland to Molly. She said as much and an old soldier told her that inside the town the streets were filthy, the people equally so, ready to rob and cheat any unsuspecting stranger. The ship, however, did not drop anchor but passed through the straits into the Black Sea with orders to join the fleet now sailing for the Crimea.

Set down by her sailor on the wet sand Molly gave him a kiss on the cheek and stood with Nell, just released from the same form of transport, to wait for the Rifle companies to form up. With his great height it was easy to see where Hal stood and she felt inordinately proud of him. Then, when they were given the order to move off, she and Nell, carrying their bundles, followed. By now Nell, nearing forty and with a gently attractive face, had told her many tales of campaigning and Molly began to know what to expect, comfort not being high on the list. They had all been issued with a blanket to which was added, as a gift for each man from General Cathcart, a welcome square of waterproof.

It seemed a bare, inhospitable stretch of ground and after four miles the order was passed back to bivouac. Molly and Nell sought their menfolk and, when fires were lit, made some sort of supper out of their basic rations. Afterwards Molly curled up in Hal's arms under his greatcoat.

'We oughter have tents,' he grumbled. 'They said we couldn't manage them without carts, but I could – and making us leave our knapsacks as well, silly, that was.'

'I know,' Molly murmured. 'Perhaps tomorrow. Oh Hal, hold me close. I don't care about the rain or anything if I'm with you.'

In the morning things looked considerably brighter. They marched into a less arid area, finding trees and fields and villages. The local people, startled and scared by the appearance of this vast red-coated army of some twenty thousand men, came out of their cottages to watch and to offer fruit, bread and vegetables, only too glad to placate these unexpected arrivals. Hal with one deft movement stowed a squawking hen into his jacket, promising a good supper that evening. Captain Smeaton passed the message along the lines: 'All goods to be paid for. No plundering.' Hal held his hen close and she, apparently deciding it was warm and comfortable where she was, did not betray him.

Bullock carts were requisitioned, men's spirits rose, the quartermaster paid for plenty of produce so that everyone might be well fed. Even so, Hal was not the only one to seize a hen, and some of the villagers refused to take the English coins, preferring to appear friendly, thankful they were not Cossacks. The Rifles took possession of one village, Major Norcott and Captain Smeaton lodging in the head man's house, while the rest tucked themselves that night into barns, hay ricks and anywhere they could find shelter. Several French officers with a company of Zouaves rode over to the village to ask if they could buy 'un morceau de tabac,' whereupon the Major sent them packing, 'As if my village had a shop!' was his swift answer.

There was a strong wind that day and the cavalry who had been expected to come up with them were delayed aboard, the landing of terrified horses impossible in such a wild sea. But it was accomplished the following day, though with some losses and as the cavalry were drawn into order to trot to their allotted position, Molly ran to watch them, fascinated by the bright uniforms and cherry trousers of Lord Cardigan's spectacular hussars. As the 4th Dragoons followed them Molly searched for a familiar face – she had long ago forgiven him for the affair on the landing. There he was in the 2nd troop, now

Lieutenant Milner, and as they passed, though he should not have turned his head, seeing a group of women out of the corner of his eye, being Toby, he did. His jaw dropped. Not daring to turn any further to be sure of what he thought he saw, she could not resist calling out, 'Good luck, Master Toby!' and laughed as they disappeared along the grassy plain.

'I used to work in his Pa's house,' she told Nell. 'He must wonder if he was seeing things.'

The whole army bivouacked, spread about four miles along the Alma river. Nearer the sea it dropped through a rocky gorge, but here the ground was flat and fertile, the river slow-moving. This was better country, a green and pleasant area, and on the far side rising heights where occasionally they caught sight of sun on steel, the Russians apparently massing there to receive the invaders. There was plenty of wood for fires, the commandeered food was cooked and eaten, and men who had been sick or tired or recovering from the fevers of Bulgaria, cheered up at the prospect of imminent action. Songs were sung, one man produced a flute and struck up a tune and there was an air of anticipation over the whole camp.

That night Molly and Hal were snug under his coat and their two blankets. Lovemaking was not easy under these circumstances and caused them both a great deal of laughter, but underlying this Hal, facing his first battle, had an urgency that Molly understood. And on her side there was real fear. So far the journey, the general excitement had been uppermost but now, suddenly, the unknown of tomorrow flooded over her. He would be going into battle and she might never see him alive again. Clinging to him she whispered a mixture of endearments and prayers. 'Be my brave Moll,' he said, 'I'll come out of it, never fear. Captain Smeaton says we'll take that great hill over the river and set our flags on the top. No Ruskie's going to knock over a feller my size.'

'You're a bigger target!' She tried to laugh but it was so much easier, she thought, to be brave for oneself than for a loved one, and even after he was breathing deeply and evenly she couldn't sleep, morning finding her still wakeful and heavy-eyed. As the sun rose behind the line of hills the awful thought came – that by nightfall she might be a widow.

At the call to 'fall in', the men turned out with enthusiasm, ready for the fight even if they only had the faintest idea of why they were here. The Light Brigade were the first to encounter the enemy at the far end of the British line. They trotted towards a solid mass of Cossacks, bearded men on shaggy ponies in an assortment of dress, but because of the fatal and ongoing quarrel between Lord Lucan, overall commander of the cavalry, and Lord Cardigan, brigadier of the Light Division, coupled with cautious orders from Lord Raglan, whose one thought was to preserve his cavalry, the 'cherry-bums' were ordered to wheel and ride back – to the jeers of the Russians and the undisguised delight of the British infantry.

Matt, being in a good position on a piece of rising ground to see something of what was going on, felt for the disappointed horsemen, but he appreciated the remark of a nearby infantryman, 'Serve them bloody right, silly peacock bastards!' Poor Toby, he thought, an ignominious retreat when for once Lord Cardigan's dash would have been the right move.

But the serious business was about to begin. Down off his hillock he could see little of the rest of the deployment which stretched in a long line for several miles. To the right Sir Colin Campbell, the most experienced leader there, had his Highland Brigade in order, their pipe majors ready to play them into action, while beyond him the smart glittering French lines waited, their irrepressible bugling echoing on the still air. But in a battle one saw only one's small section and Matt prepared to concentrate on this.

The Rifles were the first across the river, some going over by the small bridge, most wading and holding their precious rifles above their heads, going forward on the far side to skirmish fiercely on the slopes among pockets of grey-coated Russians. Orders were relayed to the 50th to cross and scale the long hillside, to which Colonel Henderson added, 'Fight well today, my lads,' and received an answering, 'Faith, and don't we always, sir?'

As usual the Colonel was on foot with his men and drew them into some sort of order on the far side where a hail of shot, shells and bullets burst on them. He ordered them flat on their faces and when the bombardment subsided had them up and on. Not a man hesitated, their colonel and their major were, they knew, both 'come ons' not 'go ons', and as they awaited the 'hookum', the order to advance, Matt remembered Wellington's words, 'Not a good-looking regiment, but devilish steady', and so they were. When the moment came the 50th stormed their section, over brushwood and stones and uneven ground, pulling down obstacles such as the remains of a stone wall. Clambering up Matt felt a shell whistle past his head and ran, confident of his men behind him straight at the line of the enemy, parried a thrust, felt his sword drive home; slashed another, was spattered with the man's blood, and leaping over a pile of stones yelled, 'Come on, lads, come on!' The excitement that was like no other was on them all, the steep climb hindering no one, so that they burst on the Russian gunners who had been told that the British would never be able to scale their heights and could be mown down like grass.

Taken almost unawares in fierce hand-to-hand fighting, the gunners were either slaughtered or took to their heels and the guns were silenced. Down one gulley and up the next slope the Colonel wheeled his men to take on a large number of the enemy esconced there. Away to the right the French were doing magnificently, only where the Turks were, did nothing whatsoever seem to be happening.

All along the line the British soldiers, soon to be nicknamed the 'red devils', were forcing the enemy to give way, guns were abandoned, every pocket of resistance cleared, while the Russian commander, Prince Menshikoff, who had brought up some ladies from Sebastopol to see the invading army defeated, hastily ordered them back to the town. In this first battle the Russians were, it seemed to Matt, taken by surprise at the determination of the British and French assault.

The fight did not last above a couple of hours from start to finish when the allied army stood victorious on the heights, the men yelling their triumph, hallooing at the retreating Russians, while one young fox-hunting captain, shouted, 'Gone away! Gone away!'

'By God,' Matt said breathlessly to Captain Marshall as they mustered their company into some sort of order, 'that was satisfactory, with I hope not too many losses'.

'All we want now is for the cavalry below there to finish the job,' the captain returned, and to Colonel Henderson as he came up to them, somewhat short of breath but without a scratch, 'Will the cavalry go in, sir?'

The Colonel stared down to where the sun caught at the shining helmets and lances of the horsemen. 'They would if I had any say in it – which I have not. But I've never seen our fellows do better. We've given the Ruskies something to think about.'

Awful frustration was to follow this superb effort. The cavalry below waited with growing impatience but again they were held back. Matt learned afterwards that the French commander, St Arnaud, who was dying of cancer, did not want to risk his cavalry division yet, and though Raglan wanted to strike at once, instead of being a strong leader he deferred politely to the French. No order was given, despite the disarray of the Russian horsemen and so a great opportunity was lost. As an ex-cavalryman Matt almost ground his teeth in fury but turned away to deal with the business of getting the wounded carried back to the river, the burial of the dead to be attended to after the care of those who could survive. When the count was done the entire British army had sustained only three hundred and sixty-two dead and some sixteen hundred wounded, having reduced the enemy by six thousand.

Below on the low ground by the river Molly had watched with Nell and the other women. There was excited chatter as their men advanced, the overwhelming thrill of it carrying Molly away. The Green Jackets were first through the river and there was great admiration as the scarlet-coated Guards went smartly up the slope to the left, 'Like in Hyde Park,' Nell said. A village to the right of the long stretch of meadowland was on fire, every cottage burning and clouds of thick black smoke mingling with that of the artillery obscured much of the view. Some way off Molly could see Mrs Henderson sitting her horse impassively, her maid on the mule, her eyes fixed on the thin red line where the 50th was in action. She had been through this before, as Nell had, and as men began to be hit, and smoke drifted to reveal fallen bodies, Molly wondered how they bore it. Was there terror in their hearts too?

The sudden silencing of the Russian guns, the shouts and yells that greeted the raising of the British flag on the heights told them of victory and Molly impulsively flung her arms round Nell. But after a few moments Nell said, 'Now we must try to help the poor fellows we can reach,' thus hiding the anxiety in both their minds as to whether their husbands might be among the wounded. 'Bring your canteen,' she added. 'We'll fill them at the river.'

Molly obeyed and they crossed by the bridge. At first she only looked for Hal and grew more relieved by the minute not to see his long legs sprawled on the grass, and it was now that the horror of war dawned on her for the first time. Some of the men who had gone cheering through the water would cheer no more. A lad lay across her path, one leg mangled by a shell. He was young and crying with shock and pain, and she recognized him as the rifleman beside whom she had marched out of Anglesey Barracks. She held his head and put her canteen to his lips. He swallowed thirstily and then gasped out, 'Am I going to die, missus?'

'I shouldn't think so,' Molly said practically. 'It's Fred Wilson, isn't it? Do you remember me?'

He looked up at her, nodding, but was in too much pain to take it in. Glancing round the long slope she could now see two staff surgeons moving about to see what they could do and she called out to one of them, 'Sir, can you come? This poor lad —'

'What the devil are you doing here?' was the doctor's curt answer. 'It's no sight for women. Out of the way and let me look.'

'I'm here because my man is in the Rifles,' Molly retorted with spirit, 'and if I can give a wounded lad a drink I will.'

The surgeon examined the wound. 'Amputation,' he said briefly. 'We've no hospital tent set up yet, thanks to general mismanagement. That flat rock will serve.' He dragged the moaning youth a few yards and then said to Molly, 'As you are here, can you bear it? If you hold his shoulders, sit on him if you have to and give him this bit of wood to bite on, I can do my work better.'

Afterwards she became inured to such things but at this

moment she never knew how she did bear it, let alone encourage the agonized rifleman who clung to her, horrible sounds coming from behind the clenched teeth. In less than two minutes the surgeon had cut the flesh above the mess of blood and muscle and sinew, brought a small saw from his bag and was through the bone, casting away the useless limb. Molly, half lying across the terrified youth, looked at it with a queer fascination. It had borne him through the river, into the fight, and now lay discarded, food for carrion birds. Fred Wilson was screaming but suddenly stopped and his head fell sideways.

'Oh!' Molly gasped, 'Oh, sir, is he dead?'

'Dead?' the surgeon was drawing the skin together, stitching rapidly and with considerable skill. 'No such thing. I know my job, ma'am. What's your name?'

'Mrs Hallam, sir. My husband's a rifleman and I was looking for him. Surely you're one of our brigade surgeons?'

'That I am, and a better bunch of men I never saw. What does your man look like?'

'He's a great big fellow, the tallest in our company.'

The doctor leaned back on his heels, wiping his hands on a rag. 'With a shock of fair hair? Aye, I've remarked him before and he's up on that hill, yelling his head off at our victory. I went up at the end, but most of the casualties are on this hillside. Well, Mrs Hallam, there's not an orderly in sight – do you think you can come with me to assist me?'

A few tears of sheer relief were running down her face, but she brushed them away. 'Yes, sir, anything – anything for the hurt men.'

He nodded. After his first burst of irritation, directed not really at her but at the paucity of medical arrangements, he had nothing on his mind now but doing the best he could for the wounded. Several Molly knew. Rifleman Black who was one of Hal's drinking companions lay tumbled on the grass, his sightless eyes gazing upwards, his chest having taken the full force of an exploding shell, but the surgeon merely stepped over him to those he could help. Molly, in a state bordering on shock, turned her head away. Hal would be sorry about his friend. But she kept going, tearing up one of her petticoats for bandages and for the rest of the daylight hours she worked with the surgeon, holding heads and hands as required, keeping limbs steady.

By now the bandsmen who acted as stretcher-bearers were bringing down the wounded to the camp below, where one of few bell tents was being hastily set up as a field dressing station, and an orderly assured her that he too had seen Hal. Dizzy with relief she kept going beside the doctor, admiring his skill, his knowledge, his indefatigable care for the men. But there were no ambulance carts, no medical supplies other than what the doctors could carry.

'What a way to conduct a war,' he exclaimed angrily at one point. 'Those men must be got back to the ships as soon as possible.'

Molly had had time to observe him now, a man in his middle thirties, with an unexceptional face but for a pair of very intense blue eyes. He gave his total concentration to what he was doing, and, not long back from India, he had considerable experience behind him. His name, he told her, was John Turner.

All over the field the wounded were being tended now. 'The dead can wait,' was his terse comment.

It seemed to her as she followed him to a man who lay groaning, fingers tearing at the turf, to be horrid mockery that the sun should still be shining out of a blue sky, the grass a lovely green where it was not stained red. This field of blood and suffering was something for which her imagination had not prepared her; it swam before her eyes, the colours all muddled, but somehow she kept going, following the surgeon, obeying his orders. At last, dazed, exhausted after such a day on top of her sleepless night, and scarcely able to stay on her feet, Molly felt herself swaying when he caught her arm.

'You've done enough,' he said. 'Go back down now, get your rations and then sleep.'

She was staring at a bloodied green-clad corpse. 'Look! His head's blown off – his wife'll not know him,' and she began to laugh wildly.

Dr Turner brought out a flask and made her take a drink of brandy and water. It was warming and steadying but even so she could not stop shaking.

'But I must go up,' she stammered, 'up there – find my husband.'

He glanced up the steep slope, scarred by rocks and stones where breastworks and low walls had been broken down. 'You will never manage it tonight,' he said firmly. 'Do as I say, go back to your friends and go up in the morning. He knows you are safe enough.' He looked at her for a moment with that penetrating blue gaze. 'Not many women would have done as well as you have today, Mrs Hallam, and I thank you. Off you go.'

She stumbled away, down across the open ground, over the little bridge, now sagging dangerously, and then without even looking for Nell or her place of last night collapsed beside a tree uprooted by a shell, to fall instantly asleep, secure in the knowledge that Hal had survived.

Waking hours later, in the first light of dawn, it was to see on the ground beside her a pair of muddied black boots and the shaggy hooves of a pony. In sudden fear that it was one of the dreaded Cossacks she was hastily scrambling up when with some relief she heard an English voice.

'So it is you! I could hardly believe it. Can I help you up, Molly? I don't even know your married name!'

Chapter Eight

Half dazed with sleep she grasped the outstretched hand. 'Oh! Major Hamilton!' Scrambling up, she took in the coat besmirched with blood, torn trousers, a bandage round his lower calf, a cut across his cap which appeared to have done no real harm.

'Shocking, isn't it?' he said smiling. 'And I've no change of clothes at all, apart from a pair of socks! God knows when our baggage will come off the ship. And this is – was – my full dress uniform!'

'You're not hurt?' she asked quickly.

'No, a mere scratch on my leg from nothing more glorious than a jagged boulder. My brother told me he had seen you and I thought he must be dreaming. But I did get a letter from my stepfather to tell me you had left to be married, only', he gave her a slight smile, 'he omitted to tell me who the lucky man was. Obviously you must have come out here as a soldier's wife?'

Explaining how it had come about she was aware that she too looked in a dreadful mess, her skirt stained with blood, and dirt where she had knelt beside wounded men, her hair fallen down. 'He's in the Rifle Brigade,' she added, 'a very big fellow and two people told me they had seen him after the fight and not hurt at all. Oh, Major Hamilton, I didn't know – I couldn't guess what it would be like. And helping a doctor with the wounded —'

He stared at her. 'Do you mean you went out and assisted the surgeon?'

'Yes, sir. It was little enough to do for those poor fellows.'

115

She gazed over his shoulder at the hillside. The wounded were almost all brought down now, burial parties collecting the dead. 'I didn't know —' she repeated.

'No one ever does until they have seen it. I'm glad you are all right.' He could hardly explain the swift pang he had felt when he saw her lying there, her skirt covered in blood. 'Molly – perhaps I should say, Mrs Hallam – when did you last eat?'

'Yesterday, breakfast I think, well, a biscuit anyway, not like the breakfasts at Crossley Lodge.'

He laughed outright. 'No, by Jove. I wouldn't have minded one of those this morning. Where's your bivouac?'

'Back there, where there's a fire. I can see my friend who's man is a corporal in our company.'

He was amused by the possessive little word. 'How long have you been married?'

'Since August, sir, and first I was in married quarters in Portsmouth, at Anglesey Barracks, and then we sailed for the war.' She returned his smile a little shyly. 'I liked that. I wasn't sick once, though most of the others were when it was very rough.'

'I'd have been very surprised if you had let a thing like sea-sickness get the better of you! Well done, Molly-all-alone, though I suppose I can't call you that now, can I? Everyone at Crossley Lodge must have been very sorry to see you go.'

'They were all very kind to me, especially Sir Charles. Is your brother safe, sir?'

Matt nodded. 'Safe but disgruntled at not being in action yesterday. I rode over to see him this morning, which I was able to do as I commandeered this shaggy apology for horse-flesh from a dead Cossack.' Disgruntled, he thought, was a poor word for Toby's disgust, for the disappointment of all the cavalry, both officers and troopers. The Light Brigade was fresh, ready and eager to pursue the fleeing Russians and to be held back was both frustrating and humiliating in the extreme. The men nick-named Lord Lucan 'Lord Look-on' and the name was to stick. Colonel Henderson was of the opinion that a vital opportunity had been lost and that if the cavalry had gone on they could have walked into Sebastopol without hindrance. Poor Toby! His dreams of glory were still waiting to be fulfilled. Looking down at Molly – the last person he expected to see on a Crimean battlefield – it seemed an extraordinary turn of fate to find their former housemaid camp-following. Yet he did not think of her like that – that she was of a different stamp to most domestic servants was more than obvious – and now that she was married he had better not think of her at all.

His smile faded a little, and abruptly he asked, 'Are you happy?' adding almost immediately, 'I beg your pardon, none of my business. You'd better go and get something to eat.'

At the sudden change in his voice she said simply, 'Yes, I am happy, sir. I've wed a good man.'

He nodded and without another word turned and walked away.

She thought him a man of odd moods and yet there was something about him, an integrity perhaps, which appealed to her and she hoped he would survive the war.

Reunited with Nell, who had thankfully heard that the corporal was safe, she drank her tea, ate some bread and an onion left over from their spoils of yesterday. A peasant had brought them some grapes and she and Nell devoured these. There was an air of celebration on this bright morning, only dampened when the chaplain, on his way to a burial party, called to one of the wives and told her she had better follow for her man had been killed. Sobbing hysterically she went with him. And then a passing orderly told them that an officer in the Guards had died last night, not of wounds but of cholera. The very word seemed to strike fear into the little group of women. Having watched the gallant advance of the Guards yesterday the joy of the morning abated a little.

Collecting their belongings she and Nell crossed the little bridge to climb the hill, finding on the far side a dip in the ground and another further climb to reach their menfolk. It seemed a long steep way and Molly wondered how men who were ill-fed, unwell and tired could have gone up yesterday like a strong red tide with the green of the riflemen skirmishing gallantly ahead.

On the plateau at the top, stretching for some miles, Lord Raglan's army was spread. The two women caught a glimpse of him in a blue frock coat, his cocked hat bearing a white plume, and accompanied by his staff as he inspected the land ahead. The men cheered him but he looked neither to right nor left without even a wave of the hand. Personal attention such as this embarrassed him. Molly thought only what a weight must lie on his shoulders. The ground abandoned by the Russians was littered with discarded camp 'usefuls' - clothes, ammunition, even food - and the soldiers were busy gleaning everything that was of the slightest use.

Two rest days had been declared, mainly because the French demanded it. Their men had fought with great tenacity in the battle but afterwards were less disciplined than the British. Here the riflemen had managed to find some green wood to coax alight their camp fires and boil their kettles, all cheerful, cracking jokes, not talking of the comrades who were missing, hardly knowing until the count was completed. The Rifles were easy to find. Hal saw the women approaching and ran to seize Molly, the two of them clinging wordlessly together. Then they sat down by the fire, Molly produced her tin cup for an unappetizing brew of partially warm brown liquid made from crushed green coffee berries.

Hal was full of the fight, his eyes sparkling as he described his part in it, how they had stormed the hill with bayonets fixed and how he had accounted for two Russian gunners, their blood spraying over the long lethal barrels. He had come through unscathed except for a powder burn on one cheek and had clearly enjoyed every minute of it. 'I'll never be anything but a soldier,' he said. 'You won't mind that, Moll, will you?'

She thought of her terror of yesterday, of the carnage on the hillside. Could she go through that over and over again, as Nell did? Yet where he went she would go, somehow, only their love making this bearable, and hers, with the more passive part, would be the hardest.

He was brimming over with a surprise. 'Look, I've a present for you. The Rooskie general, don't know his queer name, brought up some of the ladies of that place down there,' he couldn't get his tongue round Sebastopol either, 'to see us defeated and they must have had to skedaddle when we came charging up. We found all sorts of gear left lying about and I picked up these for you.' He fished in his pocket and brought out a pair of grey kid gloves.

'Oh!' she exclaimed in delight. 'I've never had any gloves. They're so soft – and they fit, see?'

'Oh aye,' he grinned at her. 'They make you a proper lady, too fine for the likes of me, eh?'

'Never,' she protested. 'I'm just a soldier's wife.' But the words struck a chord, buried deep, something she had lived with all her life. Were battles and army camps and barracks to fill the rest of it? Sitting beside Hal while he smoked his pipe she wondered if it was pride that kept her thinking about her mother and her unknown origins. Should she not put all that away from her? But she could no more forget than deny the mother she had never known but of whom Miss Plumstead had taught her to think so warmly, with pity for what must have happened to her. She was still her mother's daughter and that mother had been a lady. Whether it was pride or loyalty that kept her memory alive she didn't know, only that she wouldn't have it any other way.

In the evening the men drank from their captured bottles, sang and danced round their fires, the bandsmen went back to making music and Molly and Hal capered to the familiar tunes. Best of all she liked 'The girl I left behind me', because she had refused to be left behind. They had just unrolled their blankets, found a place of smooth grass for sleeping when suddenly he said, 'I feel a bit queer, Moll,' and lurched away from the firelight and his comrades into a patch of darkness. There he began to vomit, not once, but over and over, collapsing to his knees.

Molly fell on hers beside him. 'What is it? Did you eat something bad? Hal – Hal!'

Slowly he went down, rolled over, all his healthy colour vanishing. Springing up she called out, 'Help, oh help. Where's the doctor?'

Corporal Harker and Nell both ran over, 'Oh Gawd,' he said in a low voice, 'is it the cholera?'

Nell bent down, looked closely, saw other horrid symptoms, and put her arm round Molly. 'I fear it may be. Oh, my poor dear.'

Someone came hurrying up and Molly saw thankfully it was Dr Turner with whom she had worked yesterday – was it only yesterday? 'It happened so suddenly,' she told him, her voice

119

shaking. 'We were enjoying the dancing and then —'

'That's how it is with cholera.' He was down on one knee, his hand on Hal's sweating forehead. 'But take heart, some recover, and your man looks a strong enough fellow. I can't offer you more hope than that.'

'What can I do?' she whispered.

'Keep him covered, try to get him to drink a little water. We can't take him down for proper care until the morning, the stretcher-bearers couldn't do it in the dark, but in the morning —'

Numb with shock, she murmured, 'To have come through yesterday, only for this —'

'I know, but having seen how you bore yourself among the wounded, I know you'll bear this,' he said confidently. 'Do you have any friends here?'

'Corporal Harker and his wife,' and then hardly knowing why she added, 'and I'm acquainted with Major Hamilton but he's in the 50th.'

'What, Matt Hamilton?'

'Yes.' There was a moment while she wiped the vomit from Hal's slack mouth. 'I used to work for his family. Do you know him?'

'I should say I do.' He gave her a curious look. 'He's my cousin.'

If the moment had not been so ghastly she would have been surprised, pleased, but as it was all she could say was 'Oh!'

Dr Turner got to his feet. 'Well, we'll see how your man is in the morning. I'll be nearby and do what I can.'

In truth it was little enough. Nell had brought a blanket and together they wrapped Hal up as warmly as they could. Molly stripped off her shawl and made a pillow for his head. He was groaning and doubling himself up, and once, catching hold of Molly's hand cried out, 'I'm so sick, Moll, so sick.'

'I know,' she whispered, 'I know. Dearest Hal, it will pass. The doctor says you've got a good chance.'

But he was barely conscious, a spasm seizing him again. 'I wish I'd died yesterday,' he moaned at one point, and after that speech left him.

The news had spread through the company and the singing and jollity died down. Some of his friends came over to look,

120

to offer Molly the odd word of comfort, but there was nothing they could do and they drifted away to roll themselves in their blankets on the ground, wondering which of them might be next.

The night passed slowly. True to his word, Dr Turner came frequently, taking little sleep himself, but there was nothing to be done. Another soldier had collapsed, and Turner thought privately that by morning both would be dead. Nell brought her own blanket to put about Molly's shoulders for without her shawl she was cold in the chill September night. As the hours passed she sat on in the stench and mess of his illness, her tortured husband clearly growing weaker. She had never envisaged such a terrible disease. In the workhouse people had had consumption, whooping cough, fevers, but nothing ever like this. There were, she knew, occasional outbreaks of cholera in the slums of Portsmouth, and other big cities no doubt, but nothing she had seen was like this. He lay in all the nastiness of it because he couldn't be moved, but she tried to wipe his face and hands. Nell brought her water which one of the men had fetched all the way from the river, and Molly tried to trickle some into his mouth whispering as she did so his name over and over again, praying disjointedly, pleas for his life, for him to know her again. But he didn't seem to be aware of anything now, and it seemed an appalling tragedy that, after the triumph of the battle which he had come through so bravely, the great oak tree of his body should be felled, not by a Russian bullet, but by foul disease.

Nell had sat beside her for most of the night and as the first streaks of dawn came, she said, 'He's dying. Don't you see, Nell?'

It could not be denied. His face was a leaden colour. At last Nell said, 'Jenks is lighting a fire, I'll make you something hot to drink.'

It was very cold. Molly tried to take Hal in her arms, to hold him, expend some of her life and what warmth she had on him, but though she got one arm under his shoulders he was too heavy to lift. All she could do was crouch over him, murmuring his name, praying that he knew she was here, loving him, willing him to live. But, at last, at the end of her own strength, her head fell forward and she drifted into some sort of sleep. When the doctor came up shortly after dawn she woke abruptly. One look, and he said, 'He's dead, my poor girl.'

After that, in a daze of horror and shock, Molly never quite remembered what happened, only that somehow Nell and the doctor extricated her, rubbed her cramped limbs, got her to her feet. Brokenly she bent to kiss Hal's forehead, no tears yet. She was simply numb. Nell said, 'Come along, my dear, come with me.'

Her legs were so unsteady that Nell and Dr Turner had to guide her across to the camp fire. Orderlies were summoned to Hal, to roll him in his own blanket, a stretcher fetched to carry him to where the dead from the fight were waiting to be buried. She made a move as if to go too, but her legs wouldn't bear her.

'Not yet,' Dr Turner said. 'Don't fear, Mrs Hallam. The chaplain will wait a little longer.'

Hal was buried later that morning. Molly, leaning between the corporal and Nell, stood by the yawning hole, Hal one of seven. The chaplain, his surplice whipped by the wind, read the committal service, but though she tried to join in, to listen to the words – *'for man walketh in a vain shadow, oh spare me a little that I may recover my strength before I go hence and be seen no more ...'*

Hal had not been spared, his great strength gone in a night of anguish, and she would not see him again, nor be sheltered in his sturdy comforting arms. In this shattering moment she tried to reiterate her faith, assuring herself that the God she trusted was still and always with her. Her sorrow was not borne alone, for there was another woman weeping noisily by this communal grave, and with a great effort Molly straightened her shoulders, stood firmly.

Major Norcott had attended and when it was over he came to Molly, shook her hand and said, 'I am very sorry, Mrs Hallam. Your husband was a bonny fighter and a good comrade. We shall all miss him.'

Afterwards she sat with Nell by the camp fire, not saying much, obediently drinking whatever Nell put into her tin cup. Dinner was better than usual, for Bob had found not only a cabbage among the litter, of all odd things, but also half a hare

122

which one of the men had shot, and coupled with the salt pork Nell had made a passable stew. Molly managed to eat a little and the food put some strength into her. Afterwards as she and Nell sat alone together, she told her friend about the work-house and Miss Plumstead, the farm and Mr and Mrs Wicks, and how Hal arrived there for the harvesting, recounting how he had come into the barn and she had tumbled down the steps and into his arms. Talking of the supper, she had no compunction in telling Nell of their slipping away together, their lovemaking in the barn, and Mr Wicks coming in on them with his shotgun and dog. Between laughing and crying, she told how Hal had got some buckshot in the leg, and how funny it all seemed afterwards.

Hearing of her wretched time in Portsmouth and the kindness of Sir Charles Milner, Nell said, 'You make my life seem quite dull!'

'But you've been to so many foreign places,' Molly said. 'Now that's all over for me.'

'I have found,' Nell said, 'that one camp is much like another, except that India was so hot, too hot for me.'

The burials finished, the corporal joined them, remarking thankfully that there were nothing like so many as there might have been. 'We've quite a few wounded, poor devils, though for some it's no more than a cut or two and easily mended.'

To Nell Molly said, 'You've seen so many fights. How do you bear it?'

Nell gave her a sad smile. 'I suppose one can always find the strength for what must be done and it's better than being left at home without my man, as I have been before, though not, I'm glad to say, when he did the long spell in India.' She talked of some of her experiences there to distract Molly and the afternoon faded away. To her surprise Molly did sleep, a sleep of exhaustion and in the morning Major Hamilton rode up on his shaggy pony.

Dismounting, he said, 'My cousin got a message to me. Molly, I'm sorry.'

She had risen to her feet. 'Thank you, sir. It was kind of you to come over.'

'Walk a little with me,' he suggested, 'so that we can talk,' and when she obeyed, leading the pony, he said, 'You must go

123

home, of course. I'll talk to Major Norcott and he'll settle it with Captain Smeaton who will no doubt get you taken down to the ships as soon as possible.'

'Oh no, no,' was her instant reaction. 'No, sir, I can't go.'

'But you must,' he exclaimed. 'There's nothing for you here now, my poor girl.' Molly-all-alone again was his private thought and he felt a wave of sympathy and a desire to do something for her.

'There's naught for me at home,' she reiterated. 'I've got no home, no one, nothing of my own. Here, I've friends – the company –'

He came to a halt as they were a little apart from the men. It was the second rest day before they marched on – when the high command could agree on strategy, he thought cynically. Having little faith in the courteous but ineffectual Lord Raglan or his quarrelling cavalry commanders who had to be kept apart like spoilt children, he had just heard that Marshal St Arnaud had retired to die in peace aboard a French ship. He imagined General Canrobert would take his place but how he and Raglan would deal together he could not guess, though the Frenchman appeared to have an excellent record as a brave and efficient commander.

He brought his attention back to Molly. 'I'll write you a letter to take to my stepfather,' he suggested. 'He will help you, I know he will, find you employment, maybe take you back. I'm sure,' he added vaguely, 'there would be a bed for you up in the servants quarters until you are settled.'

This was all probably true, but she didn't want to leave, not yet. Gazing up at him, she thought he looked pale and tired, though he never had much colour. 'It's kind of you,' she murmured, 'and I'm sure Sir Charles would do what he could for me but –'

A faint smile lifted his mouth. 'A third chance, eh?' and had the satisfaction of drawing one from her.

'He's very good,' she agreed, 'but I don't want to go. I can't go.'

'Why not?'

'Because – oh because a lot of good men were buried yesterday with my Hal and the least I can do is help the ones that are left. The doctor, your cousin, said I was the right stuff to do it. Oh,' seeing the doubt on his face, she pressed on, 'ask him, please. I don't turn sick at the sight of blood, and apart from that I can cook and wash, write letters home for the ones who can't, listen when they want to talk of their wives and children and folk at home. Don't you see? I'm sure I can camp with Corporal Harker and his wife and be useful. Oh sir, please, please persuade Major Norcott not to have me sent back home. I owe it to Hal – and the rest —' Where all these ideas, this pleading came from she didn't know, it was only what was welling up inside her so that she was sure it was what she must do.

For a moment, shaken by the intensity of her pleading, he looked down at her. Then he said, 'Well, it's not really up to me, but I'll talk to Major Norcott and I know my cousin would put in a word for you.'

'Thank you, thank you.' Impulsively she seized his hand and put it to her lips, hardly realizing what she did. 'You are as good as your step-papa. I never thought that Hal – that it could happen like that - so soon —' And then all the horrors of two nights ago and of yesterday's burial overwhelmed her so that for the first time she broke into a storm of weeping. He put an arm round her and let her sob into his stained and muddied coat.

Chapter Nine

The golden opportunity had been lost. Sebastopol was not to be stormed. Instead the army began the long and tortuous march to encircle the city, leaving fatal time for the Russians to build new fortifications, which they set about at once. The allies marched off for the oddly named Mackenzies Farm, so called after the English admiral who had once lived there while assisting the Russians to construct the very naval base that was the object of the present invasion. There were several upsets on the way. One was caused by the cavalry taking the wrong fork in a forest and going down what was merely a woodcutters' track. They had to retrace their steps before they caught up with Lord Raglan and the rest of the army.

In a voice vibrating with rare rage, the Commander in Chief turned on the hapless Lord Lucan and informed him he was late; nor did Lord Cardigan escape his admonition. Not long after the staff literally bumped into a knot of Russian soldiers who had burned Mackenzies Farm and were now making their way north. They were as surprised as the English, tried a few volleys and fled before the cavalry could be brought up. Lord Lucan was ready to set off after them, but once again Lord Raglan ordered them back, from what would have been a very satisfying pursuit. Seething with resentment and justified indignation the cavalry returned and there Matt caught up with his brother.

'Don't! Don't say a word!' Toby could hardly speak for his bitter disappointment.

'I wasn't going to,' Matt answered mildly. 'I can imagine your feelings.'

'Perhaps you can,' was Toby's savage retort, 'as you were once a cavalry officer – unless you've forgotten.'

Matt ignored this jibe. 'Come on down. We've just taken some prisoners, including a Russian officer. He's sitting in a wagon, paralytic, and waving a champagne bottle invitingly at us, but I doubt if there's any left. Probably there's more of the stuff lying about.' The cavalry were all dismounting to stand waiting for orders and Toby obeyed. The champagne bottle was indeed empty, but there was an enormous amount of plunder around the farm. In the abandoned carts were boxes of food, several warm sheepskin jackets, bottles of brandy and a number of pornographic novels in French. Toby pocketed one, but his unhappy mood could not yet be dispelled.

'What is Lord Raglan saving us for?' he asked Matt disconsolately. 'I didn't think it would be like this. I imagined being in a charge, winning glorious victories.'

'Well, the infantry had one a few days ago,' Matt couldn't resist pointing out. 'Come, Toby, you'll get your turn no doubt, in the meantime Merton will be able to cook us a decent dinner tonight, so come over to the 50th if you can. By the way, poor Molly's husband is dead.'

'Killed in the battle?'

'No, by cholera.'

'Oh,' Toby said, distracted for a moment from his own troubles. 'I'm sorry. She was pretty, wasn't she?'

'More than that,' Matt answered and then added hastily, 'I mean I wouldn't call her conventionally pretty – beautiful perhaps, though not at the present moment, poor girl. But at least she didn't catch the cholera.'

'You liked her too, didn't you?' Toby asked. 'Well, now's your chance. She'll want a bit of comforting.'

The confidential moment had passed and Matt retorted coolly, 'I suppose that's the sort of remark I might have expected you to make. We should all have other things on our minds.' He waved a dismissive hand at Toby. 'I'll see you tonight and in the meantime I'd better find my men.'

Toby stayed leaning on his horse and thinking that his brother's sense of humour could not always be relied upon.

Among the smoking ruins of Mackenzies Farm, the army camped for the night. Matt's man, Merton, collected a fine

127

amount of firewood and had plans for a good dinner, but before he could start Matt sent him off to look for the Rifle Brigade. There, asking for Mrs Hallam, he found her crouched by a fire, wrapped in a blanket with part of it over her hair. Her shawl that had been under Hal's head was in too bad a state to keep and despite the fire she was cold, her face still pinched and white with shock and grief.

Since that wild outbreak of two days ago, she was calm, seemingly incapable of coherent thought. Without Hal's protection, the security he afforded, she knew herself to be alone again, to have to depend, despite her kind friends, on no one but herself – well, she told herself, apart from the two months' marriage to Hal, that was how it had always been. And all she had left from that short marriage was a pair of grey kid gloves.

Joseph Merton was a wizened little man, originally from Hackney and of indefinable age, who had served Major Hamilton for many a year. His skin brown and leathery from the sun of India, his body hardened by many campaigns he had only one purpose in his life. He resented bitterly his master's exit from the cavalry; however, he marched with him as willingly in the infantry and had come to the conclusion that it was they who won the battles anyway.

He looked down at Molly and said, 'You must be that cold, miss. The weather's turning nasty. Major Hamilton sent you this,' and he held out a short Russian sheepskin jacket.

Molly got up, dropping the blanket and without a word slipped her arms into it. A little large, nevertheless she felt warm almost at once. 'Please thank him,' she murmured, slightly overcome by the gift. 'It was kind of him to think of me.'

'That he is,' Merton told her. 'Some folk think him hard – well, he's had enough trouble to make him so – but he ain't, not underneath. When my old Ma were dying last year he sent me home with all sorts for her comfort. As for the jacket, some Rooskie soldier'll be lying cold this night. And there's this that I picked up on the way here. The Rooskies must have run off in an awful hurry!'

She took the grey forage cap he was holding out. Slightly crumpled, it was hardly woman's gear but she put it on and thanked him. 'And tell the major how grateful I am.'

'Yes, miss,' he said and disappeared into the growing dark-ness, thinking she looked mighty fetching in her plundered outfit.

Nell greatly admired her much needed acquisitions, thinking that it was some small distraction and much needed. They sat by the fire and ate a plentiful supper of pillaged food and the corporal had added a bottle of brandy to the feast, over which Molly and Nell choked and he said was the worst he'd ever tasted. But it was warming. Many of the riflemen had found liquor of various sorts and there was a good deal of cheerful drunkenness.

Molly sat by the fire in her new coat. Was its owner dead? Or had he run for his life? Either way she had no compunction about adopting it, and sticking her hands deep into the pockets, to her astonishment pulled from one a rolled-up white piece of material which when shaken out proved to be a woman's petticoat. For the first time since Hal had died, a little trickle of laughter escaped her. 'Oh look, Nell! I wonder how that came to be in his pocket?'

She had to go on, grief buried deep and somehow not be a burden to her friends. For some unaccountable reason the petticoat was so incongruous that it eased her tension; glad she had Nell to laugh with, that night she slept better, warm in her sheepskin.

The hard-pressed infantry marched on in the morning not knowing how dangerous their situation had been. So far from their ships, they were in a vulnerable position, but the scout-ing arrangements on both sides seemed equally poor, the Russians appearing not to know where they were, any more than Lord Raglan's staff had known yesterday when they almost walked into a body of enemy cavalry.

There was no sign of the enemy today and within a few miles the British came in sight of Balaclava and the open sea where English ships were already sailing between the narrow cliffs into the harbour. A single mortar was fired from the apology for a castle and one bomb landed near Lord Cardigan who controlled his frightened horse with consummate horse-manship – it was perhaps his only skill. A naval vessel sent off a swift answering fire and there were no further shots. The

Russian commandant came down to surrender, having virtually no troops, only a mere half-dozen militia. He invited Lord
Raglan to dinner and asked to be allowed to sail round to
Sebastopol in one of the fishing boats. The first request was
refused, the second permitted, he and his few men hardly
worth keeping as prisoners of war.

The village of Balaclava, it could hardly be called a town,
lay sheltering under cliffs which overlooked the long narrow
harbour already bristling with craft of all sorts, fishing smacks
and small vessels soon to be sent out of the way of the Navy.
To Molly and Nell, marching at the tail of the Rifle Brigade it
seemed a delightful place after the bleakness of the hills, with
green-tiled cottages and peasants clustering round to present
them with fruit and vegetables and one youth solemnly handed
Molly a bunch of hastily picked flowers. She gave him a
smile, not knowing his word for thanks and in return he
nodded and smiled back at her, putting out a hand to touch the
sheepskin.

'He probably wonders where I got it,' she murmured, and
Nell, looking at the ships, said, 'You could go home, Molly.'

But she shook her head. 'My Hal lies in a grave back there,
with nothing to mark it, and I'm not going until I have to. Oh
Nell, this is such a pretty little place, just a fishing village. Do
you think we might get a fish or two to cook tonight?'

The sun was shining this morning, the sea was sparkling
and it cheered everyone. Balaclava was taken with hardly a
shot fired and no one could guess at the hell-hole it was to
become, all sure Sebastopol would be stormed and taken in a
very short time.

But for the troops there was no room to make camp here.
The cavalry were settled on some flat ground above the village
but the infantry climbed the heights overlooking the
Woronzow road, and there set about organizing their camp.
'The next camp in Sebastopol, eh?' the corporal suggested.

But once again the allies disagreed. The new French
commander, Canrobert, said his men were too exhausted for
an early assault, that camp should be made here with so good
a base, while reconnaisance taken of the enemy's position.
Lord Raglan disagreed, but again deferred politely to
Canrobert and the Turkish leader, Omar Pasha.

So another opportunity was lost. For those who had no ordering of affairs it was a time of welcome respite. In a few days tents were landed and for the first time the army lay under canvas. The tents, however, were not in the best of condition having lain in store at Woolwich since the Waterloo campaign of forty years ago; some split, others tore easily and had to be mended somehow, many of the poles snapped and there was a search for replacement wood. Still it was far better than being in the open and that night Molly slept with the Harkers and another rifleman and his wife, out of the cold wind and thought themselves in luxury.

Molly lay wakeful for a while, kept from sleep by the awful longing to be warm in Hal's arms. The loss was so shattering and she had not been prepared for it, at least not so soon. Calmly giving her own life into the hands of the Almighty, it was much harder to accept that He had taken Hal instead.

Major Norcott had agreed to her staying on and settled it with Captain Smeaton, thinking it likely, as so often happened, that a personable widow would not stay widowed for long. As the days went by after the arrival at Balaclava she began to go out to do what she could for the men, beginning in a small way with a sick rifleman and another wanting a letter written to his mother. In a short while she was constantly visiting the sick, sometimes with Nell – on one occasion to help deliver the baby of another wife – but often she was alone, comforting the dying as best she could, the men anxious for wives and children at home. She let them talk, listened, wrote letters for them, soon to become a familiar figure, often asked to go beyond the Rifles to the other camps where help was needed. The men accepted her only too gladly, many having known and liked Hal, and in other camps when her sheepskin-clad figure was seen the word went round – would she write a letter home for one man, mend a shirt that was fit for nothing but the rag bag, or stitch up a split cap. Miss Plumstead's tidy was frequently in use and Molly thought of her often sitting cosily no doubt by the fire in Rosemary Cottage. Where there were sick waiting to be sent down to the newly taken over hospital she was prepared to sit by them as long as they wanted and often read little portions of the psalms from her Bible, for it seemed to bring comfort.

131

For the first few weeks, things went well. The countryside was rich in all manner of produce, the harvest plentiful, and it added greatly to the rations brought up from Balaclava. Those men sent down to collect the food often managed to bring back a bottle or two of a local and lethal brew from the Greek or Armenian traders for an extortionate amount. These merchants, having got wind of an army stationed at Balaclava, had descended on the place, sure of rich pickings. But it was not long before the farms and orchards were stripped bare, the owners long since fled. The clear streams became sluggish and brown from the hooves and boots that trod through them while the track that led up to headquarters and to the camps beyond was, as the autumn rains fell, soon churned to an almost impassable morass of mud and slime, the ruts deep and treacherous.

And everyone was impatient for something to happen. As always the High Command could not agree on strategy, Lord 'Look-on' became hated for the caution that was only partly his fault while his loathed brother-in-law, Cardigan, had ordered his yacht *Dryad* to be sailed into Balaclava harbour and obtained permission from Lord Raglan to eat and sleep on board. Officers, particularly those from India, despised him for it – Lucan at least lived in a tent with the rest of the men and shared their hardships as these grew worse.

As October passed, the bombardment began between the guns of Sebastopol and the British artillery on the heights and the noise was perpetual, the hissing through the air and whop of the shells as they fell, the constant explosions, at first unnerved Molly but it was odd how she got used to it, ducking or falling flat when someone yelled 'Look out!' or 'Take cover!' With the soldier's ability to find nicknames for anything and everybody, the shells were soon called 'Whistling Dicks', injuring men with their flying splinters. Officers were injured as they supervised the digging of trenches to overlook the enemy, and it was dreary work for officers and men alike.

'The whole affair is being bungled beyond belief,' was Matt's bitter comment to his cousin as they sat over a meagre dinner of salt pork. 'We sit here doing nothing, except for the poor devils digging the trenches, when we should have been in

Sebastopol for the winter, instead of allowing the Russians to build up their defences. Why in hell we didn't attack before I'll never know.'

'They've got women and children at the earthworks now,' Dr Turner said, 'I've seen them through my spy glass.'

'It's a damnable waste of a fine chance. One of the staff told Colonel Henderson that the quarrelling and disagreement among the officers at the top is unbelievable and poor old Raglan hates it. He leans too much towards Cardigan and that causes more trouble. He should keep "the Noble Lord" and "Look-on" apart, like spoilt children who have to be separated.'

'Thank God I am not required to attend the staff,' the doctor observed, to which his cousin added a heartfelt amen, before he asked if he had seen Mrs Hallam. 'Someone told me she is making herself useful.'

'More than useful,' John Turner told him. 'She seems to know the right way to deal with the men, both those that are sick and those well enough to be cheeky. They've nicknamed her "the Lambkin" because of that coat, which she tells me you sent her.'

Matt nodded. 'I must admit to sinking to looting, but it was too good to ignore and the poor girl had insufficient clothing for the vile climate of this place.'

'Half the riflemen are only waiting for a decent interval to pass before offering for her,' the doctor gave him a grin. 'She must look like a good wife for the quick taking in this wilderness.'

'I hope she's got more sense than to let loneliness lead her into remarrying too soon. I saw that in India where the single men jumped at the chance of an English wife. No widow was left alone for long.'

'Well, you know her better than I do,' his cousin said, 'but I've the highest opinion of her common sense, and she strikes me as a young woman well able to take care of herself. And she's found a panacea for her grief in looking after others.'

Matt was silent for a moment, listening to the evening noises of the camp, the soldiers roaming about with friends, shouting good-natured obscenities at others, the children singing out their games, and in the background the perpetual

133

noise of the guns which were seldom silent. 'I must get her to see one of my injured fellows.' Then he changed the subject by asking, 'How are things with you, Johnny?'

'Don't ask me.' There was a sudden note of irritation in the doctor's voice. 'The medical provisions are totally inadequate. I don't know what the Medical Board in London think they're doing, but no provision has been made. None of us have more than we can carry in our medical bags. I've no bandages left, no drugs. And though we're promised ambulances, not one has come. It is past bearing.'

'Let's hope supplies of all sorts will come in soon,' Matt said, 'I'm getting heartily sick of salt pork, or occasionally beef. I wonder why mutton isn't salted.'

'I've no idea. Perhaps it was tried out on the Board and even they think it uneatable!'

'Mr Russell from the *Times*, who's a dashed nice fellow and good company as well, dined with my Colonel last night, and he says he is making sure that everyone in England knows the real situation. But it's always been the same, hasn't it? The men who do the fighting are the last to be considered, and we've got some splendid men in the 50th, their health and strength being squandered through red tape and sheer folly.'

'It makes me very angry,' the doctor agreed, 'and out of patience with our so-called betters. By the way I'm shortly being sent down to Balaclava to be Depty-assistant surgeon in the hospital there, which is a long title for working under the worst conditions I have ever endured. The hospital is in a filthy state with too few orderlies to achieve much. And not even an operating table! Well, I suppose I must do the best I can. Come in and see me when you next go down to the harbour, won't you?'

'Of course,' Matt agreed, and the next day, after trench duty, went to find Molly. She was writing a letter for a young lieutenant with an injured right hand, several bones broken by a splinter of shell, but he sprang up as his senior officer approached.

'At ease,' Matt said, and gave Molly a searching look.

Handing the finished letter to the young man, she turned to him to say, 'Thank you so much for this jacket, sir. It surely

134

does keep me warm. And I'm wearing the petticoat I found in the pocket!'

Raising both hands he tilted her forage cap to one side. 'There, that's more jaunty, though I don't suppose you feel very jaunty, poor Molly.'

Yet he thought the passing of a few weeks since Rifleman Hallam's death had restored her a little, the ashen look was receding, a little colour back in her cheeks, but she had a withdrawn expression in those bright dark eyes that had not been there before. Well, life was no picnic, as he had long since found out.

However she had managed a little smile. 'P'raps the men will like it.'

'Oh, I've heard about your doings,' Matt said with an answering smile. 'Do you think you could come over to B company of the 50th tomorrow. We're about half a mile from here and Captain Marshall would appreciate it. A shell landed near us the night before last and we've several fellows waiting to be taken down to Balaclava to the hospital there, stinking hole that it is.'

She agreed at once and then asked if he thought they would be in action again soon, at which he shrugged his shoulders and said he wished he knew.

But as he walked back to his own lines he remembered his cousin's words – a sensible man, Johnny. Molly did indeed seem to have found consolation in what she was doing for the men. He only hoped some fellow would not persuade her into a drumhead wedding. It seemed to him she had moved beyond that, though he could hardly have said how. He wondered if he should speak to her, offer some words of wisdom, but came to the conclusion that he didn't have any, and in any case he thought it would be impertinent.

She came the next day and was soon an equally familiar sight among the men of the 50th as well as the 1st Royal Scots, Colonel Bell's Royals, and the Staffordshires, all of whom made up the 1st Brigade of the 3rd Division. The noise and explosions went on around Molly but left her unruffled now, even a bomb, landing dangerously near and blowing her off her feet, hardly surprised her. Several men rushed to help her up, glad to find her unhurt except for a couple of bruises.

Her life was in other Hands than her own and whether she lived through this campaign or had her bones laid in the same earth as Hal's seemed immaterial just at this moment.

That evening Matt dined with his Colonel and Mrs Henderson, Colonel Bell joining them. He was just back from Balaclava and had looked in at the hospital now taking in their own sick and wounded. 'A shambles,' the Colonel said. 'Far too few orderlies and most of those are the pensioners who were sent out to do the job, but seem to have no idea how to do it. As for the surgeons, poor fellows they are overworked to the point of exhaustion.'

'I'd sooner die under the stars,' Colonel Henderson said and encountered a speaking look from his wife. 'Don't fret, old lady. We've survived a few campaigns together, haven't we? But if the weather and the conditions here get much worse, I think I'll send you down to Balaclava. The poor folk who lived there are all fled and there are empty houses, small wretched places for the most part but better for you than here.'

She gave him a little smile. 'And I think I'll not go. Colonel Bell, have another slice of this pork. Captain Fanshawe was lucky enough to shoot a wild boar today and has generously distributed the animal's parts!'

He held out his tin plate. 'I was wondering where it came from. It really is remarkable how we all manage to hunt up the occasional treat – though one can't help thinking of roast beef and Yorkshire pudding.'

'And apple pie,' Matt said so longingly that they all laughed. Colonel Bell, a veteran in his late fifties, was, he thought, one of the most pleasant men he had ever met, and Mrs Henderson obviously enjoyed playing hostess to her husband's friends with her small travelling box serving as a table. But Matt didn't think she looked well. The perpetual rain was debilitating, causing colds and fevers, clothes always wet and a change seldom available. He had not had his own clothes off since they landed, except for washing, and yesterday told Merton to sluice his shirt in the nearest reasonably clean stream, and he wriggled a little, sure it was not really dry.

All hopes of taking Sebastopol before the winter had been

136

dashed and the French had agreed to siege tactics, digging parties setting about their own trenches, and irritating Lord Raglan with their perpetual bugle-blowing.

During the day the allied artillery caused considerable damage to the walls of Sebastopol, only ceasing when darkness fell and during the night the Russians repaired and strengthened their walls. It was a prolonged battle of nerves and the casualties mounted. An optimistic French officer, Captain St Croix, with whom Matt had struck up a friendship, wagered that Sebastopol would fall before November and it looked as though he would be forced to pay up. Several times at night a jumpy sentry had them all out of their beds, if rolled blankets could be so called, and 'stand to your arms' was bellowed along the lines, only to find it was a false alarm. The men blamed their officers for the stalemate, the officers in turn developed a contempt for the High Command while these gentlemen shifted the blame from one to the other, that they were in this sorry state.

When Matt took his leave, Colonel Henderson said, 'I'd be glad if you would go down to Balaclava tomorrow, Matthew, and see if you can wring anything out of the Commissariat. There's nothing we're not short of – God knows where my baggage is, still aboard the *Arethusa*, I shouldn't wonder. Take a couple of men and my wife's mule and do your best. Young Lieutenant Foster achieved nothing, but maybe a more senior officer will make them attend – we are owed so much. And you might see if there's any chance of our baggage arriving.'

Matt agreed at once and asked what he might bring for Mrs Henderson.

'A pair of shoes,' she said at once, 'but I fear you will be unlucky.'

He went down the six-mile track, his pony slithering in the mud. What had at first seemed a rather pleasant fishing village had now vastly changed. The harbour was one mass of ships, the landing quays stacked with supplies of all kinds, crates and boxes piled high, the ground trodden to mud, the road out almost indistinguishable. There was a great deal of bustle, some men laying railway lines to carry trucks of gear, food and ammunition to the camp six miles away. They had no idea, he thought, of the difficulties they would encounter on the broken slopes above. That was just part of this campaign – lack of management, lack of foresight, lack of scouting parties, lack of what seemed to him pure common sense.

He found the stores headquarters in three low adjoining mean-looking cottages. Two of them seemed to be filled with stores of basic rations and in the centre room stood a large table at which was seated an untidy individual with his feet on it, a cigar in his mouth and a bottle beside him.

'What do you want?' was his ungracious greeting.

Matt produced his piece of paper. 'I am Major Hamilton and this is an order from Colonel Henderson of the 50th. We are in desperate need of all these things. Our last two orders produced virtually nothing.'

'I can't issue what I don't have.' The storekeeper cast his eye down it. 'Well, I might have some of this in stock, but where I can't say. And I'm too busy just now to look.'

'Busy, are you?' Matt exclaimed. 'What's your name?'

'Mr Commissary Jones – sir,' this last added hastily, seeing the expression on Matt's face. 'As you see I am here without assistance and have a great deal of paperwork to sift through before I can fill out any orders.'

Thinking of his wretched, neglected troops and the way they bore with extraordinary patience the awful privations that were growing worse by the day, Matt's anger exploded. He came round the table, seized the cigar from the commissary's mouth and ground it to shreds under one boot.

'No doubt this was filched from some officer's home parcel! By God, I would like to have you in camp for a few days to see how you like being cold and wet, with little firewood and less clothing to keep you warm. Now get off your backside and look for what I want – for fellows worth ten times your salt. Get up, curse you.'

The Commissary's face had gone a nasty mottled colour. 'Swearing at me won't get you anywhere, Major. And I can't release so much as a biscuit without the proper requisition.'

Matt leaned over and lifted the fellow by his collar and one shoulder bodily to his feet. *'Then get it.* I'll be back in an hour and expect to find what you can raise waiting for me, or you will answer for it. And swearing at you will be the least of what I will do.'

He went out, to find his waiting escort grinning all over their faces. 'That's telling 'im, sir,' one of them said but Matt was in no mood to turn the whole thing into a joke. However he gave them a couple of coins and told them to find a liquor store, but not to dare to get drunk. Then he went off to where the Greeks and Armenians had set up their stalls and were fighting for customers with the utmost combination of wheedling and belligerence. Most of the goods were being offered at ridiculous prices. Matt looked over what was mostly trashy stuff and shook his head, but a pair of red leather Turkish slippers attracted him and after fierce bargaining he bought them for Mrs Henderson. Then on an impulse he added a similar pair in brown for Molly.

When he returned to the stores he found most of his requests fulfilled and, what was more, his own baggage and the Colonel's had now been landed. There was also at the postal sorting depot a parcel addressed to Mrs Henderson, sent by Fortnum & Mason. Mollified by this, certain of being invited to a good dinner tonight, he signed Mr Jones's piece of paper and with nothing but contempt for the man rode back to camp with his laden mule, his men shouldering almost equal burdens. He wondered if there was time to ride over to the cavalry encampment which was only a short distance to his left, but decided against it. Poor Toby, he must be suffering swift disillusionment over the realities of war.

Mrs Henderson was delighted with both her parcel and her slippers, and the Colonel with his long-awaited traps. Matt was excused trench duty tonight and went off to find Molly. On his way he passed three of the day's wounded, lying on the ground, all caught by the same exploding shell, and now awaiting attention. Pausing, he asked if they had seen Mrs Hallam.

'Oh aye,' one said. His right leg was shattered, blood seeping into the bare soil, but he managed a grin. 'God's lambkin, that's what we call her, sir. She's an angel, she is, and that good to us fellows.'

Matt nodded. 'I'll see if I can find her – and if I can hurry the orderlies for you.' Poor fellow, he thought, and wondered if the man would survive the journey down to Balaclava. The way was so steep and rocky, to say nothing of the great tracks

139

of mud that for the men who carried the stretchers made the comfort of their patients the last consideration. He hoped he would never have to make such a journey himself. Nearby another young fellow was lying moaning quietly. He was clearly in great pain from a stomach wound, but waiting patiently for help. He was dying, Matt thought, and bent over him.

'Can I do anything for you? Jenkins, isn't it?'

'Yes, sir. I only wanted a letter sent to my mother, and that lady who came did it for me.'

'That lady? Do you mean the one you all call the Lambkin?'

A faint smile crept over the grey lips. 'Aye, sir. Just looking at a fellow she makes one feel better.'

Poor boy, Matt thought, he was very unlikely to get better, but as he walked on he was thinking of Molly. The lad had called her 'that lady!' Seen perhaps a quality in her, giving her a title he himself would not have thought of, yet a quality that had been there, even at Crossley Lodge if he had but seen it. A lady and God's Lambkin! He smiled a little. Molly herself, he was sure, would have laughed off the idea of being a ministering angel. She was practical, gave the men hope and encouragement, took cheeky overtures in her stride, and slapped importunate hands. Neither did she have time for malingerers and would tell them rigorously to be about their business.

A tale had gone round the camp, repeated to Matt by Merton, that one less than sensitive fellow had lured her into his tent, talking of a sick comrade, who did not exist. Exactly what happened Merton didn't know. No doubt the fellow was lonely and an unattached woman was too tempting, but whatever did occur, the Lambkin emerged in a couple of minutes to go on with her ministrations while the next day Private Smith had a black eye. He got a rough ride from his fellows who objected to their Lambkin being annoyed by unwanted overtures, though several of them looked at her with considerable desire, a desire that met only with cheerful indifference.

When Matt found her, walking back to the Rifles camp, he swung himself off his pony. 'Molly, one moment.' Suddenly feeling slightly embarrassed, he added, 'I've been down to Balaclava,' and handed her the slippers.

Her eyes widened. 'For me, sir?'

'Of course for you. Do you like them?'

'Oh yes, yes. They're beautiful. I shall wrap them up and keep them safe.'

'Not wear them?'

She smiled at him, glancing down at the mud. 'Not here, at least not in all this dirt.' Hitching up her skirts a little, she added, 'But I've got some new boots, see? One of our riflemen took them off a dead Ruskie – well, he'd no futher need of them, had he? And they're only a little large, and stronger and better than my old shoes.'

'And a more useful gift than mine,' he said sardonically.

'Oh!' she exclaimed, colour flaming into her cheeks. 'I didn't mean it like that. I shall treasure your gift – always.'

She seemed so distressed that he touched her cheek with one finger. 'That's kind of you, Molly.'

'It's you who are kind,' she answered warmly.

No, there was little resemblance now to the housemaid who had come to Crossley Lodge more than a year ago. Suddenly he asked, 'What have you done to your hair?'

She laughed. 'Oh, it did so get in the way. I never could keep it pinned up, could I? I asked Mrs Harker to cut it short for me which is so much better with my forage cap.'

Despite the cutting it seemed to him to be curling as much as ever round the edge of the cap and he thought it suited her. 'Very sensible,' was all he said but as he remounted and rode off to his own lines he found himself thinking of how the men saw her, how good she was for them, and it somewhat changed his view of women in the camps. It was the brawling drunken ones they could do without, and in his tent he began a letter to his stepfather, describing what Molly was making of herself out here. It was just the sort of thing to be pleasing to 'Second-chance-Charlie'.

That he himself was falling more deeply in love with her every time he saw her he had yet to discover.

Chapter Ten

Toby Milner was dying. Yet he clung to his horse's mane, holding on tenaciously to every last moment of life, as a trooper led his exhausted animal away out of the thick smoke and horror of the north valley above Balaclava. All he wanted was to lie down – only not yet, not yet. Of the appalling blunders, the stupid quarrelling of the two senior cavalry commanders, of the bungled unclear orders he knew nothing. Only that the Light Brigade had charged in one glorious spectacular ride, lances couched and pointing straight at the enemy, pennons flying, to be met with a murderous flank fire from the Russian guns on the slopes to either side. He reached the guns facing them, tearing in among the astounded gunners who had never seen cavalry attack artillery before. But it was in a hail of crossfire that a shot smashed into his left side, destroying his rib cage, exposing muscles and bone alike.

At the outset he had seen Captain Nolan, shouting and gesticulating, receive a shell directly in his chest, and had heard the awful and almost unearthly shriek that emanated from him. Toby had felt sick with fear, and even hardened soldiers shuddered at the sound of it, but then they were away, the fear was gone and it was all just as he had imagined, Lord Cardigan leading them with sword raised, the finest regiment in the army, in Toby's eyes. So it was, until he was struck, and then the world went black and yellow. Now he only wanted to get back to see his brother just once more. The Light Brigade was extricating itself. Lord Cardigan who had reached the guns with unhesitating courage, charged in among the Russian gunners, slew a couple of them and then apparently thought he had done enough and wheeled his horse to ride back. It was Lord George Paget who kept with the troopers, shouting the order to disengage, and through the smoke and dust the remnant of the Light Brigade limped out. The ground was strewn with men, dead or wounded, surrounded by horses in the same miserable case, some of the men crawling to where much loved chargers lay.

At the end of the valley below the Causeway Heights, at length Toby gave way, swayed forwards and fell, and it was the dragoon leading his horse who caught hold of him and eased him to the ground. He lay there, thankful even for the hard stones under his head. Opening his eyes, he said hoarsely, 'My brother – Major Hamilton – the 50th. Find him – for God's sake, find him.'

The dragoon scratched his head. He could hardly go off, leaving what was left of his troop without permission. Only who was there to ask for it? But to go looking for an officer in another regiment, he'd be flogged for such a thing! Anyway, in his opinion, the poor lad wouldn't last long. It was only sheer courage that had kept him going this far. He muttered, 'Do me best, sir,' and easing off the shako for the dying man to rest his head on it, went off to join what comrades were still alive. Toby drifted into unconsciousness.

Matt had been on trench duty above Sebastopol when they heard the sound of musketry mingling with that of the perpetual bombardment. Undoubtedly this heralded an engagement of some sort. Colonel Henderson went off to find their divisional commander, Sir Richard England, who told him that the Russians were mounting an attack in the area of the Woronzow road, obviously targeting Balaclava.

'We are ordered to stay where we are at the moment.' he said to his second-in-command. 'Sir Colin Campbell will hold, brilliant fellow that he is, until Sir James Scarlett brings up the Heavies. The Russian cavalry is engaged and it looks like being a cavalry battle.'

Matt saw little except smoke, hearing the noise and waiting for news. Time passed as he paced the trenches until the rumour reached them by a perspiring aide on his way to find Sir George Cathcart, commander of the 4th Division. 'The Light Brigade – desperate trouble,' was all Matt needed to hear and putting Captain Marshall in charge ran back to camp to find his colonel, already mounting, the ever-vigilant Merton thowing a saddle on his master's pony. Henderson, having just despatched a private to look for his major, wasted no words. 'Along the ridge,' he said. 'We'll see there.'

Matt seized his reins and together they rode along the high point until they found the position taken up by the Staff officers, six hundred feet above the valleys below. He spoke to Lord Burghursh, Raglan's nephew, who gave him an account as far as he knew. It appeared that both the Highlanders and the Heavies had done magnificent work and with their relatively small numbers had fought with such dogged determination that the great mass of Russian cavalry wavered under the assault and withdrew. What was then needed was the Light Brigade to assist and turn it into a rout.

The Russians were desperately trying to draw off their own cannon with some of the British artillery they had taken and, seeing this, General Airey advised Lord Raglan to send in the Light Brigade. This time he did, but what followed was a succession of appalling blunders and misunderstood orders with Lucan and Cardigan once more at odds, while the impetuous young staff officer, Captain Nolan, bearing Lord Raglan's piece of paper, pelted down the slope in a state of wild excitement. What happened then no one as yet knew. Whether he pointed in the wrong direction, to attack the wrong guns down the wrong valley no one could now ask him, for he was the very first to die. Here, high above the battlefield the two valleys were clearly in sight, but on the ground visibility would have been quite different, and the Light Brigade charged into the north valley, already named most appropriately 'the valley of death'.

A ghastly horror settled on the watchers. Smoke was drifting, mingling with the dust thrown up by seven hundred galloping horses, obscuring the valley. Then the ubiquitous Mrs Duberley, whose husband was engaged below, said clearly into the silence of the watchers, 'What are those skirmishers doing? Oh God, it is the Light Brigade!'

Someone brought Lord Raglan a stool on to which he sank with one hand over his eyes. General Airey was watching in stunned disbelief. Colonel Bell, hurrying up, joined Colonel

144

Henderson and Matt. 'Good God, how could such a fatal misunderstanding happen? Do you know why —'

Matt said. 'My brother is with the 4th Dragoons,' and Colonel Bell bent his kindly and concerned gaze on the younger officer. 'I'm sorry. I pray he'll come out.'

But to the watchers above it was soon pitifully obvious that only too few were coming out of that hell below, a calamity taking place before their eyes. Horses, superbly trained, obeyed as long as the guiding hands of their riders were on them, but once these were removed the animals went beserk, galloping in wild frenzy among the survivors. In a short time when the second wave had gone in, Lord Cardigan was seen trotting out, alone and apparently unhurt and unconcerned.

As the smoke cleared, a dreadful scene revealed itself, bodies of men, the famous cherry-bums, lay sprawled all over the valley, mown down as if by a scythe; the survivors, a mere one hundred and ninety-five of the nearly seven hundred men were seen coming out of the smoke, some half-carrying comrades, some limping, staggering, a few still left in the saddle, while others tried to urge their terrified chargers out. Five hundred horses lay dead or dying in agony.

No one among the little group on the ridge spoke for a moment. Lord Cardigan appeared and began at once to accuse Captain Nolan of insubordination, among other things, Lord Raglan silencing him only by informing him he had just ridden over Captain Nolan's dead body. Lord Lucan came up in breathless haste and the recriminations began while no one thought to dismiss the survivors to their camp despite the fact that they had not eaten since the previous night.

In disgust the two colonels turned away to rejoin their regiments, and Matt said briefly, 'I must go down, sir.'

'Of course,' Colonel Henderson said, 'but not till the truce flag is up. The stretcher-bearers and the farriers won't be allowed into the valley until then. There may be pockets of Russians left.'

It was true. In these hills with their folds and bumps and valleys, pockets of soldiers could easily be hidden, but at last the flag went up, the Russians equally anxious to collect their dead and wounded. So to the melancholy sound of the farriers putting maimed and broken horses out of their pain, Matt went

145

down. Finding a young lieutenant leading a limping horse, bleeding from a cut on the side of his own head and looking totally exhausted, Matt asked him if he had seen Lieutenant Milner.

The dragoon seemed dazed, but after a moment said, 'I think he fell – back there – but there were so many. And the horses – oh my God!' And turning his face into his own charger's neck he burst into tears.

Matt laid a hand briefly on his shoulder and then hurried on. Another hundred yards and he came upon his brother quite suddenly, lying still in a pool of his own blood, his horse collapsed beside him. Matt knelt down and got out his flask. He could see there was nothing to be done, but looked round, hoping for a surgeon, seeing none very near as yet. Holding the flask to Toby's lips, he trickled some of the liquid into the slack mouth.

Toby's eyelids flickered and opened. 'Matt,' he managed to say, 'I – I was waiting for you.'

'I'm here now,' his brother said. 'Take some more rum, it will do you good,' though he doubted if it would do any good other than bring a little warmth to the dying man, for that he was dying there was no doubt at all. He had been a soldier for long enough to know that.

Toby took another sip. 'I'm – glad my fellow – found you –'

'He didn't. I saw for myself what had happened and came down to see if you were among the wounded.'

The young dragoon's eyelids drooped and he seemed to drift into sleep. It was getting cold, and taking off his great-coat Matt covered his brother with it. Nineteen and dying in his first fight – it seemed unutterably cruel.

In a little while, finding breathing difficult, Toby opened his eyes. 'It hurts – most damnably, Matt.'

'I'm sure it does, old fellow. The doctors are coming round now.' One, seeing an officer kneeling by the fallen dragoon came over, but after one look shook his head and moved on, searching for those that he could save.

Toby said, 'My horse was shot – but a trooper gave me his – that was before I was hit. It wasn't like I expected – none of it. In Hyde Park it seemed easy – drill and wheel, dress the

146

lines – drill and wheel – ' his voice trailed away.

'I know,' Matt said in a constricted voice. 'It never is as we expect when we're green. And then only believing in what you're fighting for makes it tolerable.' This he said almost for himself, and whether his brother heard it, he wasn't sure, but Toby's voice, sounding strangely distant, went on, 'It's seeing one's friends fall – blown to pieces – the fellow next to me – I liked him – it was awful.'

'Don't try to talk, dear lad,' Matt lifted his head a little to rest on his own arm, but it seemed Toby had a compulsion to speak of what he had seen. 'Do you know, Matt – what was left of him stayed in the saddle – for several minutes before falling off. Look – over there – there's part of him —' Toby raised a shaking hand.

'That's enough,' Matt told him quietly but firmly. 'Think of the good times, Hyde Park and all your shining gear and horses.'

Toby's hand gripped his with surprising strength. 'Tell them at home – I sent several of those – devils – to hell. They do screech so when they fight – don't they!'

'Enough to make one's blood run cold,' Matt agreed. 'I'll tell them at home that you fought gallantly.'

A little smile lifted the blue lips. 'That girl, Molly – we heard of – the Lambkin. Is she still here?'

'Yes, somewhere up in the camps. She does so many kindnesses for the men.'

'Weren't you mad as fire – that night?' The words came out hoarsely and when Toby tried to laugh it turned into a cough, blood dribbling from his mouth.

Pulling out his handkerchief Matt wiped away the red flow and tried to respond. 'And you were a randy young idiot. Now – you've fought like a man.'

'Did I? I'm glad.' Toby was becoming exhausted, but after a moment he looked up at his brother, a smile quivering on his face. 'I – I don't like that beard.'

'Nor do I, but it's a damned sight easier than shaving in our camp! We aren't as well served as you cavalry fellows.'

'Mama wouldn't – like it. Give them all my love. Oh, Matt – I want to go home.'

His brother bent over him, for a fleeting moment remembering a dank afternoon when he had come upon Molly holding a dying man in her arms and whispering words of hope and comfort. Lifting his brother so that his head rested against his chest, he said, 'Dear old fellow, Molly would tell you that you are going home.'

'I suppose so but – I didn't mean that – only to see Papa – and Mama. When we came out, I never thought – of not seeing them – again. Oh, God –' as a groan of pain was wrenched from him. Matt had held dying friends before now, but nothing had rent him like this. He tried to murmur something – but nothing seemed adequate.

In the growing dusk people were moving about, helping the wounded whose groans and cries broke the night silence. Two stretcher-bearers came up but Matt shook his head.

'Too late to move him – but he's not ready for his grave yet.'

A short time after the glazing eyes looked up once more 'I'm glad I came –' were the last words he spoke. There was a queer sound in his throat and then silence and Matt knew he was dead. For a long time he sat beside him, holding him and strange thoughts came to him of years past, of Toby's pampered childhood, himself a withdrawn silent boy. Jealous? Perhaps, but even though he was so much older, it made him shrivel even more into himself. It was the army that had formed him as it was changing Toby – if only he had had a chance – one of his father's chances! He stayed there, holding his brother, growing cold. Though Toby no longer needed his greatcoat Matt kept it covering him. Such a painful dying, so far from home. And for what? To fight in a pointless war for which he could see no adequate reason. Was he wrong in trying to assure himself and Toby that it was all right if one knew what one was fighting for? Perhaps the reasons did not concern them, for a soldier obeyed orders and that was an end of it.

At the first grey lifting of the darkness there Merton found him. 'I've bin looking for you, sir. Why, you're half frozen. Poor Lieutenant Milner don't want your greatcoat no more.'

Matt said, 'Leave it,' but for once Merton took no notice, picked up the greatcoat and wrapped it round his master's shoulders. 'The burial parties are coming down,' was all he could say, but he waited with Matt until they did.

It was late morning before it was all over and Matt walked back to his own camp, only one thought occupying him – that he must write to his mother and stepfather, knowing that he could not fill the awful gap left by Toby's passing. In among the rows of tents he found Molly, sitting beside a man with a broken leg, clumsily put in a splint by a comrade.

One look at him and she could only utter two words, 'Your brother?' His face contracted, and she added, 'I am so sorry, so very sorry.'

He paused. 'Thank you, Molly. I know you mean it. You've lived in our home so you've come to understand us. But he was too young —'

'Poor Lady Milner,' Molly whispered. 'She did so dote on him – and Sir Charles too. There is so little to say.'

'Exactly,' he answered, 'but I must nevertheless write to them at once, say – something.'

'May I walk with you?' And without waiting for an answer, she nodded to the young soldier and kept in step beside him, thinking how tired and distressed he looked.

Suddenly he said, 'Damn him – damn him!'

Bewildered, she asked, 'Who?'

'Lord Cardigan. He took them into that death trap.'

Not knowing enough to offer any words on the subject, she only said that she thought Merton would have something hot for him to drink. 'And then you ought to try to sleep.'

As if he had not heard her, he said, 'There'll be a reckoning one day, by God there will – somehow, somewhere, I swear it. Do you know how he spent last night, with his men dead and dying in agony in that valley? I'm told, on his yacht, eating his dinner and sleeping in a comfortable bed! The man's a monster.' In fairness to Lord Cardigan, the officer who had imparted this information also pointed out that in leading the charge, Cardigan had done no more than obey orders. But being fair to the 'Noble Lord' was the last thing on Matt's mind.

With an effort he added, 'Thank you, Molly,' though she was not sure what for, and left her at his tent. But her brief presence for a few moments had sufficed to bring him back from grief and horror to the need to eat and sleep, if he could, before he went back on duty.

149

The bombardment, the perpetual sound of the Whistling Dicks went on, and the men in the camps became inured to it. Torrential rain filled the trenches a foot deep in water and made duty there as unpleasant as it could be. Soon after the battle the Russians put out an infantry probe near the ruined village of Inkerman but were turned back, at least for the time being and there was a week when both sides drew breath, rested, took the wounded away to hospital.

When he heard about Toby's death, Dr Turner came to see his cousin, and they sat for a while together, not speaking much, until the doctor said, 'By the way, I'm going down to the hospital at Balaclava to take up my duties there, so I've said goodbye to my Riflemen. I've been their surgeon for a long time, but no doubt a good many of them will come through my hands sooner or later, poor devils. There is a rumour that a Miss Nightingale plans to bring out some nurses. Dr Forrest hates the idea, it's too new for him, but I'm of the opinion they can do a great deal.'

'They'll be welcomed by the men, I should think,' Matt said. 'I'll come down when I can.'

Bad as conditions were up here in the camps, Dr Turner half wished he was staying with the Rifles instead of going to the worst hospital conditions he had ever seen, and he left his cousin with some regret. They could certainly meet less often. Colonel Henderson, considering his wife's health was being impaired by living under canvas in the deepening cold of winter, sent Captain Marshall down to Balaclava to see if he could find somewhere for her to stay with her maid. He came back very pleased with himself for he had found a small empty house, of one storey only with two rooms and a lean-to kitchen at the back. The owners appeared to have abandoned it and plunderers had stripped it of everything that could be carried away but he made arrangements for Mrs Henderson to take it over. She refused at first to leave the Colonel and he had to insist very firmly, for she was coughing perpetually and short of breath. He thought she ought to go home to England but that she flatly refused to do. Summoned by his brigadier, Sir John Campbell, he was obliged to send her off without his escort. She had to be lifted into the saddle, and her poor mare, starved of fodder, her ribs sticking out, was in no better case.

150

The groom, Jim Reid, and her maid went with her down the long tortuous six miles that had deteriorated into a churning mess of mud. Lady May stumbled and occasionally a fit of trembling shook her, the state of the poor beast causing a few tears to run down her owner's cheeks.

'Oh Reid, do you think –'

'Yes, ma'am,' he said gravely. 'If there's nothing for her to eat in the village, I'd best put her out of her misery.'

Matt rode part of the way with them. 'Reid is right,' he said, 'but those miserable men at the stores might find some fodder.'

'Take care of my husband, Matthew,' Mrs Henderson begged him as he prepared to ride back. 'It is stupid of me, I know, but I always feel he is safer if I am in camp with him. We've so seldom been parted.'

'I know, ma'am,' he smiled at her, 'but I'll do my best to take some of the weight off his shoulders if I can, and you won't be far away, quite apart from having the entire Highland Brigade handy to keep watch over you! I hope you'll feel better when you are settled within four walls.'

When he left her he went back to his camp and reported to his commanding officer, saying, 'Awful as Balaclava is, there are stores there and I'm sure you were right to send her down, sir,' to which the Colonel replied, 'I've been trying for days to persuade her, but she's an obstinate woman. One hopes there may be better food there than our poor rations. The Fortnum and Mason parcel didn't last long, for she gave half the tea and coffee away!'

For all his cheerful talk Matt could see he was very anxious and it only reinforced his belief that officers' wives should not be in camp. Even the persistent Mrs Duberley had the sense to stay down in Balaclava.

A week passed with little activity but the rain. Molly spent her time with Nell caring for the walking wounded from the trenches, encompassing several regimental camps. Nell smiled at the constant calls for the Lambkin. When they were all home again, they would remember that name and what she had done.

But it was sad work. Molly thought often of Toby, of all the other brave young cavalrymen buried near the north valley;

she thought too of her first sight of the war, the hillsides where the battle of the Alma had been fought. Nothing had remotely prepared her, nor, she was sure, Toby either, for the disgusting awfulness of a battlefield. In the growing cold she was glad of her sheepskin for her clothes were nearly in shreds underneath and at night she slept in it, for even in the tent she shared with the Harkers and another couple it was bitingly cold. Rations were short, firewood was so scarce that the men dug up roots to burn. The military bands were silent; bandsmen, worn out with carrying the sick and wounded to Balaclava, were ill and exhausted themselves, with no heart for their instruments.

And then before dawn one morning in early November, there was the call – 'Stand to your arms! Jump to it, boys. Turn out, turn out.'

The men emerged from the tents, buckling on belts, jamming caps on their heads. One or two fortunate ones now had 'bunny coats', jackets with some fur which they had taken off the enemy dead; some were lucky enough to have Russian boots but the others were in sad case, patched and lined with any cloth or canvas they could find. Lining up they made a ragged show, but being Riflemen they stood to attention, proud of their faded green and their Minié rifles which, whatever else was worse for wear, they kept in mint condition. There was no time for breakfast, though most men stuffed a biscuit or two in their pockets. Even these were providing a poor food for those whose teeth were loosened by the growing menace of scurvy. Perhaps it was as well that they did not know there were bottles of lemon juice on a ship in Balaclava harbour that it was deemed impossible to transport up to the camps.

Molly and Nell watched the Rifles march out, followed by the 50th and the Royals. 'How different they look from when we saw them off at Portsmouth,' Molly said sadly. 'How the ranks have thinned.'

No one knew the reason for the call-out, but the enemy must be on the move somewhere, and they headed off towards the Woronzow road. It was a miserable morning, damp with a drifting fog. Molly sat with a young officer who was disgusted that he had fallen on some loose rocks, tumbled down the ridge and broken his right arm.

'Not to be able to go with the Rifles,' he grumbled. 'It's so damnably annoying – begging your pardon, Lambkin, but it is. I'd rather be out there with my company, such as it is, than sitting here in my tent. The men didn't even get any breakfast, and here I've been stuffing myself with beastly biscuits dipped in an apology for coffee.'

'It's not your fault,' she said, smiling at his indignation. 'I'm sure you didn't want to fall down that hill.'

'No, I jolly well didn't. Will you write a letter for me to my parents? You'll find paper and a pencil in my haversack.'

She fetched them and asked what he wanted her to say and he began, 'My dearest mother and father. I have most unluckily broken my arm so a friend is writing this for me. Apart from that I am well.' He paused while she caught up, and casting a glance at him, she thought how pallid and thin he looked. There was scarcely a robust man in the brigade, but those who could wrote home cheerfully enough.

He went on, 'No doubt you have heard news through the *Times'* reports from Mr Russell our correspondent, who is a very good sort of fellow, always popping up all over the place. Sir Colin Campbell saved Balaclava for us, with the Highland Brigade – I wonder if the Ruskies had ever seen a kilt before! The Light Brigade took a trouncing later on, you will read about that in the paper, I expect. There was some dreadful muddle over orders. Today the infantry are out but it's too soon to know what is happening. I can hear the guns and you can imagine how I feel not being out with my lads.'

Molly wrote down exactly what he said and wondered what his anxious parents would make of it all. His Mama at least might be glad that a broken arm kept him out of today's fighting. He had told her he was an only son, and part of her was sad that she had not given Hal a son – yet all things considered it was better not, for it would have raised so many difficulties, and Hal would never have seen his child.

Giving him the letter to read through the young officer signed it with a wobbly hand. Molly begged a piece of paper for a letter of her own. She had put off writing to Miss Plumstead for a long time, and she wanted to tell her all that had happened. She hoped it would get safely to Westbourne. It was still painful to talk, even on paper, of the dreadful night when the cholera had taken Hal from her, and she said little of what they were all enduring. Even what she read in the papers must disturb Miss Plumstead.

Returning to her own camp, after putting the letters into the bag that was collected, somewhat erratically, to be taken home by the next ship, she found Nell coaxing their fire into life.

'They will want hot food when they come back,' she said. 'Oh, Molly, this is the worst campaign I've known in all the years,' and her voice shook a little.

Molly put an arm round her. 'I'm sure it is. If they could only take that horrid town down there, it would all be over. I'll go and collect our rations.'

The camp was oddly quiet. Only a few children played, managing in the way of children to make some fun for themselves. The occasional whop of falling shells no longer made Molly jump, but from the distance the sound of guns and musketry intensified and she wished she knew what was happening.

It was hours before the surviors of the battle around the ruins of Inkerman came trickling back to the camps. Molly and Nell came out to watch, as Major Norcott led the diminished and exhausted Riflemen back into camp. He was filthy, spattered with mud and blood, but he kept the men going until they could be dismissed to their tents. Her hands clasped tightly together Nell cried out with relief when she saw her husband. The corporal was in the same state as his commanding officer, with a bandage of sorts round his head but thankfully alive. He and the rest looked totally exhausted. Nell ran to him and for a moment they clung together. Molly knew exactly how they felt, tears threatening, coupled with an awful empty feeling.

She stayed on outside, waiting to see the 50th pass through to their camp. He must come back, he *must*. She could not bear it if Major Hamilton was to die as well as his brother. But she had heard yesterday of three brothers from the Sherwood Foresters killed together and she thought of poor Lady Milner. This was an anxiety worse than she had felt at the Alma, for then she had known nothing of war and was as full of hope as the innocent were.

Dusk was falling, the fog still lingering on this dreary

November day, when the last remnants of the 'Dirty Half Hundred' came in out of the gloom, very much living up to their name. Their steps were lagging, many helping wounded comrades. At their head was only Captain Marshall, one arm hanging limply and blood running down it. Molly began to feel an odd terror – he wasn't there and she didn't know how to bear it. Wanting desperately for him to come, she prayed as desperately, not stopping even to wonder at the reason for this agony.

Then she saw Merton. His head too was bandaged, but he was on his two feet. Speeding across to him she cried out, 'Oh tell me –' He looked at her out of bloodshot weary eyes and she wanted to shake him in her desperation. 'Oh tell me – is he hurt? Wounded? But not killed? Oh dear Lord, not killed?'

Joseph Merton drew a deep breath. 'Oh, it's you, Lambkin. No, thank Gawd he ain't killed, nor much wounded neither – a slash across his cheek and a cut hand – but it's the Colonel – Colonel Henderson what's killed.'

In the midst of her relief, Molly could only gasp. 'Oh no! His poor wife – and she down in Balaclava and sick herself.'

'I know, Lambkin, and that's where the Major is – gone to tell her and then he'll have to report to the Brigadier, if he can find him. He'll be acting colonel now.'

'Oh – I suppose so. Was it a dreadful fight?'

It was a minute or so, Molly walking beside him, before he could bring himself to speak, silent men trudging with him. Then he said, 'I ain't never seen a worse – all in the fog, over uneven ground and slopes that were all covered in stones and scrub and leathery bushes that took the skin off you. All we could see were more and more of them grey coats coming at us. Fiends they are. There's nothing they like better than bayonetting wounded men on the ground.'

Molly shuddered, 'That's awful – unchristian –'

'Aye, so it is and it made us real mad. There didn't seem to be no orders from any command to tell us where to attack, only our own officers, and the regiments got all mixed up. We fought with bayonets and if they broke or were torn from us we went on with bare hands, we were that mad. I ain't never, never seen a field like it – I can't describe it, nor you don't need to hear. Except one major, both feet shot off and his poor

155

legs plunged into some gunpowder to stop the bleeding, calm as you like, telling his men he was still in command. There was an officer for you! And Colonel Yea, when it was all over, suddenly sitting on a rock and sobbing for the men he had lost.'

Nausea rose in her. 'And Colonel Henderson?'

'Oh,' Merton seemed almost overcome, the tears starting from his eyes, 'He was the right sort he was. Always fair, never flogged any of us, and always in the lead. "Old walking boots" we called him because he never rode into action but marched with us. Anyway he was in front as usual, calling to us to come on, when a shot got him. He fell on his knees and then forward on to his face – well, the Major leapt across the space between them and stood astride him, yelling at us to save the Colonel. He fought like a wild man, killing I don't know how many of the Rooskies that came at him, and if the Colonel had lived he'd have owed his life to my major, that he would. But he were dead, Lambkin.'

This frightful tale of carnage and courage had brought the tears coursing down Molly's face. 'It's dreadful – dreadful! What happened then?'

'Another company came up to help us, it might a' bin the Royals, and we drove them off at last, though we were at it for hours in that nasty fog.'

'Then we won?'

'We won all right, but oh my Gawd, what it cost us! I pray I never, never see a field like that again.'

'I pray not, too,' she murmured. 'Dear Merton, I'm so glad you are safe and the Major as well. I'd better leave you here, you must want your supper.'

'Nowt since yesterday,' he gave a feeble grin, the first sign of his old cheerful self. 'I'm that hungry and a drop o' rum'll go down well.'

She walked away in the darkness to the Rifles camp and there in her own tent went in to find Nell and Bob waiting for her.

'Oh, my dear,' Nell exclaimed. 'What is it? Not Major Hamilton?'

'No – Colonel Henderson. You know he's dead?'

'Aye,' Bob Harker took off his shako and threw it on to the

ground. 'And him one o' the best officers the army's ever had.'

'Oh Nell,' Molly flung herself into her friend's arms. 'Will it never stop?'

And then, amid all the death and destruction, the misery and pain, there occurred a miracle that changed the whole course of Molly's life.

Chapter Eleven

The men of the 50th mourned their Colonel. They had both respected and loved him because they had cause to know, many of them, how much he genuinely cared for them. For Major Hamilton they had respect, certainly in action they trusted him, but it was doubtful if they loved him. He lacked the genial bonhomie of Jock Henderson, but as the first two weeks passed after the battle of Inkerman he made it evident that behind his reserve the well-being of the regiment was what mattered to him. He endeavoured to wield the much depleted men into a closer unit, and though he never said so, their long-enduring patience, their determination throughout this dreadful winter amazed him.

For himself the loss of both his brother and the man he looked on as friend, guide and mentor, left him deeply depressed and lonely. He gave himself little spare time, often in the trenches to encourage the men, and when in the middle of November a hurricane struck the camp, wrecking some of the tents, and sending their few possessions flying, he visited each company, finding out who was in desperate need and endeavouring to get what was wanted. And the sinking of the *Prince* steamship in the harbour that same night, laden as it was with food and warm clothes, seemed something of a last straw.

Requesting an interview with Lord Raglan, he determined to go on down afterwards to Balaclava to see what the situation was there. Headquarters was in a small farmhouse between Balaclava and the Heights. Several officers stood outside and one or two, knowing Matt, called out to him, sorry for the loss of a well-liked senior officer.

A sentry saluted and he entered to find General Airey, the Quartermaster-general seated at a table covered with papers. Airey was the best sort of staff officer, disciplined, tough, sensible and an excellent man for his post – if only he had had an excellent Commander-in-chief. Much as Matt liked Lord Raglan personally, he shared the general view that the old man was not fit to command such an army in such a situation. But he had known Raglan distantly, through his father, for many years, and Lord Raglan's greeting was warm, for he said at once, 'I'm extremely sorry about Colonel Henderson, he will be much missed – with so many others,' ending on a deep sigh.

'Yes, sir, General Cathcart particularly. We all thought highly of him.'

'A fine officer – yes, yes. But now you, Major Hamilton, how are you settling in with the 50th?' for all as if he had not been with them for approaching four years.

'Well enough, my lord.' Matt had already taken in the warm fire, the remains of what had obviously been a good meal on the table. Well, he supposed the Commander and the Staff should be well maintained, but he sighed for his cold and hungry men.

'I am acting commanding officer, of course, but I came to ask if you would confirm this, perhaps write to the War Office to ask for my promotion to be ratified.'

Raglan smiled. His kindly face was much wrinkled and it bore, despite the smile, a look of permanent intense anxiety.

'I can certainly do that, but it is for them to endorse it.'

Matt sighed inwardly. 'And if I know them, sir, as we are on campaign they will refer the matter to you.'

'Well, well, we shall see.' His lordship had a habit of pigeon-holing difficulties.

'Thank you, sir. I am to presume then, that I continue for the time being in Colonel Henderson's place? Our numbers are sadly depleted.'

'I have asked for reinforcements repeatedly, and expect them every day, but the weather, you know – very bad.' And then, as if it suddenly struck him, Lord Raglan added, in his particularly charming manner, 'I have had a note from

159

General Pennefather. Apparently he observed your action at Inkerman when you endeavoured to save poor Henderson. I shall mention it in my next despatch. It should settle your promotion, eh?'

Matt thanked him and took his leave. One couldn't help but feel sympathy for the old man who lacked the mental toughness for the situation in which he found himself. He should, Matt thought, be happily retired at home in England, and not bearing this burden.

Through the mud and rain he rode his shaggy pony down the track to Balaclava. It was littered with debris, overturned and broken carts, some sunk irretrievably into the morass, with abandoned boxes, a single shoe – had some poor fellow gone barefoot back to camp? he wondered. A dead horse, little more than a skeleton, lay sprawled by the side of the so-called road and Matt was glad for once that Shalima was safely in the livery stable in Southsea. His pony, whom he had named Vladima, was sturdy and used to this awful place.

Mr Commissary Jones saw him coming, and leaving a colleague in charge, slipped out of the back door to avoid the ferocious Major Hamilton, looking even more so now with his black beard. Matt managed to extract a promise of various necessities and outside ran into Major Norcott who at once expressed his regret at the Colonel's death, adding, 'It was a damned close thing up there, wasn't it?'

'It was', Matt agreed, 'the worst I've ever seen, it could have gone either way. I tell you, Norcott, if the politicians who sit in Parliament could see such things they would not so easily call out for war.'

Norcott nodded. 'At least, thank God, Russell has seen that the newspapers print the truth of it and with Roger Fenton's photographs to back him up, no one can dare to hoodwink the British people into thinking we are all living in the lap of luxury. Not a difficult task in general, but this time maybe the truth will come out!' But then, more seriously he added, 'I'm sorry for Mrs Henderson. They were very close, weren't they?'

'Yes.' The brief syllable said it all. 'I'm off to see her now. How is your regimental mascot?'

'What, our Lambkin?' Norcott laughed. 'I tell you, Matt,

that girl is a wonder. She does so much for the fellows, but without any parade at all, as if it is the most natural thing in the world, to be struggling about army camps in mud and rain in a Russian coat! She puts heart into us, and all this after losing her own husband, poor girl.'

Matt nodded. But afterwards what? When they all went home, what would she do?

He left Norcott and went on to Mrs Henderson's little house. And what he found there sent him headlong up to the camp of the Rifle Brigade. There he came upon Molly darning a sock for one of the men, though it was more hole than sock, but nearly all the contents of her tidy were gone. She looked up as Matt came and gave him a smile before noticing how grave he seemed. And she didn't like that beard, thinking he looked much better without it.

But before he came to the point, thinking of Bill Norcott's words, he looked round the miserable little tent, Molly sitting on a rolled up blanket on a square of waterproof, for which all the Rifles had cause to bless the late General Cathcart. 'You could have gone home weeks ago,' he said abruptly. 'Doesn't anything ever get the better of you?'

She gave him a little smile. 'As to that, sir, I've not been much acquainted with comfort in my life so far. Crossley Lodge was the best.'

A moment's pause. The best? Those attics he had never visited? Then he said, 'I've a great favour to ask of you.'

She rose, putting aside the pitiful sock. 'Anything, sir. What can I do for you?'

'It's Mrs Henderson,' he explained, 'my late Colonel's lady. She's very ill, consumption, my cousin says, too ill anyway to bear the journey home. She's still in the little house we found for her which is just about tolerable, but the thing is – her maid died of cholera yesterday and Reid, her groom, can't nurse a sick woman. Nor can she go into the hospital – unthinkable. Molly, will you go down and do what you can for her?'

'But she doesn't know me, sir. She might not like it. I've seen her in the distance of course, but I've never spoken to her.'

'She will be more than grateful, I can assure you of that.'

'But the men here, they need me too.'

'I think they will have to do without their Lambkin for a while. Mrs Henderson's need is great and I owe her and the Colonel a great deal. She is quite shattered by his loss, it's as if her whole purpose in life has gone and I don't think she will survive him long.' He laid his hand on her shoulder. 'It seems as if my family is always asking difficult things of you, Molly, but – will you go?'

'I was glad to stay and care for your mother,' she said stoutly, though she had often thought since that it had robbed her of a few more weeks of marriage to Hal, before it had been so briefly terminated. But she didn't say this. She only looked up at him, seeing how much it mattered to him. 'Of course I'll be glad to go down for as long as it's necessary.'

'Thank you.' He gave her a quick smile. 'I thought you would. Merton will take you and show you where the cottage is.'

She had hoped for his company, though she understood that, commanding a regiment, he would not be able to spare the time to escort the likes of her down the track. So the next morning she packed up her few goods, said goodbye to Nell and as many of the men as were about the camp and set off with Merton. He beguiled the long cold tramp by telling her of their time in India when his Major had been in the cavalry.

'And a brilliant horseman he were, same as that Captain Nolan, poor fellow. I ain't never seen better and it all came to naught because of that Lord Cardigan – may he rot in —' he caught himself up. 'Beggin' your pardon, but it were wicked the way he hounded my poor master. And yet – well you never know, do you – he told me the other day that serving with Colonel Henderson was one of the best things that had ever happened to him. And now he's lost him as well as poor Master Toby. It's hard for him, Lambkin.'

'I know,' she blinked back sudden tears. 'I'm glad he has you to look after him, that was a piece of good luck for him,' and Merton went quite pink with pleasure.

They reached Balaclava in the afternoon. The harbour was full of ships, many of them damaged in the hurricane, though, perversely it seemed to her, Lord Cardigan's yacht, the *Dryad*

162

seemed not to have suffered. All traces of the quiet fishing village they had first seen last autumn was gone. It was now a British base, an army depot, and Molly looked at it with a great deal of curiosity, so many lives having been spent on the keeping of it. It seemed to her a hive of muddled activity, farriers, sutlers, sailors and engineers, all about their business while dark-faced Turks lounged idly, Greek traders shouted their wares, and dominating it all the grey, unappealing bulk of the hospital. Molly glanced curiously at it and hoped she would see Dr Turner some time.

Merton led her to a cottage just a stone's throw below it, a small single-storey building with a green slate roof, which had once belonged to a fisherman, long since fled to Sebastopol. He showed her into the main room, dreary enough with a rickety table and a couple of stools, a dresser bare of all necessities such as bowls and plates. A bed was made up on the floor by the far wall. To the side of this was another door. Merton indicated this and Molly knocked. A tired voice bade her enter. Inside the small room was a bed made on a wooden base, Turkish fashion, and in it, under a couple of blankets, her head on her own pillow that she had brought from England, lay Mrs Henderson.

Molly stood hesitantly in the doorway, thinking how dreadfully ill the poor woman looked. Perhaps she didn't want to live now that her husband was gone. The weather had cleared and a pale winter sunset cast a gleam of light through the window and on to Molly's face as she pulled off her forage cap.

Mrs Henderson gave a sudden low cry and managed to raise herself on one elbow. 'Marianne! Oh, Marianne, you've come back to me!'

The room seemed filled with sunset light as Molly heard these amazing words. For a moment she stood rigidly still by the door, not knowing what to say. Then, bracing herself she came forward. 'I think you're mistaking me for someone else, ma'am. I'm Molly Hallam. Major Hamilton sent me down to look after you.'

Confused, coughing a little, two fever spots burning in her normally pale cheeks, Olivia Henderson collapsed back against the pillow. After a moment she murmured, 'Yes, yes, a mistake – a trick of the light.'

'You don't look very comfortable.' Molly set down her bag and began to remake the bed. Mrs Henderson's own travelling box lay under the window and Molly thought she would look into it tomorrow to see what she could find for the sick woman's comfort. In the meantime, lifting her a little, she pumped up the pillow, feeling how thin the poor lady was, saying as she laid her back, 'There, isn't that more comfortable?'

'Much more, thank you. Since my Rosalie died two days ago I have not had a moment's ease. And though Reid is an excellent groom, he's not a nurse.' She tried to smile up at Molly.

'I'm sorry about your maid. My husband died of the same horrid sickness.'

'So Matthew said. Rosalie had been with me for nearly twenty years. She was French and we had got used to each other. First my husband and then poor Rosalie, and yesterday – yesterday Reid had to shoot my poor Lady May.' The loss, lesser among the greater, brought the tears to her eyes.

'Life is very hard to understand sometimes,' Molly said simply. 'Harder for some than others.'

'And sometimes you wonder – ' Mrs Henderson's voice trailed away and Molly thought of Merton's description of how close the Colonel and his lady were after some twenty-five years of marriage. Would she and Hal have been like that? She was no longer sure. The Crimea had changed her, she knew that. And that when they all went home she would want different things, better things.

To Mrs Henderson, she said, 'I'm quite free to stay here for as long as you want me, ma'am. Now I'd better go and see what food there is in the kitchen.'

'Reid has gone to look for firewood, but I don't know —'

'I'll see to everything,' Molly told her cheerfully. At the door she paused. 'By the way, ma'am, such an odd thing. I've always been called Molly, but my real name is actually Marianne!' With a little laugh she slipped out, leaving Mrs Henderson gazing after her in amazement.

Molly set about inspecting the little house. The bed in the

other room had been stripped and the blankets washed, for lack of better facilities, in the harbour, by the sensible Reid. Until these were dry she thought she could make herself reasonably comfortable with her own, having slept on the hard ground for months now. Going through to the back room she found a tolerable kitchen. A fire was laid, ready to cook the evening meal, and here there were at least some tin bowls and plates garnered, she supposed, from Mrs Henderson's store and Reid's knapsack. A cupboard yielded some salt beef, the inevitable biscuits and a few rather odd-looking turnips. There were insects on the floor, cockroaches and no doubt fleas, lice and mice, but at least they didn't seem to have breeched the cupboard. She closed it carefully, determined tomorrow to scrub out the whole place.

Reid appeared, with a bundle of wood under one arm and a jug in the other hand. He was a small man in his fifties, lean and wrinkled, but as she was to discover, surprisingly strong, and with the ability to make the best of the worst situations. Setting his burdens down on the table he said, 'You'll be Mrs Hallam then?'

Molly nodded. 'Did the Major tell you?'

'Aye,' he began to kindle the fire, blowing on the embers. Glancing at her and at the sheepskin jacket he added, 'seen you about the camps. I know what they call you.'

Smiling a little, she said, 'I expect you have and you are at liberty to call me Lambkin if you want to.'

'Aye. It's as well you're here, I can't do what my mistress needs.' This was quite a long conversation from Reid who, as she was to discover, preferred talking to the horses he loved than to his employers, and he had not recovered yet from having to put down Lady May. Reaching in one pocket he produced a dry head of garlic.

'Oh!' Molly exclaimed. 'Wherever did you get that? It will flavour our stew nicely. I'll get on and make it now the fire's going nicely.'

He unbent so far as to give her a hint of a grin. 'I ain't no cook!'

Molly went in to Mrs Henderson and finding her in a somewhat alarming state, restless, feverish and coughing, all with her eyes shut, she asked Reid to go to the hospital and see if he could find Dr Turner.

165

He came at once. 'Ah, Lambkin, I'm glad to find you here. I hoped my cousin might send you down, but what's all this? I thought Mrs Henderson quiet this morning.' He bent over the bed, examining his patient, who was barely conscious.

'I'm sorry,' Molly said, 'but I thought she seemed very bad – and her maid died of cholera, didn't she?'

'Well, this isn't cholera. It's inflammation of the lungs, poor woman. I doubt she'll see England again. But how long she will linger, I can't tell. Only I'm desperately needed at the hospital and there's little I can do for her anyway. You'll stay? A woman's care is what she needs.' A surprisingly perceptive man, John Turner, under the snappishness.

'As long as I'm needed.' Molly assured him.

He straightened and, in a less irritable tone, said, 'Good girl. At least I know you're well able to care for her. Losing her husband has been a dreadful shock to her. I wonder what got her into this state today.'

'When I came in,' Molly explained, 'she seemed to think I was someone else and it must have brought back some bad memories. She was quite upset.'

'Delirious of course.'

'Yes, I expect so.' And Molly added a little tentatively, 'Did you hear how Major Hamilton acted in the battle, trying to save the Colonel?'

'A couple of wounded fellows from the 50th could hardly stop talking about it. I'm not surprised, that's Matt for you.'

Feeling a sudden warm glow, she murmured, 'Thank you for coming.'

'It's I and my cousin who should thank you. Well, she may last the night, but she may not. I wish I had a better supply of medicines, but we are virtually without any over at the hospital. I shall have something to say to the Medical Board when I get home. If you really need me in the night, send Reid for me.' Giving her a little smile, he patted her shoulder and went out, a tired man expending all his stamina and knowledge on his patients without even the barest necessities, and Molly thought that only in the direst need would she call him over.

In the morning Mrs Henderson was still alive, though barely aware of anything. She muttered her husband's name, over and over again, and 'Marianne' several times, but for the

166

most part was unintelligible. Molly bathed her face and hands, spoke soothingly to her, for she had found with the soldiers that even if they were unconscious, should they recover they seemed to recall any kind words.

Dr Turner came again in the evening, and by this time, thankfully, the fever had broken and the sick woman lay quiet. 'Well,' he said, after a brief look, 'I believe she may do now. Well done, Lambkin.'

'I did little enough —'

'You did what was needed. Now it's our job to get her fit enough to travel home – as long as she doesn't have another relapse. Would you consider going with her?'

It was a question she had not yet even considered, but, much as the men needed her, it was unthinkable to abandon Colonel Henderson's lady, and she murmured, 'Whatever you think best, sir.' She could indeed take Mrs Henderson home, but what then?

Within a few days Molly and the silent Reid had settled down very well together. Molly nursed the invalid, hoping the doctor was right, and that some life and strength would come back. She soon had the little house into some sort of order, though she had to fight an ongoing battle with the cockroaches. Scrubbing out the kitchen, the walls and the floors, with sea water, that being all that was available and fetched by Reid who thought she took cleanliness a little too far, she went down into the harbour area herself every morning to bring back any foodstuffs she could find. Bartering with the Turks, to whom she took a strong dislike, for she found them dirty and dishonest, as neither she nor they spoke each other's language it was a case of bullying and cajoling. Mrs Henderson seemed to have sufficient money, but she was not going to waste it on cheats. However, every day she managed to come back with something to eke out their slender rations.

One morning she saw Mrs Duberley coming down the gang plank of the ship in the harbour where she was presently living, and without hesitation approached her.

The situation explained, Mrs Duberley, a bright bouncing little woman, who thought nothing of riding up to watch a battle and follow her husband wherever he went, did not hesitate. 'My husband has told me about you,' she said. 'What do you need?'

'Anything for an invalid,' Molly explained. 'Mrs Henderson finds it hard to swallow more than a mouthful of the meat we get. She did get a parcel from a London shop, but I'm afraid that's all gone.'

'I'm not surprised. Come and see me tomorrow morning and I'll see what I can find. Had you heard that a lady, a Miss Nightingale has arrived at Scutari with a party of nurses and is trying to set that place to rights. Perhaps she'll manage to do something for us here – now that's good news, isn't it?'

Molly hoped it was, though the workhouse had given her a poor opinion of women who took up nursing, and needed a bottle of gin before they would start, but if this Miss Nightingale was a lady she might manage to improve things. Mrs Duberley was as good as her word and the next day a package was ready for Molly, containing some arrowroot, a packet of tea, a small bag of white flour – an unheard of luxury – a little sugar and some salt. Molly nearly wept with gratitude and Mrs Duberley promised to come to visit the patient. The first thing she did on reaching home was to make up some of the arrowroot and Mrs Henderson was able to swallow it and drink some tea, her own supply having long since run out.

As the days went by, Molly was aware of the sick woman watching her as she came in and out of the room, in a peculiarly searching way, her eyes seeming to follow Molly whatever she was doing. Then one dull afternoon, Mrs Henderson thought she could sit up for a little while, and Molly propped her as comfortably as she could, fetching her own blanket roll as an extra support.

After a moment, Mrs Henderson said, 'Won't you sit down by me, Molly, here on the bed? That's right. I feel better today, which I owe to your care, so won't you tell me a little about yourself?'

'It's not very exciting ma'am.' Molly gave her a sad little smile. 'I came here with my husband, who was a rifleman, and now, like you, I'm a widow. He died of the cholera.'

'It struck down so many good men. Yes, Matthew told me that, but I mean before – where were you born? Tell

168

me about your family. It's very strange that you should be so very like the friend I mistook you for – and to have the same name!'

'I know, ma'am. I've been thinking of that too, but I come from a different sort of place from you and your friends.'

Mrs Henderson leaned back. 'Then tell me.'

Molly meant to leave nothing out, but she had got no further than the workhouse, and Mrs Plumstead telling her about her mother when the invalid reached out and grasped her by the wrist.

'Tell me again. Where was this workhouse? And when were you born?'

'I shall be twenty in a few months, so it was in March 1835 – that's why they called me Molly March. My mother was brought in, very ill, and barely conscious. The only thing she told them was that her name was Marianne, and she died just after I was born, but Miss Plumstead, who taught us girls, always told me to remember my Ma was a lady. The only thing I have of hers is my wedding ring. Miss Plumstead took it off her finger and gave it to me, so that I could wear it when I got married, which I did.'

Mrs Henderson took hold of her hand, touching the plain gold ring. 'And the workhouse, where was that?'

'In Westbourne. It's a little place between Chichester and Portsmouth. What is it, ma'am? Are you feeling worse? Perhaps I'm tiring you.' She made as if to rise but Mrs Henderson had hold of her wrist, sudden colour in her face. 'No – no – oh my dear, don't go. I think – no, I'm sure – I know who you are.'

Even afterwards Molly remembered that dark afternoon in the shabby little house, deprived of all but the most basic needs, and a sick woman declaring the most astounding thing. For a moment colour flooded her own cheeks. Stammering a little, hardly aware of what she was saying, only disconnected words came out. 'Oh, ma'am, how could you? So long ago – I mean – I'm a workhouse girl – Miss Plumstead thought – but – how can it be? No one ever – it's only the name made you think —' Aware that she wasn't making sense, she saw that there was a sudden warm and astonishing light in Mrs Henderson's eyes, her distress giving way to excitement.

169

'My dear child, I believe, in fact I'm certain now that your mother was my closest friend!'

Molly gasped, shaken by wild emotions. 'But - I don't understand - you can't —'

Mrs Henderson had hold of both her hands now. 'I've watched you since you've been here with me, and you are so like my dearest Marianne, it's uncanny. Not only your features and your hair, but the way you walk, your hands —'

'They're red and chapped, not a lady's hands,' Molly murmured, her mind coping with the small thing in the middle of this enormity.

'They're beautiful hands, or soon can be. Oh my dear child, I can hardly believe it either, but I know that it is true.'

Struggling to assimilate all this, Molly managed to say, 'Won't you tell me how - how you can be so sure? Do you know how my mother came to that workhouse?'

The sick woman smiled, for perhaps the first time since Matt had ridden down with the terrible news from the Inkerman heights. 'I hardly know where to begin, it's such a long story. Perhaps you would fetch me a drink of water before I start.'

'Have a rest first,' Molly begged, though she could hardly bear to wait. 'You look so tired. Tomorrow - '

'I don't think either of us can wait until tomorrow,' Mrs Henderson said perceptively, and when Molly had fetched her some water, she began.

Chapter Twelve

'Your mother and I went to the same school, an Academy for Young Ladies! She lived in a little place called Marlow on the river Thames and we were close by in Henley. Her father was Sir William Penberthy and they had a house facing on to the river which used to flood every winter, the garden anyway!' Seeing the shock and astonishment on the girl's face, she was mentioning the trivial things to ease the moment, but the rest of the story had to be told.

'When she was seventeen she fell in love most disastrously with a man in his late twenties, a charmer if ever there was one. He came to Henley one summer, ostensibly to row in the river races, and we all met him on the bank where there were marquees for refreshments. He seemed to be everything that was delightful and he soon became a regular caller at both the Penberthys and at my home. He told us that his widowed mother lived in York – I think the only piece of truth he ever gave us – that he had been to Oxford, a lie of course, and was about to take up a lucrative post abroad, attached to the Foreign Office, another lie as we discovered later.'

She had Molly's riveted attention now, and went on, 'It was a magical summer. At all the balls he danced with Marianne and they did make a handsome couple. He gave the impression that he had plenty of money and at the end of the summer season he asked Marianne to marry him. Of course she said yes.'

'What was his name?'

'Geoffrey Sefton. Oh, he took us all in, Marianne most of all, and she was deliriously happy. Sir William, seeing his daughter so deeply in love, was moved to give his permission, on certain terms. He wrote to the Foreign Office to ask if the young man had good prospects. The Foreign Office had never heard of him. Sir William pursued other lines of enquiry, all equally revealing, and he told Mr Sefton that he was a charlatan and a liar, and forbade him the house, making it plain to his daughter that the affair was over. Marianne was dreadfully upset, as you can imagine, and there were some unpleasant scenes. She had a will of her own – like you, I should think, dear Molly.' With eyes glistening Molly gave her a smile. 'I suppose so.'

'Well, your finding your way on to the troopship tells me that. Anyway we all thought that was the end of the matter, but we had reckoned without the determination of the lovers. Afterwards we found out more about Mr Sefton. He had done this sort of thing before, persuaded a girl to elope with him and then demanded that the father concerned should pay him off. He realized of course that Sir William was wealthy. Marianne had a brother, Gerald, and he was enraged by the whole thing, even more so than his father. He told Marianne he would throw the young man down the steps if he ever came to the house again. I don't know that I have ever disliked anyone as much as Gerald Penberthy. Sir William told his daughter that if she didn't give up Mr Sefton at once he would send her away to an aunt in Wales, that if she disobeyed him he would never wish to see her again. It was all bombast we thought, because he adored her and was driven to the end of his tether because she would not give up her lover. Marianne, as you can imagine, caught in the middle of all this, was in a wretched state. She came to me and sobbed in my arms. I begged her to give Mr Sefton up but she wouldn't listen. She refused to believe the tales they told her of him!

Eventually Marianne gave her father the slip and the two eloped, going through a form of marriage in some obscure chapel in Reading. She was under age, you see. For weeks we heard nothing. Then a letter came from Mr Sefton demanding money. He gave the address of an inn and although Gerald went there to look for his sister, they were not there. The landlord said he was only told that if there was a reply he was to keep it until Mr Sefton called. Another demand came and

Sir William threw that on the fire. You can imagine, Molly, what my feelings were.'

Molly nodded, understanding only too well the emotional turmoil her mother must have endured. 'What happened then?'

'Well, we heard nothing for a long while. Was Marianne happy? Did he have any genuine feelings for her? I don't know. But months later, further enquiries had revealed him as a drunkard and a gambler as well. Marianne had taken all her mother's jewels so I presume he used them to fund these habits.' Exhausted, Mrs Henderson lay quiet for a moment, but when Molly made a move to leave her to rest, she opened her eyes to say, 'No, don't go, my dear. Let me finish. There's not much more.'

Molly sat down again and she went on, 'We had no idea where they had gone. We wondered if he had taken her to his mother in York, but that proved a false trail and in the end every possibility came to a dead end. It broke Sir William. He had already lost his wife, and Marianne was his only daughter. You see, he never did get on with Gerald. He became a recluse and Gerald took charge of everything. He cared for nothing but money and position, and he was so angry that Marianne had caused a scandal, I think he was even glad that Sir William had cast her off, even out of his will. My father thought the whole thing very badly handled and we saw little of them after that.'

Another pause and then Mrs Henderson said dreamily, 'Not long afterwards I met my Jock. We married a few months later, when he was posted to India. If only my dear Marianne had met a man like him.'

The poignancy of it all, seeing the girl who looked like her in such a sad little drama, Molly felt like weeping for the first Marianne. 'Did you never hear from her again?'

'Yes, one letter, which my brother forwarded to me in Bombay. Of course she didn't know I had left the country and being so far away I could do nothing myself. Anyway she didn't give me an address. I could tell how wretched she was, everything seemed to have gone wrong. Mr Sefton was gambling heavily as usual and eventually had the police after him for embezzlement. Poor darling Marianne. By this time they were living in Portsmouth though I don't know where.

Apparently he found a sort of living there, fleecing sailors home on leave and easily parted from their money. He had sold all Marianne's jewels and when his funds were totally exhausted he disappeared. She believed he had boarded a ship, perhaps for America, or maybe somewhere like Shanghai, but there she was, expecting a child and very near her time, abandoned in Portsmouth. She couldn't pay her rent and was turned out of her lodgings, but that was the end of her letter. What she did after that I don't know. She only said she hated Portsmouth and wanted to get away. I wish I could have written to her and told her to go home, but from such a distance it was impossible. Maybe she did write home, I don't know.

I wrote to my brother and asked him to do what he could, but of course by the time he got my letter and went down there the trail had gone cold. She must have been in the area of Westbourne when she was taken ill, though how she got there we'll probably never know. But I believe it was my dearest Marianne who was brought into the workhouse that night to give birth to you.'

Molly was crying between grief and joy and somehow found herself, the strong one, being enfolded in Mrs Henderson's bony arms and it was inexpressible comfort. At last, stemming the tears, she sat back a little.

'It is so strange, after all these years, to know who I am, who she was. For of course you must be right. Oh dear Mrs Henderson, you were my mother's friend, almost family. I have someone of my own at last. Can I really believe it?'

'I think you may, dear child. The strangest thing is that we should have been so close all these months and only ever saw each other in the distance!' Mrs Henderson kissed her forehead, but the telling of the tale had exhausted her and she closed her eyes, murmuring, 'Sit by me a little.'

Molly obeyed, but after a while, sure she was asleep, she rose and in a daze walked out of the house. It was a clear evening, a single star in the great dark bowl of the sky and hardly knowing where she was walking she tried to take in what had happened. If only she could go to Miss Plumstead, tell her this wonderful news! But she would write soon – tomorrow – to tell her that her grandfather was Sir William Penberthy, her mother his daughter, from a place called

Marlow, wherever that was, and she had a family at last. Even if she never saw them, they were there! As for her poor mother's tragedy, it was heart-breaking, but she had always known it must be something of the kind, and now there was a bond, an awareness that was new. She too had known the hardness of life – at the workhouse, the débâcle at the farm and the miserable days in Portsmouth, and come out of it. Even the losing of Hal subsided a little in the face of this stupendous happening.

Two riflemen, passing on their way up to the camp saw her and one called out, 'Hullo, Lambkin, have you deserted us?'

'For a little while,' she answered, and the one who had spoken to her wondered what had put that radiance into her face.

The army had to face the fact that in spite of their stupendous but costly victory at Inkerman, there was not the remotest sign of Sebastopol falling and a whole winter here was now inevitable. Some reinforcements arrived, a company for the 50th composed of fresh-faced lads who gazed in astonishment and some horror at the scarecrows who inhabited the trenches. More supplies were, however, at last coming in, to everyone's relief. Captain Marshall was now acting major while the new young captain of the reinforcements, who had bought his promotion, began to look as though he wished he hadn't. After a week spent attempting to integrate the new arrivals, Matt took a few hours respite to ride down to Balaclava and the green-tiled house.

Molly opened the door. 'Come in,' she said at once, 'Mrs Henderson hoped it would be you.'

On the threshold he paused. 'You look different, no sheep-skin jacket. What's happened to the Lambkin?'

She laughed and beckoned him in. 'Mrs Henderson kindly gave me this dress and as I'm thinner than I used to be it fits me quite well – only a little short. My jacket is safe enough but I don't need it in here, Reid keeps a good fire going when he can.'

Matt followed her in. Olivia Henderson was lying propped up in the meagre bed, still pale and very thin but the fever spots were gone and her breathing sounded to Matt's mind much less laboured. It seemed she was going to live and she must owe it to Molly's care. Taking the stool Molly put for him by the bed, he said, 'You look better, ma'am, and I'm glad to see it. My cousin sent me a message to say as much and I've come down as soon as I could.'

'You've a great deal to do,' she said appreciatively. 'Tell me, where was my Jock laid to rest?'

'On what we call Windmill Hill, with General Cathcart and General Strangeway. Their graves are marked.'

'Ah,' she leaned back on a sigh. 'One feels sad that so many are buried with no mark to say where they are resting.'

He hesitated, finding it hard to express what he felt and she added, 'Dear Matthew, do you think I don't know how much you cared for him? I just have to thank God that we had so many years together, that he survived so many campaigns.' Pausing she gave Molly a little smile and then went on, 'It is very odd, but something has happened, a miracle if you like, that has changed everything for me, and for Molly.'

Matt looked from one to the other. 'What —'

'Molly will tell you. I find talking tiring and I did a great deal of it yesterday.'

But he could see at once that she no longer looked so distressed, indeed almost happy, and he turned to Molly. 'What can it be that makes you both look so - so —' He could find no adequate word for what he saw in their faces.

Molly came close to the bed to take one of Mrs Henderson's hands before telling him the whole amazing story, and when she had finished, he was for a moment totally bereft of speech, his brain reeling. If this was all true, and he saw that the two women believed it, then Molly was the granddaughter of a country gentleman living in Buckinghamshire and gently born. And it seemed to him, looking at her now, that she had visibly shed the last of the workhouse.

'Well!' was the best he could do. 'Well!'

Mrs Henderson smiled and Molly could not keep back a laugh. 'We really believe it, because it all fits.'

'And', Mrs Henderson added, 'although Molly is, I'm sure, much thinner than she was when she came to the Crimea, and pale in this dreadful climate, she is still the walking image of my dear friend, and will be even more so when we get back to

England's healthier weather. There is no doubt of the truth of it, Matthew.'

He contrived to find his tongue though nothing seemed adequate. 'I'm glad – glad for you both. It is quite – astonishing.'

'I've something to live for now, you see,' Mrs Henderson said. 'Molly is going to call me Aunt Olivia, which is what she would have done if things had been otherwise, aren't you, my dear?'

'If – if it is not too familiar,' Molly murmured. 'I've never had anyone to call aunt before. It's just wonderful. Major Hamilton, Mrs Duberly has brought us a great luxury, a bottle of Burgundy that she wheedled out of the captain of that ship that anchored here yesterday. We've no such thing as a glass, but three tin cups will serve us, won't they? I think it is just what Mrs Hen – Aunt Olivia needs.'

He left the two women a little later, glad of their joy in each other, but he was hardly part of it and somehow his depression grew as the short November days died.

For the two women in the little house below it was a time of discovery, of getting to know each other. To her delight Molly found several books in Mrs Henderson's travelling box and she read aloud to her in the afternoons, holding the book by the window to catch the last of the light. Dr Turner pronounced himself pleased with his patient's progress. She had acquainted him with the news that had given her the will to live and his remark was, 'Well, some good has come out of this miserable shambles. You'll soon be well enough to go home.'

Molly and the invalid were indeed developing a rapport, a great liking for each that cemented the extraordinary turn of fate. Molly found in the older woman a character she could appreciate, unsentimental but strong in her attachments while Olivia in her turn wanted to know every detail of Molly's life in order to understand the events that had shaped her into the girl she was. They talked of their husbands, Olivia Henderson sympathizing deeply with Molly.

'At least I had nearly twenty-five years with my Jock,' she said reflectively, 'and I must indeed be grateful that we shared so much, had the same tastes, so that our lives fitted together.

177

Only just the one sorrow, that we had no children. Nor did you, poor child, but perhaps it is better this way as you had so short a time together and must make a new life when you go home.'

'Yes,' Molly admitted, 'It's better as it is. And in a strange way, though I loved my Hal, indeed I did, I've come to see that – apart from loving we shared so little. I can see now he would have lived for his soldiering, and so for me it would have been life in an army camp or barracks. Well, I could have done it, but I've seen how hard other women find it, having their babies in such conditions, and trying to rear them without any sort of home. I wouldn't have wanted that and the only alternative would have been lodgings somewhere while Hal was far away. And you see, I'm beginning to want other things, to read more books, to learn, to discover – oh, ever so many things.' She hesitated. 'I hope I'm not being disloyal to his memory.'

'Of course you are not,' was the practical answer. 'You are so young and I'm sure your Rifleman would not have wanted you to spend your time looking back. It is time for you, for us, to move on, my dear.'

'Yes, I suppose you are right. But as to going home – I don't know what I'll do or what lies ahead.'

'But of course you will come home with me,' Olivia said as if stating an obvious fact. 'When I'm ready to travel we'll go together, won't we? I'm going to need you.'

'I'll be your maid,' Molly said in sudden delight. 'Oh, I'd like that.'

'Certainly not! I can't have a maid who calls me Aunt Olivia.' The funny side of this struck Molly and she chuckled, while still wondering what was to come next.

'You will travel home as my adopted niece,' Olivia went on, 'and I would very much like you to come to live with me. You see, Jock and I bought a house in Kensington, oh many years ago, so that we would always have a home whenever we were in our own country, and we had begun to think it was time for us to settle there. He had given the army so many good years – but it asked the final sacrifice at the end.' A moment's wave of grief, and then she added firmly, 'It could be our home together, couldn't it?'

178

'Oh!' Molly's eyes filled. 'Oh, Aunt Olivia, do you really think – I lived such a rough sort of life.'

'Which is showing less and less every day.' Olivia gave her a warm glance. 'My dear, a few months together quietly, and then when we come out of mourning, you'll be a young lady ready to go into society.'

'Me?' Molly was quite overwhelmed. 'I don't know what to say, how to thank you. If you think I can —'

'You have so much of your mother in you, and it is what she would have wished me to do.'

Molly took her hand and held it to her cheek. 'I will try to be what she would have liked me to be. And finding you – I never dreamed – a miracle in this horrid place. And – oh, dear we've been talking so long and I must get our rations and see if I can find anything different to do with them. At least your appetite is better.' She gave her aunt a quick kiss and went out, so happy that she wanted to sing as she picked her way through the mud and down to the harbour.

Up on the bleak ridge above, Matt was far from the desire to sing. Snow was falling, making trench duty even more unpleasant. There was no letter yet from home in answer to his unhappy one, it was too soon, but the sorrow at Crossley Lodge weighed heavily on his mind. At this time his friend Captain St Croix was quietly supportive, inviting Matt often to dinner in the French camp, where they were now hutted, every man under cover, a large prefabricated hut for a hospital, all kept clean. The French also had replacement clothes, unlike their British allies, still shivering in their torn garments. They were also fed from field kitchens, great pots of soup always simmering. After a particularly good dinner Matt said, 'You must visit me after the war, André, and I'll give you a really good English dinner, which is more than I can offer here.'

'I shall surely come, *mon ami*. I've always wanted to see London. And you will, I hope, come to Paris. There's a little restaurant I know in the Place de l'Opèra,' he kissed his fingers to it in a very French gesture, and Matt said, 'All we seem to talk about in camp is when we shall get a decent dinner. Eating with you is the nearest thing!'

'I shall buy a house near the Bois and you shall bring your

179

wife and come to stay with us.' St Croix said firmly, and laughed when Matt said he had not as yet got a wife. 'Then that is the first thing for you to do when you get home, *mon brave*. A man is only half a man without a wife. My Sidonie is the greatest blessing I ever had.'

Matt shrugged. 'I haven't yet found a blessing like that!' But he enjoyed the Frenchman's company, both determined not to lose touch when the war was over, which was odd considering their fathers fought on opposing sides at Waterloo.

Trying to integrate the new arrivals, and walking one morning knee-deep in mud and snow, he had a word for most of them, well aware that some of the old stagers were grinning. 'What greenhorns,' he said in a low voice to the sergeant. 'Are any of them shaping up?'

'Quite a few, sir. You there, Jones – get your head down or a "Whistling Dick" will take it off for you.'

'The batteries are quiet this morning,' Matt remarked, and had no sooner said it than the Russian barrage started up again. 'Finished their breakfast,' was the sergeant's comment. 'Lucky fellows if they've had some.'

But it was nearly time to end this detachment's turn of duty and Matt climbed out of the trench to walk back. There was another distraction always on his mind at the moment. He was glad for Molly and for his Colonel's widow, of course he was, but where would it lead them? Away from him almost certainly and his depression and sense of loneliness grew. Perhaps St Croix was right. And perhaps it was these thoughts that induced a moment's carelessness of the bombardment going on around him, so much part of every day, that he neither saw nor heard the particular shell that struck him. The blast hurled him a considerable distance before flinging him senseless to the ground.

Molly saw the stretcher-bearers bringing another wounded man down from the Heights, as she was walking out to collect the day's supplies and was near the hospital as they came up. From the look of the poor fellow lying on the blanket slung between two shafts she thought he was more likely to need a burial party. He seemed unconscious; one arm hanging

180

limply, blood welling from one thigh, his trousers soaked with it, and she thought the journey down must have caused him great pain. His face was blackened by powder and Molly felt a moment's deep anger at so much loss of life. His field cap lay on his chest, put there by one of the bearers and half hiding the great wound torn in his shoulder. And then a second glance wrested a great gasp from her.

Running across the short distance between them she cried out, 'Oh, wait, wait – Major Hamilton, you're hurt!' Which seemed afterwards an unnecessary thing to say.

'He ain't conscious,' one of the bearers said. He usually played the cornet in the 50th's regimental band and was obviously greatly distressed to be bearing down his commander. The other added, 'We must get him into the hospital, Lambkin, not that he'll last long, but that's our orders.'

Sick with dread, she said, 'I'll come with you, find Dr Turner,' and bending she caught up the dangling hand, meaning to lay it across his body. To her astonishment the bloodied fingers entwined themselves round hers in a fierce grip and he opened his eyes, dark with pain and far from unconscious.

'Molly?'

'I'm here,' she reassured him. 'Lie quiet, sir.'

He was looking straight up at her. 'I always hoped – I'd never come down – like this. Dead up there – or on my own two – feet.'

'Don't talk,' she begged him. 'Save your strength. I'll look for your cousin.'

He seemed to approve though his eyes closed and she thought that he was really unconscious now. But his hand still lay in hers and holding it firmly she walked with the bearers into the hospital.

It was the first time she had ever been inside this grim building, and there, used as she was to dreadful scenes, the place appalled her. There was filth and dirt everywhere. No facilities, no bedpans, no bedding other than a dirty straw mattress. Each man had to sleep under the blankets, mostly in a disgusting state, in which they had been brought down. There they lay in their own mess until they died. Only a few of the very toughest survived. There were two or three elderly

181

orderlies, the few doctors endeavouring to save at least a few of these poor wrecks. The air was foul and filled with the groans of the suffering, a single shriek from a youth enduring an operation with nothing to kill the pain. Molly felt bile rise in her throat and fought it back. Then, with enormous relief, she saw Dr Turner. He had just finished amputating, the poor fellow having mercifully fainted. She called to him and when he saw her and the stretcher, some intuition sent him headlong over to her.

'Matt? Oh Good God! You fellows,' to the bearers, 'carry him into the officers' ward, at the end there.'

This was a smaller room, scarcely any better, where a dozen officers lay on the straw mattresses. One or two had extra blankets over them, and here there was, thankfully, one bedpan, being wielded by an orderly so unhandily that Molly could see he was part drunk.

'May I come?' she asked the doctor. She thought he looked shaken but in a moment it was the doctor not the cousin who was uppermost. 'He doesn't seem to want to let go of my hand.'

'Come then,' Turner said, 'only don't get in my way. Sorry, Lambkin, I know you better than that.'

Matt was laid on a mattress and the bearers disappeared to collect another victim. The doctor worked on him with speed, calling an orderly, 'Get me a bowl of water, *now.*'

'I'll try, sir,' was the answer, 'but I think they're all – '

'Oh, for God's sake, do as you are told,' John Turner snapped. 'I need water. Get it in the major's hat if you have to.' Then to Molly he said briefly, 'Release your hand if you please, and cut his trouser off that leg,' handing her a pair of scissors out of his bag, while he set to work on Matt's jacket.

Molly obeyed but as she began to cut, the injured man moved his hand weakly in protest, his eyes open now. 'No – no —'

'Don't fret, sir,' she was beginning gently. 'I've done this often enough,' when the doctor broke in; 'For heaven's sake, Matt, this isn't the time for modesty. Get on with it, Lambkin.'

But she understood his embarrassment and bent over her task, not looking at him. The gash was long and deep across

182

the top of his thigh, but not, she thought, likely to be dangerous. By this time John Turner had got part of his cousin's coat
away from the injured shoulder, drawing in his breath at the
damage he saw.

'The epaulette,' he said to Molly. 'I'll get what I can off
now, but it'll be the devil's own job to extricate all those bits
of metal. Yes, my poor fellow,' as the patient let out a groan,
'it must hurt like hell. Take his hand again, Molly, he'll bear
it better if you do.'

She obeyed and the thin fingers gripped hers again. He was
quite conscious now as his cousin snipped away the last
remnants of his jacket, one epaulette churned by a large shell
splinter into a mess of blood and flesh, the gold strands driven
deep. In a moment's pause, Matt managed to say, 'Those
damned things cost me – fifteen guineas.'

His cousin gave an appreciative grunt. 'You'll do, Matt my
boy. It will be a long job, needing more patience than I think
you've got, but no doubt the Lambkin will help you.'

'Of course,' Molly said, trying hard not to let the rising
tears tumble down her face. Somehow she had never thought
to see him like this – others had gone this way, but not him,
not him.

Dr Turner was dressing the wound. 'No need to put more
pain on him now. I'll start on those bits of wire tomorrow.
Now you can wash his face while I take a look at his leg.'

Molly wrung out a cloth in the water brought by the
orderly, washing away the black powder, while the doctor
cleaned the wound. It was high up, dividing the flesh where it
was deepest, smaller splinters buried further down, and as he
worked he said, 'We can thank God for Miss Nightingale. She
has sent us two crates of bandages and sutures and a great
many other things which are still being unpacked. I think
there's even some laudanum and if so I'll give him a few
drops.' But the stitching was the last straw and Matt had
fainted. 'Best thing,' his cousin said. 'Go home, Molly, and
tell Mrs Henderson what has happened, but be sure she under-
stands that he has a good chance. She's very fond of him.'

She was reluctant to leave and he gave her a surprising
smile. 'Now you know better than to argue with me. I'd rather
have you than a dozen orderlies who are mostly as dense as

they come or drunk or both, but you'd better go back to Mrs Henderson. We've done what's needed for now, and he can rest until tomorrow morning. You can come back then.'

She went home with lagging steps and had hardly explained what had happened to a shocked Mrs Henderson when Merton arrived, the word having got back to camp. He was beside himself and, on seeing Molly, burst into tears. 'Oh miss, to lose the Major what I've served for more'n fifteen years, and him the best master a fellow could ever have. I can't – '

'Stop! Stop!' Molly exclaimed. 'He isn't dead, Merton. He's badly wounded and has lost a lot of blood but Dr Turner has attended to him and he's very hopeful.'

This renewed Merton's sobs, but eventually, snuffling into his sleeve, he said, 'Sorry, Lambkin. They told me he was dead.'

'I thought so too when I first saw him on the stretcher, but we must just pray now that he will live. I'm sure you can go over to the hospital to see him. And if you like you can sleep on the floor in the kitchen, as Mrs Henderson's groom does.'

He thanked her, almost inarticulate with gratitude, and then went off to the hospital, only to come back even more dejected, convinced his master was dying. In the morning John Turner sent over a message to say Matt had had as good a night as possible, and thinking Merton needed something to do, Molly sent him off to the camp to bring back the Major's possessions. She doubted if he would be going back there, certainly not for some time, and despite her hopeful prognostications coupled with Dr Turner's encouragement, she knew his chances were slim. Settling her own invalid as comfortably as possible she went over to the hospital, wanting only to do something, anything, to be of use.

Chapter Thirteen

At the hospital, she was torn with sympathy for the poor broken men stretched out there, waiting most of them, for death. One or two she recognised and stopped to speak to them, with a few encouraging words. They could never, she thought, have been in so foul a place before.

In the officers' ward she found Major Hamilton lying with his eyes closed but whether asleep or unconscious it was hard to tell. Merton was there, having come in with a spare shirt – something of a luxury – from his baggage, but it was impossible to put it on over so shattered a shoulder and upper arm, so Merton and an orderly had merely stripped off his wrecked uniform and laid it over him.

'He ain't said much,' Merton whispered, 'but he do seem to know I'm here.'

'I'm sure he does,' Molly assured him. She took hold of the hand belonging to the uninjured arm for it seemed a way to reach him. 'Good morning, Major. I hope you managed to sleep a little.'

The familiar voice penetrated his confused mind and he opened his eyes. 'Molly? I don't know – such odd dreams – I was floating somewhere – not in this damned – bloody awful place.'

She gave a little laugh. 'When you begin to swear I know you are more yourself.' But he was right. The young lieutenant in the next bed was threshing about in agony from a stomach wound and crying out, calling over and over, 'Mama – Mama, oh do come.' In another bed an older officer lay shaking uncontrollably with shock after an amputation. The others were in no better case and it was, as the Major had said, an awful place, and she was thankful to be able to say cheerfully, 'Here's your cousin to see you.'

'Come to torture you, poor fellow.' Nodding to Molly Dr Turner added, 'Glad you're here. You can hold on to him while I get to work,' and to Merton: 'You'd better wait outside.' Then he removed the shoulder dressing, in itself a painful business and began to work on Matt's wincing body. Molly thought it must be agonizingly painful, but though he gripped her hand like a vice, he only let out an occasional gasp.

Several gold strands were pulled free from the tangle of torn flesh and dropped on the floor for lack of any medical receptacles until at last, after about ten minutes, a protest was wrenched from the sufferer. 'For God's sake, Johnny, enough, enough!'

The doctor stopped immediately, but retorted with grim humour, 'I was only just getting started. Well, I'll leave you in peace for now, but the arm is in a bad way. I may have to take it off.' He came out with this in a casual tone but it hid an enormous anxiety on his part.

'Damn you, no,' Matt whispered. 'Don't – I won't have it —'

'I'll do my best,' his cousin assured him, 'but I thought it best to prepare you. If our revered Commander-in-Chief can do without his right arm so can you. Lambkin, if you go into the main ward, you'll find an orderly with a jug of water and lime juice which, thank God, came off a ship yesterday. Take his mug and get him a drink.'

Releasing her hand, Molly obeyed and was soon holding his head while he drank thirstily. Leaving him, she hoped, to sleep after the exhausting performance, she was about to go back to the cottage when Dr Turner stopped her in the corridor.

'He can rest for today, but I must work on him again tomorrow. There's no chance of saving the arm if I don't get the metal out. Can you come back, about this time? It clearly helps him. I've known men buck like stallions under the probe and yet be much more composed if there's a woman there, which there seldom is, poor lads. Our pride perhaps.'

'Perhaps,' Molly gave him a quivering smile, but after

another painful session the next morning, which left the patient totally exhausted, she hurried home to Mrs Henderson. 'Oh, ma'am – Aunt Olivia – it is so horrid in that place, so – so disgusting, and I've been thinking. Could we not have Major Hamilton here? He could have my bed, if you don't mind me sleeping on the floor in here —'

'No, of course I wouldn't, but wait a moment.' Mrs Henderson was slightly taken aback. 'Have you thought, my dear – he will need attentions that really are not suitable for you?'

'I've thought of that,' Molly murmured, 'but his man Merton is here and has brought down all his things. So he could do what is necessary and I'm quite able to dress the shoulder, if Dr Turner will come over, perhaps once a day. And Merton can rig up some sort of screen to cut off the corner where the bed is.'

'You have thought it all out!' But Mrs Henderson was smiling. 'And you are quite right. If Dr Turner agrees we will look after dear Matthew here.'

Dr Turner's first reaction was perhaps predictable. 'My good girl, do you think I've nothing better to do than make calls on you every day!'

'Well, you do come quite often to see Mrs Henderson and it isn't far,' Molly pointed out. 'Is once a day enough until all the pieces are out? And at least the cottage is clean and the air fresh. It's not as if there's much at the hospital that we can't do better for him here.'

'You're right there. I'll see how he is tomorrow and if I think he can be moved over.'

This was the best she could get out of him, but as she left he added, 'I wouldn't trust him anywhere than where he is now unless it be with you, Lambkin.' Which left her quite touched. Matt was not asked, simply told of the new arrangement and he accepted it in a dreamy way, being too weak even for discussions. Nor did he know that his cousin had found time to write to his aunt Lady Milner to tell her what had befallen her elder son, keeping the letter as hopeful as he could. Poor woman, he thought, she and Sir Charles had had one awful blow and must now endure the wait for news, but he didn't see he could do other than inform them.

Two orderlies brought the Major over on a stretcher, an operation that caused him so much pain that he no longer cared where he was being taken, if only they would put him down. When they had gone and he was safely settled by Merton in his new quarters, he lay with his eyes shut and Molly left him to rest. Mrs Duberley had come over and brought them a rare treat, a loaf of white bread. Molly was so transported that she actually hugged the bearer, and Mrs Duberley laughed and said, 'Well, we ladies must stick together, mustn't we? My dear Mrs Henderson, you do look better today.'

'I am, thanks to this dear girl.' Olivia Henderson had already told her visitor of Molly's history. 'I hope I shall be able to get up soon, when Dr Turner lets me.'

'What a dragon he is, but so kind really. I'll come again in a day or two. My dear Duberley is so cast down by all our losses that I must go up to him as often as the weather will let me.'

Lady Errol was another visitor, and when the new arrangement was explained to her, she laughed and said, 'I'm sure, Mrs Hallam, you sleep quite as well on the floor. I do. My husband has the camp bed, his need being greater than mine!'

She added quite a note of brightness to Mrs Henderson's room and a few days later Captain St Croix arrived, having ridden over to see his friend, found he had been injured, gone to the hospital and been directed here.

'You are a crafty *camerade*,' he said, sitting on a stool by Matt's bed. '*Ma foi*, if I am injured, I cannot imagine I would be lucky enough to be nursed by this – *agnelet, n'est-ce pas?*'

Matt managed a smile and said firmly that they were not surrendering their Lambkin to anyone. She had not seen him so relaxed since he was brought down and she blessed the Frenchman for his easy manner.

'I have brought you a bottle of eau-de-vie,' St Croix added, 'Poor enough stuff, but it might put some warmth into you, *mon pauvre*.'

Within a week Dr Turner professed himself satisfied with the experiment and with the progress of both his patients. 'Though they need feeding up,' he added, 'and there's precious little of what's required. And what there is, is ridiculously expensive. Five shillings for a small ham!'

'Those horrid traders care for nothing but to cheat us.' Molly said vehemently. 'But Merton was out for a long time yesterday and came back with a hare, so we will do well for a day or two.'

Without complaining further the doctor came over every morning to work on his cousin, Matt so drained that the inevitable pain made tears course down his cheeks and dragged words of protest from him. 'I didn't know – I could be – such a coward.'

'Nonsense,' Dr Turner retorted. 'It's nature's way of easing you.'

And then at last, after more than two weeks, he extricated the last of the pieces of metal with quite an air of triumph. 'There, that's the end of it. Old fellow, you've borne it well and thank God you've not developed gangrene, so you shouldn't need to lose the arm.' And at that Matt turned his head away, unable to stem the tears, of relief this time.

But it was a long slow process. His body was so debilitated by the loss of so much blood coupled with the constant pain that at times Molly began to despair. He would lie for hours not moving, hardly speaking, but one hopeful sign was that he was beginning to develop an appetite and, one morning, when she told him that tomorrow would be Christmas day, he looked up at her with a gleam in his eye and said, 'Roast goose and stuffing? Plum pudding? Nuts and mince pies?'

'Oh stop!' She was laughing. 'I can't bear to think of the table set at Crossley Lodge last year.'

But she did her best, with a few little treats. Mrs Henderson still had sufficient money for bargaining down at the stalls and wanting to add her own offering to the feast, she brought out a few of the last coins in her purse. Returning with some fresh meat and a cabbage, a small bag of currants, a few brown rolls of uncertain age, a little flour, some butter, rancid though it was, she nevertheless managed to produce what amounted to a feast, including the last of Captain St Croix's brandy which they had saved for Christmas. Mrs Henderson sat at the table, and Matt insisted on being propped up in bed, claiming that he was tired of Merton spooning his food all over his face and managing very well with his left hand. It was the best day they had all had for a long time.

The nights were the worst time for the invalid, for he could not find any position to sleep in; on his injured side it was impossible to lie, and on the uninjured side it meant lifting the hurt shoulder which caused a great deal of pain. Matt only tried it once and gave up very quickly, while on his back every bone seemed to be aching. It was Merton who found the solution. He went off, returning with two large flat stones and these, with Jim Reid's help he placed under the side of the bed, top and bottom, where the injuries were, so that his master was tilted to one side but without any pressure. Matt proclaimed it a great success, had better nights and Merton went about with a satisfied grin on his face.

On this Christmas night, when Matt was settled so much more comfortably and Merton gone off to the comfort of the kitchen floor, Molly looked in behind the curtain before seeking her own bed. He seemed to be asleep already, black shadows under his eyes, his face colourless, and longing to see him more like his old self, she offered a brief prayer for him to the Christ Child.

On the following day Merton and Reid went off into the village and came home very late and very drunk, trying to be quiet but inevitably tripping over things in the kitchen. In the morning, aware that he had for a rare moment neglected his duties, Merton apologized to Molly, but got a warm smile in return.

'Merton, you've been so good, and so clever with his bed, I'm sure the Major wouldn't begrudge you a spree. How's your head?'

'Like a pudding.' He grinned at her. 'Sorry, Lambkin. I'll get the water for washing him now. He's better – ain't he?'

'Yes, oh yes, Merton, I believe he is.'

'P'haps we'll be able to take him home soon, so's his Ma and Pa can look after him.'

He went off to get the water and Molly stood very still. Somehow she hadn't thought of that – the Major out of her care, back at Crossley Lodge. This truth, hardly bearable though it was, had to be faced. He would no longer be hers to care for as he had been here and she didn't want that thread broken. He was still asleep and she stood looking down at

190

him, wanting only to cradle his head in her arms, kiss that deep crease between his dark brows, cherish him back to health – but when he went home she would lose him, for what could he be to her? She loved him so much, so deeply, she knew it now, and silently cried out 'Oh Hal, forgive me. I didn't mean for this to happen, but it has, it has!'

The winter days passed. For the wretched men in the trenches it was a miserable time, operations confined to the exchange of gunfire, though the army was somewhat relieved by the arrival of considerable French reinforcements who took over part of the siege lines. But the worst of the weather was passing and by the end of February ships began to arrive containing warm clothing for the soldiers, thick coats, woollen caps to pull over their heads, boots by the hundred. Food stores mounted up, parcels from home by the crateful, for the Government had at last woken up to the state of things in the Crimea and what their army was enduring. And not only the Government. There was scarcely a town or village in England that did not now have its Crimean fund to send out comforts for the soldiers; some people lacking imagination even contributing smoking jackets and velvet caps. The road to the camps was properly laid and railway tracks were now the method of sending up trucks loaded with food, ammunition and other necessities, even transporting passengers, the trucks pulled by either mules or some seventy sweating men. An air of cheerfulness began to pervade the camps and one day Molly had a visit from Corporal Harker who told her that huts had arrived, quick to put up so that the men could get out of the still chilling wind. 'A proper little village we've got now,' he said, 'and Nell, bless her, thinks she's in heaven!'

For the little household in the green-tiled cottage a simple routine was now established so that Mrs Henderson remarked that it was surprising how well one could manage on only the barest necessities. Those days thankfully were passing, food available in the proper shops now set up, so that the opportunist traders and their stalls were vanishing. A parcel came for Matt from a store in Portsmouth, which was taken up to the camp and brought down again before its recipient was found. To Matt's delight it contained among numerous foodstuffs, a box of cigars, though the first one made him feel slightly queasy, and Dr Turner told him to wait until he was better to enjoy them, taking a couple for himself and blessing Sir Charles who had organized the parcel. Molly started to read *The Tale of Two Cities* aloud in the evenings and both her listeners clearly enjoyed it, though Matt often fell asleep in the middle, and Molly thought sadly of poor Hal who made such heavy weather of any kind of learning.

Olivia Henderson was now getting up every day, though taking an afternoon rest, and she enjoyed Mrs Duberley's visits and the little treats she occasionally brought. Ben Marshall had come down to report on the state of the 50th, temporarily taken over by a lieutenant-colonel newly arrived from England.

'So much for my promotion,' Matt pulled a face.

'Oh, you'll get it,' Captain Marshall insisted. 'Colonel Bell told me this other colonel is only a stop-gap, thank God, and he had that from Airey himself. By the way Colonel Bell is going home too. His health is causing great anxiety, and he must be near sixty. He doesn't want to go, old campaigner that he is, but the regimental surgeon has told him he won't answer for his life if he doesn't. But everything is better in camp. Give a soldier shelter and decent food and there's nothing he won't do.' All this news made Matt long to go back up to his camp but there was, his cousin assured him, no chance whatsoever of that. His arm was healing slowly but he could not lift it above elbow height and it was obvious he could not use it in a fight or for much else for that matter. Major Norcott came down to see him and to exchange a word with Molly, assuring her that the Rifles were now in good heart. But as Matt's health began slowly to improve, in the way of convalescents his temper did not. One morning she heard him shouting for Merton. 'Come and get this damned beard off me. I've had enough of it.'

Merton's voice came in swift response. 'Sir, you don't want to be bothered with that now, eh? It becomes you, really it does.'

'Stow that. Get it off me now,' and then as an afterthought, 'you can leave the moustache.'

Molly and Olivia exchanged amused glances and both

192

thought when they saw him later that though more deathly pale skin was visible, they liked him better without his whiskers, though approving of the neatly cut moustache. And every little incident like this only made Molly love him more, to rejoice in every small thing she could do for him. But it was hopeless to love him and she forced herself to face the fact, bury her feelings deep. How could he turn to someone who, despite recent discoveries, had been a servant in his parents' house? So she hid her feelings, successfully, for her nature was naturally cheerful.

Hating the slowness of his recovery Matt insisted on getting out of bed, only to find that he could scarcely stand, but his cousin promised him that he was doing well and a few more months would see him greatly improved.

'Months?' Matt groaned. 'Good God, not months?'

'Of course months. You need time to replace all the blood you have lost, asking a great deal of your body, I assure you.'

'Can't you find me better news than that?'

'Yes. You're alive,' the doctor said tersely. 'And you have your limbs pretty well intact.'

'If I hadn't I'd have to go on half-pay and become as sour as Henrietta!'

His cousin gave a brief laugh. 'Poor Henrietta. Her own nature is her worst enemy. You do as you're told and I'll have no worries about you. I'm sure the Lambkin will see that you do.'

Matt fell suddenly silent. How long indeed would he have her to care for him?

It was Molly who said, 'He's quite right,' when the door had closed behind the doctor. 'You must try to be patient,' to which Matt replied, 'Don't you start,' but had the grace to give her a weak grin.

She left him and went outside where the spring sunshine was beginning to have a little warmth, and pushing up through the hard earth behind the house, despite war and destruction, she found a few yellow crocus, and had a sudden desire to kneel down and kiss them. Instead she took her aunt out to see them. But the improving weather brought a growing dread into her heart, for there was now positive talk of going home.

Matt was helped by Merton into an odd assortment of

clothes, summer trousers, a camp coat and his only decent shirt. He would spend part of the day sitting by the table, then sleeping on his bed in the afternoon – to his own disgust. 'Like an old gentleman,' he said wrathfully. The three of them now ate their dinner together at the table, which Reid had made considerably less rickety.

'Much more civilized,' was Matt's comment. 'Molly, you're wearing the slippers I bought you.'

'There's no mud in here,' she smiled across at him, 'and they're so comfortable. I only put my boots on when I go out. That dead Russian will never know how I have blessed him for his boots.'

'Thank God the men are now getting proper clothing. I wish I was up with them, drunk or not! Barrels of beer are getting up there now, so Merton tells me.'

She could see he hated being an invalid, feeling he had deserted Colonel Henderson's regiment which he had kept in such good shape. The Colonel's widow told him briskly that he must not bemoan what he could not help, and she entertained them with stories of her husband's long career, of his days in India and Canada and the West Indies, for she seemed to take comfort in talking of those old campaigning days.

Eventually a long argument ensued between the cousins, Matt trying to insist that he should go back to his regiment, while the doctor refused point-blank to sign his release from medical care.

'You've not the strength for it,' he said bluntly. 'It's all very well here with the Lambkin and Merton to take care of you, but you get back up there and you wouldn't last a week. Come back in six month's time if you must, but you're going home now.'

Captain St Croix came down to say goodbye and impart an item of news. 'By the way, there's a very passable restaurant, French of course! opened in Kadekoi, that village just along the road. I'll stand you dinner there, if you do come back, if not, it will have to be the Trocadero in London. Oh yes, I know some of your London restaurants!'

Lord Cardigan had given up and, suffering from bronchitis, had sailed for England in his yacht before Christmas, while in February Lord Lucan had, to that gentlemen's amazement and fury, been recalled to England. 'Thank God, we don't have to go back on the same ship as either of them,' was Matt's heart-felt comment. 'I've a feeling Lord Raglan will be glad to see the back of both of them.' But he knew as everyone did, that their Commander-in-Chief was far from well, a sorely tried and anxious old man. Yet he never for one moment lost his courtesy and care for the people under his command. One day to the astonishment of the occupants of the little house in Balaclava, he dismounted outside and knocked on the door.

Opening it Molly saw a tall man in a plain blue frock coat, the empty right sleeve pinned up, an odd sort of cream-coloured straw hat on his head. To Molly he said, 'I'm Lord Raglan, my dear. Is it possible for me to see Mrs Henderson and Major Hamilton? I understand they are here.'

Rendered almost speechless, Molly bobbed a hasty curtsy and ushered him in. There he sat at the table, told Mrs Henderson how he regretted the loss of her husband, enquired after Major Hamilton's health and when told he was ordered home by Dr Turner, said, 'Quite right, quite right. You have served the 50th well, and I shall see to it that you get your promotion.'

'Thank you, sir,' Matt said warmly. 'I mean to come about as soon as I can.'

'I'm sure you do, but please God, we'll take Sebastopol this spring and there will be no need to return here.'

He stayed for half an hour and before leaving he said to Molly, 'Major Norcott has told me about you, that you have been doing a great deal of good for my poor soldiers. They call you the Lambkin, don't they?'

Astonished that he should know this, she looked up at him, saw the kindest eyes imaginable. 'Yes, my Lord. It was because of my jacket. And it seemed only right to stay —'

He patted her shoulder. 'Well, take the thanks of one old soldier for all the others,' and when he had gone Molly said, 'I'm so glad to have seen him. People say such unkind things at home, so Dr Turner told me, but I think he's a dear, gentle old man.'

It was arranged that the little party, with numerous other disabled men should go home aboard the *Herald,* a steamer which had docked at the end of March, bringing more supplies of warm clothing, 'Better late than never,' being the obvious comment. The day before they were to leave Molly settled her charges and went off at first light to walk the six miles up to the Rifles camp. However some trucks were about to set off, and one man called out, 'Hop up, Lambkin, we'll give you a ride.' So she went up in style, much amused when a newly arrived corporal of the Engineers, grumbling about the unsteadiness and dirt in the wagon, was told in no uncertain terms that 'if he didn't like it, any Johnny-new-comer could bloody well get out and walk'.

Once there she found Nell, though the corporal was on trench duty, and they said a fond farewell.

'We've seen so much happen,' Molly said. 'Oh Nell, I have missed you, and I hate to leave the men.'

'And it's not the same here without you,' her friend assured her. 'The men grumble that their Lambkin has gone. But it was time, you know. You looked worn out. Anyway things are much improved now. Come into our hut. We have a stove and I can make us a cup of tea.' Molly was touched by the welcome she got, and gladdened to see the great improvement in conditions, even the bombarding from the trenches was no longer constant. There were fewer casualties, Nell told her thankfully, 'And you'll never guess, on Christmas day in the evening several Russians came over to our lines, asking for lights for their pipes. They were so friendly; they said *"Anglichanin – harasho"* – that means "Englishman – good", and they all shook hands!'

'I never expected to hear of that,' Molly said. 'It makes you wonder why we are fighting them.' Most of those in camp crowded round her, expressing the hope that she was back for as long as the war lasted.

'Well, I can't stay running after you fellows for ever,' she said in her old bracing way. 'But if I see any of your ugly faces in Portsmouth I'll want to know how you are getting on.'

Now why, she wondered, did she think she'd be in Portsmouth? Going home with Aunt Olivia, would it not be London? But Portsmouth, Crossley Lodge, and Miss Plumstead had been part of her life. She was glad to find

196

Captain Smeaton in camp, though Major Norcott was down at headquarters, and after explaining that she was taking Mrs Henderson and Major Hamilton home, she added, 'Thank you so much, sir, once again, for allowing me on that ship last year.'

'For allowing you to come to this wretched place, lose your husband, and then go short of food and just about everything else?' he asked almost gruffly.

'That was only part of it,' she gave him a little smile with less sadness in it than might have been there a while ago. 'I've learned so much and been able to help a little.'

'That you have. Good luck, Lambkin, wherever you go. We'll all miss you.'

'I'll pray you come safely home, all of you,' she said and went down for the last time through the gathering dusk.

Back at the little house Molly packed up the few possessions she had left. Her wedding dress, worn during the voyage out and the first warm weeks on shore, was so stained and torn that it had had to be used for useful rags. Her other dress, a warmer one, was hardly in better case, but Mrs Henderson had insisted on giving her one of her own, and she still had her Russian petticoat and the grey kid gloves. Holding these for a moment against her cheek, she gave a long sigh. Hal had been so proud, giving them to her and calling her a proper lady. Sadly she laid them in her bag with her Bible – that too was badly stained, *David Copperfield* not much better. Nothing to come, she thought, however bad, could be worse than the winter that had just passed – but it had brought her unlooked-for joy as well and it was with very mixed feelings that she walked down to the harbour, a matter of only a hundred yards, with Matt leaning heavily on Merton's arm.

For the journey down the companion way to his cabin, he was hesitating for a moment when a large sailor said, 'Sure an' I'll help you, sorr, 'and before Matt could protest he was lifted up bodily and carried down like a child.

Dr Turner came to see them settled on board and in the tiny cabin Matt was to share with another wounded officer, as well as four great bags of coal, this being stored in every available place, begged his cousin to behave himself. 'I haven't worked on you all these weeks for you to go off and do something

197

daft,' was his admonishment. 'Give my regards to my Aunt Milner and tell Sir Charles he is to keep his eye on you. At least three months' leave – I've written to the War Office to say so.'

'That's going behind my back! Curse you, Johnny, how can I ever thank you for what you've done?'

'If I see you fit and healthy and with some flesh on you when I come home that is all I ask. Though when that will be God knows. At least Miss Nightingale has brought in many improvements that are going to save dozens of lives, and her nurses here in Balaclava are a willing set of women. The place is cleaner than when you were in it and we have six bedpans. There's progress for you!'

Matt laughed and said, 'Come home in one piece.'

'I intend to.' Taking his cousin's left hand the doctor shook it firmly. 'That girl will look after you so do as she tells you, you young reprobate,' he added for all as if Matt was still a schoolboy. He went out, but put his head back round the door to say, 'I'm having a small wager with myself that when I get home from this pestilential hole I shall see you married to the Lambkin!' He then departed, leaving Matt in a state of shock.

What on earth made Johnny say such a thing? He sat on his bunk looking out of the small porthole. Of course he had known for a while now that he loved her as he had never loved in his life, not even the fickle Maria. He had been a boy then and this was a man's love. All these weeks that he had lain in the little cottage on that very uncomfortable bed, he had watched Molly as she went about the place, caring for him, for Mrs Henderson, and his love had grown day by day. But he was partly crippled now; his cousin had warned him that the bone might be ankylosed and that he would never have full use of the arm again. He had been more than fortunate that Johnny had saved it. But marriage! Could he even think of it? Out here everything seemed different, but once back in England their ways must part, at least for a while. She would go to London with Mrs Henderson and he must go home, try to get his strength back, go on half-pay, useless! She was young and lovely enough to turn plenty of heads while under Mrs Henderson's wing in London. The thought taunted him, depressing in the extreme. He had to get his life into some sort of order, but the future seemed shrouded in mist and he had no desire to contemplate it at the moment. And she – what did she feel? There was something there, he was sure of it. The thought of her as their housemaid no longer troubled him, she had changed so much, but he was shrewd enough to see it might cause friction at Crossley Lodge. It was not hard to imagine Henrietta's reaction. No doubt it would be better for the moment to say nothing to his family, at least until he was well enough to settle his own affairs.

With all these thoughts brought out into the open in his head, it was not surprising that he was in an unreceptive mood when a middle-aged officer hobbled into the cabin. He was, he said, Captain Trumble of the Royal Artillery, and after they had shaken hands, added, 'Both of us on the shelf, eh?'

Somehow this stung Matt into retorting, 'You may think so, but I'll be damned if I'll be left there. Even if I have to camp out on Horse Guards Parade, I'll make them give me something.'

'You have youth on your side,' Captain Trumble said gloomily. 'I've missed my shot somewhere along the line. Nearly fifty and still a captain, and now with a gammy leg into the bargain. What a waste war is and this one! A shambles in my opinion.'

This diatribe had, contradictorily, the effect of quite cheering Matt up. The pessimistic fellow needed a dose of the Lambkin, he thought, and was pitched into another channel altogether. Marry her? What was Johnny thinking of? And yet, suddenly, it seemed the only thing he wanted to do. But suppose she took him out of pity? His pride shuddered at the very idea. Yet he had thought, during that quiet time at the cottage, that she had looked at him in a different way from when she bent over an injured soldier in camp. Only that could be just his fancy when he lay weak and in pain.

Tossing restlesly, he wanted the ship to move out of the harbour, perversely wishing himself back in the cottage. Pity? It was his own self-pity, he thought in disgust, and heard the screws start up with relief. Perhaps everything would look different away from the Crimea – if only he were not tearing himself in two over his abandoned men. And if he thought his companion was sunk in gloom, he himself was hardly enlivening company for the poor fellow, having far too much on his mind.

On deck the two women were standing by the rail, among the many sick and injured going either to Scutari or home, all of them looking their last on Balaclava as the ship slipped between the tall cliffs. 'We shall never come here again,' Mrs Henderson said sadly. 'If only I could have visited my Jock's grave, even taken him home, but he will lie here for always, with so many of his friends and comrades. Your Hal too.'

'His grave isn't even marked.' Molly caught one last glimpse of the made-up track out of the village, the newly laid railway line to serve the camps above, signs of spring in the sprouting vines here and there, everything brighter and more hopeful. Nevertheless she said, 'Part of me says I ought to stay to the end, do what I can.'

'You've done more than enough,' her aunt thrust a hand through her arm. 'The worst is surely over. And everyone thinks it will end this coming summer. You are going home to a new life, my love, so much ahead for you.'

For a moment Molly leaned her head against Mrs Henderson's shoulder. 'I wonder what? It is like a dream to be going home with you. What I would have done on my own, I'm sure I don't know.'

Mrs Henderson smiled. 'You would have found something. You are a survivor, Molly.'

Both stood side by side as the *Herald* slid between the cliffs and out into the Black Sea. Neither turned back to look at the vanishing shores of the Crimea.

Chapter Fourteen

The voyage home was uneventful. The weather for the most part was calm, and Molly remembered how sick poor Hal had been on the outward journey. The sea air and the good food were working wonders for the men being sent home and Molly and Olivia got some colour back into their cheeks. Even Matt began to look less haggard. Meals were taken in the wardroom and it seemed like being in civilization again.

Molly seldom saw Matt alone now. Merton looked after his needs in the small shared cabin, and during the day he was often in the wardroom talking with the ship's officers or the army wounded who were being repatriated. He walked about the deck now and then, sometimes with Molly or Mrs Henderson, but he still found the companionway difficult to climb and in the afternoons, obeying his cousin's injunction, took a nap on his bunk, which was hardly the most comfortable of places, being a few inches too short for him.

For herself Molly spent of the idle hours with the men on deck, occasionally visiting a few wives on the lower deck. One rifleman in particular was glad of her company for he had lost a leg and found it hard to walk about ship even with his crutches. They talked sometimes of the campaign, but mostly of his wife and the child born after he left.

'And what about you, Lambkin?' he asked one morning when a sea mist seemed to deaden all sound. 'It was a shame you lost poor Hallam, but a bonny girl like you won't have trouble finding a man.'

Molly looked out over the grey waves. She nearly said, it was more a matter of getting the one she wanted, but bit back the rash words and said instead, 'I think I'll wait a while before I settle down.'

'Well, good luck to you whatever you do,' he answered. 'You deserve it for what you did for us.'

Later, standing by the rail she thought of his words. The voyage would soon be over, and the future seemed hidden in the misty whiteness that surrounded the ship. Sometimes, in the wardroom, she would glance at Matt, wondering how he was feeling, now that home was so close, and she too could almost have wished them all back in the green-tiled cottage.

Mrs Henderson, though she gave nothing away, was none the less very much aware of the true state of affairs. Both Matthew and her adopted niece were absorbed, deep in love. Though it was not openly acknowledged, of that she was sure, nevertheless she felt it and was glad, thinking of how pleased Jock would have been. But Matt made no move, he and Molly were never alone, and she made up her mind that she would take a hand in the affair, and as soon as Matthew was well enough invite him to stay in Kensington. In his present state she perceived that marriage was probably the last thing on his mind.

The twentieth of March was Molly's birthday and the day that they docked at Malta. Olivia took her shopping and bought her a bonnet and a beautiful Spanish shawl, shoes and gloves and a reticule. Molly was quite overwhelmed, particularly when her aunt purchased a length of grey silk and some black velvet ribbon, ordering a dress to be made up at once as they were sailing the next day.

'Quite suitable for half mourning,' she said, 'and nice for you to wear when we land in England.'

It was duly sent the next morning and Molly threw her arms about her aunt. 'How can I thank you for everything? I shall look respectable once more, but I don't think I can ever part with my sheepskin jacket, even if I never wear it again. Nor my forage cap. I doubt if that is suitable wear for Kensington!'

Matt had not realized it was her birthday until after they had gone, Merton having had it from Reid, and he was chagrined that he had nothing to give her. Writing a note of exactly what he wanted, he sent Meron ashore with five guineas almost the last of his funds. Merton showed surprising taste and with his master's note to guide him came back with a gold locket edged with pretty filagree work. More than pleased, Matt knocked on the door of the cabin opposite and Molly opened it.

'Come in, Matthew,' Mrs Henderson called. 'We are both ready for dinner.'

'Before we go, I've a present for Molly,' he said and brought out the small package.

More touched than she could say, Molly opened it and exclaimed. 'Oh how beautiful. Look, Aunt Olivia, isn't it lovely? Thank you so much, sir. You've both been so kind to me.'

'We rather think,' Olivia said, echoing the rifleman's words, 'that you have been kind to us.'

In the wardroom her health was drunk, and a young lieu-tenant, obviously rather smitten, having a day's shore leave had come back with a small bouquet of flowers for her, so that Molly went to bed glowing with the pleasure of the day. She had never had a birthday like it.

On the last evening, the ship due to dock at Southampton on the following morning, she wrote a long letter for Miss Plumstead, to tell her that they were home and explain the whole wonderful business of finding Mrs Henderson. It could be posted ashore in the morning. By the time she had finished Mrs Henderson was asleep and suddenly beset by a tangle of emotions, she slipped away up on to deck.

It was a clear night, with a crescent moon hanging in the dark sky and she stood there trying to realize that tomorrow she would be back in England. The Crimea with all its horrors was behind her, Hal lying in his lost grave, and she was going home with her mother's closest friend, incredible though it might seem. But oh, there was another side to this. The man she now loved so burningly, would he go on his way, further from her than just going home? Did his gift which she would always wear, mean anything more than a birthday gift? She didn't know. Sometimes she had thought, when he looked at her, that there was a hint of – something, but perhaps it was only gratitude for her care. Slow tears trickled down her cheeks. She wanted only to spend the rest of her life with him and despair seized her so that she leaned against the bulkhead, her hands spread on either side of her.

Some of the wounded men were preparing for sleep on deck, preferring it to the stifling lower regions and now and then sailors passed about their work but she was in shadow and hoped not to be noticed. There was a step on the companionway. Whoever it was she hoped he would not see her. But then a voice said, 'Molly! What are you doing up here?'

With a swift attempt to brush away the tears she managed to say, 'I wanted a breath of this lovely sea air before I went to bed.'

'So did I.' He paused and then added, 'When I first saw you on the landing at home you were standing like that – at bay. Why are you at bay now, Molly?'

'Was I? I don't know – oh, perhaps I do. So much has happened. Going home, so many poor fellows still out there – it almost seems like running away. But Aunt Olivia needs me.'

'Of course. Where is your jacket?'

'I – I forgot it.'

He had his left arm in one sleeve of his greatcoat, the other slung about his injured shoulder. 'Come here, Molly,' he said and opened it wide, and when she obeyed wrapped it round her, enclosing them both.

With a long shuddering sigh she leaned her head against the uninjured shoulder.

'What is it? What's the matter?' he asked in a strangely gentle tone.

How could she say that he was the matter? Stumblingly she whispered, 'Life in England will be so strange after – after everything that happened out there.'

'Losing your husband?'

'That – and other things, like the baby Nell and I delivered who died in a few days, poor little thing, the mother too, and the men, one or two who died in my arms, as Hal did.'

'Did you care very much for him?' Matt asked and thought perhaps it was too private a question, but she answered without hesitation.

'Oh yes, at the time, though now I think a little differently. He was a good man, but how it would have been for us – I don't know. I've changed – and it's all in the past now. I know I have to look forward and thanks to Aunt Olivia I have a future I never expected.'

He had listened, standing very still and now let out a deep breath. 'I must too. Molly, look at me.' And when she raised her head, she saw that in his face which riveted her. Swiftly, his mouth came down on hers. After a moment, he raised his head for a moment to look at her and then kissed her again, the kisses growing deeper every time. Taken utterly by surprise, she stood still under this onslaught, but when he paused again, she freed one arm to put round his neck, reaching up to him, her lips parting under his in a moment of incredible joy.

At last, a little breathless, he said, 'I have wanted to do that since I first saw you, when that rascal Toby had the same idea.'

'Then? Oh, sir, I didn't think – I didn't know —'

He gave a low laugh. 'Molly! After what has just happened between us, how can you still call me sir? Matt, if you please.'

'Matt,' she murmured obediently, a little shy of using his given name. Having always thought him too exalted for her, this feeling was nevertheless dissolving rapidly. Did he really love her, or was it only the same kind of desire that Toby had?

As if to answer her, he said, 'All these months in camp, watching the Lambkin, I was falling in love with her, though I hardly knew it. And then, lying ill in the cottage, I thought I had never known a woman like you, Molly.' He kissed her again, intensely, as a man who had long been starved of love – her eyes, her cheeks, her hair, before her mouth once more. After that they stood still, wrapped together in the greatcoat, knowing a deep content.

But after a while he said, 'Do you really love me, Molly, or is it only that you are sorry for me, being so kind to me?'

A little laugh escaped her. 'I suppose it began when I was so anxious every time you went into action, and after the battle at Inkerman I was in an agony until I knew you safe. All the things I heard about that fight, and you, and Colonel Henderson, made me pray you'd never be in such a fight again. And then you were hit in the trenches. When I saw you brought down, I thought you were dying and I didn't know how to bear it.'

'But being you, you held my hand and came to the hospital with me.'

205

'I wasn't sure if you were conscious of that.'

'Oh, I was conscious,' he said grimly, 'of every damned jerk as they brought me down'.

'I was so sorry, so —' there wasn't a word for what she had felt, 'but I was praying for you, all the time.'

He did not move. 'As you were for so many other poor devils, no doubt. Wasn't I just another wounded soldier?'

'How can you ask that? Why – '

'Pity,' he said savagely. 'Are you mistaking pity for love?'

'I sometimes think one is near the other, but, Matt – ' she used his name hesitantly, 'you must know tonight that I love you. I wish I could come home with you and go on looking after you, but – it's not suitable, is it? What would I come as? Not, I think, one of the housemaids! A nurse, which I am not and you don't need now? In any case your mother, Miss Henrietta – '

'For God's sake,' he shifted a little, his leg tiring after standing so still 'Molly, you would come as – as what I want you to be.'

She laid her head against his chest. 'It would be so awkward for everyone, don't you see? I must go to London with Aunt Olivia – she does need me.'

'And I don't?'

'You'll have your family. Oh Matt,' tears stung her eyes again, 'you're not well yet, you know Dr Turner said it would still take months to get your strength back. I – I wonder if you are still thinking of me as the Lambkin going about the camps? It will all be different now, and when you are well, maybe you will wish you'd said none of this.'

'You don't place much confidence in my love,' he protested.

'I want to, oh I *do,* but I'm just so afraid that when – when you have spent time at home and are well again, you won't see me as you did out there.'

'That damned place is behind us now. Molly, I love you, I adore you. You must believe me.' He was kissing her again, holding her close, pressing her against his body, and she in her turn clung to him, wanting never to let go of this moment. But in the end it was she who drew back.

'And I love you,' unable to keep her voice quite steady, she made the swift avowal, 'Only I would be taking advantage of you if we settled anything now. Don't you know,' she forced a smile, 'men often fall in love with the women who look after them when they are ill? Yes, they do,' as he made a deprecatory movement. 'I had three proposals in camp, which they might have thought better of back in England! But I'm serious. There's so much to consider – your family when they know about me, even where I really come from. Did it make a difference to you when you found out?'

Matt took this as seriously as it was meant. 'It made a difference, yes, but only in that it enhanced what I had already learned to love. Beloved girl, to me, you are you.'

'But not to your family. They will still think of me as their housemaid, if they think of me at all. Don't tell them about us yet, please, not yet.'

'They don't matter, and you don't have a family, apart from Mrs Henderson. We are free, you and I.'

'No one is ever quite free,' she murmured. 'Your mother and Sir Charles do matter. And you are going to a house in mourning. Think what your poor mother has been through, and Sir Charles.'

'And do you think Second-chance-Charlie wouldn't welcome you?'

She smiled at the memories brought back by that name. 'Perhaps, because he can't help being kind!' And for a moment she saw herself going home with Matt, loved, respected, the past forgotten. But it wouldn't, it couldn't be like that. At least not yet. She had to be firm for him. 'Matt,' she said very gently. 'I do love you, in a way that I never loved poor Hal, I promise you that, but I do think we must wait a little. I'm not going to take advantage of this moment. We've been through so much together while you were ill, weak, which you still are —'

'Good God,' he interrupted. 'Do you think I'm weak in the head as well? Molly, I've waited years really to love a woman enough to want to marry her and I'm not going to let you go for a scruple, unless – oh dear God, unless this means it really *is* pity.'

'I've told you it's not. I loved you long before you were hurt. When your brother was killed – oh, I wanted to take you in my arms and comfort you. Grief like that is awful, as I should know, but I – I wasn't sure you would like it at all. And then when you were ill and not being a soldier any more, then – then I had gone far beyond doubting it, though I saw no future for myself with you.'

'My poor darling.' He tightened his arms, feeling the scars pulling, but not caring. 'If that is all true, why can't we —'

She put up a hand and touched his mouth. 'You know why. Go home and get well, while I go to London with Aunt Olivia and learn to be a lady.'

'As if you were not!'

She gave a little laugh, and then said in her workhouse voice, 'Oh sir, I could go back to bein' a housemaid and forget to talk proper and bob a curtsey if I saw her ladyship on the stair.'

'Stop that,' he broke in sharply. 'I won't have it. That's not you as you are now. They'll understand, of course they will.'

'Even Miss Henrietta?'

'I'll deal with Henrietta. Georgy is much the nicer of my two half-sisters, and she will welcome you. But I keep saying none of that matters. You will marry me, my darling, won't you?'

'Yes, I will, but not yet. After the loss of your brother, how could I go straightaway with you to Crossley Lodge? To be so happy, getting married – no, it would be too soon, too unkind, too hurtful. Stay with them, give them time, let the wounds heal, both yours and theirs.'

He looked steadily down at her. 'You are a wise woman, my Molly.'

'I'm just trying to be sensible for both of us.'

'My prosaic love. Little as I like the idea of being parted, I believe you are right. I owe it to my mother to be with her for a while, even if I can't be Toby to her. We'll have a summer wedding.'

'Yes, but quietly,' she murmured. 'Only what is fitting,' And then in a rush, 'I don't like leaving you tomorrow either. I want to be with you, see that you drink your porter at lunchtime and Burgundy in the evening, mind.'

'Very well, Lambkin! But when I've got myself well again, I shall want a wife, although I can never quite forget the Lambkin.'

'Oh yes, Matt, yes. That's all I want – to be your wife.'

They clung together under the greatcoat until she became aware that he was swaying, and drew back. 'You've been out here too long. And there's a spot of blood on your shirt.'

'I felt one of the scabs break just now. It's nothing, but I don't think I can stand on my feet any more.'

'Of course you can't. Let me help you down and then Merton can get you to bed. Perhaps I'd better take a look at the wound.'

'It's nothing,' he insisted. 'Merton will see to it,' but he was exhausted. At the door of his cabin, he kissed her again, lingeringly. 'My love, my darling, I am the most fortunate of men. I wish I had the strength, and an empty cabin, to make love to you now, but I do know that we must wait. I've no idea where I shall eventually be sent or what I shall do. I'm not a rich man, but I don't think you are the woman to care for that.'

She shook her head, caressing his cheek. 'Wherever they send you I don't mind as long as I am with you.'

He touched some stray curls, blown by the night wind 'I always loved your hair. It was one of the first things I noticed about you.'

'And it would never stay under my cap!' She added with new confidence, 'My dear love, you look so tired. Do go to bed.'

With one last kiss he said lightly, 'Johnny told me to obey you, so I'll go.' In the cabin, wishing for other company than his gloomy captain, he wanted only silence, to taste the joy that had come to him, not Merton fussing over him, nor his opinion being asked on the comparative merits of grape and round shot.

In her own cabin, glad her aunt was soundly asleep Molly sat on her berth, not attempting to undress, experiencing the same joy. It had not been quite like this with Hal, for with Matt she shared other things, quite beyond poor Hal's capacity. A great surge of gratitude welled up in her for such joy; after all they had been through, it seemed another incredible miracle. To have to leave him tomorrow was one of the hardest things she had ever had to face, but for the moment she had to let him go, to trust that all would be well in the

209

end, keeping with her the memory of his mouth on hers, his warm kisses, his words of love.

The little party broke up on the quay at Southampton. Merton found a hired carriage to take his master to Portsmouth but Matt lingered before climbing in. 'I feel I should be escorting you ladies to London but —'

'Of course you can't even think of it,' Olivia told him. 'Reid will look after us, but when you feel able, come and stay with us in Hyde Park Gate. You know you will always be welcome.'

To Joseph Merton Molly said, 'Take good care of him. I wish I was coming with you.' To which Merton perceptively replied that he was sure it wouldn't be long before they were all together again, not even countenancing that the Major might ever do without him.

At the door of the carriage Matt turned back to kiss Olivia on the cheek. 'That's for the privilege of having served with Old Walking-Boots,' he said softly, which brought a lovely warmth to her angular face. Then he caught Molly to him, kissing her lips before smiling at Olivia and saying, 'Now you know!'

'My dear boy,' she answered, 'As if I hadn't known for some while.'

Hesitating as if he couldn't bear the parting, it was Merton who held wide the door saying, 'If you please, sir, the horses is getting frisky,' and he carried away with him the look on Molly's face. But he was torn between incredulous happiness that she was going to be his and a very real dread of going home to the grieving household in Southsea.

It was late afternoon when he reached Crossley Lodge. In his surprise Frederick so far forgot himself as to wring the Major's hand. 'Sir! Oh sir, to see you back again!' But the butler was shaken by the appearance of this pale, thin man, so unlike the one whom he had seen marching away at the head of his men through the streets of Portsmouth, and his thoughts went to his mistress upstairs. The master was not back from the courts yet, he said, and Miss Henrietta was gone to the lending library, but Lady Milner was in her sitting room.

210

'Shall I go up, Sir? Prepare her?'

Matt shook his head. 'No, I'll go alone.' But he had not climbed a flight of stairs like this since he had run down them on the morning of his departure and now with a quarter of that strength had to lean on the banister to get his breath back. He wanted Molly, not the scene that he dreaded was awaiting him.

His mother called in answer to his knock, and he went into the well-remembered room, nothing changed. There lying as usual on her chaise-longue, he saw for one moment a wholly unfounded hope flood her face, only to fade equally quickly.

'I'm sorry,' he said in a constricted voice, 'the wrong one has come back.'

There then faced Lady Milner a choice such as she had never before had to make. For years, cosseted, waited on, fussed over by her family, she had become totally self-absorbed and the shock of losing her younger son had devastated her. Her first instinct was to indulge in hysterics, but instead, dimly, she realized that something was actually demanded of her. Though unable to stem the tears, what was needed rose in her and she held out both arms.

'Oh my dearest, dearest boy – to have you safely home! Come – oh come.'

He went on his kness beside her, felt her arms round him and they wept together. Then she set her hands about his face, kissing both his cheeks.

'My darling Matt, don't think I ever loved you less. It was just that Toby —' she brought out the name with difficulty 'was so young, so vulnerable, while you were always strong and in command of yourself. Or so I thought. But let me look at you. My poor boy, you're so white and thin. That moustache makes you look even paler. Tell me – '

He got up, not without some difficulty and sat beside her, the tears dry on his face. 'Did you get Johnny's letter?'

'We did and thankful we were to have it, not that he told us much. Your shoulder, he said, and one leg.'

'And a few other what he called minor cuts, but which gave me a great deal of pain then though not now. I'm healing, only I wish it wasn't so damnably slow. But I believe Johnny saved my life. He had to get most of an epaulette out of me and a

211

number of shell splinters. But you will want to hear, to know about Toby.'

She stopped him. 'Not now, not tonight.' And with that new perception she added, 'and not until your Step-papa and Henrietta are present. You won't want the pain of telling it all twice.'

'Thank you, Mama,' was all he could manage.

'I shall get Dr Lingwood to see you tomorrow,' she said and when he murmured that he no longer needed a doctor, she brushed this aside. 'Of course he must see you. There's nothing of you compared to the Matt who went away. Cook must order some extra cream. Oh Charles,' as her husband came in, 'look who has come back to us'.

'Frederick told me below. My dear boy, welcome home. Are you really flesh and blood? We have been so anxious.'

Matt stood up to take his outstretched hand, wincing a little at the grip. 'Flesh certainly, but a little short of the red stuff.'

Sir Charles eyed him. 'A little short of clothes too, by the look of it. When I think how you looked in your regimentals!'

'It all got pretty desperate in the winter. We had nothing but what we stood up in, the quartermasters having been ordered by the powers-that-be to leave our gear on board ship and what we had was soon threadbare. Only our greatcoats got us through, those of us that did survive.'

'Was it as bad as Mr Russell reported in the *Times*?'

'Worse,' Matt said, and the single word said it all.

Lady Milner had risen to stand with her hand through his arm. 'I don't think he should tell us all we want to know until tomorrow, do you, my dear? He needs a hot bath and a good dinner.'

'And a bed,' Matt put in. 'I've not slept in one since we landed in Bulgaria, and I don't call a ship's berth a bed, too short for me for one thing. Mostly it has been a blanket on the ground.'

Sir Charles rang the bell at once and when Frederick appeared he ordered up a bottle of the best claret in the cellar. 'A bottle a day for you, my boy,' he said, and to Frederick, 'You had better have the front guest room made ready. The Major is not fit to climb two flights of stairs to his own. I imagine one has been enough.' And when Frederick had disappeared he asked, 'Did you ever come across that girl we had here? Molly? She married a rifleman.'

Matt looked out of the window into the garden. There were tulips in the beds, blossom on the cherry tree, a lilac in flower. 'Yes,' he said, 'Her husband died of the cholera after the battle of the Alma, last September.'

Lady Milner murmured, 'Poor girl, how sad for her. Has she come home?'

'Yes, Mama.'

Sir Charles said, 'Well, I'm sure she knows I will give her a helping hand if she needs it.'

Thankfully, as far as Matt was concerned, Henrietta came hurrying in, having been informed below that her brother was returned and no more was said about Molly, except when Henrietta, on being told by her father that Molly had been left a widow, remarked that she had always thought the marriage too precipitate. 'And the girl rather too forward.'

Matt held back the instinctive retort, and changed the subject, asking after his younger sister and her family.

It was Frederick, escorting the newly returned hero – in his eyes anyway – to the hastily prepared room, who enquired most assiduously after Molly, saying that the staff below stairs would like to know what had befallen her. Matt kept it simple, rather worn out by all the emotion engendered by his home-coming, but he did say she had done many kindnesses for the soldiers in the Crimea, which information Frederick took back to the servants' hall.

'I can't say I'm surprised,' was Cook's remark. 'She was a rare good girl, that one.'

Tired by the journey, his leg aching, Matt was thankful to be alone, and he saw that Molly had been right, that this arrival home was not the time to talk of their love. Giving himself up to the luxury of a hot bath and clean linen to be followed by the best dinner he had eaten in a very long time, it was bliss later to sink into a real bed. But he missed his Lambkin and drifted off to sleep thinking of the time to come when she would lie beside him.

In their own room Sir Charles found his wife at her dressing-table, and when she had sent Sylvia off, he said simply, 'That was very well done of you, my love. It can't have been easy.'

213

'No,' she murmured, 'not easy, but when I saw him – oh Charles, I could only think how awful it would be if we were to lose him too.'

'We'll see what Lingwood has to say tomorrow, but I don't think we need fear that, though he may be a long time getting back to his old self. And we owe it to your nephew that he has come through it at all.'

'Dear John, always so sharp and yet so kind. And I do thank God Matt was with our darling boy at the end.'

'Something of a miracle. I can imagine what it must have been like, searching for one man in the aftermath of a battle, but we shall hear it all tomorrow.'

'Yes, tomorrow, if we can bear it,' she whispered and Sir Charles turned away with a long sigh. Fond as he was of his step-son, Toby had been his only son.

The telling of Toby's death, traumatic for them all though it was, reducing the women to quiet tears, somehow brought an easing of grief, the truth clearing away the worst of their imaginings, and his mother blessed her elder son for being with his brother at the last. Sir Charles went to wring his hand again, his feelings beyond speech, but when Matt hastily held out the left one, tucking the right into the breast of his coat, he said, 'Hey, what's this? Your hand too?'

Matt explained that the splinters had gone a good way down his arm and that even writing a letter would be a painful process so that from then on his stepfather made it his business to communicate with the War Office, and do any other practical things that were needed.

In the weeks that followed Matt obeyed his cousin, finding he had little inclination to do anything else. He began the day with a sumptuous breakfast brought to him in bed by Frederick and when the weather was fine lay about in the garden, reading the papers, *Punch* and the *Spectator,* sleeping a great deal. Merton fetched Shalima from the livery stables and she gave every sign of recognizing her master, whinnying and nuzzling her nose into Matt's shoulder, though he wished she wouldn't show a marked preference for the injured one. It was some time before the family physician, Dr Lingwood, tut-tutting over his injuries, would allow him to ride, but when he

214

did Matt took a few gentle excursions along the shore and into the summer countryside. But he was annoyed to find himself still so weak. He wanted to go to London to see Molly and would have done so except that he realized it was quite beyond his powers at the moment.

'You can't lose the amount of blood that you have, young man,' Dr Lingwood told him, 'without the direst consequences.' He had treated a number of the wounded returned to Portsmouth and knew what he was talking about.

So the early summer drifted by, cheered by Molly's letters, which he answered laboriously, though with greater ease each time. These he gave to Merton to post, having adjured him not to talk too much of her below-stairs. There was no need to explain to Merton who understood the situation very well. He told Molly that she had been right and that he had said nothing as yet to his family. For the moment they were too engrossed in the loss of Toby and the need for every detail he could tell them. His own affairs, he said, must come later, but one piece of news he had to impart to her was that the War Office had written to him confirming his promotion to Lieutenant-Colonel on the recommendation of Lord Raglan. Molly wrote back to say how pleased she was. She in her turn was missing him every day. She added that Aunt Olivia had brought her a whole wardrobe of clothes and what was more had opened an account for her at Coutts bank with a monthly allowance of fifty pounds. She couldn't imagine what she would spend it on but admitted that the London shops were very tempting, which made him smile. She also added that a great many relatives were calling at the house, glad to see Mrs Henderson back, while commiserating with her over her loss. One of them was a nephew whose name was Edward. He had come to London looking for fame and fortune and though he had as yet apparently found neither, he appeared to be enjoying himself hugely. Soon she and her aunt would go into society again and Edward had offered to escort her anywhere she wished to go.

Reading this Matt was aware for the first time in his life of a strong feeling of jealousy. Were London and all the new experiences turning her head? No, she was surely too sensible for that, but she was after all only a girl, just twenty. This Edward – was he more exciting than a thirty-one-year-old

215

disabled soldier? He began to fret and took himself off to visit his younger sister. Georgy and her amiable husband made him very welcome but it was a noisy household and after a week of his nephews, of whom he was really very fond, sliding down the banisters, hallooing round the house, and begging him for tales of the Crimea to be re-enacted round the garden, he withdrew to the peace of Crossley Lodge.

'Don't blame you, old fellow,' his brother-in-law said, 'Our house is hardly a convalescent home!'

But the visit told him he must be patient a little longer and Matt was not by nature a patient man.

Chapter Fifteen

By the end of July Dr Lingwood, somewhat reluctantly, agreed that his patient was well enough for the journey to London, being of the opinion that the major would more likely fret himself into a fever if he was kept at home any longer. Matt's instinctive response was to fling himself on to Shalima's back and gallop all the way. However, Sir Charles scotched this idea immediately and insisted that he travel at a respectable speed on the railway. Lady Milner prepared to part with him only if he promised a letter as soon as he had some idea what the army would do with him.

On his last evening he and his stepfather retired to the study where they sat companionably with their cigars and port. Through a cloud of smoke Sir Charles said, 'Your mother has borne the grief all the better for your being home. I hope, my dear boy, you are going to have a more settled life now.'

'I doubt if I can go into active service, at least for the time being. Johnny held out little hope of my ever regaining full use of my arm and Lingwood agrees with him, so it's no use grumbling about that. But I don't want to leave the army. Lord Raglan, rest his soul, managed very well with one arm.'

'I'm sure he is much missed by the army.'

'Yes,' Matt said with a touch of his old cynicism. 'When he died after that frightful attack on the Malakov redoubt, which was from all accounts a knock-down for us, everyone discovered that they actually loved the old fellow. After the way the Press treated him, and the Government, the recent tributes have all come a bit late. I think that last defeat broke his heart. Johnny wasn't there, but he talked to Raglan's physician afterwards and he said in his last letter that cholera was not the cause, whatever the papers say, the old man was simply worn out. I'm sorry for his wife, she hadn't seen him since we sailed last year, but that's the way of the army. I shall badger them until they can find me something to do. At least I can use a pen now.'

'I hope they will, but I was thinking more of your having a home of your own, a wife and family, if Georgy's uproarious ménage has not put you off!'

Matt laughed. 'They are pretty wild, but no doubt one's own brats would be tolerable. And yes, I would like now to be more settled, though I had thought once to end my days a crusty old bachelor-general reliving past campaigns with anyone who would listen!'

Sir Charles blew out a cloud of smoke. 'I am, by nature of my profession, more perceptive than your mother, who has much on her mind, or Henrietta who doesn't see beyond the end of her nose. My dear boy, I believe you have lost your heart to Molly March, strange as it may be.'

Matt leaned back and released a long breath. It was almost a relief to have someone to whom he could speak of her.

'I was going to say something about it, but she said I should not, that it was not the right time, but I can't deny that we love each other. At one time I thought I would never stand on English soil again, and it's entirely owing to Johnny and to her that I have come home. We hope to marry soon. That is, if —'

'If what?' Sir Charles gave him a penetrating glance. 'You are doubtful because of the position she held here?'

'It's only partly that.' Matt got up and began to prowl restlessly about the room. And then he explained the whole story of Molly's true parentage, of Olivia Henderson adopting her, setting her up for going into London society, even the ubiquitous Edward. 'Damn him! He seems to be escorting her everywhere and I'm afraid – afraid she might have been influenced by circumstances in the Crimea, the way we were thrown together, that her new life will wean her away from me.'

'Then I think it is a very good thing you are going to London tomorrow to settle the matter for yourself.' Sir Charles surveyed his stepson. 'But if I am any judge of character, if Molly says she loves you, then I don't think it likely that this fellow will supplant you. Sit down, dear boy, and fill your glass.' Broadminded as Sir Charles was, there was no doubt he was happily impressed by the story of Molly's true parentage, 'I am intrigued by what you have told me, though not entirely surprised. One could see there was quality there.'

'You will find her very changed now from the girl who worked here. She is emerging into what she should always have been.' Unable to keep a note of pride from his voice, Matt refilled his glass and sat down again. 'Mrs Henderson says she must have some relatives and is trying to trace them, though her grandfather and her uncle have gone from the Marlow house.'

'Poor Molly, after that wretched childhood it would be good for her to be restored to a family.'

Matt supposed so, but he wanted to take her away, have her all to himself. He could see unknown relatives bearing down on her, bringing her 'out', finding her a rich and more suitable husband. It would be unbearable. To his stepfather, he said, 'If you please, sir, I would rather you said nothing of any of this to Mama and the girls, not yet. When I've seen Molly, after these months away from each other, talked to Mrs Henderson – well, I hope I may bring her home. But there's a lot to be considered.'

'Yes, I can see that and it shall be as you wish. I'll say nothing. But what an astonishing girl! When I think of all you have told me about what she did out in that dreadful place, well! I always thought her out of the usual run.'

A smile crossed Matt's face. 'Oh she is, sir, I assure you.'

The housekeeper at the house in Hyde Park Gate told him regretfully that Mrs Henderson and Mrs Hallam had gone with Mr Edward to spend a few days in Ruislip with his father, Mrs Henderson's brother. She expected them back tomorrow afternoon.

Disappointed and beginning, quite unreasonably, to thoroughly dislike the unknown Edward, Matt turned away and took himself off to the War Office. He was asked to wait by the sergeant in the entrance for nearly half an hour which did not improve his temper, and was then shown into an office where a very young, very smart lieutenant sat behind a desk. He did leap up and salute, but made Matt very conscious of his second-best uniform. He sat down while the lieutenant began to shuffle through his papers. 'I don't seem to have any information on you, sir. Should I have?'

'I have been on sick leave from the Crimea. I've had confirmation of my promotion, which Lord Raglan asked for; since then I've written twice without the courtesy of a reply.'

'Oh, I see, then we must know – though I don't seem to have your documents to hand. So many officers coming back, you know.'

'Not so many as lie dead out there,' Matt said tartly. 'Lord Raglan himself wrote home concerning me and you will kindly take me to a more senior officer.'

By this time the young man was rather pink about the ears and hastily disappeared into an inner room. Conducted there, a fellow colonel was more co-operative, but he said he had no orders yet from the Commander-in-Chief, Lord Hardinge, who studied all Lord Raglan's despatches personally, and since his death had been inundated with a mound of correspondence. Matt handed over his medical release but it was laid on one side without apparent interest. In the meantime the desk soldier, as Matt silently dubbed him, suggested that Colonel Hamilton should wait, on half-pay of course, until his papers came to light and some decision could be made concerning him. Did he have an address in London?

Unhesitatingly Matt gave that of Mrs Henderson in Hyde Park Gate. But he went out angry at the red tape, the insensitivity of War Office officials, and no longer wondered at the incompetence with which the campaign had been conducted. Shaking the dust of the place off his feet, he hailed a hackney and had himself driven to the office of his friend, Captain Tuckett, he who had once been shot in a duel with Lord Cardigan by the windmill on Wimbledon Common. He still ran his business in the Poultry, dealing with the East India Company and he welcomed Matt warmly, taking the proffered left hand.

'I'm very glad to see you back, old fellow, though I can see you've taken a knock or two. Your arm, eh?'

'It's tiresome, but I'm pretty well again generally. How's that young rascal, Simon?'

'Still gracing the *Agamemnon* with his presence. Nothing would wean my brother from the navy and he was delighted that his ship had the honour of carrying Lord Raglan and numerous bigwigs to the Crimea. He's only sorry that the task of bringing his lordship's body back to England was given to the *Caradoc*.'

'Give him my best when you see him. And you, Harvey, is all well with you?'

'Well enough. Where are you staying?'

'I was hoping to plant myself on my late Colonel's widow in Kensington but she's away until tomorrow, so I must look for an hotel.'

'You'll do no such thing. Susan will be delighted to see you and you'll find our girls have half grown up since you last saw them, while Tim and Jeremy are a pair of little fiends. But I like boys to have spirit. Come, if you can stand the racket.'

'If I can stand trench warfare I guess I can manage your quiverful.'

'Then that's settled. We're living quite near, in Bloomsbury Square. But first, what do you say to lunch at the Army and Navy Club?'

In the cab bearing them thither Harvey Tuckett wanted to know all about Matt's injury and his being invalided home, and finally Matt told him of the morning's interview in Whitehall.

'Those fellows!' Tuckett snorted. 'They sit on their arses all day and don't have the slightest idea of what's going on. Lord Cardigan by the way came home to a hero's welcome, but before you choke on your spleen, let me tell you that didn't last very long. The papers turned against him and since Lord Lucan has been sent home there have been a stream of angry letters exchanged between them via the daily papers. I think they deserved each other more than the army deserved either of them.'

'I agree with that,' Matt said with feeling. 'Toby died in that charge at Balaclava last October.'

'So I saw in the casualty lists. A damned shame for such a young fellow. Something else to lay at Cardigan's door, eh?'

'I suppose it's not entirely just but that is how I feel. God, how I loathe that man.'

221

Putting Lord Cardigan out of their heads, they ate an excellent luncheon, exchanging news and discussing the latest reports from the Crimea. Matt found several acquaintances at the club, all of whom had a disposition to give his hand a hearty shake until he tucked it into the breast of his coat, proffering his left. Afterwards they sat in the window, smoking their cigars and watching the world go by, and Matt began to feel it was good to be in civilization again. He had had a letter from Ben Marshall who told him he need not fret about his men because they were now all hutted and well fed and the summer weather cheered everyone up. The bands were performing again, the men playing football and cricket in their spare time and everyone was striving to forget the awful winter. A new colonel had been appointed to command the 50th and he himself had his promotion to major (acting, in brackets) in Matt's place. The trench shelling continued, on both sides, and an attack on a Russian fortification had caused a great many casualties but thanks to Miss Nightingale the men were less in dread of being sent off to Scutari. He added a postscript, that everyone missed the Lambkin. Assimilating all this, Matt half wished himself back there, but only if she were with him.

At last, reluctantly, Captain Tuckett said he ought to get back to his office, the young clerk being new and inexperienced. Coming out into the bright sunshine they stood together at the top of the few steps and there most unfortunately, coming up was Lord Cardigan, with a young man beside him.

'A good position to be in,' Tuckett muttered. 'Always overlook the enemy.'

Lord Cardigan, appearing old now and very thin, his cheeks rather sunken, surveyed them with all his usual truculence. 'You!' he directed his first salvo toward Matt. 'I thought you had left your bones at Balaclava.'

'It is my brother who lies there, after the charge you led into the Valley of Death,' Matt retorted. 'You, I believe, rode out and left it to Lord Paget to retrieve the remnants of your command.' This was treading on dangerous ground but he no longer cared. Not having spoken to his lordship since the incident of the handkerchief, he could not have restrained himself now if he had wished to, which he didn't.

His lordship gave him a nasty look and glanced at Tuckett. 'I suppose you two would keep company together,' and to his companion added, 'keep away from Indian officers when you are enrolled, Vincent. They are of no use except as cannon fodder.'

'After what has passed in the Crimea, I find your remark offensive,' Matt said icily. 'However two can trade in insults so permit me to tell you, sir – ' he omitted the title, 'that in my opinion high rank and preferential treatment do not prevent a man from being vain, ignorant and unfit for command.' He should not have said it, and he knew it, but it was very satisfying to see Lord Cardigan's eyes bulge as they always did in his rages, his face turning dark red.

'You insufferable cur! By God, if I were younger I would call you out for that.'

Tuckett laughed. 'As you did me! Wimbledon Common, eh? But it was outlawed then, and must be more so now that men of sense realize the stupidity of it.'

'In any case,' Matt added, 'if it were possible it is I who have a score to settle.' But standing here, looking down on his old enemy, he saw only a bewhiskered arrogant old man hardly worth expending his hatred on.

His lordship, deep in the rage he had never learned to control, tried to push past them to enter the club, but as his sword clattered on the step, his nephew tripped over it, upsetting his uncle, so that Cardigan sat down plump on the step.

'Buffoon! Clown!' he roared. 'Get me up, damn you.' It was clear he could not rise unaided, and the young man trying without much success to get him up, glanced at Matt who was nearest. It took only a moment's hesitation, for Matt to come down, put his left hand under the Earl's other arm, and between them they got him up.

To receive a favour from an 'Indian' officer was the last straw. His lordship raised one hand as if to strike out at Matt, but his nephew, showing some common sense, caught it. 'No sir, no. Not here – you can't.'

'No, but you could. Does the honour of the family mean nothing to you?'

The poor young man nearly fell over again in his amazement. 'You want me to challenge – no, no, indeed I couldn't.' And to Matt, 'Excuse me, sir, if you will be so good ... I ... I wouldn't dream of ...'

Several people in the street were watching the little scene, as well as one or two officers at the club window. Somehow the unhappy young man got his uncle inside, while Matt and Tuckett fled down the steps, trying to control their laughter.

'Oh by God!' Matt exclaimed, when he could speak. 'How are the mighty fallen!'

'His bolt is shot,' Harvey Tuckett agreed. 'That was extraordinarily satisfying.' He had never seen his friend so relaxed. 'But your magnanimity amazed me.'

'It surprised me too.' Somehow the incident had settled the score, the indignity pricking Cardigan's balloon, and Matt felt light-hearted as he had not done for years. What did he care for old scores now? The future was what mattered, and Molly was his future.

His friend was still chuckling. 'I must admit that at one moment I did think he really would force that poor young fellow to challenge you. What would you have done?'

'Put him across my knee!' Matt said promptly.

They spent a riotous evening at Captain Tuckett's house, recalling old times, laughing at remembered incidents and the following afternoon Matt presented himself in Hyde Park Gate. Mrs Henderson and Mrs Hallam had not long returned, the butler told him, and were in the drawing room. He showed Matt in and it was a reunion he would never forget. They exclaimed on his improved looks and for his part he could scarcely take his eyes from Molly. Olivia Henderson had excellent taste and Molly's cream-coloured gown, matching lace decorating it, the sash a russet colour were just right for her. He thought she looked enchanting and had to drag his attention away to answer Olivia's question.

'Yes, I went to the War Office yesterday as soon as I arrived. I saw Lord Hardinge's secretary, though I got little joy of the interview for he didn't seem able to find my papers. I doubt if I will be in command of anything more than a desk, if they can find one for me!'

At that moment a young man came into the room, giving such a feeling of energy that he could almost be said to have bounced.

'All safely in, Aunt Olivia,' he said cheerfully. 'oh, I beg your pardon, didn't know you had a visitor.'

'This is your uncle's second-in-command, Colonel Hamilton, who was wounded a few weeks after Inkerman.'

'I say, sir – how splendid! I mean – to have fought there! I do hope you are recovered.'

Somewhat amused by all this enthusiasm, Matt gave him his usual left-hand shake. A puppy, he thought, amiable enough but a puppy for all that. He merely inclined his head in answer while Edward then reminded Molly of her promise to let him drive her round the Park.

'Oh, I think Molly will want to postpone that now that Colonel Hamilton is returned,' Olivia said smoothly. 'You shall take me instead and you needn't look so crestfallen. Come along, I need you to help me sort those books your father gave me.'

She swept him, somewhat reluctantly, out of the room and the door had barely closed before Matt had Molly in his arms.

'I've missed you,' the words came out between kisses. 'My God, how I've missed you. Let me have a good look at you. How elegant you are. And your hair —'

'It has been specially cut and dresed by such a smart hair-dresser in Bond Street. The fashion is to have it parted in the centre and straight to the sides, but nothing will make my hair straight, so he settled for this style which he said was French.' She was smiling up at him. 'Aunt Olivia spoils me.'

'You are due for some spoiling, and I intend to carry on the good work! I shall write to Johnny and tell him he has won his bet with himself.'

'What bet?'

'That we would be married before he came home! When he does he will hardly recognise the Lambkin.' And holding her at arm's length, he said, 'I can hardly wait to take you home. They won't know you! I have told my stepfather about you, but not Mama and the others. Not yet, as you bade me.'

'Dear Sir Charles,' she murmured, 'if it hadn't been for him I would never have met you. Darling Matt, I've missed you every day.'

'Despite this Edward fellow?'

'I do believe you're jealous?'

He drew her to him again. 'Of course I am, but I can see he's only a boy.'

Chuckling, she said, 'So he is – the same age as myself!' Then looking critically at him, she added 'You do look so much better than when I last saw you, when we said goodbye in Portsmouth – how horrid that was. And you look somehow different, as if something good has happened. Has it? More than us being back together?'

'Of course it is having you in my arms again, but for another thing I as near as anything fought a duel yesterday.'

'Matt! Stop funning. No one fights duels these days.'

'I know they don't and you needn't look so horrified. I'd no mind to be clapped up in Newgate.' But he told her about the incident with Lord Cardigan. 'And I can tell you it let a great deal of resentment out of me. The fellow's not worth so much bitterness. I'm too much in love to want to hate anyone, even him!'

'What a tale. If you had fought either Lord Cardigan or that nephew of his I should have been very angry. Doctor Turner and I didn't work on you all those weeks in Balaclava to have you come home to risk your life, behaving like a school-boy. As if you could do it anyway. I never heard anything so silly.'

'I'm sorry,' he tried to look penitent. 'Did you know I am as good a shot with my left hand as my right, something my father taught me. But I can't tell you what it has done for me. All those years, nursing so much bitterness, it's all gone. Seeing Lord Cardigan sitting on the steps of the club, Harvey Tuckett and I could hardly stop laughing. I remember years ago, when I was at school, the old Duke fought a duel with Lord Winchilsea. No one was hurt and we thought it rather a lark.'

'Well, I don't,' she said severely. 'Don't you know how precious you are to me?'

There was only one answer to this and the kiss helped her to recover herself.

Over dinner, Edward having gone home, Olivia asked him where he was staying. 'I have had the impertinenace to have my bags put in your hall,' he said, 'and sent Merton to your kitchen. I hope that's agreeable. You did say —'

'Of course. I would be very sorry if you should think of going anywhere else. I'll tell Starling to take your luggage up. And now,' Olivia looked from one to the other, 'what are your plans for your wedding?'

'We haven't any yet,' Matt said, 'but soon. I don't want to wait a moment longer than we need, but I'm somewhat in limbo at the moment. The War Office were singularly unhelpful. If we find lodgings here in London they'll probably send me to Timbuctoo.'

'Then I have a suggestion to make. Why don't you marry in Holy Trinity church in the Brompton Road, it's not far from here, and then live in this house until you can make a more settled home. Goodness knows there's enough space.'

They looked at each other, the thought crossing Matt's mind that it must have been hard for Olivia to come back here without her husband, and he could see why she needed Molly so much for the first few months. He said at once, after Molly had given him a little nod, 'I think we would like that very much.'

So it was settled. Molly wrote a long letter to Miss Plumstead, telling her news of her engagement and the forthcoming wedding, promising to bring Matt soon to visit her.

He took her to Bond Street to buy her a hoop of pearls for an engagement ring and they called on the vicar, arranging for the banns to be read.

Walking home, sorry that her glove hid the beautiful ring, Molly said, 'I wish I did have some relative to ask. Aunt Olivia has had a detective trying to trace my mother's family for weeks now, but all we have learned so far is confirmation that my grandfather sold the house in Marlow and they moved away.'

'Do you want so much to find them?'

'I don't know. Oh yes, yes I do, although Aunt Olivia did so dislike my uncle. But if I had a grandfather, I would like that very much. It would give me —' she searched for the word, 'some family substance, if you know what I mean.'

He nodded. A year ago she would not have used such a word. But these months in the company of her adopted aunt had been an education, while the daily use of the large number of books in Colonel Henderson's study had extended her knowledge and vocabulary. She told Matt she had read Sir William Napier's vast history of the Peninsular War, unusual enough for a young lady, but just what she would choose, Matt thought. She said she had loved every word of it, and Matt had a private smile over this, thinking of the romantic novels which were Henrietta's choice from the lending library.

It was a week later that they came in from a drive in the Park to find Mrs Henderson sitting in her chair with an open letter on her knee. She was looking very serious.

Molly stopped in her tracks. 'Oh – is something the matter?'

Her aunt picked up the paper. 'This is a report from the detective I employed. He has found your uncle. Apparently he now owns a wine business and is living in Watford.'

'And my grandfather?'

'He is dead, my dear. I was afraid it might be so – twenty years is a long time.'

Molly sat down beside her while Matt took the Colonel's chair, which seemed to have become his own. He was watching Molly's face.

'Well,' she said resolutely, 'I can't grieve for someone I never knew, but I'm sorry for I would like to have at least seen him. And my uncle? Does he know about me?'

'Oh no, my love. I wouldn't think of his being told before speaking to you.'

'Do you think I should see him? You said he was very unkind to my mother, didn't you?'

'It is for you to say, of course, and you musn't be influenced by what I felt so long ago, but I don't think you will be content unless you do.'

'I think I must,' Molly said. 'Will you come with me?'

Mrs Hendeson hesitated. 'I've been thinking about that, and I don't believe I will. I did dislike him so much and when your mother ran away I quarrelled most dreadfully with him. He may have changed, I hope he has, but I can't go with an open mind. If Matthew had not been here I would have done, but as it is – you will take her to Watford, won't you? I think that better than inviting him here.'

228

'Of course,' Matt said at once. 'But should we not write first?'

'I've thought about that too,' Olivia said slowly, 'but I think it better not, for several reasons.'

Matt nodded perceptively. It was better that the man should not have warning, nor time to consider what he would say to Molly. And it was quite possible he wouldn't accept their story. He held out his hand to her. 'I think we should get this over at once. Would you like to go tomorrow?'

'I think so,' she agreed. 'The sooner the better. But, dear Aunt Olivia, suppose he should be sorry for what he did, suppose I should like him?'

'Then I shall be glad for you, and perhaps the wounds can be healed.'

'Oh, I do hope so,' Molly said at once and gave her aunt a kiss.

But in the carriage which Mrs Henderson had set up on her return, with Reid driving them, she said, 'I can see Aunt Olivia is not happy about this. Don't you see, she felt she had to try to find my relatives, for my sake, but she would rather not have done, and now I'm beginning to wonder if it is all a mistake, this visit, if we should not try to dig up the past.'

He had her hand in his. 'My darling, I think you would always have wondered about them if you hadn't faced up to it.'

'I used to think it was the one thing in the world that I wanted but now – I'm glad you're with me.'

'Olivia clearly thought – ' Mrs Henderson had insisted that Matt should use the more familiar address now that they were all so close, 'it would be better for me to take you.'

The house in Watford was a villa of modest size, set in a garden surrounded by laurel bushes. An elderly servant answered Matt's ring.

'I'm sorry, sir. Mr and Mrs Penberthy are out, but I expect them back about four o'clock.'

There was nothing for it but to say they would return. Matt left his card and enquired about a respectable hotel where they might get luncheon, the butler sending them down the road for half a mile where they would see the Cedars Hotel. It proved to be a typical suburban establishment, but the food was good.

The delay increased Molly's nervousness and she was without her usual appetite.

Once she said, 'I thought perhaps it would be wonderful to have an uncle, maybe cousins. Now I'm not so sure. Maybe they won't want me?'

'As if they wouldn't! But now we are here, I think we have to see them,' Matt sounded positive, but he was anxious for her. After luncheon they sat over their coffee for a long time. The afternoon was sultry, overcast and very close, and the longer they waited the less sure of herself Molly became, but he cheered her as best he could and waited for the time to pass. At last he paid the bill and they left, presenting themselves once more at the door.

Yes, the servant said, the master and mistress were returned and in the drawing room and he had given them the visitor's card. Opening the door he ushered them in.

The moment he saw Gerald Penberthy Matt was sure that they would have done better not to have come. A dark countenance, cold and disinterested faced them. Mr Penberthy was about forty-five, his wife much the same age, a pale woman, small, and giving the impression of a frightened rabbit.

He bowed slightly. 'As far as I know, sir, we are not acquainted, so I have no idea why you wish to see me, though no doubt you will enlighten me.'

'I will, but first I must present to you – Mrs Hallam.'

Mr Penberthy turned and there was no doubt he received a shock. His mouth opened and closed again, while his wife gazed at Molly, clearly at a loss. She had only met Marianne Penberthy once shortly before Marianne's disappearance, not long before her own wedding, and the likeness did not at first strike her.

The effect on her husband was quite different. He cleared his throat, hardly able to take his eyes from Molly's face.

With an effort not to show an uneasiness growing by the minute, he said, 'Good afternoon, ma'am. How may I serve you both?'

'I think you see a resemblance,' Matt's reply was straight to the point. 'This is your niece, your late sister Marianne's daughter.'

Mrs Penberthy gave a little cry of dismay and put a hand to

her mouth, causing her husband to turn to her and say in a low sharp voice, 'Be quiet, Lilian. This is no concern of yours.' And to Molly, 'What an extraordinary thing to suggest. You surely don't expect me to believe such an improbable claim. What evidence have you?'

'I was baptized Marianne after my mother,' she told him. 'She died the night that I was born.'

'We can see by your face that you suspect the truth of it,' Matt added. 'Perhaps we may sit down, for this needs discussion.'

Their unwilling host motioned them to the settee, but did not sit down himself. 'How did you come to connect me with this – this ridiculous assumption?'

'Because Olivia Henderson told us about you. You remember Olivia Manners? It was she who told us of the circumstances of your sister's elopement.'

He was clearly disconcerted. 'Olivia? *Olivia* told you?'

'Yes, your sister's closest friend. She married an army officer, Jock Henderson, you recall him?'

'Henderson? Tall, sandy-haired? Yes, I remember him but I fail to see —'

'He commanded the regiment I served with in the Crimea,' Matt broke in, 'and Mrs Hallam was out there with her husband. He was in the Rifle Brigade and died of the cholera after the battle of the Alma. Mrs Henderson was convinced the moment she saw Mrs Hallam.'

'There's a trifling resemblance, I grant you, no more.'

'Oh, I think there's a great deal more and you know it. Mrs Henderson says she is the image of her mother. Perhaps you have a portrait?'

Molly glanced round the overcrowded room, but the only pictures were of landscapes. Mrs Penberthy who had been listening in growing alarm to this exchange, suddenly said in a quavering voice, 'I said – I did say you shouldn't have got rid of it. There was one and oh, yes, I can see —'

Her husband seemed to be searching for the way to handle this. 'I had no desire to keep a portrait of the sister who had disgraced us all, but enough of that. If, I only say if this is true, why have you come to me? What are you after? Money, I suppose. Well, there was no mention of my sister in my father's will. She was always his favourite but her behaviour shocked him and I don't wonder.'

'As if that's what I would come for,' Molly said indignantly. 'but I'd like to have known my grandfather.'

He gave her a sour look. 'You've not established any right to call him that.' He moved to the mantelshelf and took his stance in front of it. He was clearly disconcerted. 'I can see why you have come – a passing likeness, a silly woman's concocted tale.'

'I would imagine, if you knew her, you could hardly apply that to Mrs Henderson,' Matt said. 'We have gone into it very carefully and Mrs Hallam is surely your niece.'

'And what, pray, is any of this to do with you?'

Matt ignored the insolent tone of this query. 'Mrs Hallam is engaged to me, so her welfare is very much my concern.'

'And you come here to blackmail me, eh? Well, it won't wash. I don't believe the story, and this young woman is not my niece.'

'I think you will find I am,' Molly retorted, 'all the facts fit.'

'What facts?' he demanded but a note of unease had crept into his voice. 'There can be none.'

'Oh there are,' Matt assured him, 'and I shall enlighten you, if you will listen.'

Seeing her husband about to expostulate, Mrs Penberthy said in a faint voice, 'My dear, should we not listen to what this gentleman has to say? I'd better ring for some tea.'

'They are not guests of my inviting,' her husband retorted sharply. 'If you wish to retire —'

She shook her head. 'I'd – I'd better not,' and she cast an anxious look at Molly, who smiled at this obviously frightened woman.

'Don't be alarmed, Mrs Penberthy. I mean no harm to anyone, and certainly I did not come looking for money, only to find out if I have any relations. You see, I grew up thinking I had no one of my own.'

'Yes – yes, I understand,' Mrs Penberthy murmured, 'But—'

'Lilian, I have told you to keep out of this,' her husband's anger was rising. 'This young woman wants to prey on us because of a slight resemblance, blackmail us, no doubt. As if I should listen to a girl from a workhouse.'

232

Chapter Sixteen

There was a sudden and awful silence. Mrs Penberthy gave a little shriek. Matt stood up, glancing at Molly in her pretty summer dress.

'And how, sir, do you know that? I hardly think Mrs Hallam looks like a workhouse girl.'

The man was in a corner and he knew it. 'Oh, one can't tell. A few good clothes —' he tried to bluster, but his wife had sprung up.

'Don't lie, Gerald. It's too late. Don't you see, they *know*!'

'Yes, we know,' Matt said. 'I think an explanation is due to Mrs Hallam.'

Gerald Penberthy's face was ugly with anger. 'I owe you nothing. Get out of my house, you pair of charlatans.'

His wife, for perhaps the first time in her life, turned on him. 'Stop it – stop it! We can't lie any more.'

Molly too had risen, and slowly she said, 'Are you saying that you knew – you knew that I, your own niece, was in the workhouse and you did nothing about it?'

Mrs Penberthy broke into hysterical sobs. 'Yes, that's it. That's just it. I said no good would come of it and God has punished us by not letting us have any children of our own. I wanted to fetch you home, adopt you as our own child, but he wouldn't let me and we have lived with this awful guilt ever since.'

'Don't talk such utter rubbish.' Her husband turned on her. 'Be silent, woman. I'll have no more of this.'

Molly gazed at the truculent figure of her uncle as the truth faced them all. Then she said slowly, 'Do you mean to tell me that knowing all along that I was your sister's child born in that workhouse, you left me there? All these years —'

He almost snarled at her. 'After the way my sister behaved, disgracing the family, bringing shame on us all, why should I want to take her bastard into my house?'

'And that's a lie too.' Mrs Penberthy ignored her husband. 'Oh my dear,' to Molly, 'he's lying to excuse himself. Sefton's wife was dead. We found that out afterwards. Your mother, to her grief, was indeed married to him. I wanted to bring you home, to adopt you, but Gerald – Gerald wouldn't let me.' She was rocking to and fro in her agony and Molly went down on her knees beside the distraught woman.

'Please don't distress yourself. You at least have told the truth.'

For a moment Mrs Penberthy clung to her. 'You are like your mother, I see it now. Oh, how I wish – but forgive us, at least forgive me.'

'My God, what a mawkish scene,' her husband jeered. 'Well, so you may be Marianne's daughter, but nothing to me.'

'You are quite despicable.' Matt helped Molly to her feet. 'Come, my dear, we had better go.'

'Yes,' she said, 'yes,' and to Mrs Penberthy she added, 'I can see it was not your fault. But one thing I must know. How, Mr Penberthy, did you know about the workhouse?'

He gave her a nasty look. 'Oh, two can play at detectives. Months after Marianne had gone, my father had a stroke and he became obsessed with finding her. As far as I was concerned she had made her bed and she could lie on it, but he insisted that I should look for her. Anyway I eventually found myself in Portsmouth and traced her to a lodging house, but there I was told her husband had left her, without paying the rent, and she had been turned out of her lodging, even though she was expecting a child very shortly. A chance meeting with a young man on his way to enlist in the Navy, told me that he had seen a woman answering her description on the Chichester road. We have some cousins there so perhaps she thought to take refuge with them. The young man said she looked on the verge of collapse and would never get there in her condition so he very sensibly informed a constable. The most likely place for her to be taken was a workhouse and I learned that there was one in Westbourne. It was very late so I slept the night at Emsworth in an intolerable inn.'

'Oh?' Matt queried. 'You thought your night's rest more important than your sister's plight?'

Penberthy ignored him but having started went on, albeit unwillingly. 'In the morning I went to Westbourne to continue my search. As it happened it ended there. When I arrived Marianne was dead and buried.'

'And me?' Molly asked.

'As far as I was concerned I saw no reason to remove you.'

'And you abandoned me? How could you, how could you?' Rage seized her, combined with disgust and loathing she had never felt for anyone. Clenching both fists as if she would strike him, she cried out, 'You are a monster. A cruel wicked monster! You —'

Sure that some ripe soldier's language was about to ensue, Matt restrained her. 'Come, he's not worth it. And you need never see him again.'

'But what about my grandfather. Didn't you tell him about me?'

He shrugged. 'The old man died soon after I got back. I saw no reason to bring Marianne's brat into the house.'

'You are beneath contempt,' Matt said, and glancing from the angry belligerent man to his shattered wife, he added, 'I wish you joy of your miserable lives. It's no thanks to you that Molly has survived as she has. Whether we take the matter further depends on her.'

Mrs Penberthy wept. Her husband said, 'Get out, the pair of you. You'll get nothing out of me. And don't think, Colonel, that your rank frightens me.'

Thankful that he had always had a good left hook Matt planted a facer on him. Taken completely by surprise Penberthy went reeling backward, crashed over a small chair and sent a table flying with a vase of red roses. His wife screamed.

Matt took Molly's arm and propelled her out of the room. In the hall he took his hat and cane from the manservant who had heard the commotion and was hurrying towards the door. 'You are probably needed in there,' he said and led Molly outside to hand her into the waiting carriage, signalling to Reid to drive off.

She sat on the edge of the seat, shaking. 'I'm glad you did that. If you hadn't hit him I would have done.'

'I thought you might!' He put his arm about her. 'So it seemed better if I sent him flying. Despicable cur.'

'I feel sorry for Mrs Penberthy married to such a man, though she doesn't seem to have the courage of a pea-goose. Aunt Olivia was right and I'm glad she didn't come. With all her memories she would have been so distressed by such a scene.'

'She would indeed, but thank God none of us need ever have any further dealings with them.'

'To think he could have condemned me to all those years in the workhouse, without anyone to care tuppence about me, except for dear Miss Plumstead, and then that hard labour on the farm – wicked! Wicked! He must have been eaten up with jealousy because my grandfather loved my mother best. I can hardly credit it that anyone could be so cruel to a child, his own flesh and blood.'

'I have an idea that when your mother ran away the old man changed his will, and when Penberthy found you, it was his greed that made him abandon you, to stop you sharing in whatever inheritance there was. But it's over now once and for all, and we must try to put it behind us.'

'Yes,' she agreed in a low voice, 'but he's robbed me of the only chance I had of knowing my own family. I've thought, hoped for so much since Aunt Olivia told me about it all back in Balaclava.'

'As my wife you will have mine,' he assured her and she wished she felt as confident.

Rain had begun to fall, beating heavily against the glass window and as darkness fell the rain made it all the blacker.

'I'm beginning to wonder whether, after all that delay, we'll get home tonight,' Matt was peering out. 'Reid will do his best, but – '

And at that moment as if to reinforce his doubts there was a sudden jolt, the carriage veered to one side and Reid brought it to a halt. A moment later he came to the window, soaked to the skin.

'Sorry, sir, the off-sider's lost a shoe.'

'Damnation,' Matt said. 'Have you any idea where we are?'

Reid looked uneasy. 'Well, never havin' bin down this road before I think we've took the wrong fork back a few miles. This is just a country lane, not what we should be on.'

'Then what do you suggest we do? Sleep in the coach?'

'No, indeed, sir. I can see a light ahead and I thought wi' a bit o' luck it might be an inn.'

It was an inn, of sorts. They got there at a snail's pace, Reid leading the limping horse, but at least there was a stable when they got there. A creaking sign told them that the very old and low building was the Black Cat. Rain was still falling and Matt helped Molly down to hurry her across to the door, pushing it open and ducking his head to follow. It was a poor enough place, a few benches round the walls, stools and a table bearing a sconce of candles in the centre of the room. A bar was in one corner with ale jugs and a barrel. Two farmhands sat on one bench, tankards in their hands and they looked at the new arrivals with considerable curiosity.

'Sit on this bench,' Matt said, 'while I go and rout someone out.'

Molly gave him a wan smile. 'It's not your fault. I suppose we'd better spend the night here, if we can.' She was still too shaken by the afternoon's shock and distress for this small mishap to worry her.

Matt disappeared into the nether regions shouting for the landlord who had been conversing with Reid, while one of the yokels observed to Molly that it was a rough night.

'Very rough,' she agreed.

'Come far, miss?'

'From Watford.'

'That's a tidy step,' the other one put it.

'I think we took a wrong road.'

'You won't get nowhere tonight,' was the opinion of the first fellow.

'No, we won't for sure,' Molly agreed and there the conversation lapsed.

Matt came back to say that they could stay and Reid might sleep in the room above the stable. 'I've sent the landlord to bring up a bottle of his best wine from the cellar, not that it's

237

likely to be any good in a place like this. His wife says she has a stew on the fire, so I suppose it might be eatable, and she's gone upstairs to make ready for us.' He bent on the two farmhands the sort of look he would have expended on a couple of soldiers who might be better elsewhere. They seemed to take the hint, saying regretfully that they'd best go home and bidding this commanding man and his lady goodnight, went out into the rain. He waited until the door had closed and then sitting down opposite her said somewhat tentatively, 'The only thing is, there's only one room. I introduced myself as Colonel Hamilton and said that you were Mrs Hallam and she must have thought I said Mrs Hamilton because she assumed we were husband and wife. I suppose I could sleep on that very uncomfortable settle or perhaps there's a chair in the bedroom.'

Molly laughed for the first time on this rather horrid day. 'Oh Matt, if only you could see your face. You're trying to look apologetic, but at the same time – oh dear love, we're to be married in two weeks! I hope you said it would suit very well?' And seeing the light in his eyes, she added, 'Don't you know how glad I'll be not to be alone tonight.'

His grip tightened though he refrained in so public a place from the kiss he wanted to set on her mouth.

Mrs Bellows, the landlord's wife, came down the stair at the end of the room and asked if they would care to come up. It was a small room, low under the rafters, the bed nearly filling it, the only other furniture being a washstand with a basin and one stool. A few hooks in the wall served for a wardrobe.

'It ain't much,' she said, 'but you're welcome, sir, ma'am, specially as it's Tuesday,' she added darkly.

Not having an idea what this might portend Molly refrained from enquiring and merely gave her a smile. 'It's very acceptable on a night like this.'

'I'll send up hot water, I got the kettle on the hob, and a towel.'

She went out and Molly surveyed their quarters. 'Well, you could hardly sleep on that stool. I wonder if the sheets are damp.'

'We'll warm the bed,' he said and took the overdue kiss. 'Molly, what can I say?'

'About tonight?' She was looking up into his face. 'Only that it was meant to be. We didn't plan it, did we? For one awful moment, when he said I was a bastard, I saw myself as Molly-all-alone again.'

'You didn't really think that would weigh with me? Even if it were true, which it isn't. Never, never while I live.'

A knock on the door parted them and a tousle-headed boy stood there with a steaming jug and a towel which he set down on the washstand.

'Ma says supper's ready any time these ten minutes,' after which cryptic statement he disappeared.

'Like mother, like son,' Matt exclaimed and both were reduced to laughter, but as she washed Molly thought fleetingly of the barn and Hal, remembering the dreadful guilt that consumed her afterwards. This time it would be so different. With her wedding so near, and the circumstances what they were it just seemed right, the two of them hidden away from the world, and without a qualm she took his arm and went down the stair to the taproom.

A portly farmer was enjoying a tankard of ale and though he bade them good evening he left it at that, merely observing them with interest. The supper was adequate, except for the potatoes which were undercooked. Uncorking the bottle with a great flourish the landlord poured out two glasses of the wine, it not having reached him that gentlemen liked a taste first before accepting it.

'I've drunk better in Balaclava,' Matt said when Mr Bellows had gone back to the kitchen, 'but after two or three glasses it may become tolerable.' Mrs Bellows produced a raspberry tart which was the best part of the meal, the cream thick and a rich yellow.

They were drinking coffee when Reid came in to say there was a smith in the village barely a mile down the road, and he proposed to take the horse there to be shod at first light. Matt bought him a pint and a plate of supper and he went off happily to the stableroom. Mr Bellows, who hadn't had quality in his inn for a long time, waited assiduously on his unexpected guests, but at last Matt said they were tired and would go upstairs, Molly telling Mrs Bellows that she was a very good hand at pastry and asking if the raspberries were out of her garden.

239

In their tiny room where the bed had been turned down Molly inspected the sheets and pronounced them dry, 'Though folk aren't always careful about airing them. Still, compared to sleeping in a blanket on the wet ground —'

'Oh damn the sheets,' Matt said, and she saw at once that he was trembling, in a state of nervous excitement. She went at once to him to hold him close and say lightly, 'I suppose I shall have to go to bed in my petticoat and you in your shirt as we've no baggage. Let me help you off with your coat as there's no Merton to do it. Tell me if I hurt your shoulder.'

She had understood. Having told her of his youthful love for Maria, and of the broken engagement, but of no one since, she realized he had poured all his energies into his soldiering, suppressed his emotions, ridden himself on a very hard rein with no time for the gentler things. And now that he was in love at last he needed most desperately the expression of it. When they were ready she went to him, running her hands soothingly up and down his back, yielding herself. He gave a long shuddering sigh and then sank his mouth on hers.

'The candle,' she whispered. And then they were in the bed. She thought fleetingly of Hal, so different, so straightforward and simple like the man of the soil that he was, enjoying his lovemaking in the way of all natural creatures. But this man beside her was different. There was an intensity in his loving, a longing that was of the mind as well as the body and now her needs matched his. And then he was above her and all thinking turned to sheer joy.

A little later, while he still lay over her, still within her, he murmured, 'I never knew it could be like this. My love, my love, my love.'

She had her hands about his head in an ecstasy of giving. 'I'll love you, always, always.' Gently he rolled on his side, cradling her in his good arm. 'I've never been so happy,' and she whispered, 'Nor have I, not as we are.'

He slept soundly and late, waking to see her standing by the tiny window, a shawl about her shoulders. For a few moments he watched her and then said, 'Why are you standing there? It's not warm yet. It must be very early.'

She turned to smile tenderly at him. 'I've always woken early. And I was remembering Ruth in the Bible, what she said to Naomi. *Intreat me not to leave thee, or to return from following after thee: for whither thou goest I will go ... and thy people shall be my people ...* Only will they? I'm afraid they may not want to be my people. And my uncle certainly doesn't want me, nor do I want him.'

'Come here,' he said softly and opened wide the coverings. She came to slip into his arms again and he went on, 'None of that matters. You and I will begin our own family. I hope we shall have sons and daughters and grandchildren, make a new dynasty of Hamiltons!'

She gave a little laugh. 'Oh, I hope so. But – but – with Hal I didn't —'

'My darling girl, all told, you only had a few weeks with him. We have all the time in the world, and seeing you by the window, I seemed to see you with a child in your arms.'

'Oh,' for a moment tears stung her eyes, 'that's something I long for now. I shall pray for it.'

'And you're rather good at that! We shall be a family and make up for all your sad past, for my long years of being alone. Do you know, I worried myself into a lather at home in case you should have changed your mind about me. I'm not a rich man and they might send me to some God-forsaken place. Life may be hard, uncertain, though never, please God, as bad as the Crimea.'

She laughed and snuggled closer. 'As if I would worry about that. I can always get out my sheepskin jacket and my forage cap, can't I? You know I don't care anything for hardship.'

'Ah,' he gave a long sigh. 'I've waited a long time for you, my darling, and now I shall never let you go.'

She touched the crease between his brows, that suddenly seemed to have lessened. 'It's like a miracle, that we both need each other so much.' She was showering kisses on his cheeks, his mouth and there was only one end to this.

Later there was a knock on the door and when Matt got up to open it, the boy stood there with a jug of water and, waiting for another cryptic message, he was not disappointed.

'Ma says was you wantin' breakfast soon, only the chickens is making a racket – well, they ain't in a hurry, are they – and the bacon's frying.'

241

'And very good it smells. We'll be down directly.' Matt told him, giving him a friendly cuff on the shoulder, so that the boy was grinning as he ran off. To Molly he added, 'I shall remember this place and its extraordinary conversations. Why do you suppose the chickens aren't in a hurry?'

Molly laughed and said wisely, 'Because it's market day, I should think.' They ate in the taproom, bacon, eggs, fried potatoes and sausages, and had nearly finished when Reid came in to say the shoeing was done and should he put the horses to? As they drove away Molly gave a deep sigh. In the daylight the place looked small and seedy, but she said, 'I expect we'll stay in better places, but not one I'll remember more dearly.'

'I shall take you to Brighton for our honeymoon,' he said, 'to stay at the Old Ship, a favourite place for army officers. Old Wellington liked it. But I was thinking, my darling, we ought to go down to Portsmouth first. We can't keep them in the dark any longer. My mother won't be able to travel up to the wedding, but I'm sure my stepfather will.'

'And your sisters?'

He shrugged. 'I'm positive Georgy would like to but she's expecting again. As for Henrietta, she's an unknown quantity. Don't worry about it, my darling. My mother will love you, you know.'

But she was worried and the following day in the train to Portsmouth she was very quiet. What would Frederick call her when he opened the door? Molly? Mrs Hallam? Ma'am? He had after all given her away at her previous wedding and it was a very odd situation. But of course it was silly to worry about that. As long as she had Matt with her, surely everything would be all right. She braced herself and in the carriage on the way to Southsea he sensed the inevitable tension in her and held her hand firmly, trying to impart his strength and support.

Molly thought briefly of their arrival back in Hyde Park Gate yesterday. Olivia, being a sensible woman, had not worried, guessing something unforeseen had occurred. The possibility that they might have stayed the night with Gerald Penberthy flashed across her mind and she was thankful to be soon disabused of this idea. When she heard the whole tale her

242

comment was that his behaviour was only what she had expected, but his abandoning the baby Molly to the workhouse was an infamy worse than even she expected. When they bade each other goodnight she said, 'Molly, my dear, I wish I had not found him.'

'I'm glad you did,' Molly said, 'even if it was so awful. I would always have wondered and now I know I never want to see him again. I hoped there might be a portrait of my mother but Mrs Penberthy said he wouldn't keep it.'

'You have only to look in the mirror,' Olivia said affectionately. Yet it was obvious now to her that the unhappy interview of yesterday was not uppermost in either of their minds. They had come home with a glow, a content about them that told the perceptive Olivia that wherever they had stayed it had been together. The only thing she said however, as they kissed goodnight, was, 'I've never seen Matthew so happy, and that tells me a great deal.'

'You see a great many things,' Molly whispered and gave her a long hug. 'No mother could be more loving to me than you are.'

'My dearest. I think that's the nicest compliment ever paid me. And you, oh you are just the girl for dear Matthew. Jock felt he needed to be married, that his life was too austere. I did try to promote possible brides but to no avail. He could I suppose have married a shy little society miss and been tolerably content, but he needed a girl like you, someone – what's the word I want? robust, courageous, and not afraid to speak her mind. Not easy to find, and I believe he knows how lucky he is.'

It was strange now to be drawing up outside Crossley Lodge, very white in the summer sunlight. Her stomach was behaving oddly and she thought she had never been nervous like this before. Dressing carefully this morning in a summer gown of pale green poplin and tying her straw bonnet with matching green ribbons under her chin she looked long in the mirror, until her aunt smiled and told her the outfit was just right for the occasion.

Frederick opened the door with his usual, 'Good morning, sir, madam – ' and then was bereft of speech.

'Yes, it's Mrs Hallam,' Matt said with an irrepressible

touch of pride, for he thought she looked particularly beautiful this morning. 'Hard to recognize, eh? Are the family at home?'

Being highly trained, Frederick recovered himself at once, got over the necessity of calling her anything and answered the question by saying they were in the drawing room and luncheon would be served shortly.

Feeling her hand tighten on his arm, Matt said in a low voice. 'Suppose I go in and break the ice?' And seeing her grateful look, added, 'Frederick will take you down to see Cook and the others, won't you?'

'Of course, sir.' The butler gave her a quick smile, but hardly had Matt disappeared into the drawing room than he was called away to deal with the arrival of a consignment of wine. Molly was glad. She didn't really want to talk to any of them below stairs until the present situation was resolved. She told him she would wait in the hall and sat down on one of the straight-backed chairs that she had once had the duty of polishing.

There was a murmur of voices from the drawing room, for Matt had not closed the door firmly enough. It was open a chink and suddenly she heard Henrietta's voice, raised to a high pitch and carrying into the hall.

'You must be out of your mind! For heaven's sake, Matt, she was our *housemaid*! You can't mean to do this. What about the servants? How are they to treat her? As a lady? Or do you suggest we dismiss them all and engage new staff? And what about our friends, people who've dined here? Oh, it is too bad. I can't think —'

Molly waited to hear no more. As Frederick came back into the hall, she said hastily, 'Please tell the Colonel I've gone to visit my old friend in Westbourne.' And before the astonished Frederick could answer, she had opened the door and was gone. Knowing where to find the cab rank she hired a hackney and gave her destination.

'I don't usually go that far,' the driver grumbled. 'I don't go out o' the town.'

'I'll give you double fare if you take me at once,' she insisted and greed got the better of him. Sitting on the edge of the seat, longing for Matt's presence beside her, she remembered that Aunt Olivia had called her strong and able to deal with anything, but at the moment she felt utterly crushed, tears running down her face. It was no good. They would never accept her. She would be the cause of a dreadful rift in his family. Hadn't she known all along that Henrietta would be disgusted, refuse to accept what had happened? What was Matt saying to his sister at this moment? What would he do, what *could* he do? Marry her and cut himself off from his family, especially his mother? It was unthinkable, especially after the loss of Toby. Poor Matt – perhaps she shouldn't have deserted him, but she couldn't stay, she couldn't ...

Wiping away the tears, she blew her nose defiantly and at Westbourne paid the more than satisfied cabby. Winifred opened the door in answer to her knock and as her mistress came out of the sitting room merely said, 'A lady to see you, miss.'

Miss Plumstead stood stock-still and then held wide her arms. 'A lady indeed! Molly, my love, I can't believe it. Oh, you look quite wonderful. What a surprise! Have you had luncheon? No? Winifred, set up a tray, at once. Now come in, come in.'

In the little sitting room she gave Molly a long embrace, surprised to find Molly trembling and clinging to her. 'Why, what's this? You wrote to me such lovely excited letters from London and you seemed so happy with your Colonel.'

Molly sat down beside her on the sofa, trying not to cry again. And then she poured it all out, the awful meeting with her uncle, followed by the necessity to face the Milners, ending with Henrietta's diatribe.

'What can I do?' She begged for an answer. 'What should I do? If I marry Matt I shall take him from his family, and if I don't – I think it will break his heart – and mine.'

'Well, we can't have that,' Miss Plumstead was smiling. 'Dearest, you both deserve your happiness and no doubt his family will come round. They always do. And when they know who your grandfather was – well, I always said your mother was a lady, didn't I?'

'But – but I was a housemaid there. Nothing can change that.'

'From what you tell me of Sir Charles I would not think he would mind that.'

'No, not him perhaps,' she admitted, 'but the others – '

'It's your Colonel's opinion that matters, isn't it? I very much want to meet him for he sounds just the man for you.'

'Oh he is, he is.'

'Well, then —'

Winifred came with a tray and Miss Plumstead sat Molly down at a little table to tackle the cold meats and fresh salad from the garden. 'How he will scold you for running off like that,' Miss Plumstead added with a teasing look. 'It will all come right, you see if it doesn't. In the meantime, tell me about Mrs Henderson. She sounds a very lively lady, and so kind.'

Molly needed no prompting to talk of her adopted aunt and the miracle of their meeting in the little house by the harbour. That led to a description of the mud and the rain and snow of that winter. 'I'm afraid my poor Bible got very wet at times and muddy, and even stained with the blood of a poor dying fellow.'

Miss Plumstead looked quite horrified, 'Honourable scars, I'm sure. You must let me give you a new one – for your new life.'

'Thank you,' Molly said warmly. 'I would like that. But I'll never part with the other one. You gave it to me and you don't know what it meant to me out there and to so many of the poor soldiers that wanted a crumb of comfort.'

Miss Plumstead was clearly staggered by the revelations of what Molly had endured so far away, and she murmured, 'Tell me more about that place, where you nursed Mrs Henderson and the Colonel.'

Graphically, Molly went on and it wasn't until an hour had passed that there was a knock on the door. She jumped nervously, but Winifred came in to announce that the vicar was in the hall. Miss Plumstead said regretfully that she had forgotten he was calling about some parish business, and thinking this was the last interruption Molly wanted at the moment, suggested she should go out into the garden while she dealt with her visitor.

Molly went only too readily. The little garden was bright with roses and marigolds and cornflowers and in the vegetable patch beyond the first scarlet runner flowers were appearing on their trellis. She had walked here with Hal, just a year ago, so much happening since, confusing her, tearing her one way and another, and when at last she had found such happiness two nights ago, it seemed cruel that it should be snatched away from her.

Pacing up and down, her hands clasped, time slipped by and she was so deep in her anxious thoughts that she did not hear a soft footfall on the grass. Then he was holding her shoulders, a little away from him so that he could look down into her face.

'You foolish, foolish girl! How could you run away from me?'

She let out a little gasp. 'Matt! Oh, Matt!'

'Don't tell me you didn't expect me?'

'But – I heard – your sister – she said – '

His smile widened. 'I can't believe that the Lambkin who faced the worst the Crimea could inflict on us, ran away because of my sister's sharp tongue? Frederick told me you must have heard, and of course I knew at once where you had gone. I'm taking you back with me now.'

'How can you? Yes, I did run away, but only from them, not from you – oh, Matt, not from you. Was it silly of me?'

'Very silly. Come and sit down on this seat. Now – after you had gone we had a long family conference – ruined the lunch! But my stepfather gave Henrietta the worst dressing down I have in all my years heard him give anyone. In the end I was quite sorry for her. She is much chastened.'

'Oh,' Molly murmured. 'Oh, I didn't want —'

'It was time she learned a few home truths. Anyway the upshot of it all was that she asked me to beg your pardon and to say she is looking forward to seeing you.' He cocked an eyebrow. 'I think she meant it, as far Henrietta can eat humble pie. I believe my throwing Sir William Penberthy into the conversation helped a little! On the other hand, my mother is delighted and says she is waiting to welcome her new daughter. She always did like you, you know.'

'And – and Sir Charles?'

Matt's smile widened. 'He came over with me and is at present with your delightful Miss Plumstead whom I left trying to press a glass of her cowslip wine on him.'

'He is here, he came with you?' she asked in wonder and he kissed her lips fleetingly. 'Indeed he did – and there he is coming up the path.'

Molly turned and there was Second-chance-Charlie, his round face one beam of pleasure. Holding wide his arms he said, 'Another chance for us all, eh Molly?' And without hesitating she ran straight into the warmth of his embrace.

You have been reading a novel published by Piatkus Books. We hope you have enjoyed it and that you would like to read more of our titles. Please ask for them in your local library or bookshop.

If you would like to be put on our mailing list to receive details of new publications, please send a large stamped addressed envelope (UK only) to:

Piatkus Books, 5 Windmill Street
London W1P 1HF

PIATKUS

The sign of a good book